Where the Mockingbird Sang

A Novel of the Civil War

By

David Wilson Atwood

Printed in the United States of America

First Edition, second printing July, 2010

Atwood, David Wilson

Where the Mockingbird Sang, A Novel of the Civil War, David Wilson Atwood. – 1st ed.

ISBN 978-1451538823

1. Unites States – History – Civil War, 1857-1868 - Fiction

To my wife, JoAnne Rebecca Atwood, and all eight of my children who stand on the same shoulders of the same giant...May you all see farther.

Dr. Evans Atwood (C) Washington Co. Historical Society / Shiloh Museum of Ozark History

Evans Atwood (Circa 1857-1860)

The Sunny South

Take me home to the place where I first saw the light

To the sweet "Sunny South" take me home;

Where the mockingbird sang me to sleep every night---

Ah! Was I tempted to roam.

I think with regret, on the dear home I left;

Of the warm hearts that sheltered me there;

Of my wife, and the dear ones, of whom I'm bereft---

And I sigh for the old place again.

Take me home, to the place, where my little ones sleep

Where my Father lies buried close by;

O'er the graves of the loved ones I long for to weep,

And among them to rest when I die.

Take me home to the place where the Orange tree grows,

To my cot in the evergreen shade;

Where the flowers on the river's margin bloom;

Where in sweet childish glee I have played.

Attributed to 2nd Lt. Evans Atwood CSA

Prisoner of War, Place and date not specified

Forward

The story of Evans Atwood is told from his journals. In keeping with the spirit of journaling, there are many excerpts, real and fictional, used in the telling of this story. Evans copied many of the letters he received along with many he wrote in his "copy book". From this correspondence, I was able to piece together a narrative. All letters and journal entries are outlined.

The fictitious entries are written in the same spirit that I think he, or the person he was corresponding with, would have written. I have been as true to the story as possible.

I have changed some of the language. It was a naïve and sentimental time, and the men spoke in windy phrases. Things written were often poetic and wordy. I have made them more modern while making every effort to stay true to the time. All interpretation of character and fact are mine, hence, I lay claim to all mistakes.

Where the Mockingbird Sang

David Wilson Atwood

1) The Battle for Port Gibson, Mississippi

Thursday, April 30 – Friday, May 1, 1863

I shiver in the late night chill of the last night of April, first day of May. The dusty scent of pine resin mixes with the sweetness of magnolia and honeysuckle to bid me sleep. The pines provide a soft bed of needles that entice me to yield to bone deep weariness, but I can't. Six thousand men in the fields and woods to our rear are counting on us to be the first line of defense; the sharp point of the sword, the warning shot.

We six of Company A, 15th Arkansas Infantry of the Confederate States Army are assigned picket duty. Our post overlooks Rodney Road along which we force marched hours ago from Grand Gulf on the Mississippi River. The road crosses Bayou Pierre southeast of the town of Port Gibson, a mile or two to our rear. This is the road Grant's invading army will use as they march inland from Bruinsburg where they landed unopposed. Their objective is Vicksburg, about thirty miles to the north. This is where we have to stop twenty thousand Yankee invaders.

I say into the dark, "Midnight?"

"I figure."

My platoon sergeant, Buck Buchannan keeps no truck with officers and the trappings of rank, so there is no "sir" offered in his reply and none expected on my part. We've been together too long for that.

The clop of horse hooves on the hard packed dirt of the road to our rear draws our attention. We wait. A challenge is issued, "Who goes there!"

"General Green; what unit, and who are you?"

"Private Bill Fiedler of the 15th Arkansas, sir!"

"General Green?" Buck questions in a whisper which is only a little less than thunder.

I can make out the Brigade commander in the light of the near full moon. He is a lean, tall man standing over six feet and sits his horse with his long legs seeming to touch the ground.

"Who's in command here?" He asks into the dark.

"Lieutenant Evans Atwood, down the road a piece, sir."

"Can you hear me Lieutenant?"

"Yes sir," I reply. "Do you have orders sir?"

"General Green; out here?" Buck whispers again.

The general rides closer, "No orders; I'm riding to make sure you pickets are awake."

I am as confused as Buck; a general checking pickets? I hear Buck shift and know he's looking at me with a "what's this about" look. Does the general know something we don't? "We're ready sir. I was told we're not expecting Yankees until morning?"

"That's right lieutenant, but we must be prepared."

"Yes sir; we're ready."

"Very well; carry on." He turns off the road and into the woods riding toward the pickets of the 12th Arkansas Sharpshooters. They have the same duty across the road to our north and west of a large home owned by the Shaifer family whose land we are on.

"It's a nervous general who checks his own pickets," says Buck.

"Yeah, I don't like it. What does he know?" I say louder, "Be alert men". I get various affirming grunts and mumbled "Yes sirs" from down the line. They're already alert; they know what a General riding pickets means.

"You think the Yanks'll attack in the dark?" Buck asks.

"They don't know we're here."

"They know we're somewhere."

"They'll send skirmishers to probe and find us. Then we worry about an attack."

"If it happens, we ain't fallin' back over that plowed field in the dark without getting picked to pieces."

"We'll make our stand here Buck. We can't let them by, or we'll be cut off. We're going to stay put right here and fight."

"I don't like it."

"Nobody does. Our advantage is having seen the lay of the land in daylight, and we've got surprise on our side. We can hold them 'til dawn then we'll be able to see. Pray the Lord shows a way." I pause a moment, "Try to get some rest."

"Yeah, rest; you're a bigger fool than I know you to be".

Our whispered conversation seems to boom in the still dark. We've not fought a night action, and the prospect is not a happy one. Battle is confusing enough when you can see. Tonight, if it comes, will be like fighting blindfolded. I try to picture the road as I saw it this afternoon, but in the dark, nothing is familiar.

There's a knot in my stomach. I've got to think clear or get us killed. The cold coupled with my extreme fatigue makes it hard for me to focus. Across the road, in the woods, I hear the 12th's challenge to General Green and imagine a conversation similar to ours. The general rides toward the Shaifer house.

There's lantern light there and I can see movement in the yard through the trees. People are crossing back and forth, in and out; women and children loading a wagon.

We sense more than hear noise on the road from the west where it shouldn't be and our attention is shifted. It comes closer, moving around the corner two hundred yards from us, and materializes into black forms spanning the road bed.

Behind me, General Green assures the folks loading the wagon that they're safe until morning, "The Yankees won't attack at night," I hear him say; "you can rest easy." There is no way to warn them without giving away our position. They'll know soon enough.

The apparitions materialize into the enemy. We can hear their commands as they move toward us. Someone up front of their formation says, "There's nobody here."

My mouth is dry, and my hands are sweating. Even in the cold, the anticipation of ambush has me wishing I could shed my coat. My heart pounds as I watch them come nearer. "Come on, come on; just a little further and you're mine." I hear the muffled cock of Buck's rifle. I cock my Springfield and slide it forward in the same motion. Sighting down the barrel, I target a Yankee on the far side of the road; closest to the stake I placed as a range marker. He'll be first.

General Green and the ladies exchange pleasantries as the general departs. The Yankees hear it and halt. One of them says, "It's only the women in that house. There's nobody here; move out! Let's go."

I hold my breath and feel my heart pounding against the ground. My hand moves from the trigger and wipes sweat from my brow. My hat feels like it weighs a ton. I re-sight on the Yankee closest to the stake. When he's past the stake, there will be five targets within the range. I wait. It seems like forever as they grow closer and closer; Buck shifts again. We're anxious. I see six, one each. When we fire, we'll lose our night vision from the muzzle flashes and be firing blind. Our boys have hunted enough at night to know that. Hopefully, that's another advantage over the invading factory and mill workers. They're closer.

Forty yards now; they're moving with confidence, weapons loose; not ready; cocky. Wait...wait, they're at thirty yards now; it's time. I breathe deep, hold it, aim, and squeeze the trigger. The muzzle loading Springfield roars with a flash and cloud of smoke, blinding me from my target as I absorb the rifle's recoil. I move up on my knee to reload. As I do, I am deafened by the near simultaneous roar of five more rifles. Loading the Springfield is automatic and has to be in the dark with compromised vision. I try to see the road to assess the damage, but the smoke and flash prevent it. Screams of wounded men tell me we've been accurate. Some of the smoke lifts and with the aid of muzzle flashes, I make out the enemy moving. They're firing everywhere, but not near us. How could they have missed our muzzle flashes? Then I know; we downed the forward troops; this is their second line. They're confused and afraid and are firing wild. Good.

"Aim at their muzzle flashes," Buck yells!

"Fire and move!" I shout. The enemy will overcome their confusion soon and will be firing at our muzzle flashes too. The second volley sounds. Our men shift.

Across the road, there are shouted orders from the Twelfth to form a skirmish line and move forward. They open fire on the Yankee flank. The Federals in front of us hear the increased firing from their left and fall back. We continue to pour lead into where they were, but we're making more noise and smoke than danger. The battle is moving away from us.

The 12th break contact and fall back to their position. We both celebrate with shouts and comments directed at the parentage and heritage of the Union soldiers. The smell of gunpowder hangs heavy as I shout, "Causalities?"

"None," Buck says in a voice boosted by the thrill of combat.

I am shaking. The probe lasted minutes, but seems like hours. "Those were their skirmishers; now they know we're here. We'll soon see if they attack or wait to morning."

We hear the Yankees reforming and moving into position. Horses whinny and neigh in the dark, working under a burden. They're bringing up artillery. "Sounds like they ain't content to wait," someone offers. Our big guns are located on Foster Ridge, the next ridge back from our position here by Magnolia Church on a ridge of the same name. They're on higher ground and have the advantage of having laid out fields of fire before dark.

"They're comin'. Our big guns should start any time now," says Buck.

Boom! Thunder, lightning, and iron shatter the night as they flash over the road into the gathering Yankees. We hear the crash and whistle of canister shot as it thrashes the trees. Moments later, Boom; an enemy answer.

Buck moves to me, "Fall back, or stand?"

"Stand; they're going to disperse in the ravines below us, but the only clear way to come is the road. Move everyone up and spread out facing that way." Buck goes to carry out my orders.

The artillery continues its deadly work. The firing of each piece sends gunpowder born thunder rolling over the fields, gullies, and washes where troops of both sides lay hidden. The earth trembles and shakes from concussion of firing and impact. Shells scream over our position on the way to their final destination in some Yankee gun crew's belly. It is savage work. The flash of exploding gun powder, the screaming of the wounded, the bursting of shells, the rattle of grape shot crashing through fences and timber, assault the senses, striking terror that only training and experience can subdue.

The muzzle flashes of artillery light their positions as well as ours, and we are able to choose targets, fire, and move. The cries of their wounded tell us we are effective. As they return fire, we target their muzzle flashes, and continue our skillful, accurate, death dealing work. The enemy fire is inadequate and inaccurate. They aren't as we good as we are.

The battle continues for over an hour with no break. My mouth is parched from the gun powder as I rip open the cartridges with my teeth before pushing them down the barrel of my rifle, but I cannot stop to open my canteen and drink. The right side of my face is stinging from the repeated blasts of caps into the chamber and the back flash. I rub dirt over my face to ease the pain, and to prevent further burns. My nostrils and throat are raw from the smoke laden air.

The Union artillery pieces are silenced one by one either by our cannon fire, or their ineffective fire and desire to conserve powder and shot until daybreak. They did not expect this spirited a resistance and choose to break off the engagement and reorganize; wait for daylight. Their skirmishers fall back too. We can hear hundreds, maybe thousands regrouping along the road and in the woods. We are panting from exhaustion. The physical strain of battle deepens the fatigue from our forced march.

The Blue Bellies feel worse than we do. They have been forced to yield. We have not given up one inch of ground, nor lost one soldier to wound or death. I fear it won't last.

Looking around, I see Buck crouching off to my right, and I make my way to him.

"Fine mornin' ain't it Boy?" Buck's teeth show bright white in his black bearded, gun powder marked face as he grins at me in victory. Nathanial James Buchannan is much older than my twenty-six years. He enlisted to fight the northern insistence that the south change their ways, and he's very good at it. His passion swept me along and we joined together.

Even though he's over forty, he and I are close. We've know each other since I was six, and before the war, we traveled and adventured . We're opposites in most ways, and are good and bad for each other.

Buck is honest, hates liars, cheats, and thieves as much as I do, and has never said anything he did not mean. It takes him awhile, but once he reasons it out, if he speaks it, it'll happen.

"I guess we showed those boys how Arkansians can shoot!"

"We made some Yankees wish for home, that's for sure, and some we sent a great way beyond." The men gather round, pass around canteens to drink and wash hot faces, and wind down from the night's battle. Buck cuts it short with, "What are your orders Lieutenant?" He has a way spurring me to action while letting me think it was my leadership, not his, that got us where we needed to be.

It's darker now as the moon has dropped below the tree line. We can't be certain of where to go if we could go. The Magnolia Church is a shadow on the ridge. "We don't have orders to fall back unless pushed off this ridge, so we're going to stay." Everyone is quiet and listening. "We're going to take up positions facing the road. Their skirmishers are on the next ridge or in the gullies and may come to try us again." Turning to Buck, "Sergeant, I figure it to be about 3:00 in the morning; that gives us three hours before first light. I suspect we'll have company then. Organize a rest and watch schedule including me. Each man needs time to take care of himself, get water, and sleep a little." Chuckles from the men; all know there will be no sleep tonight. "How we fixed for caps and cartridges? Give me a count." There is fumbling in the dark as each man checks. We tally a number, or as close to it as we can get. "We don't have enough ammo. Buck, assign two men to go to the rear and get as much as you can. Make some noise when you come back, or we're likely to shoot." The detail is sent, and the rest of us take time to go to the creek, wash our faces, and fill canteens, answer nature's call, and rest.

The woods calm, an owl hoots while crickets, frogs, and other critters are heard again. The Yankees are milling around down the road. There'll be no sleep in their camp either. It's almost as if the battle was a bad dream. The stinging on my face and the moans of their wounded tell me otherwise. I lay back to relax and let my mind wander home.

2) Home, April, 1863

April the 22nd, 1863
Shilo, Arkansas

My dearest Evans,

It is with greatest love, and deepest sadness that I take pen in hand.
Love, because I miss you so. Sadness, not only because of your absence,
but the extreme loneliness that is on me as a damp cloak presses one
down to smother. The loneliness is not from being alone, for I seldom
am. I have our two beautiful children to love and care for, and I do. No,
the loneliness is due to my empty arms.

I know you think you are answering a high, patriotic call, and are
doing what you can by sending money when able, but it is not enough. I
need someone to hold me, to love me, to be here.

I could not have made it through the past winter without the aid of
your sisters Jeretta, and Harriet, as well as your mother, Eliza. Jeretta is
in poor health and is very unhappy. She seems melancholy and speaks
often of wanting to leave this life. It distresses me so.

Our beautiful Martha Jane had her third birthday the 3rd of this month.
Of course, you know that. She asked about her Pa, all day. She is a
beautiful, bouncy, doll; full of energy and mischief like you. She has my
hair, and your green eyes. I am so jealous of her long eye lashes, just like
yours! It is so unfair that a man should have eyes as beautiful as yours.
Looking at her eyes makes me miss and want you so!

James Calvin is eighteen months old this month. He has grown so
since you were last here. Of course he would, since he was a new born
when you left. He is pulling himself up on things and trying to walk.
Martha Jane cares for him a great deal and he tries to chase her around.
As long as she stays along the walls or furniture, he goes after her. To
tease him, she moves to the center of the room and beckons for him to
come. He squeals and bawls until she comes back in range. One of these
days he will be running after her and she will be sorry for her teasing.
The winter was hard on James. He is so thin, like you, and seems to catch
every cold that comes along. He has my blonde hair, but it is coming in
fine like yours. He will, I think, have my eyes, but again, he is blessed
with your lashes.

I keep the photograph of you on the wall by the fireplace. We talk
about you every night before we go to bed. You look so fine in your
uniform. I suppose now that you are an officer, it is even more
spectacular. We always remember you in our prayers.

Oh Evans, where are you on this starry night? Where are you to lay your head? I worry about you, and you are never out of my thoughts. I know you write when you can, but it is never enough.

Patsy Robinson, Steven Wayne's betrothed, shared her last letter from him. He seems a pompous ass even in his writing. Patricia allows me to call her "Patsy" now since, "Your husband serves under my 'soon to be', it is only proper that we are friends". I don't like her. I am certain she is entertaining other gentlemen on the sly.

Dear husband, when will this terrible war end and you come home to our little cabin with me and our beautiful children? Its years past the "six months, no more" declaration you and Buck made when you enlisted. I know you are doing what you think you should, but is it worth all this suffering? I pray this will soon be over. I weary of concern for the coming winter. I don't know if I can make it without help. Oh, do pray for me. Do you love me? How selfish of me, of course you do. I just want you home so…

Your loving wife,
Lucy Jane

Lucy Jane Roberts Atwood frowns and lays her quill pen aside as she bends to blow across the page covered with her practiced hand to dry the words written in berry ink of her making. She sighs and as she does, the only candle on the only table in the small cabin she and Evans built and call home, flickers, throwing odd shadows on the walls.

She is comforted by the breathing of her sleeping babies across the room. Martha Jane in the "big bed" as she calls it, and James Calvin on the trundle. They are her joy, her anchor in the storm of war. If it were not for them, she thinks, she would go insane, but how long can she protect them?

The fires need tending, and she goes about it; setting a large hickory back log in the fire place and banking the fire in the cook stove against the cold of the April night. Spring comes slowly to the Ozarks; winter is not yet defeated.

The small fatherless family has already read from the family Bible, said evening prayers, and read stories from the many books Evans has left. She is afraid. What if he never comes back? What if he's dead, rotting in some common battlefield grave unknown to anyone? She shakes her head to clear it of such thoughts and clings to the hope, the visceral knowledge that he is alive. If he weren't, she would know.

She also fears for herself and the children. A woman alone with men about who did not answer the call to war is not safe. She has no lack of male attention, but it is undesirable. She married Evans to better herself and that is what she is going to do. This war is an obstacle to her eventual goal, but she will overcome it. When Evans returns, things will be much better and better is what Lucy wants.

She looks around the simple cabin and declares all to be well. It is time for bed. She stands near the bed against the back wall of the single room, loosens the sash holding her simple, pale blue dress, raises her arms over and behind her head to undo the three buttons. Thus unencumbered, she slides the dress over her shoulders, and off, followed by her other garments. The cabin, with the fire stoked and burning bright is warm and lighted.

She lifts her right hand to her hair, removes the blue tie pins and shakes it free. Her long, blonde locks fall around her bare shoulders and cascades down her back. She sees her reflection in the darkened window likes what she sees.

Even with the birth of two children, she has the figure God graced her with, which she has used to capture the fancy of many and the heart of one. Her slender form is well muscled from hard work, and shows no fat. She smiles at her reflection.

Lucy moves to look closer. Her gaze settles on her eyes. They are her most powerful feature. They stop men in their tracks and frighten women. They pierce to the heart of anyone who is daring enough to engage her stare.

She sighs, "Someone this beautiful", she says out loud, "should never have to go to bed alone." She turns, and moves to the bed, stooping as she goes to retrieve her discarded garments, folds them and places them on the chest at the foot of the bed. She contemplates opening the chest and taking out her flannel sleeping gown, but decides against it. Her bed may be empty, but it doesn't have to be cold. She blows out the candle, pulls down the covers and slides onto the chilled cotton undercover. It is cold to her fire warmed skin. She pulls the quilt, a wedding gift from Mother Atwood, up to cover herself then slides her hands over her body enjoying her own touch and whispers, "Evans, good night my love where ever you are. I hope you think of me as I do of you." She smiles at her touch and the thought.

3) The Battle for Port Gibson

May 1st, 0400 - 0530

May 1, 1863
Port Gibson, Miss.
Sometime before dawn

I fear no one will read this. I am writing in predawn light; I see the page as a shadow. We, my outpost of six men have been awake all night. We've tried to rest, but with the massing of the Yankee forces to our front, it has been a futile effort. After the terror and confusion of the night action, the enemy has made no further probes of our lines.

We listened to the Yankee wounded moaning and crying until a detail came to their aid. They sought permission to retrieve their men which was granted. We risk nothing by being compassionate. The men were suffering. I hope they will extend to us the same courtesy when the need arises. As they were leaving, their leader yelled, "Thanks Reb! Good night to you!"

I yelled back, "You're welcome blue belly. We'll see you at sun up!" His answer was a valuable piece of information as he called back, "You sure will, we're coming for you!"

One of my men yelled across, "Where you boys from?"

"Iowa".

I could hear someone chew the Yankee out for telling us when they would attack, and what unit they were. It wasn't like we didn't expect the attack, or care where they were from; but now we know. I sent a dispatch to Steven Wayne, our company captain, with the information. In return, he had no orders but to stand our ground until attacked then fall back. I have observed that the toughest, hardest, soldiers in either army, when wounded, call for their mothers, and it was no different tonight. Mothers are comfort and protection. When you are in terrible pain, nigh unto death, you call out to the one person who has always been there, the one who could always make it better. Oh, dearest Mother, I do love you. Please forgive the pains I have caused.

The reason I fear no one will read this is that we are going into battle. It will be fierce and terrible; the most awful yet. We have been outmanned for every battle we've fought, but have never faced such an army. Grant's army is said to number 20,000 or more. I hope that number is the result of rumor. I fear for my men, and my army, and myself. If I should fall, I pray this journal is recovered, and sent home. The Yankees are massing on the road west, and spreading into the woods in front of us. We can hear their pickets about a hundred yards out, and see their fires flicker through the trees. The sounds of preparation for battle intensify as more and more of them arrive. Our small forces have the advantage of knowing how the ground lays which is our ally. We know where the ravines and washes run. They are filled with cat's claw and berry vines, honey suckle, and such, and are an ally and advantage to us.

It won't be for long. I hope and pray that the end of this day finds me still among the living and able to finish this entry. I pray the Lord's protection on us...

I put the journal inside my coat, secure in the pocket there. Its pages have become worn and water stained from sweat, rain, and crossing of creeks. If I fall, it will be with me. I have given Buck instructions to remove it and send it home to Lucy or Ma. He says to take it home myself, but I know he'll do as I ask.

Buck, with his best effort at quiet says, "Light soon."

"What time you figure?"

"Five or so."

"Yeah."

It's quiet between us, but I can tell that my sergeant, my friend has something on his mind. Traveling together as we have, you get to know a man. I wait, knowing he will speak when ready.

"I got a bad feeling 'bout this one."

"Yeah, I know."

"No, I got a <u>real</u> bad feeling about this one."

"Buck, what're you trying to do, scare me more than I am? I gotta lead these men, and I don't want to do it with piss running down my leg!" He chuckles; I can almost see his big, round, fur covered face do its familiar bob as he laughs. "Go on and check the men. Make sure they're ready and have plenty of ammo." Buck turns to leave, "Get 'em to eat and drink; it's going to be a long day."

Buck's hand waves in my face. I smell before I see the pieces of hardtack and jerky. "You'd better eat too," he says, as he heads down the line to check the men.

I stretch out to rest, close my eyes and feel the warmth of my home and watch my beautiful wife and our children sleeping. I want so to sleep with them. I can almost hear their breathing and match mine to the cadence in my head. I drift further away. Coffee, I smell coffee. How

long has it been since I had a hot cup of coffee? I walk to the stove and
reach for the pot. It makes no sense for the pot to be on in the night, and
fresh and hot, but this is a dream and I can have what I want.
My hand is almost on the handle when I start awake. I see a flicker of a
small fire, and smell coffee, real coffee, not chicory root, or barley
toasted in a pan, real coffee. I think I am dreaming again, and inhale; it's
real.

I hope it isn't pilfered from the civilians about. I do not countenance
pilfering. If we ask and they give, that's one thing, but stealing from our
own people is wrong. The southerners would rather give it to us than
have it taken from them by the Federals in exchange for a worthless
receipt.

One of the men from the fire asks, "Do you want some coffee
Lieutenant?"

"Praise the Lord, yes, please," I pass my cup, "where did you get it?"

"When you sent me to take the dispatch to Captain Culpepper, he had
it and shared it out. He said Mrs. Shaifer gave it to him as she was
leaving." Although Steven Wayne is betrothed to Patricia Ann Robinson
back home in Shiloh, Arkansas, he is a ladies' man. His skill has paid off
many times in additional rations. The men appreciate his way with the
women; he never seems to be turned down, but they make sport of him.
When he is near a woman and he himself is on foot, his limp from a
wound sustained at Corinth, Mississippi becomes more pronounced. It is
an effective ploy, but comical. There are wagers on when he will use a
cane.

The coffee's passed and my sincere thanks offered. I savor the aroma,
and luxuriate in the warmth of the cup in my cold hands. With the first
sip, I close my eyes and try to imagine my love, my life, my wife lying in
our bed warm and safe. I long to be there; the smell of the coffee takes
me home.

I see flashes of Lucy Jane moving about the kitchen in the early
morning in her gown, stoking the fire from last night's embers, and watch
the flames dance alive with the kindling that she lays on. She breathes
life into the fire as she exhales into it. Light flares, making her gown
transparent; silhouetting her curves though the fabric. I watch as she
turns back to our bed and feel her slide in the covers beside me…

"They're coming!" Buck drops next to me.

I take a gulp of the coffee, and pass it to Buck who finishes it with a
grunted, "Thanks." I chew more jerky, sucking its juices; a cool drink
from the canteen and I'm ready. The men put away their mess kits and
kick out the fire. Within seconds; we're waiting.

This is the hardest part of battle, the waiting. This is the time when all men are certain they are cowards, and hope it isn't so. This is the time when you cling to the yesterdays and hope for a tomorrow. This is the time you think of God and talk to Him just in case. You plead for that tomorrow. I have never known a man to not. This is the time when you feel like your bladder is about to burst and your guts feel weak. More prayers are offered. This is the time when those new to battle throw up anything they have eaten, and sometimes let go of what they were praying not to. This is the time when your mouth is so dry a river can't quench the thirst. This is the time to fight. All of your senses are tuned up sharper than ever before. You will never feel like this again because every time is different. You are aware of every heart beat, every breath, every movement, every sound. This is the time when all life is more brilliant, glorious, and beautiful. The colors are more vivid, the air is more precious, and the water is nectar from God. Your skin is so sensitive, that you feel everything, but acknowledge nothing. This is the time that makes the man next to you your brother. You can hear his breathing and hope to again when it's over. This is the time when a reassuring touch, even a word carries a message never to be forgotten; you are not alone my brother, you are not alone. This is the time; are you ready?

We hear them before we see them. The light is coming, but their blue coats blend into the yet night and shadows of the woods. They're close; from the sound, they number about twenty to our six. We're outnumbered three to one; nothing new; the only time we had the odds in our favor was at the Battle of Pea Ridge; we lost - bad leadership. We don't have that problem now; General Bowen's a genius at making a few into a lot. "Steady men, steady," I hear myself say in what I think is a whisper but hear returns of, "Ready, sir," "Ready here," "Let 'em come." Two last commands, "Don't fire until I say, we will fire one volley. When you withdraw, remember your sequence. Make every shot count, or they will be on us too quick to move." Our future, if any, lies in each other's skills and courage. They won't let me down, but will I be the weak one today?

Yankees are in the woods, just the other side of a wash that they do not see. They're right in front of us; within range, but I want to make sure we can't miss. We'll fire at thirty yards. They'll return fire wild as we move away from them.

I think, "Ten more yards, four more of your scared little steps and you will die." My thoughts are not Christian. Those are not men over there, they are enemy; more like deer in the woods than men; deer that I am hunting, except they can kill. They won't have the chance. They aren't as good as us; we have more to lose.

Two more steps... Boom, crack, boom, boom, boom, firing from the 12th's position; screams and cries of Yankee wounded; ragged, rippling cracks of rifle fire. The 12th will be falling back. It has started; 5:30 is my guess. Now is the time. I take a deep breath and with every bit of pent up tension, scream as a man possessed of the devil, "Fire!" There's a thunderous roar from the voices of my six who join me in the Rebel yell, followed by six rifle blasts as they discharge close enough to be simultaneous. With the hot lead, and fire, there is a cloud of smoke from the discharged gun powder that covers our controlled, rapid withdrawal.

As soon as the triggers are pulled, we are moving. I hesitate a heart beat to allow my men to get ahead of me. I am first in the covering fire sequence. We stagger our retreat to cover for each other as we fall back. I'm surprised at how well I can see. My LeMat pistol is in hand; I will not try to reload the Springfield while I run. The LeMat is a heavy, durable, and lethal weapon with its nine .40 caliber bullets cylindered over a single, short, 16-gauge shot barrel. It isn't accurate at much beyond twenty yards, but I can get off a series of shots that are more effective with their noise and smoke than one rifle shot and maybe I'll drop one of them.

We are in the open, on plowed ground, stumbling along as fast as we can in the night shadows. Buck is steps ahead of me, and I am about to overtake him when he turns and drops to one knee facing the advancing line of the enemy. I turn and do likewise, but at a distance from him to make a smaller target of both of us. Buck is reloading; I am covering him with the pistol. He takes less than twenty seconds; a good rifleman can reload the Enfield three times in a minute. I am watching the enemy advance.

Their skirmishers are struggling through the ravine and up the steep slopes. The cat's claw vines, greenbrier, poison ivy, and honey suckle are grabbing onto their wool clothes. The thought of those Yankees fighting through the tangle gives me a chuckle; they're going to have a miserable next few days itching and scratching. "Welcome to the South, boys; if the bullets don't get you, the bugs, critters, and noxious plants will!" Buck laughs.

"Ready," he shouts as he brings his rifle to his shoulder.

We hold our fire until the first five or six are topping the ridge, then I say, "Fire." We open up; Buck with his single, accurate rifle shot, and me with three shots from the LeMat. I see dust jump off a blue coat as the man tumbles back into the ravine. I see another drop, maybe two, but

I don't know if from our fire, or they are dropping into the ravine for cover. It doesn't matter, the results are the same; we are clear to run.

Buck's moving across the uneven ground in an erratic pattern. He'll run forty yards to make twenty, but he is a master at it. He says he learned the skill chasing rabbits as a boy. I'm doing the same in the opposite direction; both of us heading for the next man in line, Briggs. The Yankees are out of the ditch, we can hear bullets ripping the air apart and kicking up dirt beyond us as they fire wild trying to move over the furrows of the field.

We get to Briggs and he is ready to fire. Instead of running to the rear, I halt and turn. I have six more shots to spend with the LeMat; which means I can fire two shots here with Briggs, two more with Wilson, and, if I need to, fire two with Feidler. I hope I won't need them; the LeMat is a great weapon but takes a long time to reload. Buck stops with me, but I signal him to go on to Wilson's position. He nods and goes.

Briggs fires sooner than I planned. The blue bastards are close. I whirl and fire. I am not concerned with hitting, but stopping them. The Yankees are dropping to the dirt as I fire and hear one of my shots thwack into meat. That'll stop 'em for awhile. Briggs and I run.

He is much faster, and even with erratic running, he is pulling away. I don't take the time to look back knowing that over the uneven ground; I stand a good chance of falling. He has five yards to go to my ten. I see Martin Wilson's rifle raised and ready, but pointing at me and tracking me as I run.

Martin is Susan Wilson's younger brother. He begged to go with Buck and me as we enlisted. It had been two years since I married Lucy Jane instead of Susan when we agreed to take him with us, but right now I wonder about Martin's level of acceptance. I asked him right in front of both families before we left, "Martin, if you've got any hard feelings about me not marrying your sister, say so now," and before he could reply, "I don't want to have to be watching my back with the best shot in two counties lurking around; so what is it now?"

"No Evans, I want to go for my own reasons. If Susan don't hate you, and she can forgive, I can too." So it is that he came with us, but every time Buck or I try to get it out of him why he enlisted, he avoids the discussion. Right now, as I stare down the .54 caliber muzzle pointing at me, I have my doubts about his level of forgiveness.

I look at Buck watching me, and then back at Martin whose aim has not wavered. Buck follows my line of sight and realizes the situation. I see Martin's finger on the trigger and the barrel swing wide of me.

A split second before I arrive, Martin fires. I feel the concussion which deafens me as I am even with the muzzle of Martin's rifle. I close the final yards to Buck's side, panting and wiping the sweat out of my eyes. It is still cold, but war, wool, and running warm me up in a hurry. I spin around and prepare to fire. Buck yells in my ear, "What'd you want to do about this?" He is gesturing toward Martin who was reloading from the prone position.

I don't have time to sort it out. My options are clear, shoot him, or keep him with me. "You and Briggs drop back, I'll keep Martin with me, now go!" Buck fires off a round as does Briggs and they are running to the next position. I turn to face the enemy wondering if I have one on my side of the line. The Yankees are within thirty yards and closing; their bullets are cracking through the air over our heads. They can't get steady to fire with any accuracy; thank God. I fire off three quick but aimed shots as Martin fires again. We have done some damage; their advance is halted.

Martin is standing beside me; our eyes meet; there is no malice as I expected to see, or any sort of challenge; there is nothing; just an obedient stare waiting for orders. I give one, "Run!" We both sprint toward the next fall back position. We zig-zag as we run; cutting wide swaths, but the Yankees are not firing. We halt where Private Johnson is prepared to cover our retreat, but he doesn't have to. The enemy has halted their advance.

I am breathing like a horse after a two mile race. I take my hat off, wipe my face and head with my sleeve and turn about to assess the situation. I feel the sting of the sweat in the powder burns on my face and swipe with my sleeve again. Johnson has his rifle at the ready, and Martin is in the final movements of the chorography of loading. His eyes never leave the battle front as the rod runs down the muzzle, tamping the charge home; back out, and secured in its tube under the barrel. His face shows only a fierce, ready soldier willing to fight.

The Yankees have decided that we pickets are not worth the effort and leave off the pursuit. They're regrouping for a concentrated assault. We fall back unchallenged to our lines. I find Buck with the rest of our platoon. We drop behind the cover of a wooden fence line.

"How many of 'em, Lieutenant?"

"As many as you saw yesterday, we're outnumbered as usual." This is Grant's main invasion force; what the South has feared for a year and a half. "We've been outnumbered before; remember they're invading our country. Our cause is righteous." I sound like a preacher, but with what is facing our small army today, a preacher is what we need.

There is quiet. We wait. Martin Wilson moves to rejoin his squad. I take him by the arm, ready to defend myself if necessary, and turn him to me, "Martin, you stay with me." The boy does not seem to have any malice in his heart. If he did, he's not showing it. If I had been caught aiming at an officer, and had been foiled in my attempt to assassinate, I would show the fierce anger that had brought me to the point of pulling the trigger. Martin does not; quite the opposite; he acts as if nothing has happened.

Still holding his arm, I say, "Martin, come over here a minute," and lead him away from the rest of the men. I nod to Buck, who joins us. When we're apart from the men, who are watching and trying with all their might to hear us, I ask, "Martin, what was that all about back there?"

"I'm wondering the same thing Evans." I have a difficult time requiring "sir" from someone who was, at one time, almost family. "What was Buck doing putting the muzzle of his rifle against my skull?" He's incredulous as if it were he that has been wronged.

As calm as I can, trying to control my pent up anger and emotion from the skirmish and near miss, I ask, "Martin, is this a joke?"

He looks at me with complete incomprehension, wrinkles his brow, frowns, and shakes his head. "No, Evans, what's going on?"
I look at Buck who shrugs. He's as bewildered as I am. "Private Wilson, you had me in your sights as I was running across the field to your position. What was that all about?"

"Evans, I don't know what you mean. My eyes never left the Yankee who was chasing you. He must of know'ed you was an officer, because he was making a bee-line right at 'cha. I guess that explains why you slowed down don't it?"

I stare at him; then look at Buck who is staring at me. "Did you see a Yankee chasing me?"

He shrugs; baffled as I am.

"Why do you think I waited so long to fire? That Yankee was right on you, but tripped and fell. I swung my aim away then 'cause I didn't want to shoot you! It took him awhile to rise up, but when he did, I popped his head like a dandelion off a stem!"

I look at Buck, "Did you see this?"

"Hell no, I was moving my ass out of there. I ain't as fast as you young 'uns, I got to get me a head of steam going! But Boy, I believe him. I don't think there's a hateful bone in his body, and he sure as hell ain't mean, but he is one damned fine shot!"

"Excuse me, sir," comes a tentative voice from off to the side; it's Fiedler, "I can't but help think you think Martin done something bad, but sir, I was the last position, and I saw it all. Why, he saved your life, sir!

If that blue belly hadn't fallen, Martin would have had to shoot him in the ear, sir, and he could have done it too! Martin would never hurt you, sir. Why, the reason he come in the army was to take care of ya! He said he had to make sure you get home to Miss Lucy and them babies of ya'lls. He said Miss Susan told him to! He's just doin' what he promised his sister, s'all. Leave him be sir, he loves, ya; hell, we all do! Please…sir."

I'm speechless. Since I was honored by being elected to be the men's leader, they making me an officer, I have wondered about their loyalty and their willingness to follow me. Now, there's no question.

Buck's kicking a dirt clod and looking after it like it was the first one he's ever seen. Martin's staring at the clouds and sniffing like he has a cold, and Fiedler's just standing there slack jawed waiting for me to answer him. "You're dismissed Private Fiedler."

"Uh, uh…"

I glare at him.

"Yes sir." He moves back to the line.

Loud rippling fire, a volley from the 12th, re-focuses our attention. We turn toward the sound and watch the smoke rise over the trees in front of the Shaifer House. I can hear the cries of the dying and wounded as the thunder of a hundred rifles fades away. The cries are engulfed by a massive return volley from the enemy. It was much louder, and rolls over, and over the land like peals of thunder. The attack has begun.

I look to our front; the enemy is advancing in huge numbers. They come out of the woods looking like trees in the early morning light. There are so many, it looks like ants from a hill. "Boys, we ain't got time for this! Buck, to your men! Martin, you're with me the rest of this day; do not leave my side! Do you understand?" I look at both of them. They're staring at the Yankees, anxious to go at 'em.

"Yes sir!"

"Go to your positions!" They hustle off until Martin remembers his specific order and returns to my side.

"Evans, I'll die before anything happens to you! You don't worry; I swore an oath, I ain't going to break it…ever!"

"You swore an oath; to who?"

"Susan," he says, "I'm sorry Evans, but she still cares about you, and made me swear that since I was coming to war no matter what they said, that I would watch out for you." He looks up at me, "The whole family loves you; I ain't goin' to break that oath."

"O.K., Martin; let's us kill us some Yankees!"

"Yes sir, let's kill us a bunch!"

4) Shiloh, Arkansas
April, 1863

Across a fertile valley, high on a hill overlooking that valley, sits a house large enough to be named. The actual gate to this edifice is at the foot of the hill in the valley. The stone gate posts hold matching bronze signs which announce, in raised, ornate script, the name "*Spring Dale*".

Numerous springs dot the lands of the estate below the hill, or dale as its pretentious owner, Hubert Rodney Robinson loves to call it, each with its own drainage, and hence, the name, "*Spring Dale*". All of these lesser creeks flow into a larger waterway which provides Spring Dale with its northern boundary and is named Spring Creek.

The springs are the source of the abundant water supply which lend the valley its fertility, and from hence, the wealth, and the pretentiousness of the Robinsons. The valley is capable of growing any number of crops, and does, but the money crop, as it is all across the south is the white gold, cotton.

The economy of cotton requires intense labor from the plowing and planting in the spring, to cropping, the process of thinning to allow one hardy plant per foot of ground, to hoeing, to the harvest in the fall, all of which is intensive, and expensive unless you own the labor. Thus, Rodney Robinson is a slave owner; the largest in Washington County. Depending on the season and the need, there are as many as twenty-five workers on the property at any one time.

There was a time when Mr. Robinson leased slaves from other owners, but has now entered into an agreement with a fellow cotton grower, Congressman Clifford Wade Yeller, the wealthiest man in the state, from all the way over in the southeast corner of Arkansas, on the Mississippi River to exchange slaves as they are needed, thus cutting by half, the expense of ownership and upkeep. The growing seasons from the southeast to northwest Arkansas are sufficiently staggered to allow for the transport of ten to fifteen slaves between the two plantations depending on the demand.

It is just such a trip that has brought young Horatio Thaddeus Yeller to Spring Dale this April. It is the first that Congressman Yeller has allowed his youngest and most frivolous son to take. Thad's three older brothers are fighting for the cause leaving worthless, young Thad to schooling and the tutelage of the congressman. Thad is delighted with the arrangement.

He does not care about the cause of the Confederacy and cannot imagine why all the fuss over a few slaves. His main goal in life is to have a good time, with good whiskey; have money, not make it, and adventure if it comes without danger, hence his strong aversion to war. He is the reason that Patricia Anne Robinson's bed is, unlike Lucy Jane's, not empty, nor cold.

She is the only child of Rodney and Sarah Anne Robinson, and is, because of her ability from birth to manipulate daddy, spoiled beyond redemption. Sarah tried over the first twelve years of Patsy's life to instill discipline and manners in her daughter, but Patricia would have none of it. She has always gotten everything she wants regardless of what her mother says and Sarah finally took to drink and let Patsy find her own way with her father.

Patricia Anne has the morals of an alley cat. It matters not a whit to her that she is sharing her bed with young Thad while betrothed to Steven Wayne Culpepper.

There is a guest house built over the twenty stall barn, just behind the main house, which is used to accommodate the overseers as they transport the labor pool. Since Patsy's education in Atlanta has been interrupted by the "terrible war of northern aggression", as her father makes almost constant reference, and since she is forced to be subject to his protection, Patsy insists on maintaining her quarters in the guest house. The arrangement serves to give her an illusion of independence, and affords her the dalliance she has just engaged in with young Thad Yeller.

Even with the chill of an April night, Patricia Anne lays in the dark covered with a sheen of perspiration that captures the light from the fire, giving her a red-orange glow. Beside her, Thad, a year younger than her eighteen, lays on his back, right arm over his eyes, panting. Thad is in an all out sweat.

Patricia is basking in the glow of fires both internal and external. It is a wonderful moment until Steven Wayne Culpepper intrudes into her thoughts. She pouts and grows cold. "Why won't he just go away," she thinks to herself. Her mood is ruined. She draws the covers to her chin. The gesture is not brought on by modesty or guilt. Patricia Anne has no compunction whatsoever about her behavior. Her remorse is only that the situation is so complicated.

She had just turned sixteen when Steven Wayne, the son of the banker handling the Robinson holdings, swept into her life wearing the tailored uniform of a Confederate Captain – a commission and rank that his father's influence and money bought him. He was dashing, handsome, charming and she was taken with him at first sight. Daddy approved of the courtship, and allowed it for two reasons.

First, Steven Wayne was going to be wealthy some day, and the son of the owner of the bank that he dealt with; well, it just could not hurt to have him at least close to the family if not part of it. The second reason, and by far the most important of the two, Steven Wayne was going to fight for a cause that was close to Rodney Robinson's heart; the continuation of the time honored system of slavery which is a major part of Robinson's wealth. The fact that Steven Wayne did not give two hoots in hell about the institution of slavery, and if truth be told, opposed such a thing, did not change the fact that he was going to war, and since he was going to fight, in Rodney's mind, it might as well be for the cause dearest to his heart; wealth which equated to slaves.

Daddy had made it easy for Steven Wayne to court Patricia. He knew the relationship was going too far in some regards, but for the sake of prosperity and posterity, he was willing to turn a blind eye.
Patricia Anne's mother, Sarah Anne, took a very dim view of the situation and voiced her complaint to Mr. Robinson but once. He explained his views and the necessity of the relationship to her in his most persuasive manner and they came to an immediate understanding. After the explanation, Sarah Anne took to her bed with the vapors for several days. Although Patsy did not see her mother, the house slaves talked and said that Miss Sarah was not at present ambulatory, but the bruises and marks would be healed in time for the betrothal festivities. They were not. Patsy scarcely noticed her mother's absence.

Patricia Anne was so thrilled at being engaged to such a wealthy, handsome, war hero, that not much else mattered. She did not love Steven Wayne for she had no inkling what loving someone entailed. No one would ever usurp her first love, herself. She begged and pleaded with Steven Wayne to not go to war, to stay home, make the rounds of parties and balls, and be at her beck and call, but he was passionate in his belief in the cause of the Confederacy, and against her, and her family's wishes, he went.

Daddy and Steven Wayne both assured the young girl that if she would wait for, "just a few months, a year at the most", this inconvenient war would be over; the arrogance of the north would have been quashed, and the South's, along with the Robinson's, prosperity would be assured. All would be back to normal in just a short while, if she could just wait. She would not.

She managed the better part of a year, but was not allowed to go back to school in the fall of 1862. It was obvious by then, that the war was not going to be over in "just a few months, a year at the most", and Patsy grew restive. At home, there were not the distractions of study, or music, although Patsy cared not for learning, nor playing piano. Going to classes was for her, a social event allowing her to glory and gloat at her classmates' expense about being engaged to such a fine, wealthy, gentleman, and a company commander too. No such distractions existed at Spring Dale, leaving only one to entertain her; the numerous young men who came to call for the sake of courtesy and curiosity.

She is dutiful in writing Steven Wayne once a week. She would chronicle her activities; who said what, to whom, and about whom on a daily basis. She closes the letter on Saturday, posts it, and begins a new one on Sunday.

Patricia is impressed with, and careful to remark on Steven Wayne's heroics in battle that he has shared in his letters. She glories with him in his victories, and mourns with him in defeat, but is very uncomfortable with the tenor of his correspondence. It seems Steven Wayne has discovered a side of himself that he never suspected; he can lead men in battle. He's very good at it and regales her with details that do not interest her in the slightest. She feels that Steven Wayne is far too passionate about something that does not include her. She is not the center of his universe, and that will never do.

His letter informing her of his wound suffered in Corinth, Mississippi by a Mini' ball in the hip causes a great deal of consternation on her part, and she spends two entire pages brooding and agonizing over his condition. His health and well being serve to occupy her mind for almost the entire week before she strikes on the possibility of his wound being severe enough for him to come home. She's excited about the prospect and insists that he forsake the cause and come home to obtain superior medical care and be where she can nurse him back to health. She waits with girlish anticipation for his reply, knowing it is a wonderful plan, and will fulfill her needs. At long last, it comes. She hurries to her rooms, rips open the aged letter and reads…

March 2, 1863
Corinth, Mississippi

To:
Patricia Anne Robinson,
Betrothed of Steven Wayne Culpepper
Capt. 15th Arkansas Infantry

My dearest, darling, Patsy,

How grateful I am to be in receipt of your letter posted last month. It raises my joy to be graced with your fine hand and extensive entries. I do look so forward to your letters. They are the brightest light in the dreary life of this worn soldier. I pray there never comes a time when they cease.

My heart breaks at the thought of your loneliness. I cannot imagine the grief this war has weighed upon you. All of us in our dear country are called to sacrifice. I promise you on my word as an officer and a gentleman, that your endurance and patience will be rewarded tenfold upon the successful conclusion of this conflict.

I realize that the duration has been longer than anticipated, but endure we must. The light at the end of this dark, dreary, path is that of freedom, glorious, unsullied freedom; for that we must persevere!

In answer to your plea for release from your burden of care and woe for my condition, and for your loneliness, I cannot comply with your wishes. I am committed to the cause of our country and will not forsake my oath to defend our infant nation, no more than I would walk away from a starving baby.

I cannot leave my men at this dark hour. The war does not go well in Mississippi. The news of Grant's invasion and the fall of New Orleans are most trying. The men are counting on me to be their leader. How can words written or spoken ever convey the brotherhood of men who have served in arms? I know that I am inadequate in my attempts. Suffice it to say that for men who have fought for it, freedom has a different meaning that those who have not stood in battle cannot understand. I do not love this war, but I do love the cause.

Please do not tempt me further with pleas for me to leave my men, my army, and my country in their hour of darkest peril. I know of your needs, but cannot comply with your wishes to abandon these sacred duties.

My most precious love, please realize that I am fighting not only for our country, but our way of life, and most importantly, you and I, and our future. I beg your continued loyalty not only to our cause, but to me. These bitter moments will soon be behind us and the glory of our loving future looms before us. I implore you to keep your eye on that goal, and never wasver.

I close with undying love. I never dreamed that I would find a love of such angelic qualities while living on this earth. You are more than I ever dreamed of and your visage occupies my every thought and dream. What I do, I do for you and your precious love. I long to be with you, but only in honor.

My eternal love,

Steven Wayne Culpepper

Commanding Officer, Company "A",

15th Arkansas Infantry, CSA

"Steven Wayne Culpepper, *Captain* of the Confederacy, you will live to regret those words!" She hisses and spits her curse with all the venom of a Cotton Mouth Moccasin. "You speak of causes; *I* am your only cause!"

It does not take long for word to spread that Patricia Anne, is available. Yes, she's engaged to the banker's boy away at war, but she is not rebuffing advances or invitations. She wears his ring, but is being seen more and more with any number of eligible young men. Few of the suitors satisfy the second requirement in Patsy's limited list that of being well to do, but all fulfill the primary requirement of being a man.

Horatio Thaddeus Yeller is the latest in the parade, and he almost fulfills both requirements. He is a man, trying to be, and with training, can and will do all she asks and he is wealthy, or will be thanks to his trust fund. Patricia does not know the dollar figure, but she is certain it will be sufficient for them to start a life together. Thad's trust will also be released upon his marriage.

She is certain that it is a marriage dear Daddy will approve of. There is already the relationship of the families through the years; this union would only serve to strengthen that bond with one of the most powerful, influential, and wealthy families in Arkansas. Who is there to object? Daddy may champion the cause of Steven Wayne for a moment or two, but when his darling Patsy explains all the ramifications of the marriage, his practical side will see the light and his honorable side will follow. Patricia demands, "Horatio Thaddeus Yeller."

His head lifts at the formal tone and commanding voice of his paramour. "Yes, my lovely?"

"Do you love me?"

"Oh, my dearest, yes, of course I love you!"

"If we are to continue such activity," reaching for him to make her meaning clear, "to protect my honor, we must get married".

"Yes, I would like that very much. We should as soon as possible".

She rolls away and in the dark, Patricia Anne slips a particular ring off her left hand, reaches to lay it on the table beside the bed, turns back to Thad, pulls him to her, and says, "Show me how much you love me," thus ending her engagement and betrothal to Captain Steven Wayne Culpepper.

5) The Battle for Port Gibson
0600 – 1000 hours

Martin and I make our way to the rest of the platoon. We see Captain Culpepper on his horse, waving from twenty yards away. "What Captain?" I shout; the formal courtesy of "sir" to a superior officer is a thing of the past between us. Truth is I've never called Steven Wayne "sir". He is far less experienced than I am, as well as being two years younger. I was elected to my rank by the men, which is customary in the CSA, but Steven Wayne was a captain from the moment he "enlisted". He cups his hands and yells, "We're about to be attacked…"

I can't believe what I'm hearing. Does he think only company commanders on horseback can see what's coming?

"…they're going to try and flank us! When I signal, we're going to move deeper along the ridge to the south!" Steven Wayne is a walking dichotomy. He's a natural on the battle field, but a jester off.

As a commander burdened with the day-to-day running of a company, he is a bumbling buffoon. Most of his orders are countermanded by me or Sergeant Buck, and the men look to either of us to confirm anything Steven Wayne says. It is an embarrassment to him, but we have all grown accustomed to it. In a fight, he is a demon. Something comes over him and he has such clarity of thought that Colonel Reynolds, the regimental commander defers to him. Like a chess master looking over the board, he can see three moves ahead, and he's never been wrong.

"I got it Steven Wayne, we'll be ready!" I join my men, walking behind them, reloading the LeMat as I go. "Steady boys, steady; wait for my command, wait…" I look out to the front and the Yankees are standing like they want us to take our shot. Maybe they're trying to scare us with their numbers, but we're not going to waste a volley. We might kill a few, but we need more than a few, we need thousands, we need them in the kill zone; less than fifty yards. At that range, we boys from Arkansas can shoot squirrels without missing. We sure as hell can kill men in blue jackets.

The battle near the house is intensifying. The 12th Sharpshooters are giving them hell. I can tell by the smoke and the noise that the Yankee line is falling back. Our boys see the same, and stand to let out the terrifying, warbling, battle cry of the south, the Rebel Yell! It strikes terror into the hearts of the boys of the north with all their high ideas, thinking to show us how to live, and how they're superior. They have no idea how animal a human being can be when he and his family, and country are backed into a corner. The yell teaches them. We see the fear on their faces. Most are mill and factory workers from the cities and have no notion of what life is like in the south. They just got a taste.

The same cry erupts as the 12th pursues the Yanks. They've pushed them off Rodney Ridge and are moving to join our line and reinforce the road. The yanks in front of us wait.

An officer, a colonel, struts behind his troops on a white mare, wearing a white plume in his hat shouting encouragement to the northern boys who are pissing their pants. "Martin, see that peacock on that horse?"

He grins at me, "Yes sir…"

"Take him down a notch, will ya'?"

His smile broadens as he goes to fetch his Whitworth Rifle. It is a rare and expensive weapon imported from England at a cost of over $100. It's equipped with a telescopic sight that adds to its value. Martin seldom uses the weapon as it has a hexagonal barrel and bore requiring a special and expensive .45 caliber cartridge. The advantage of the Whitworth is that it's accurate and powerful at extreme ranges. Stories abound of the Whitworth killing at over a mile. I think it is less than that; more like a thousand yards, but in Martin's hands, anything is possible.

Our intended target is making a show, moving up and down the line. He's got his field glasses staring right at us, right at me. I don't know how I know, but I do and cannot resist a salute to him. He doesn't know it, but he's about to die. I watch as he signals one of his troops and points in my direction. Martin adjusts his sights and looks at me for confirmation; I nod and watch his target only two hundred yards away; an easy shot for Martin and the special rifle.

The colonel is joined by a color guard. There are the Stars and Stripes; and the battle flag of the 21st Iowa. From where I am standing, I can make out a dark blue field, with an eagle, and stars arrayed across the flag above the eagle. "Boys, that's a pretty flag their sportin'; I want that flag; I want their colors!" My shout elicits another demonic yell which is punctuated by a single shot. Fire, smoke, and thunder belch from the muzzle of Martin's Whitworth along with a near half inch piece of lead. The colonel tumbles off his mount, taking the unit colors down with him. A cheer goes up muffling the return shot that knocks me back as I am whirled around by a force striking my left shoulder. I stagger back several steps, but do not leave my feet as I clutch the wound. The shock from the round passing through my thick coat knocks the wind out of me, but I will not bend. I won't give the yanks the satisfaction. I am hurting; I clench my teeth, squeeze my eyes shut as tears come. After the shock, the wound burns like the fires of hell. I pull my hand away and see blood. It is not the first time I have been bloodied in battle, but the first time I've been shot. My whole arm is numb and burning at the same time. I count myself blessed that the Yankee shooter does not have the Whitworth and is not as good as Martin. I raise my right hand to the men and shout the yell myself; they join the chorus. We are ready!

Dawn, and I feel as if I have lived a life time. The early sky indicates a hot, clear day is coming. It's unnatural quiet as we wait. My heart's pounding with the shock of my wound. So many things have happened in the last two days that it's a blur.

Night before last, we were in an artillery battle with Grant's invading armada over in Grand Gulf on the river. It raged till dark when our forts were successful in knocking out several ships and disabling an iron clad before the Federals broke off and turned south. The victory wasn't much of one as the Yanks landed at Bruinsburg unopposed. Their landing caused us to force-march to Port Gibson yesterday, arriving in the late morning. We've slept little and today will offer no chance of rest.

The Yankees move forward. Their numbers are staggering. They stretch from the road, a hundred yards to my right, to the far left, the south, and disappear into the trees. There are more ravines over there, so flanking will not be as easy as they think. They will have to fight nature's redoubts of tangled vines and steep slopes in the washes and ditches.

From behind us, near the road on Foster's ridge, our artillery opens up on the now advancing enemy. It is terrifying what artillery in the hands of well trained men such as the Pettus Artillery of Missouri can do to standing troops. The enemy lines, which just seconds ago were well formed, uniformed, and flagged by the ensign and their battle colors, are now jagged heaps of screaming men destined to death or the agonizing torments of being left on the field. Their artillery returns fire, but they are far down the road firing up hill and through dense, tree lined ridges. The Yankees keep coming; thousands of them.

I shout the order, "Form ranks!" The men fall in and stand at attention in one, long, gray line. If the men are afraid, they do not show it. "Forward rank, kneel!" Half the men drop to one knee with their rifles ready.

They have picked a target and I can hear the discussion; "I got that tall feller there" or, "Red whiskers is mine", and "Fat Boy's gonna die!"

The Yankees move into range seeking cover as they come. The ridge is heavily wooded, but not enough to afford each of the enemy a hiding place. It's time for a lead storm; "Forward rank, fire!" There is a rippling roll of noise and smoke as units fire close enough together to be indistinguishable. I feel the earth shudder. Our vision is impaired by the billowing smoke from six hundred rifles of the 15th Arkansas. There is no breeze in the early morning and it hangs over the field. The acrid smell of burning powder sears my lungs. The boom of artillery sounds disjointed and odd as I stand enveloped in smoke. I can make out the forward rank falling back and reloading without taking their eyes off the front. The second rank has taken their position. "Second rank, fire!" Another blast, more smoke, more blindness, but this time it is punctuated by the sound of bullets cracking and whistling around us and through the air. I did not hear the enemy's return volley, and brace for their second. My men have gone to ground. In the smoke and confusion, the Yanks are firing high and into the trees around us. One of my men is hit by a falling limb and is rubbing his head as his fellows laugh.

The Yankees are breaking off and moving back into the trees. The first encounter is ours and we enjoy it, but I fear it will be short lived; there are too many of them. The cheers from our ranks drown out the sounds of their artillery moving into a better position.

"Causalities," I bellow over the field in front of me. The smoke is clearing as I hear Buck's booming voice declare, "None," then laughs adding, "…except Phillips; some squirrel dropped a limb on him!"

No casualties; what a relief.

We reload and get ready for the next attack. Enemy officers are milling around, colors being restored as more men move into position behind the enemy's ranks. The cries of the wounded are awful. Rifle fire cracks from the 12th Sharpshooters on our right flank as they keep everyone in blue honest.

The sound of horse hooves heralds the arrival of Steven Wayne. "Lieutenant, that was a probe; they're just feeling us out. They're massing for a major push. We have to hold this ridge. If we don't, they'll have the higher ground."

We cannot hold this force with four artillery pieces to their dozen or more, nor with our six thousand men to their twenty thousand plus, but what we are forced to give, they will pay dearly for.

"Sergeant Buchannan!"

Buck smiles as he launches a stream of tobacco juice, "Gonna be hot in a few minutes!"

"Yeah, in more ways than one. You make sure everyone has a full canteen, a full belly, ammo pouches, and cartridge boxes. We're in this all day."

"You got it Boy; I'll take care of 'em. You watch your own self," then to Martin, "Little brother, you take care of him you hear?"

"I got him." Martin stays, Buck goes.

More Yankees join those already in front of us. There's a ridge to our left with cane breaks that'll protect that flank if we don't have to give up the ridge here by the church. Ours is a good position. The sun is up now; I make it to be 6:30 or so.

The pain in my arm draws my attention. The enemy is still milling around in the woods. I strip out of my jacket to check the wound. It's a cut, but the bleeding has stopped. The area surrounding the wound is turning reddish purple. This one's going to hurt for awhile. I strip out of my shirt and pour water over the gash to clean it out. The bleeding starts again.

I find a cloth strip in my haversack that I use for bandages; I am struggling to tie it on when Buck comes back. "Let me help you with that." He moves my hand out of the way and takes over. "How bad is it?"

"Not bad; just a scratch."

"Yeah, I can tell it's 'just a scratch' by all the blood here," he says looking at me with his one eye closed as he does when he thinks I'm not being as truthful as I ought to be.

"It'd stopped until I cleaned it; it'll stop again. It for sure ain't worth going to the hospital for. Where's the hospital set up?"

"It's at the Shaifer House; ours for now, but both sides will be using it."

"You're always ahead of me Buck. You should be the leader of these men."

"I don't want the responsibility, I ain't good at it. I can't make decisions like you. You're good at seeing the end, I just get us there." He snug's the knot down, "We both have our place; we're strong where the other'un ain't."

"Damn Buck, ain't you waxing philosophical this morning? Lord, if I didn't know better, I'd think you been reading again!"

"Shut up, Boy. Don't you be tellin' anybody about that. I'll kick your skinny ass so hard, you'll have to reach over your shoulder to scratch it," as he wags a threatening finger in my face. "I don't want the boys to go thinking I'm better than they're."

Buck taught me to fight; and I've taught him to read. I'm proud of my pupil. He loves reading and attacked the task as he would an opponent in a fight, with a vengeance. He's proud of his accomplishment, but thinks it separates him from the men.

"You got it wrong; they already know. They admire that you wanted to better yourself. It's a tool to better your life, and the lives of the men."

Buck's helping me back on with my jacket, "I reckon; but just the same, you got your job, I got mine. One ain't no better than the other, ain't no worse, just different. That's what makes it work, I reckon." He steps back as I put on my belt and other necessaries. I don't have time to respond. A bugle from the enemy calls us to battle.

The men are calm, eating, and sharing out some more coffee. My mouth waters at the smell but I don't have the luxury; Yankees are coming, and there are more than I've ever seen.

"Get ready boys!" Even a blind man would know they're coming; you can feel the tramp of their thousands of feet as they march onto what will no longer be a farm field, but one of battle, one of death. What we harvest today will not feed a soul, but by the grace of God, save a nation.

We look down from our ridge and marvel at the sight. Drums beat a tattoo as the blue line with its banners and flags move forward. Their officers are riding high and proud behind the line; minus one. Our battle flag is raised by a boy of no more than sixteen. Next to him, the "Stars and Bars" flutter as it unfurls on the slight morning breeze accompanied by another chorus of the Rebel Yell. Every unit up and down the line tries to best the other and results in a cacophony that must be what Dante describes as the wailing of the souls of hell. It has its desired affect; there is a hitch to the line of the boys in blue. Their officers encourage with shouted orders, but they feel the fear. No man on the field, given an honorable alternative would chose to stand against us. It is our land we are set to defend and die for, but before we make the ultimate sacrifice, there will be dozens who fall with each of us.

The union forces continue to come. I feel as Moses on the shores of the Red Sea when the Egyptian armies were descending on him. I pray for a miracle, but fear that today, there will be no parting. We must do the work of the Lord.

I shout encouragement as I move behind the men. Martin is shadowing me. "Steady men! Make ready! Look at the fear in their faces! When you see their eyes, it'll be time!"

I am amazed again as I look at the men that voted me their leader; any one of them is a better soldier than me, and my guess is that they know it. It is an awesome trust that these, my brothers, place in me.

Steven Wayne rides up behind me and shouts, "Lieutenant!"

He is riding with the 15th's battle flag anchored in his stirrup. It gives us a thrill and will provide a rallying point when things become confused in the next few minutes. We all answer his hail with a fist in the air, and the fiercest yell we can muster. He smiles and rides the line raising the spirits of the rest of the company. Steven Wayne is ready for battle; he is at his best. I think about the colonel Martin dropped; was he their "Steven Wayne"? There must be one in every army.

The Yankees dip into the small gulley we crossed on our retreat and seem to halt.

"First Rank!" They come to attention; "Make ready!" They kneel. "Second Rank!" They respond ramrod straight; "Make ready," and they fall into gaps or behind the first rank.

"Where do you want me sir?" Martin is at my elbow looking at me like an eager child ready to do something truly terrible and exciting.

"I want you right next to me Martin. I need you here. This is going to be fierce and long. If I need a messenger, I'll have to have someone I can trust, someone who won't be afraid to go it alone. Is that you?"

He smiles through his powder stained, sweat-streaked face, nods his head, "Yes sir."

"Let's get in line." We step to the ranks. It seems an eternity before the Yankees' heads appear above the edge of the ditch. As they do, I can see the men fighting the urge to fire. "Hold, let them get up the slope. Aim low, and for center mass!" The Enfield and Springfield rifles have a tendency to shoot high and right, but we know how to compensate.

The Federals show from the waist up. I see out of the corner of my eye Steven Wayne prancing on his stallion, and hear Martin breathing in gasps as we wait. Steven Wayne lets hell loose as he cries, "Aim for their balls boys; FIRE!" My repetition of his order is swallowed in the blast of our twenty-six rifles joining the deadly chorus of six hundred more of the regiment. A blast of the four guns comprising our artillery on Foster's ridge adds percussion bass to our symphony; the movement and work of death has begun.

The second rank has fired and is reloading. Our position is masked by the smoke of our double volley. The morning breeze is at our backs blowing into the face of our enemy. I hear enemy shouts to aim low. "Down!" The men drop to the ground as the crash and concussion of their volley rolls over us. I hear all around, the sound of hot, fast moving lead hitting yielding flesh, and the cries of the wounded. Our artillery booms again leaving a cloud over the field. The smell of sulfur hangs heavy as our men struggle to rise, reloading as they go. The smoke burns my throat as I shout, "Fire at will!"

Our men, released from the constraint of ranks, seek cover where they can fire, reload, and fire again. Martin and I are doing the same. The booming thunder of our artillery is soon exceeded by the number of guns the Union batteries bring to bear. Huge geysers of earth shoot skyward as the Yankee guns fire for range. Dirt showers down around us, but we keep up our fire.

We fire blind through the clouds of smoke. It is terrifying not being able to see the enemy. The smoke, noise, and cascading dirt and rocks disorient even the most disciplined man. In the confusion, troops become separated from their unit even if the man next to him is within reach. The wind gusts from behind us clearing the battlefield for mere seconds and we acquire targets, laying down a withering fire into the unending mass of blue coats.

Our artillery is having the better of the big gun battle due to their being on higher ground. The Yankee batteries shift their fire to our gun emplacements. It gives us some relief, but is hell for our gun crews. Somehow, they manage to keep up the fusillade, and aid us with the Yankee attack.

It is becoming clear that we are going to have to yield, and is confirmed when Steven Wayne rides up shouting, "The left flank is about to give way. The union troops have breached the ravine and are moving to flank us. Fall back to the woods on the ridge to our rear!" Any other orders are lost in another Yankee volley, and our return fire.

"Sergeant Buchannan, organize a withdrawal and get us out of here!"

"Already done Boy, you go first!"

Martin and I begin to fall back and the remainder of our platoon moves with us, we fire to cover the retreat, and are met with an accurate, hot volley from the still advancing enemy. The unmistakable sound of lead hitting a body punctuated by a grunt from the wounded soldier comes from my right. Private Johnson yells, "Mustain's hit! I've got him; I'm headed to the hospital!" We've lost our Corporal responsible for our right flank.

"No you don't," I bellow, "hold that position!" It is against the rules of engagement for a man to relinquish his place in the line of battle to aid another. I cannot allow Johnson to aid the wounded Mustain and leave us vulnerable on the flank.

Buck weaves his way rabbit style to where Johnson is while the rest of the men fall back. We've only got seconds to retreat; bullets are hitting all around us, and past us, but we cannot panic and run. We will lose more men if we do. I do not know, but suspect that is what happened to Mustain; he stood, turned to run and was hit in the back.

We are moving to the woods when Buck appears through the smoke with Johnson by his side. There's blood on Johnson's shoulder. I yell, "You hit?" He shakes his head. His face is pale, sick, and white even under the powder and dirt coating.

Buck guides him past me and says as he passes, "Mustain's dead. Shot in the back; broke his spine, probably got his heart too. Johnson was trying to carry him over his shoulder, that's where the blood came from." Now we are twenty-five.

It takes what seems like an eternity to reach the cover of the woods. I stand and shout, "Shiloh here, Shiloh here!" Shiloh is our home and has served as our rallying cry since we've been together. The name is a comfort to us as the place where the tabernacle stood during the reign of the judges and as a name referring to the Lord. We will not survive this day without His grace.

The men gather to Buck and me as he takes up the cry. We are safer here, but we have given up a superior position. The Yankees are moving onto higher ground. They have broken off fire as have we. Their artillery will have command of our gun crews and us when they move into position. "Roll call," I cry out.

Buck and Martin Wilson start calling names. Buck turns to me and reports, "The Smith brothers are not here!" His voice is raspy from inhaling the gun powder and the lack of water.

"Where are the Smiths?"

"They're wounded and have gone to the hospital," someone shouts, "they both got a round in the right shoulder or arm, and are helping each other there. There's a lot of blood Lieutenant; I wouldn't count on them back. Their arms were just hanging limp like." Now we are twenty-three.

"Anybody else?"

Buck and Wilson both reply, "No," and Buck adds, "all present and accounted for."

"O.K. men, we're in a fight. They've got three of us, but we've gotten a lot more of them. Sergeant, get a count of each man's remaining rounds and distribute the rest of our cartridges equally. We're going to need 'em...."

At the sound of a galloping horse, we turn to see Steven Wayne rein to a halt, dirt spraying up off the stallion's hoofs. The horse is lathered in sweat, rolling his eyes, and tossing his head side to side. "Lieutenant, prepare your men for a counter attack! We must have that ridge! It will never serve for us to stay here. Colonel Reynolds is moving men to the left flank to secure that position, and Colonel Tracy is sending some of his Alabamians to reinforce us; just pray they are here in time. As soon as they are in place, we are to attack. Watch for me to signal. This is the turning point boys! If we don't retake that ridge, the day is lost, and maybe the war! Remember, Company "A" is the best of the best; all are expecting us to lead. When you charge, charge with all the hell you can muster! God be with you all!" Steven Wayne spins his horse in a gallant pose, spurs him and rides further down the line to issue similar orders.

Someone says, "When he gets in the spirit, he gets caught up don't he?" There's a ripple of laughter, but all are moved by Steven Wayne. In battle, he is a commander, a leader, a fierce warrior we have learned to love.

"Men of Shiloh," I am caught up as well, "we are the best of the best, we will not fail, and we will lead and conquer!" The men take their positions on the line. "Fix bayonets!" Every soldier hates that command. It means we are going to look the enemy in the eye as we kill him. It is one thing to kill at long range, but to watch a man's face as he breathes his last at your hands is a terrible thing. I smile as I see the weapons drawn from their scabbards and flash in the sun as they are fixed over the muzzles of rifles. There is not a bit of rust or tarnish on any one of the blades. I know from talking to prisoners taken in other battles that when they hear our yell, and see the shine off the metal of our weapons they know they are facing a superior foe. We are few in number, but we give an undeniable account of ourselves on the field.

We stand ready. Martin is at my side with a grim look on his face. Now we wait again; the horrible anticipation. The dry mouth, the stomach wrenching fear that eats at your core and makes you weak. Several of the men, myself included, step away from the formation to relieve ourselves. It doesn't help much.

We hear the shout of, "Charge!" coming from our left flank. They will be in the bloodiest of it. If the flank fails, we are doomed. Steven Wayne echoes the command, "Charge!"

We do so with our fierce cry, firing as we go. The fierceness of our charge stuns them; we are half way across the field with no response. Their troops are milling around, confused. Elements of their line are being organized, their battle flags rise as rallying points, we move faster, yell louder, loading as we run. Others down the line spur their troops to seize the moment.

As we make our way across the field, I see that the victory will not be ours today. We are outnumbered at least four to one. The only thing for us is to survive. We cannot hope to move the massive blue army. All we can do is delay until Bowen can send reinforcements, but I fear that they will arrive too late.

We press forward, down the ravine that we held this morning, and up the other side. It is exhausting. Sweat is streaming off me; I am blinded by it and the sting of burning gun powder, and acrid smoke. Our yell is choked by lack of wind, and fatigue, but not by submission. We battle up the slopes of the ravine only to be met by a deadly and withering fire from the organizing enemy.

Men fall around me; some from wounds, others for cover. It is our turn to be confused and disorganized. I hear cries of the wounded, and pleas for aid. Fire from the enemy intensifies. Our artillery opens up and ranges short. The blast is not five feet to our front. I am hurled back with Martin into the wash. We are both stunned. I am deafened by the blast of the exploding shell, otherwise unhurt. There is confusion and disarray all down the line. Buck is sprawled fifty feet from me not moving. I can see his chest rise and fall as he breathes. I stand, rally the troops and head back up the slope; pressing the attack.

The chaos is worse to our left toward the weak flank. We have troops from other units among us, moving up to the edge of the ravine. We top it again, but one glance, a blast of gun fire, a concussive wave, and a cloud of smoke roiling toward us, and we know it is lost. I pull Martin off the top and roll to the bottom of the ravine. Dirt tumbles into my mouth and eyes. Men are struggling up the opposite slope in full retreat. I have heard no such order, but give it now, "Fall back, fall back, move out of here now!" Some of my men make a valiant, but useless stand. I move closer to them to make myself heard over the sound of the rifle fire from the Yankee lines, artillery explosions, and the cries of the wounded. Amid smoke and chaos, with shouts and hand signals I make my orders understood. They scramble up the slope we just came down.

I stay in the bottom of the ravine. Martin is gone. I remember Buck. To my right, toward the road I see him. He is trying to rise as I reach him, but push him down to assess his injuries. He fights me and sits up. He is dazed. I yell to be heard, "You've been hit!" There is blood running down the right side of his face, soaking the collar of his jacket and shirt. I retrieve his hat, locate one of my bandage strips, tie it around his head, clap his hat on to hold pressure against the wound, and move to pick him up.

"Lieutenant!" It's Martin above us on the edge of the ravine; "Lieutenant, get out of there, we've lost the flank and they're moving this way. We're going to be cut off, hurry!"

I look over my shoulder toward our left flank and see blue coated troops moving down the defile in our direction. We have been flanked, but the way to the road is still open. I see only Martin of our unit.

"We've pulled back," he yells, "get out of there!"

Many of our wounded are crawling up the slope and onto the field. Our losses are heavy. We fought well; many expending their last round of ammunition, but to no avail. We held but the reinforcements did not arrive.

"They're coming Evans, they're coming! Get out of there!"

"Martin, Buck's wounded; I'm gonna take him down this ravine to the road to the hospital." He starts to protest as he looks to the advancing enemy, and back to me. "Martin!" He focuses. "Go, rally the men, then find Captain Culpepper and tell him what I am doing." He hesitates. "Go now! That's an order!" In a much calmer voice, "Tell Ma and the families what happened when you get home." I don't know why I said it, and I don't know if he heard, but he looked resolved and went to obey. I turn my attention to Buck.

"Can you stand?" He looks at me, dazed and confused. There's more blood down his right side. The bleeding from the head wound has stopped. We have to move. "I'm going to get you on my left side so I can use my right to fight, do you understand?" He nods. I get to my feet, move to his right side and bend to lift him. There's a lot of blood.

I get him to his feet; he looks at me puzzled. "What happened? Am I hit? Where are we?"

"We don't have time, we've got to move; come on, let's go!" I drop my rifle. I can get another if we survive this day.

"Where you taking me?"

"Hospital," I say, dragging him half walking toward Rodney Road.

"You can't do that," referring to the rule of assisting a downed man, "the men…," he trails off.

There is no way I'm going to leave Buck, but we're moving too slow. I can feel his blood soak my left side. He's getting faint. "Buck I'm going to have to…," I never finish. He blacks out and is dead weight. I get my right arm under his legs and use his momentum to swing him up and into my arms. Rules of engagement be damned, I won't leave Buck on the field. I have to get him out even if we both die.

With a surge of energy from fear, or combat, or whatever, I am able to move faster than we had been staggering along. The strain hurts, but there's no doubt that he would do the same for me. I keep moving; my lungs burn with every breath. Sweat runs in my eyes blurring my vision. My arms and back ache. My legs burn with the exertion, but I keep putting one foot in front of the other. I hear myself saying, "Hang in there Buck. It ain't far now. I can see the house through the trees. Come on Buck, hang in there. Oh, God help me!" I stagger blind, but determined; we round a curve, and it doesn't matter anymore.

"Halt!" Is the command from in front of me, but I can't see for the sweat in my eyes, so I keep moving. "Halt, or I'll blow you to hell you worthless rebel!" The enemy is in front. They're already at our rear. I have no choice, it's over, and I stop. "Drop that rebel piece of flith you're carrying, and raise your hands!"

We may be captured, but there is still fight in me, "I will not drop this man!" I am not in a position to negotiate, but shout again, "I will not drop this man!" My vision clears and I see that I am facing two Yankee soldiers. One is not pointing his weapon at us, while the other, the voice I presume, is. He looks angry and hateful. I am struggling with the weight of Buck; my legs are shaking from exertion. Fear, pleading, or cowardice will serve nothing but to stain my honor and I will not dishonor my friend, or the uniform of my country.

Buck whispers, "Put me down boy, and let's kill these bastards!"

"No, it's over. We're done; just be still, and we might get you to the hospital."

"Or we can die."

"Shut up! Drop the man or I will shoot you both where you stand!"

"Since you've made that declaration, and I have stated my position, we are at an impasse. Please, get on with the shooting, or step aside so I can take my sergeant to the hospital." I have no idea where such bravado came from; maybe I have been listening to Steven Wayne too long. I smirk a little. The man moves his already aimed rifle to bear on my face. His finger starts to tighten on the trigger.

"Hold it Hank," speaks his companion, "don't go off half cocked."

"He's daring me to shoot him, Ike!"

"Let's just be calm here. He ain't going to hurt us standing there holding that man like that."

The voice is familiar, "You the Iowa boys?"

"How'd you know?"

"Just a guess; I saw your banner this morning across from us. Were you on the detail to retrieve your wounded this morning?"

"Yeah, I was; are you the one that gave us permission?"

"One of them, yes. If I am not mistaken, I believe we exchanged pleasantries as you departed." I smile.

"Yes, we did. I got my ass chewed good!"

"Yeah, I could hear." He was smiling too. Hank, the angry rifle man had yet to lower his weapon. My hopes began to climb; we just might survive.

"Thanks for letting us get our men. You are a gentleman in spite of being a traitor."

"You're welcome. Would you be of a mind to reciprocate?"

"What?"

"Will you allow me to pass and take my man to the hospital?"

"He must be real special to you, you standing there shaking and not putting him down. Are you willing to die for him?"

"Without the slightest reservation; he is my sergeant, and my particular friend."

"Will you surrender?"

"I had hoped to get around that unpleasant prospect, but if that is a term of being allowed to assist this man, I do indeed surrender."

Buck squirms and says, "Put me down. If we have to surrender, let me do it on my own."

"My sergeant is conscious and wants to stand. May I put him down?"

"Slide him down gentle like. If you go for a weapon you will die," says a voice from behind me.

I turn and look into the barrel of a .44 caliber Colt Army Revolver in the hands of a Union Lieutenant. I ease Buck to the ground and hold him steady as he gets his balance. His right side is soaked in blood. I too am covered.

"Are you injured Lieutenant?"

"A flesh wound in the arm. All of this," gesturing to my blood-soaked left side, "is from my wounded comrade. To whom do I have the honor?"

Without lowering his firearm, he says, "First Lieutenant Carlton Sykes, 21st Iowa, and you?"

"Lieutenant Sykes, I am Second Lieutenant Evans Atwood, 15th Arkansas Infantry. This fine but injured man is my Sergeant, Nathanial James Buchannan. "

Buck, still whispering asks, "What you going to do next, kiss him?" I ignore him, "How come you always use my full name, and never yours, and how come you're talking all fancy like, like you do when you're teaching school?"

"Hush Buck, and stand up straight."

"Lieutenant, I heard your surrender to Private Hansen," Ike nods, "and Private Dubois," Hank scowls, Lieutenant Sykes pauses, "Are you amenable to the terms?"

"That we surrender on condition that I am allowed to take this man to the hospital and secure his care; are those the terms?"

"Yes, Lieutenant, those are the terms."

"You are most gracious and generous. We accept, and with thanks. May we take our leave now sir?"

"No, you may not. I will need the surrender of your weapons; especially that fine LeMat pistol. Do you have any others that I can't see?"

I hate the idea of parting with the LeMat and my Arkansas Toothpick, but I won't lie; they'll find them anyway. "Yes sir, I do."

Sykes speaks, "Private Hansen."

"Sir," he snaps.

"Relieve our two guests of their armament."

"Yes sir." He moves to Buck first who is growing weaker. His head is slumping and he is leaning on me. Private Hansen removes Bucks Toothpick, cartridge box, and ammunition, turns to me and does the same. Hansen takes our weapons to Sykes who takes a long hard look at the Toothpicks, recognizing them for their unique work.

"Lieutenant, please let me assist my friend to medical attention. I fear for his life without assistance."

"Shut up scum," spews hatred from Private Dubois, "Do you really think we give a hoot in hell about your friend?"

"That's enough Dubois!" Sykes shouts. "If it hadn't been for this man, your brother-in-law would be dead now instead at the hospital!"

Dubois raises his voice, "If it hadn't been for this scum rebel son of a bitch he wouldn't be shot and without an arm!"

"Dubois, stand down! That will be quiet enough! This man is an officer and you will treat him with all the respect due his rank regardless of his allegiance, do you understand!?"

"Do I have to salute the bastard too?" Dubois is barely under control as he responds in the mimicking voice of a whiney, petulant child.

"Private, you will stand down from this duty. Private Hansen, you will escort Mr. Atwood and his sergeant to the hospital and report with him to the rear holding area. General Grant's staff will have questions. Now move." He turns to me, lowers his weapon and in tones meant only for Buck and myself says, "Lieutenant, it was a great service you allowed us this morning, and I thank you. You may keep your haversacks and personals." He waits a moment, and in a louder voice says, "Private Hansen, take charge of the prisoners."

Lieutenant Carlton Sykes, who I will never be able to repay, turns and walks away. I shoulder my near unconscious friend, and with the humiliating assistance of my enemy, we limp toward Shaifer House and captivity.

6) Home Sunday, April 26, 1863

The Atwood and Wilson families sit down to a shared Sunday dinner as they have since the Atwoods arrived in Washington County, Arkansas along Wilson Creek in 1850. The families became instant neighbors in the physical sense, then the spiritual (the Wilson's are strong Baptists and practice the admonition of the Lord to "love thy neighbor as thyself") within hours of the Atwood's arrival when they broke bread together and the sharing has continued.

Sunday meals after services at The Friendship Baptist Church have alternated between families each Sunday and are attended by Reverend Claiborne, along with anyone else in need of fellowship and a full belly. The gatherings were, at one time, festive and happy occasions. As of late, clouds have settled over the gatherings.

The foremost reason is the passing of John Wesley Wilson, patriarch of the Wilson clan. He was working alone in his black smith shop along the creek on a cold, blowing day the first of February when he was set upon by bushwhackers and murdered. There were no witnesses and little evidence; only the foot prints of five men. The alarm was sounded, but the scum had done their deed, and nothing was ever found, nor voiced about. John Wesley was forty-nine years old and left his wife, Rebecca, and ten children. The two oldest boys were in various parts of the county, and one, young Martin was off with the 15th Arkansas Infantry serving in the same company as Evans Atwood who is the other cause of melancholy and uneasiness.

The Atwoods are proud of their son and brother, and would love to speak of his exploits, his election to the officer corps and share the most recent letter, as well as discuss the possible outcome of the war and Evans' and Martin's homecoming, but they cannot. It would put half of the attendees ill at ease.

Lieutenant Atwood is married to Lucy Jane Roberts Atwood and is the father of her two children. The nature and circumstances of this union are no longer subjects on the gossip circuit, but are the basis of tender feelings.

The Wilson and Atwood families have been neighbors for some thirteen years. Evans and the Wilson's number three child and first daughter, Susan Jane, have been hard fast friends for as long. It was understood, perhaps since they first met as children, that Evans and Susan would marry. They were both of like education, attended services and school at the Friendship Baptist Church, and enjoyed singing together to Susan's accompaniment. Their marriage seemed to be predestined.

Susan Jane is a dark haired, brown eyed, white skinned young woman of average height and weight. She is not remarkable in her looks, but is on the strong side of pretty, and as she ages, pretty is giving way to beautiful. She carries herself with grace and confidence. If there was one word to describe Miss Susan, it would be smooth. Everything she does, from the most menial chore to the most elaborate work of Bach, or working on one of her much desired needle points, is smooth.

She is graced with elegant, long hands and fingers that look too fragile to do any sort of manual labor without snapping. Her hands are her deceit; they are wonderful, strong, and powerful. She has a prodigious grip that many a man has envied. She is a hard worker in the field, the kitchen, caring for the sick, in school, or at the piano.

All who met the couple knew within minutes that Evans and Susan loved each other. They were never heard to have a cross word, and it is said by both families that they seldom needed to speak. They knew what the other wanted to do or not do. They communicated on a different level and it seemed to always have been so.

Evans taught reading and penmanship at the church several days a week. One day, and it proved to be a landmark day in the history of the Wilson/Atwood relationship; Lucy Jane Roberts walked into class.

The Roberts family was a recent transplant from Eastern Tennessee. The Roberts did not socialize. They remained strangers in a community where such was unknown. No facts were available concerning them, so the gossips filled in the blanks.

When blonde, statuesque Lucy Jane walked into school seeking further instruction beyond her rudimentary knowledge of reading, Evans was awe struck. He knew who she was and the talk, but when she stood before him, he was stunned at her beauty and what she stirred in him.

Lucy recognized her shortcomings in education and was willing to take her place in a class with students that were half her age. She knew that being able to read well would open doors to her; the doors to a better life. Better things were Lucy's goal.

Lucy Jane had nothing, but wanted more; a lot more. She is the oldest of six and is the result of her mother having a little too much "shine" at a dance while being courted by her now husband ,Maxwell. There was a tryst with a handsome boy from over the mountain and beautiful Lucy Jane was conceived. Maxwell has always suspected, if not known, that Lucy is not his, and uses the knowledge of her parentage to justify his treatment of her.

God leaves none of his children without gifts, and He most assuredly gifted Lucy. Her looks and figure are her assets, but her gift is the knowledge, the instinct, to use them. She does not flaunt her figure in a wanton way; any prostitute can do that; Lucy wants better. Her gift allows her to be able to show enough physical charm, along with tasteful coloration and clothing to match her mood or the emotion she wishes to project. Her most powerful asset, her coup de grace, is her eyes.

With her eyes, she can speak poetry or profanity and never move her lips. If she had lived in Massachusetts in the late 1600s she would have been burned as a witch. Her eyes allow the viewer to see deep within her. She is an open book but the pages are blurred unless she wants you to see. Thus was the power over Evans.

Evans Atwood was not only a wonderful, handsome man, but he had potential. Lucy saw his star rising and wanted to ride along; which is what she set out to do.

It was a subtle seduction. Lucy had heard that if you were to put a frog into boiling water, that he would fight like crazy to get out; but if you placed him into a pot of cold water he was as happy as can be; and would grow tolerant of gradual temperature increases until the water was boiling, and never struggle. Such was her plan for Evans.

Lucy did not flaunt her attributes. No, it was not sex with which she would win Evans, it would be a slow process involving her other talents, her mind, her strength of will, and her eyes. It was for this purpose that she went to Evans' reading class and became his pupil, and later, his master.

It started in the spring of 1856. She had the friendship between Evans and Susan to overcome, and a social ladder to scale that had been unavailable to her. The process involved reading, learning music, and going to church; none of which she had ever done before. She worked and molded herself into what she knew Evans could not resist.

It had taken three years to accomplish and was almost thwarted by Evans confusion. In 1857, Evans had gone wandering, adventuring he called it, alone, to sort things out. All who knew the situation knew that Evans wanted an escape from Lucy Jane's attentions.

During all this, even the year Evans was gone, Susan managed to stay above the fray and maintain her dignity, poise, and smoothness. She knew that Evans and she were destined to be together, and even when it was clear that she was losing the battle to Lucy, she kept faith that Evans would come to his senses. Even after he had his fling, and his adventuring, she had confidence that things would work out in her favor. After all, Evans and she were in love; both had professed it, and both had accepted it. But Lucy had a trump card that Susan would never stoop to match.

When Evans returned in April of '59 wanting to settle into a life with Susan Wilson, Lucy's situation grew desperate. She could no longer

tolerate life with her family. The attentions and demands of her
stepfather were growing heavy handed and threatening, and her younger
brothers were at an age to be lustful. Under the encouragement of their
father, they had become a threat. She had to get out.

Evans had bought a piece of property close to the White River, near to
his family as well as to the Wilsons, on which he started a cabin. He had
made no commitment to either woman. His idea was that he would build
his home and the situation would sort itself out without him having to do
anything. Nature abhors a vacuum, and where there is inactivity on the
part of one, there will be redoubled activity on the part of another to fill
the void.

He had cleared the land with the help of his brothers, and some of
Susan's family, but with spring planting coming on, they could not be
counted on to help. Evans set himself to barking the logs he would use
for his cabin, measuring out the foundation, clearing brush, and all the
things necessary for construction. He wanted it finished in seven or eight
months, November or December, before it snowed, but without help, he
wouldn't be able.

Lucy Jane heard that he was back and since her situation had become
untenable, she formulated a desperate plan. She took a horse in the
middle of the night with her few clothes and some food bundled into a
piece of canvas that would serve her for a ground cloth or a shelter if it
rained, and turned her back on the only life she had ever known, setting
her face to an uncertain future. Lucy was shot of her family and going to
make her own way. Her plan included Evans, and if her plan did not
work, she would make her way in the world as best she could, but she
would never return to the shack called home.

She arrived at Evans' home site fearful of the outcome due to her
desperate state. She knew she was playing from a point of weakness.
Any who have ever played poker know that even a royal flush in the
possession of a desperate player is a loser. The play is to not let the other
players at the table know how desperate you are. Besides, if Evans
shunned her advances, she always had…well, nothing. She had nothing
to fall back on but her wits and her determination that she was not going
back to be a field hand and more to her step father.

Evans looked up from stripping one of the felled trees of branches and
bark. He could not make out the rider sauntering into his camp. There
was a mist hanging in the early morning hindering identification. The
rider made no attempt at greeting. Evans shaded his eyes as he looked at
the rider silhouetted by the rising sun and moved his head side to side
trying to determine who it might be. He moved closer to his muzzle

loader and reached around his back to touch the Arkansas Toothpick secreted there.

"Good morning," he called out with a bit of challenge in his voice. There was no answer. He spoke louder, this time the challenge was clear, "Who are you, and what do you want?" The rider did not slow, nor acknowledge the greeting. There were fifty yards between them, and unless the rider was deaf, Evans knew he had been heard. He took up his Kentucky rifle and laid it across his body from right to left, cradling it in the crook of his left arm, his right hand resting on the stock, not yet on the trigger. "Halt right there, get down, and tell me who's calling!" The rider plodded on.

The light had shifted, making Evans' angle better. He could see the rider was small, yet tall in the saddle, and wore a non-descript, shapeless, black hat. It flopped in such a fashion as to hide all facial features. The mount was of no quality; a dirt farm nag more accustomed to plowing than being ridden. Evans impression was that this was a desperate rider looking to increase their lot in life at the expense of another, or... he wasn't sure there was any other conclusion.

Lucy Jane was afraid. Her heart was pounding at Evans' first greeting, and then it increased its rate with the less cordial second. She feared he could hear its tattoo as he commanded her to halt. She knew she couldn't; she had to keep moving.

Lucy was close to giving in to her fear, but with her head still bowed and her heart still pounding, she rode on. She drew closer; raised her head and halted thirty feet from Evans and met his stare. He was raising the rifle to his shoulder when she reached up and removed her hat. The blonde curls fell around her face, and with the early morning sun behind her, cast a gold light onto Evans. She sat still and locked her eyes onto his.

The vision froze Evans. With the light behind her she looked angelic and fragile. He had never seen Lucy like this and his voice belied his confusion as he asked, "Lucy, is that you?" His mind began to sort it out. The mysterious rider was female and might be Lucy Jane. The rider was slight of build, but rode upright and tall, and that cloth bundled over the horses mane could be the skirts of a dress, and the golden blonde hair, the elegant face, and...then the eyes. Looking into them, he was mesmerized, and captivated. There was no doubt. He stated with finality and gentleness, "Lucy".

When he spoke her name, Lucy Jane lunged off the horse, rushed to Evans flinging herself into his arms. She clung to him with desperation, buried her face in his shoulder and sobbed, "Oh, Evans, oh, Evans; please don't make me go back." Tears and desperation flooded from her.

"Lucy, what are you talking about? Go back where? What's the matter? I don't understand!" Confused words tumbled from him as tears did from her. She sobbed and he babbled. All he could do was hold her and wait. Evans and Lucy had never before engaged in such intimate contact.

There had been occasional pecked kisses on cheeks and holding of hands, but never an embrace; nothing like this. It felt good, and he hoped she could not feel his eagerness. He found himself running his hands over her back, patting her and reassuring her with soft words one would use with a hurt child, but she was not a child; she was a grown woman, clinging to him as if her life depended on it. She seemed fragile and weak; something he had never suspected.

Lucy stepped back and looked at Evans. Her eyes held him; she felt his desire and could see compassion in his face; her confidence rose. The tone of her voice expressed her relief at not being rebuffed as she pleaded, "Oh Evans…" It all spilled out as the dam of prohibition against her dark secrets burst. She told him everything as a torrent of emotions cascaded from her. All the anger, frustration, humiliation, fear, longing, flowed from her unabated. She had never been this open with anyone; there had never been anyone to be open with. She said things that she did not know she had ever thought. She and Evans found themselves sinking to the ground as the catharsis of confession shifted the burden from her to him, leaving both weak and drained. She pleaded, "…and I so don't want to burden you, but Evans, you are my only friend, my only hope." She finished with, "If you turn me away, I fear it may be to my end", revealing her desperation and fear. She was then silent; hanging her head, spent, exhausted.

Evans was overwhelmed. He let the silence settle on them, too stunned to speak. It would take hours, maybe days to process what she had revealed. He had had no idea about her circumstances, no idea what a hell her life had been; no idea that a human being could do the acts she spoke of.

No one had ever spoken to him of such and in this manner. This powerful girl had laid her soul bare and begged him to be her savior, her champion. What should he do; what could he do? He wanted to ask his parents, ask Buck, but knew he couldn't. What Lucy had revealed was in confidence, and he could not betray that confidence.

The silence stretched on. Her eyes never strayed from his face; his wandered. He looked at Lucy, the horses, at the lean-to shack that was his temporary dwelling, he looked into the woods, at the cabin site, toward the river, and back into Lucy's eyes before saying, "Lucy, I don't know what to say…I'm so confused, no one has ever…what am I to do with this?" He paused, looking at the ground and then said with a sigh, "You are safe with me."

"Evans!" She shouted as she lunged from her sitting position opposite him, knocking him backwards, throwing her arms around his neck and falling on top of him, "I knew you wouldn't let me down, I knew you would be my salvation!" Her lips found his as she expressed her gratitude in the only sincere way she knew.

Evans' words had betrayed him. He had meant to convey only that her revelation was safe with him, but she had heard more. In his wanderings, he had become acquainted with the wiles of women, and had known the temptations, but never in his limited experience had he ever felt such emotions. He wanted to hold her and possess her. Her desperation and dependency was a powerful elixir. Sensations surged in him that were beyond his understanding. The embrace was not only physical; it encompassed his spirit as well. It was pleasurable, but was it right? The intense warmth of Lucy's body against him had its natural effect as he squirmed beneath her. What to do, what was he to do? It was so new, and so exciting. "I want more," was his first thought, his second was, "but it's not right, or is it? I am so confused! Let me have more! This has to be love. I've never felt like this before. No, I can't take advantage of her like this, this is the only way she knows to show gratitude. It has to mean more than this." Thoughts of Susan and his family caused him to squirm more.

His hands fumbled at her shoulders and he began to push against her. Her strength was surprising; she did not want to break the kiss or the embrace. Evans changed tactics; pulling her tight against him, he rolled over on top of her. Lucy's legs spread and Evans knees met the ground. He released her, put his hands palm down against the earth, and pushed himself upward. It took a great effort to break free of Lucy, but he did, and rose to his knees.

"No," he said with a gasp, "this is not right. This is not the right way."

She looked up at him. Desperation was in her eyes again. Random thoughts raced through her mind, "Have I gone too far? Have I misread him? Of course I have; he doesn't want me! This is all my own doings, no one as decent as Evans Atwood would ever want a used, abused woman. My life is to be that of a common whore. There is nothing left; Evans has shunned me. Well, I'll make a damned fine whore! I'll be the best there is! She burst into sobs of real grief.

"Lucy, stop this. Get hold of yourself. I have no intention of not helping you. I don't know what you need, or want I can give. I'm confused. It'll take awhile to work this out." Evans got to his feet and extended his hand to assist her. "I won't let you down. Your secrets are safe with me."

She took his hand and rose. With genuine relief, she said with more desperation than she intended, "I've got no place to go; no friends, and I will not go back to my family. I don't know what else to do."

"You've come here seeking help and I'll help you." Evans looked around his rough camp and all the work before him. He did not have much to offer. "You can stay here today. I need time to sort this out. I need to talk to my ma and pa; they'll know what to do." His eyes met hers, which even red and swollen still held power. He could tell no one, he could not betray her confidence and trust. This was a burden he alone would have to bear.

"I'll help you work on the cabin," she said in a soft voice, "I can cook, mend; work a team better than most men. I'm strong, I can lift...," she trailed off, "I want to stay...please?"

"You can stay today. I can surely use the help, but I don't expect you to 'pay me'. You are my friend. We'll work this out. I won't hurt you or mistreat you."

"I know," she said as she brushed herself off. She looked up at him and smiling she asked, "Where do we begin?"

The "we" did not escape Evans, or the concept of "beginning". "What have I gotten myself into?"

7) Captive

Buck and I, guided and guarded by our captor, Private Ike Hansen of the Union Army, make our way to Shaifer House which is now behind Union lines. I had hoped to be rescued en route, but it is not to be. Escape will have to come later if at all. Buck's wound makes his status questionable, but mine is certain; I am a prisoner of war. "Private Hansen, before we get into the hospital, I wish to thank you for your kindness and help."

"It's payback Reb; without your compassion, many of our men would have died."

We are silent the rest of the trip to the hospital.

The Shaifer House is a beautiful, sprawling, white domicile that reminds me of my family home. It stands on an acre or more of cleared ground covered by a lush lawn that occupies a good third of the clearing. The rest is used for out buildings, and a large garden. There is a white flag flying from the peak of one of the gables informing all who enter the area that they are under a truce.

"Please remember Lieutenant, you have surrendered and are my prisoner."

"I gave my word as a gentleman and an officer to Lieutenant Sykes. I fully intend to keep my word. You need not question it again." We walk in silence to the hospital grounds.

Buck is weaker and I have to carry him. His bleeding has stopped, but he has lost a lot of blood as my uniform jacket will attest. My wound is throbbing and picking up my friend is a painful reminder of the morning's action which seems part of a distant past.

In the yard of the Shaifer house, there are soldiers of both armies lounging on the grass. Hansen is bewildered. "Your first time to a field hospital?" I ask.

Shocked at what he sees, and smells, he says, "Yes it is," then observes, "I take it this is not your first."

"No, I have been obliged to check the welfare of my men at such facilities. I have had too many occasions that have required such distasteful duty."

Some soldiers on both sides have no visible wounds at all. These are the shirkers; those who fake an illness or injury to avoid combat. They are by themselves, not welcome, nor willing to mix with those who have braved possible death facing an enemy. The more serious cases are inside, or are on the shaded porches awaiting treatment. The most serious are under the knife inside. As we get closer, we can hear their moans and cries. Hansen pales.

Near the woods, downwind from the hospital, are the dead covered by ground cloths and blankets to keep off the flies. I note that there are more blue coats than gray, but fear that will change before the day ends.

The buzzing of flies is louder as we get closer, and the smell of the place assaults us. There is a pile of amputated limbs in the space between the front and rear sections of the house. A crew of field assistants from both sides, with bandanas and handkerchiefs tied around their noses and mouths are digging a hole in the woods near the dead to bury the gore.

"My God," says Hansen, "I would hate to have to come here." His voice is subdued and is hard to hear.

"It is not a pleasant place to be."

"Have you had to be at a hospital before; I mean for yourself?"

"No, not before today."

"You're wounded?"

"Yes, my arm, it will need attention."

"I don't know about that; my orders are to…"

I interrupt, "Under the rules of war, you cannot deny a prisoner medical treatment."

"I'll have to confirm your wound."

"If that makes you comfortable, you are welcome to do so."

It is not unusual for Union and Confederate medical staffs to occupy the same facilities. After "Stonewall" Jackson captured a Union hospital at a battle near Winchester, Virginia, and returned the medical staff to the Union lines, he proposed a new policy. General Jackson's reasoning was that medical personnel were not in the armies to make war, but to relieve suffering, therefore were not subject to its penalties. It became a "rule" on both sides.

Medical staff and field assistants wear special badges that identify them as non-combatants and, in theory at least, are not to be shot at. Another rule developed is that a combatant, someone carrying a weapon, cannot cease hostilities and care for a wounded comrade. I have broken that rule, which many do; yet it is a court martial offense.

The Confederates, because we were first at Shaifer House are on the front lawn, while the Union occupies the area behind the house. There is considerable mingling of both sides. Tobacco of the south and coffee from the north are bartered and enjoyed. Food is shared around without regard to allegiance. Some of these men could be related.

The chatter quiets as we come into the yard. We are an unusual sight, two confederates being escorted by a Yankee; I, an officer, Buck enlisted, being carried by me. There are times when rank is unimportant.

I am struggling with Buck and the pain in my arm as I begin to climb the steps to the porch. I fail to inform Private Hansen of another rule of hospitals in combat zones. The thought makes me smile.

We cross the porch and enter the front door. Across the room, positioned to capture light from both the east and south windows, is a surgeon wearing a blood soaked apron. His hair is graying and disheveled as is his full beard. His head is bowed as he works to save the leg of a Union soldier. His well tailored coat denoting his rank of colonel in the Confederate Army hangs on the wall behind him. I know this man, and smile.

He looks up, puzzled for a moment before the spark of recognition brightens. "Lieutenant Evans Atwood!" Then seeing my burden asks, "How bad?"

"I don't know sir. He's got a head wound, just a bleeder, and one in the right side or shoulder. He's lost a lot of blood, and fades in an out. He walked part way, but I carried him the rest."

"Over here," he gestures with a bloody scalpel toward an elegant dining table. It is covered by a tarp from which drips blood onto the saturated and sanded floor. I lay Buck on it, steady to avoid slipping in the blood. I am relieved to have Buck in capable hands, and there are no better than Dr. William McPheeters.

He looks at me and asks, "Any of that blood yours?"

"Yes sir, a little on the arm. It was from a high powered rifle and did some damage."

"In that case, get your coat off, roll up your sleeves and get to work. You know what to do."

"Yes sir, I do. I'll be glad to assist." I had first met Colonel McPheeters when I had been checking on my men at the battle for Corinth, Mississippi. He, seeing my interest, recruited me to assist through the night until the last of the wounded were cared for.

I remove my coat and roll up the sleeve of my shirt revealing my wounded arm. The flesh is discolored but nothing is broken. I am glad that it looks worse than it is as I show it to Hansen; he blanches. I flex my arm, wash my hands in a basin of bloody water, and stand ready for direction from the doctor.

Hansen has been lost in this exchange. He stands in the doorway with his rifle resting on his foot. His confusion is evident as he sees one of his fellow troops in the hands of a Confederate surgeon who is on a first name familiarity with his prisoner. Blood is everywhere. The sickening, sweet smell abounds and causes Hansen to pale further. Flies buzz in, out, and around everywhere.

Colonel McPheeters notices him and points, shouting an order, "Get that God damned instrument of Satan out of this hospital at once!" He sounds like a revival preacher, and comes by it natural. His brother is a prominent Presbyterian Minister in his home city of St. Louis and shares the faith.

I smile at Hansen's confusion as he stammers, "What, me; what?"

"That weapon, you logger headed fool! Don't you know this is a hospital; a non-combat zone? Did you not see the flag? You heathen, do you not intend to honor the sanctity of truce, or of a hospital? Where are you from private...?" The last is a question, wanting Hansen's name.

"Hansen sir, from Iowa sir, the 21st..."

"I don't give a pea-bread muffin what cursed unit you are from; knowing you are from Iowa is quite enough to explain your barn yard behavior," then turning to me, "and they call us of the south, crude and ignorant." Turning his attention back to my captor, he shouts in his best hell, fire, and brimstone voice, "Get that weapon out of here!"

"But sir..."

"Are you deaf private? Is that the trouble? Get that weapon out of here!!"

"...he's," pointing an accusing finger at me, "...my prisoner!"

"Prisoner?" The doctor turns to me, "What is this Mr. Atwood?"

While Hansen fidgets, I explain about the battle telling how I had picked Buck up and assisted him to the aid station.

"You broke the rule..."

"Yes sir, I know I did, but I was not going to leave him on the field in enemy hands where he might have bled to death."

"And you were captured during the course of this rescue?"

"Yes sir, I was struggling to carry my man off the field and we were surrounded."

"And you surrendered?"

"That is correct sir."

"You're willing to risk death by leaving your weapons and further risk going to a Union...," he spits with emphasis to let his derision and disgust with the Federal government be known; he has reason, and continues, "...prison for the duration of the war?"

"Yes Colonel, he is my particular friend sir, and would have done more and better for me." I smile and add, "I acted from principle."

His eyes meet mine; Dr William McPheeters understood the statement; I have quoted him and his brother. The phrase is a result of his harrowing life in St. Louis under Union occupation and the events that led him to be in this place. He smiles, laughs a short laugh, and says, "I see." He walks back to the patient on the table and goes back to work. Without looking at Private Hansen, he says, "Very well private, you are dismissed. You may remove yourself and your weapon from this hospital. Lieutenant Atwood will be assisting me until I say otherwise."

"But sir…"

Still working on the leg, he says, "Private, are you so dense that you cannot see that the rules of war do not apply within these walls and on these grounds?"

"No sir, but…"

"I will vouch for Mr. Atwood. He needs medical attention, which he will get. I need help which he can offer." Turning to me, he said, "Lieutenant, are you able?"

"Yes sir."

"Are you willing?"

"Yes sir."

"There you have it private; your prisoner will be released to you when all is taken care of, and that will be when I say."

"Sir…"

"Private, weapons are not allowed in here, nor are those who carry them. You will leave at once under your own authority, or I shall call for a provost and order him to work whatever violence he deems necessary to cause you to obey my orders, is that clear?"

Hansen turns to me and says, "I'll be waiting outside for you."

"Yes you will, with your Bill Yank brothers. You will see where weapons are stacked, I suggest you take advantage of that storage, or risk losing your arms."

His head jerks up.

"Oh, I am so sorry; I meant your weaponry, of course."

The doctor chuckles as he continues his operation.

Private Hansen turns and leaves the house. We burst into laughter. It's a great release from the tension of the past twenty-four hours. A lot has happened in that time, but now I can relax. As I do, fatigue sweeps over me like a heavy blanket. I am just able to find a chair that I fall into.

"Are you alright Lieutenant?"

"No sir, I feel…"

I wake lying in the same room I had brought Buck into. My arm is clean and bandaged and I smell of moon shine. I am looking around sniffing the air when Dr McPheeters looks over at me.

"Feeling better?"

"Yes sir," I start to get up, but fall back, dizzy from the exertion, or maybe I'm drunk. "Sir, have I been drinking?"

He laughs at me and says, "No Evans, I am using the purest alcohol I can find on wounds now. It is a new thing I'm trying. It stings like the very fires of hell, but it keeps infections down, and I am able to save a lot of limbs that would normally have to be amputated. I think I have served you well."

I lay back down and rest for a moment. "How is your family sir?" It is a tender subject, but he shared the story with me in Corinth. When men who are away from loved ones are engaged in work such as amputation, or worse, they talk to ease the pain.

"I don't know Lieutenant. After my brother's ministry was ruined and he was forced to leave the territory, and my possessions were stolen from me by the Federal government, and my child died during the process of seizure, and I was forced to escape to Carolina, I have heard little of them. It's rumored that my wife and three remaining children have been banished from Missouri and are on their way to, or are already in Arkansas via the Mississippi River."

I remain silent, waiting. William McPheeters and his wife Sallie were prominent citizens in St. Louis for over twenty years. The doctor had a profitable practice and was teaching at the university when the war broke out.

Dr. McPheeters, and many others such as his brother were opposed to slavery, but proponents of the right of the south to chose its own course; the right to self determination. The two are linked being that slaves are a necessity to the economy of cotton, but the issue for many, including myself is freedom; the fundamental right of a people to choose.

When Missouri and St. Louis came under martial law, freedom became basic. The citizenry, including the McPheeters, were required to sign an oath of loyalty to the Union, and when they refused to do so; force was attempted.

Federal troops appeared with papers and confiscated their possessions. Dr. McPheeters and his brother before him had refused to sign the oath both declaring, "I acted from principle" which was widely reported in newspapers throughout the country.

Their adherence to the principal of self determination cost them. Both families lost much and may never recover. Reverend McPheeters was forced from his large congregation and had to flee into Kentucky. The good doctor was forced to abandon his wife and children and flee to the state of his nativity, North Carolina where he offered his services to the Confederacy. He was assigned to the Army of the West in hopes of being close enough to effect a rescue of his family if necessary. Such is now required.

"What is your friend's name I am working on here?"

"He is Nathanial James Buchannan, sergeant; Company 'A', 15th Arkansas Infantry. Home is Benton County, Arkansas." The details are for a clerk keeping a ledger.

"Interesting," says Dr. McPheeters, "interesting indeed."

"What's interesting doctor?"

"Would your friend be known as 'Buck'?"

"Yes sir."

"Is he from Kentucky?"

"Yes sir, his father brought him to Arkansas when he was a boy, after his mother died."

"Would you know his mother's name?"

"No sir, he spoke of her only once."

"How did she die?"

"Some disease; he has never very clear about it. I got the impression that he isn't clear about it either."

"Would it surprise you to learn that she was killed in an Indian raid?"

"The information doesn't, but you knowing it does. You seem to speak with confidence. How do you know?"

He smiles and says, "I shall answer with a family history lesson, then you will know more about this man's family than he does." He pauses to do something in Buck's right side that is laid open.

I cannot see from where I am, so I move closer. Buck's chest wound is on the outer extremity and low. The doctor has opened him to expose ribs and is probing between them, attempting to retrieve a shell fragment. Knowing I am there, he says, "Take this instrument and put it between his ribs and push them apart. I do as instructed and within seconds, Dr. McPheeters has the offending piece of iron in a set of large tweezers. "His lung is nicked, but should heal. He's going to require hospitalization, but should make a full recovery. Pneumonia will be the danger. The head wound is as you suspected, a scalp cut that bleed disproportionate to its severity."

"Your arm wound is going to be painful. I cannot keep you here for the wound, but you are still needed as an assistant. That should buy you some time to eat and rest. You are not going to shake yourself from that bull dog. He stalks by the windows looking in to see if he can spot you. He hasn't worked up the courage to come in yet, but he will."

"Do you have news of the battle?"

"Only that there are now more grey coats out there, but blues still outnumber them. It's not going well, but we're killing more of them than they are of us. There are just so damned many of them."

"Sir, you were speaking of a family history lesson; am I to assume that you are speaking of your family?"

"Oh yes, I do get distracted; no, my wife's family's history. She is a Buchannan from Kentucky. I am almost certain that your friend here is a cousin to my wife."

As he closes Buck's wound, he picks up the story. "She tells a story of an uncle who was restless by nature; always pushing further from civilization, always looking over the next mountain. He had a family that was left alone a good deal of the time due to his wandering. He came home once to find his wife and daughter gone. There was a great deal of blood, but no bodies. He found the little boy hiding in the woods, but according to the tale, could not, or would not ever shed any light on what happened. The father, my Sallie's uncle, took the boy and moved further and further west. No one was ever certain as to his whereabouts. It seems he was not that far away from Missouri." He paused, looking at Buck then me before he asks, "Does Buck have any family?"

"No, his wife died before the war. That's how we became friends. I was wandering from a situation at home and was working on a river boat when we met. We traveled together for the better part of a year, and have been friends since."

"Yes, the challenges of frontier travel can bond men closely. Does he have property in Arkansas?"

"Yes sir, he left his place to be looked after by one of my younger brothers. Before you ask sir, I think I can speak for Buck; he would consider it an honor to be of service to you and your family."

"Lieutenant, I will take the matter up with Buck, but for now, we have wounded to treat; let us get to the task. Please, lend a hand with your rather large friend. We must move him to make room for the next patient."

Buck moves, opens his eyes and asks, "What in tarnation is all the fuss about? If you want me to move, just ask."

I am surprised to hear him, "How long have you been awake?"

"Long enough to hear you give away my home to this saw bones cousin-in-law of mine. I heard about having a doc in the family, but this is one hell of a way to make your acquaintance." He offers his right hand to the doctor, then winces and withdraws it. "Sorry cousin, the hand shake will have to wait. What my young friend here promised you is in fact what I insist you do. If I can be of service in any way, I will."

"You need to lie down and rest, let us work. Then we can formulate a plan. You are a surrendered prisoner of war, but I think it is possible to lose you in the shuffle. You cannot be taken today, beyond that, you will be forgotten. You however," gesturing to me, "are another story. I cannot hide you. As an officer, you are of value to the enemy and…"

"I gave my word; I will honor it. If I can escape, I will and make my way to wherever I can find you, but I will not dishonor my family or my country by breaking my word."

"I respect you for it…"

"You're going to some stinking prison for me?" Buck interrupts.

I look at him and keep silent.

"Boy, you can't do that!"

"Yes I can, and must. I will probably be exchanged in a couple of months, then home to regroup with you. In the mean time, you can further the cause by assisting Dr. McPheeters and his family."

"What about your wife and those babies? Don't you care about them?"

"Buck, don't insult me; of course I care. Why do you think I am here fighting? I'm counting on you to assist the doctor; he is a good friend to me, and family to you. Then go home and see to Lucy Jane and the children."

William McPheeters watches us as a father watching two sons reason out a disagreement. He smiles and says, "Gentlemen, I believe we might come to a workable solution, but right now, I have many who need my assistance, and I need yours," pointing a bloody surgical instrument at me. "Sergeant, you need rest; go on the lawn, find a shady spot and relax. Before you go, drink this."

He hands Buck a crock jug like you find in every farm house in Arkansas. They usually hold shine liquor; as does this one. Buck takes a big pull, gasps, and succumbs to a fit of coughing. "What in the name of Satan is that?!"

The doctor smiles and says, "You should feel it any second now. It is the purest alcohol I can find and has many wonderful uses. Now, before you fall down, go find a tree to sleep under."

Buck takes another pull on the jug, and says, "Boy, you take care and remember all I taught you." He turns to go then stops. I keep my head down concentrating on the operation Dr. McPheeters is doing. I cannot bear to part with my friend, and I am frightened to be without him. He has always watched my back. I'll have to do it for myself now, and it will be a hard thing to do where I'm going. "See you friend."

"Sooner than you think," I don't lift my head and listen to the receding footsteps of my friend. I may never see him again.

"That's a fine man going there," says McPheeters.

"Yes sir, none better."

"I know one."

8) Evans' Property, 1859

Evans and Lucy worked and talked, talked and worked, and before they knew it, the sun was near down. They washed at the river and set about cooking from Evans' stores. They ate and talked, and as the stars began to show, the awkward subject of where Lucy Jane would bed that night arose.

Evans was first to bring it up. "I am sorry to not be able to provide you with anything better than my simple shelter. I did not expect a guest, certainly not a woman. The shelter has a door fashioned to it; you should be safe and fairly comfortable. I have built a cot up off the damp ground."

"Evans, I could never dream of..."

"Lucy," he interrupted, "this will not do. You will have the shelter; I will put down in the wagon."

"But...," Lucy started.

"This is not subject to debate. This arrangement is temporary until we can work out something more appropriate, but this I promise you, you will not have to go back."

She smiled, and said, "Thank you Evans," reached up, kissed him on the cheek, "good night." She turned and went into the shelter. Evans waited until she lit the lantern inside and watched her shadow move across the canvas that served as a door. His imagination and libido were fired. With considerable effort, he turned away to his cold wagon.

The next day she worked side by side with him, and the next, and the next, and the next. A solution other than the current arrangement did not seem any closer, and the longer they worked together, the less urgent a solution seemed. Evans became more dependent on her help and she became more dependent on his support.

They were blessed with a run of good weather and the cabin grew where before there was only the hope, but spring rains will come, and they did. Evans could deal with a brief shower in his wagon shelter, but in a deluge it was hopelessly inadequate and the skies had opened. After a frank discussion concerning their relationship, it was agreed that Evans would share the shelter on inclement nights, but when the weather broke, he would resume sleeping in the wagon.

With each passing day, Lucy was succeeding. She thought she might be in love, but having never been exposed or experienced what love should be, she wasn't sure. Evans not demanding sexual privileges and his willingness to protect her indicated, by her simple reasoning, that he was in love with her.

They granted each other as much privacy as the conditions and Christian morals dictated, but it was difficult. Lucy was not vigilant in regard to her modesty and knew the effect it was having on a strong, healthy, virile young man. Morals can sustain a man for just so long.

The rains ceased, but the cohabitation did not. It was too convenient. May 1st, a Sunday, arrived and the days were warming up. The cabin was coming along and both were proud of it. It was a brilliant day. They both knew that they should be in church, but justified not going because of the distance, clothing, work, and a dozen other excuses, but not one reason. If they had been honest with themselves, they were living wrong and knew it, making church difficult.

Evans worried, not knowing what he was going to tell his family. He had not been home in several weeks, and his brothers or Susan's would soon be calling. When they discovered Lucy's presence, it would be difficult and awkward to explain. But if he went and did so now, he would have control of the situation and reveal as much as he deemed necessary. Rumors would abound, but what had he done wrong? He had helped a friend in distress and kept her from danger. It was best to be open and honest and do it now, but something nagged at him all the more.

So it was on that churchless, sunny, Sunday, Evans announced to Lucy Jane that he was going home to visit his family. She could stay on the place if she wished, but he had to go to them and explain the situation before they came to him.

Lucy was surprised, and seeing the possible end to her salvation and scheme, demanded, "What are you going to tell them?"

"The truth; I am going to tell the truth".

"Which is…?"

"That you are a young Christian woman who, due to your family situation, find yourself in danger and have asked for help from a Christian man who is obliged to offer it."

This seemed reasonable to the young woman, but she needed control too; "And what do you think they'll do?"

"They'll either disown me, or offer to let you live with them. This is no place for a woman or a situation for a lady. I mean, we're practically living like we're married!"

A door had been opened. "Is there something so wrong with that?" Lucy asked with a coy smile.

"It's just not right, and I want it to be right, at least with my family."

"What of Susan Wilson?"

Evans had been dreading this. He knew what had been nagging him and had been able to ignore it, but now it was out in the open and he had to face it. He did not want to hurt Susan; he loved her, or thought he did.

He was becoming more confused about love as the days progressed. His feelings for Lucy had grown. He was her protector and she needed him. No one had ever needed him before and the instinct to protect her was strong. Would Susan understand? He dreaded knowing, but it had to be done. "She will hear the truth too". Evans worried how much Christian charity Susan or any of the combined families would have. It did not matter; it had to be done, and he was going to do it, and do it today.

He rode away dressed in his best and did not look back. He knew if he did, that the power of Lucy Jane's will and her eyes would turn him around. This had to be done and he must be man enough to face the consequences.

He hoped to time his arrival for the beginning of the Sunday dinner, but to which house should he go to? He had been so distracted that he had lost track of whose house the meal would be held. He had half a chance of getting it right, and since he wanted to face his family and not anyone else, he would go home.

The closer he got, the more anxious he became, the more his confidence waned, and the more the trip became a bad idea. He wished that Lucy had never ridden into his camp, or that he had turned her away, but that would have been more cowardly than not completing his appointed mission today.

He wallowed in self pity as he rode, becoming miserable. How had he ever gotten caught up in this? He was smart enough to see what he was getting into, or was he? The ride was giving him time to examine his feelings, but his thinking was clouded. He could not get images of Lucy Jane out of his head.

Because of their living conditions and Lucy's scheme of seduction, he had seen her in various stages of undress. These images interrupted his thoughts. He recalled how Lucy at work would bend at the task and her shirt would fall open reveling two of her most charming assets. These thoughts were not wholesome or Christian. He was head over heels in lust. He was doing what he knew to be right, but with the images flashing in his mind of Lucy's breasts, he was weakening fast. He needed help; so as he rode, he prayed.

He was thus engaged, pouring out his heart to the Lord, paying no attention to where he was going when he heard a booming voice like that of God say, "Boy, you must be all fired troubled…"

Evans jerked and shouted with a start. He looked around and saw not God, but his wandering companion and closest friend Buck Buchannan. "What…, uh, the hell! Where did you come from?"

Buck laughed at his young friend, and slapped his leg, "Boy! You were somewhere far off! Hell, I've been riding next to you for five minutes, tailing you for ten, maybe longer. If I was a bushwhacker, or a Cherokee, I'd have your life, scalp, horse and all! What the hell you thinking about so deep, and who were you talking too?"

Evans was flustered by Buck's appearance. He smiled as he thought, "So Lord, this is how you have answered my prayer?" Buck would love the irony. Evans rode looking down at his saddle feeling like a man caught with his pants down.

Buck leaned forward in his saddle, trying to look into the face of his road mate. Evans turned away in an attempt to reveal nothing. Buck laughed again and it rang through the woods. His black beard bobbed with his mirth as did his large belly. "Uh-oh, Boy, I've seen that look before! Who is she; anybody I know?" He punched Evans in the arm in an attempt to get him to turn around, and almost knocked him out of his saddle.

Evans' stallion skittered sideways and he fought to get him under control. He hoped the activity was enough to distract Buck, and tried to change the subject by asking, "Where you headed this fine Sunday? I know it's not to church".

Buck was a God fearing man, but having spent most of his life from the time he could shoot a rifle wandering with his Pa, and never knowing his Ma, she being the victim of some disease, or so was the story, Buck was given too much to the pleasures of the flesh to go to church. He had no use for organized religion; nature was to him the grandest of cathedrals and most likely where the All Mighty would be found. "I reckon I'm going the same place you are; to get fed, am I right?" Evans did not answer. "Come on boy; quit trying to change the subject; what's her name?"

"How do you know it's a girl?"

"Boy," Buck, never in Evans' memory had called him by his given name unless they were in danger or Buck was mad at him, "we've been too many miles together for that. I could tell riding up behind you that you're thinking of a woman. Do you love her?"

"Aw Buck, I don't know. What do you know about love any way?"

"Some, but it ain't the kind of love in them books you're learnin' me to read. I don't know any love like that. Never did, even when I had a wife, but I do know a sight about how a real man feels who needs a woman, and son, there ain't a fool on this planet that can't see you got it bad. He paused a second, then in a voice one would use with a child who was in trouble, "Now, come on and tell ole' Buck all about it. Maybe I can help."

And Evans did, he spilled it all, every detail even his feelings concerning both Lucy Jane and Susan Wilson. Buck didn't say a word;

just listened. When Evans finished, Buck waited to make sure the end of the tale had come before saying in a voice full of pathos and wagging his head, "Boy…," and that was all. They rode in silence, neither looking at the other. Evans was feeling low, and confused, Buck was speechless; something that was alien to both of them.

He finally said, "Do you love her?"

"Who?"

"Well, either one, I guess."

"I don't know Buck," Evans said in an exasperated sigh, "I really don't know. I don't feel the same with Lucy Jane as I do when I'm with Susan. When I'm with Susan, it's calm, and nice, real peaceful like. When I'm with Lucy, it's exciting, hot, intense, and she needs me," he hesitated, still thinking, "she needs me real bad."

Buck pulled up his horse, and Evans did likewise turning to face Buck who looked him in the eye and asked, "Which one feels right?"

"Which one feels right?"

"Yeah, which one do you feel right with, and stop repeating my questions, just give me a damned answer! You're avoiding the issue and Boy, it ain't going away, and I'm telling you, you had better get it together because when we make that next bend, your folks house is just down a piece, and there's going to have to be some explaining."

Evans had failed to keep track of where he was and the surprise and shock showed on his face. Buck laughed, "Boy, you got it real bad! This is going to be fun to watch! The question's still there, and you have to answer it, 'Which one feels right?" With that, he reined his horse around and headed on down the road. Evans followed.

When they rounded the bend, the Atwood place spread out before them down at the bottom of a gentle slope. Simeon, Evans' father, and all the boys had always kept the house in prime condition. Simeon was an excellent carpenter and had built the house with the help of all the children and Eliza, his wife, along with the Wilsons, and other neighbors. It was a proud place. Simeon was fond of declaring, "A man's house, even if poor, and poorly built, does not have to look it". The entire house, gables and all was painted with real paint as far as it went. It was white washed in the spots where the paint had worn thin, but unless you were right next to it, you couldn't tell. It had a porch that ran all the way around on three sides with several doors opening into the house. At the rear, the porch dropped to ground level with a six step staircase on either corner that led down to the yard. The porch was covered with a gabled roof and looked as if it were built at the same instant with never a thought of adding on. It fact, the house been added onto so many times that

Simeon and Eliza disagreed as to the number. It was open, welcoming, and home. Evans didn't want to be here.

In the yard and in front of the barn were wagons and horses a-plenty. His heart sank. The feast was here. Buck looked back, saw Evans' face and laughed as he rode into the yard, dismounted under the trees with the other horses, and tied up. Without looking at Evans, he walked around the side of the house to join the gathering.

Evans could hear the called out welcomes of both male and female voices, and hear Buck's booming response. He was welcome most everywhere he went, but especially at the Atwood and Wilson homes. Both families gave him credit for getting Evans home from Texas safe and sound. Neither Buck nor Evans ever gave them any reason to think otherwise under the assumption that what they didn't know couldn't hurt them. That was not going to be the case today; they were going to know, and the results could be damnable.

Evans, not in any rush to face the families and the girl he loved, or at least thought he did, made his way to the back just in time to hear Susan Wilson ask, "Buck, have you seen or heard from Evans?"

He was turning to leave when he heard Buck's too loud voice ring out, "Ya'll ask him yourselves..."

"Damn you Buck...," Evans thought to himself.

"...he's coming into the yard right behind me!"

"Double damn you Buck," this time under his breath as he turned the corner to face his and her families and his future.

They were gathering for the meal, the food was in the final stages of preparation. There were platters of beef, and a little pork, bowls of potatoes, both white and sweet, pinto beans with slabs of salt pork, and cornbread.

There are shouted greetings all around, hugs from the women and some of his brothers, handshakes from the rest, kisses for, and from his mother and Mrs. Wilson. Susan stepped up and hugged him for just a tad longer than was comfortable. He is sure that everyone noticed, where in truth, no one did. He is also certain that everyone could see his consternation and his sin written on him as the scarlet "A" in the popular Nathanial Hawthorne novel. He weakens and sickens a little at the thought of the tragic end of those characters who have committed adultery. "Is lust as great a sin as adultery, or are they one and the same?" He does not have time to contemplate the answer before space is made for him around the table across from Susan and the chatter, laughter, and love resumes.

Evans tries to focus on the blessing being said, but his thoughts are interrupted by the intrusion of Lucy Jane's image. He wants to be there with her, he catches her scent as if she was right next to him. His mind replays the scenes of her exposure as Reverend Claiborne drones on, "...and Father, as we ask Thy blessing on this bounty that Thou hast provided, we further beseech thy blessing on those of each family represented here, that they will have Thy comfort and protection, and that they will soon be able to join in fellowship again; in the name of our Lord and Savior, Jesus Christ, Amen."

"Amen," chorused all. "I hope the protection part works," Evans thinks.

"All right, don't stand on formality, you're all family, dig in and pass to your right," spoke Simeon, the patriarch of the Atwood family.

All the chatter that accompanies a call to chow raises a din that drowns out most all Evans' thoughts. He is quiet and grows more anxious as the meal progresses. He hopes that the inevitable will never arise, but knows it must. He's not ready when it does because it comes from the one person who he thought was a spectator.

"Boy, where've you been keepin' yourself? I guess it's been close to a month," said Buck in his usual robust, hear-me-across-the-county, voice.

"I am going to start calling him 'Judas'," thinks Evans wondering how messy it will be to kill his friend at the dinner table. He wants to go home to Lucy Jane. "That's the first time I've thought of my place as 'home'. Is Lucy Jane part of home? Should she be?" He looks up from his plate with a prayer in his heart and a smile on his lips, right into the wondering eyes of Susan Wilson. "How can I do this to her? Wait a minute, what is it that I am doing? I haven't done anything. Have I already made the decision to be with Lucy Jane? If I have, is that wrong?"

"Buck, my good, faithful friend, if you'd ever come by my place, you would know what I am up to. I could always use a strong back and weak mind to lend a hand," Evans said with a chuckle.

"Are you working on your cabin, dear?"

He looked at his mother and smiled. "Yes ma'am, it's coming along, thank you; no thanks to my big mouthed friend over there," gesturing with his fork full of beef in the direction of Buck.

"Boy, you know I'm too old for that kind of work, who's helping you out there, anybody?"

There it is; the question he has dreaded, but is relieved to hear. No sense putting it off; be a man, tell the truth, no excuses. He raises his head, sits tall, smiles at Susan, and looks up and down the table, meeting each eye while he says, "Lucy Roberts has had to leave her family for safety and decency, and has been staying on the property helping me."

There is silence. Neither Susan, her father, nor her brothers look at him. Both mothers meet his look. His father is boring holes in him with his stare.

His mother asks, "Why you, son; why not a female friend?"

Everyone with the exception of Buck and the Reverend who are busy stuffing their faces pretending to have no interest in the conversation, but both hanging on every word while not looking at him, is waiting for his answer. "Ma, she came to me because, I suspect, I'm the only friend she has. She came to my reading class before I went wandering, and I taught her, and we became friends. Her circumstances did not allow her to make many acquaintances outside her family, and when there was trouble she came to me. I did as you taught me; I extended the hand of Christian charity."

Simeon spoke, "What kind of trouble's she in son?"

"Pa, I can't say. It would be breaking a confidence. You'll have to trust me; it's something bad; something the whole family ought to be run out for, but I will tell you no more than that." His confidence growing, he looks around. There are more eyes meeting his, including John Wilson; he presses forward, "I couldn't turn her away. I am convinced she is alone in the world. That's why I'm here today. It ain't right for her to be with me alone on the property. The only solutions I can see are that one of you come out there with me," gesturing to his and Susan's brothers, "or one of you two," this time gesturing to his parents, and Susan's, "take her in. She's strong, and works as hard as any man; harder than some," casting a sly look at Buck.

John Wilson, having made eye contact with Simeon says, "Evans, of course either your folks or us will take her in. That ain't the question. The question is son, why did you wait so long to bring this up?"

Why had he waited so long? "Mr. Wilson, I guess I felt like I was protecting her, like a wounded bird or something. She was desperate, and I could help. The truth is, I grew to like her company, and it was sure nice to have the everyday help with the place."

Both fathers wait.

"She is better now, and I think she should be in a family situation to heal properly. I'll tell her she's welcome here or at your place," nodding to Mr. Wilson.

John Wilson asks, "How long's she been out there with you son?"

"A little over three weeks, sir," is the reply. Evans does not look away.

"She won't be welcome at our place," says the, quiet, smooth, but firm voice of Susan Wilson. The table is silent. "There's more to consider here than charity." She rises from the table with the dignity of a lady, and with her customary smoothness, gathers her now empty plate, glass, and utensils and makes her way up the six steps onto the porch and on into the house without a backward glance.

Evans follows her with his eyes. After the door shuts, he turns his attention back to the table and finds everyone staring at him. He does not know what to say, or do, and feels his face redden. He looks at Buck who is the only person looking at him with any sympathy. Buck is hurting for him, but Evans' misery is his alone to bear.

The silence is broken by his father, "Son, we'll take her in, like we said, but you've got some decisions to make and some more explaining to do," there was a pause before he, gesturing with his head toward the back door says, "go on now; do what's right."

Evans gets up, the antithesis of Susan. Where she had been dignified, graceful, and smooth, he is ashamed, clumsy, and rough as he gathers his dishes and makes his way up the steps as if they lead to a gallows. He's aware of being watched and moves slowly to the kitchen, manages the door, and goes into the house.

Susan is standing with her back to him cleaning the dishes. She does not turn around. He stares at her back. "Susan, I..."

"Evans, you owe me no explanation, but you do owe me the courtesy of making a decision and not make me look the fool." Her voice is quiet, but her customary kindness is absent. She takes a deep breath and lets it out before saying, "Evans, I don't know what you are thinking. Maybe you don't either, so just don't say anything." She turns to face him. He looks at the floor as she speaks again, "I have loved you since we were children, and as much as it grieves me to admit it, I will probably love you all my life and beyond, but I will not let you make a fool of me. If you want Lucy Jane Roberts, if you think that is what love is, you go ahead and have her, but don't come crawling to me when she is through with you..." She stops, letting the last word hang, "unless you come on bended knee". There's a long pause. Evans cannot look at her. She walks to him, stands on tip toes to reach him, and kisses his cheek. "Go, on now; do what you think you must." She turns her back and goes to the sink saying, "Get!"

As a school boy dismissed from punishment, Evans obeys. He turns to go and hears one sob; just one. That's all anybody will hear.

9) Prisoner of War

Friday, 7:00 PM, May 1st, 1863

I am pleased and surprised to still be in possession of my journal. Pleased that I am allowed to keep it, and surprised to find it stained with my good friend's blood. It was in my uniform jacket pocket on the same side Buck leaned as I carried him. I fear and pray for my friend.

I am shocked at what goes on in the field hospitals. I do not know how men like McPheeters manage to remain sane. I expressed dismay at the conditions under which we were working. In reply, the doctor offered a quote from a Federal Surgeon at Pea Ridge, one of our first battles, "I am fully convinced that no army was ever sent into the field in such destitute condition as ours, except the one it fought and conquered". The conquered army would be ours.

It is much later, but this is the first time I have been left alone to be able to record the happenings of the past few hours. Private Hansen was less than amiable at having to wait all day and into the night to secure his prisoner, but as much as I had hoped he would abandon his post, he did not. I have to say he is a good soldier. He now has the task of finding his unit in the dark, having no idea where they are.

The battle is lost. We were out numbered. I am told that we held to the field until after 5:00 PM before we gave up the cause as lost; the Union has secured the road to Port Gibson, hence the road to Vicksburg. General Bowen held off a force four times our strength and delayed their advance to be able to save as many of our troops as possible. Our forces will fall back and do all we can do to delay the Union advance to Vicksburg and join the garrison in fortifications there.

I have been removed a few miles to the rear, where I have found several of my command assembled, and closely guarded. There will be no escape tonight. On the way to the rear, a great many of the Federals wanted to know what kind of fortifications we had where we had been fighting, and when I informed them we had none but what nature had furnished, many were surprised and believed otherwise. I am left to think that they are amazed at the zeal with which we defend our homeland.

I saw General Grant, who questioned me as to the number of casualties of our command. I gave him as little information as possible. He was cordial, but when he realized that no intelligence was forthcoming, he dismissed me and I was taken to be with the other prisoners. There are about two hundred of us.

I am pleased to say that we have been treated reasonably well. We have been fed, not well, but enough. We officers have even been able to enjoy coffee, although I do not expect that to continue. I was even offered and received care for my wounded arm. The doctor who treated me must have smelled the odors of the hospital and asked if I had been there earlier that day. When I replied in the affirmative, he smiled and asked if I were considering medicine as my field of study after the war. I think I would like to study medicine when the nightmares of imprisonment and war are over. First, I have to survive.

We were kept at the rendezvous until about 10:00 or 11:00 at night, when we were started to Bruinsburg, on the river, the place where the Federals had landed the day before. We were well guarded on the way, although I did look for an opportunity to slip away in the darkness. I so want to go to Buck and escape with him to home and assist the doctor with his situation, but it isn't to be.

We arrived at Bruinsburg the next morning (May 2) about sun up. We stayed there that day. During the day, the captured officers were taken on board the gunboat *Louisville;* then in the evening, we were taken up the river within three miles of Grand Gulf, the scene of our artillery victory.

Sunday, May the 3rd

We were taken up by Grand Gulf and landed that night at a plantation, a few miles below Vicksburg on the Mississippi River.

Monday, May 4th

We took up the line of March for Miliken's Bend, twenty five miles above Vicksburg. We met General Sherman and his staff and were questioned by them as to the size of our force. We did our best to give a confusing account of our units and numbers. Their intelligence is woefully lacking, but they are counting on the size of their army to make up for it. They seem reluctant to commit their troops to battle. Do they think to win this war without causalities? From what we have heard from the east, Virginia, that is the case. The Union leadership is afraid to commit to battle, to lose men.

Saturday the 9th

We are bound north accompanied by gunboats as an escort. We passed Lake Providence, a little town on the west bank of the River, fifty miles above Milikin's Bend. In the evening we passed a boat loaded with armed Union soldiers of "African descent".

May the 11th
About 12:00PM, we passed Napoleon, a town near the mouth of the Arkansas River, and about 4:00 PM, we passed the mouth of the White River as it dumps into the Mississippi. (I've written a letter to Lucy about this moment; I pray she has received it)

Sunday, May the 17th:
We arrived at St. Louis in Missouri. My thoughts turn to Dr. McPheeters and his family and wonder if he and Buck were able to assist his wife and children. One of General Bowmen's adjutants, a captain, is among my fellow prisoners and related that McPheeters is going to be assigned to the Army of Tennessee which is operating in Arkansas and Missouri. This will allow him to be as close to home as possible and aid whenever duties allow.

Our boat is anchored out in the river for a few hours. No prisoners are being allowed to communicate with persons on either shore, but they have allowed us to post letters. I have written to Lucy and to Ma and Pa. I hope Buck is able to assure them of my condition should the letters not get through. I pray that Buck will get through.

At 6:00 PM we "weighed anchor" and proceeded up the River. At about 9:30 PM, we steamed up to the wharf at Alton, Illinois.

We are ordered on shore in front of the massive walls of the old state penitentiary and soon its huge gates were thrown open to "receive the Rebels", who with sad hearts and woe-be-gone faces tell our abhorrence of the place in the strongest terms to those who would deign to listen. To describe the place now would be imprudent, but of its unsuitableness as a prison in point of health and comfort, we might exclaim that the half has not been told.

10) Sunday, May 1st, 1859 4:00 PM

An hour has passed since I was dismissed by Susan, and left the family gathering. I am miserable as I ride. The sting of embarrassment is still on me. I rode out acknowledging no one; not even Buck.

I'm alone and sorry; sorry for everything, but most for myself. Alone is my choice, but it does seem that everyone turned their back on me. I talk to myself, "Why, what did I do? I told the truth. That's what I'm supposed to do; that's what I believe in, and look where it got me! I'm alone; shunned. I can never go back there, but they are my family. How could this happen? What have I done to deserve this? I did the right thing, and they turned their backs! Maybe I turned mine," I admit.

The closer I get to the homestead, the deeper I sink into despair. After all I have been through; I'm no closer to resolving the question of what to do with Lucy Jane than I was before. I can't send her to my family, even though they said otherwise. Such would cause a rift between us and the Wilson family. I can see no solution. In a way, I feel better that there isn't. I can stop worrying and let it take care of itself.

Turning off the road in the late spring afternoon; traveling the rough lane to my cabin site, my mood changes. I'm anxious to see Lucy. She will greet me with her glorious smile, shine her countenance on me through the power of her gaze, and all will be well. I'm smiling, looking forward to her embrace, and realize that the first thing she will do is ask, "How was your dinner?" That'll be followed by, "How's the family?" Those two, I can handle, but when she asks, "What are you going to do with me?" For that, I have no answer.

When the cabin site comes into view, there is no Lucy. "She's in the shelter," I think, but that makes no sense; it's too pretty a day for her to be inside. "Maybe she left too, but where would she go?" Not home, and who else does she know? That question will have to wait. I need to find Lucy. Her horse is in the corral, so she didn't leave.

At the corral, I dismount and tie my horse. "Lucy," I call; silence. I look around. The golden rays of the lowering sun are filtering through the trees and the light scatters about the yard. It's beautiful, and I want to share it with Lucy; where is she?

"She *just might* be gone, but how?" I think. If she has left, that would be a solution. Didn't I think that the only solution was to let the problem solve itself? Maybe this is it! I get an empty feeling in my gut. I will be alone if that's the case, and I don't like the idea.

I have been so self indulged that when the thought of something untoward having happened to my Lucy comes to mind, I gasp, my eyes bulge with fear, and I call her name louder, "Lucy!" Again, silence. "Did I just think of her as 'my' Lucy?" I don't have time to examine the thought, or its implications; I have to find her. "Lucy! I'm back! Lucy, where are you?" My shouting disturbs the natural sounds of the woods and the resulting silence is oppressive and frightening. My search becomes frantic.

I run to the shelter, throw back the canvas covering and stare into emptiness. Her things are still in place, and show no signs of a struggle or violence. That's good news, but where is she?

I run to the cabin. As I go, images of a hurt, broken, blonde girl lying unaided race through my head. I envision her coming to the house, not wanting to waste the day, and while working, she falls, or something falls on her. Did she break a leg; something hit her on the head, is she…? I would not allow myself to think that thought. I race through the cabin looking as I go at the open roof, the just started window cuts, and the open back door. The walls are about four feet up, so I have to go back outside to search the perimeter. She's nowhere to be found, which is a relief, but where is she?

If she had been in the woods, or at the trench we dug to answer nature's call, she would have answered, or would have appeared by now. I stop and think.

The earlier question of what to do with Lucy is gone. It doesn't matter if I can't find her. I'm becoming desperate and feel the deep dread of never seeing her again. I want her so bad that tears well up. I have no conscious thought of love for her, but I must if I feel this passionate at her absence. "What to do?" If I find her, I'm never going to let her go again; damn what others think.

I force myself to relax, sit on a stump, catch my breath and think. I will myself to concentrate on the problem saying, "Think, Evans, think! She has to be somewhere!" I look around and focus on every sight and sound. I hear the river. Maybe she's there!

I bolt down the path through the woods that leads to a small cove cut into the bank by the action of an eddy in the current which has formed a gravel and sand beach twenty yards wide with part of it shaded by huge oaks and willows whose branches reach to touch the river's water. The beach is never covered even at flood stages and is an area that we use for washing and bathing.

I am praying as I go, hoping that Lucy is there. I race past signs of her presence, oblivious in my worry. Her clothes are hanging from the lower limbs of the trees. I am desperate to find her. It never occurs to me what she might be doing here.

I top the rise just before the beach and skid to a halt as I call in desperation, "Lucy, Lucy; where are you?" I'm looking everywhere, but I am winded from my run and miss her entirely.

"Evans, I'm right here," she answers with coyness and seduction that my fear addled brain does not comprehend.

The sun is not low enough to be hidden by the tree line on the opposite bank of the river, and as I look due west, it's full in my face, blinding me to the scene before me. I shade my eyes with my hand, lower my head and peer at the water. There she is; standing in the river with her bare back to me, smiling over her shoulder. I'm speechless. I stand staring and pant. "Lucy," then breathless and soft, "Lucy, Lucy..." I drop my head from weariness, relief, and modesty. I raise it up again for all the opposite reasons.

She is an apparition with a back-lighted ethereal glow to her. She turns to face me. Her eyes never leave my face nor does the smile from her lips as I take in the beauty before me. She rises and begins to come toward me. I at last speak, "Lucy?" The word asks more than one question.

She is a nymph rising from the ocean, blonde, smiling Lucy Jane, streaming water. She locks me with her gaze and asks, "Miss me?"

"No, uh, I mean yes, but not then, I mean, I do now, but... Oh, Lucy, you are so beautiful! What are you doing?"

She laughs, "I'm coming out of the water," and indeed, she is.

"I was worried about you."

"You were worried about me; why?" She smiles, standing closer and placing her hands on my chest. "I've been here all afternoon, alone; just me and nature."

I am in her power, and happy to be. "What are you doing?"

"I'm getting you out of these filthy clothes; you smell like horses. Don't you want to join me?"

The answer is too obvious.

The morning sun's earliest rays catch us in each other's arms. There is no work done that Monday. We are seldom out of sight or touch. We explore all day; eating, sleeping, wandering the woods, swimming in the cold river.

Late that night, as we lay exhausted from the vigor of the day, Lucy asks a question she has been keeping for the right moment, "When do I go to live with your family?"

"Lucy Jane," I reply just this side of sleep, "you are never going to leave my arms."

She lies snuggled against Evans with her head on his shoulder, scarce moving. As his breathing becomes deep and regular, she smiles. Her future is secure; the "better life" is within reach. The seduction of Evans Atwood is going well.

Lucy stays on the property, and the work on the cabin, their cabin, progresses, but the labor is not as tedious or demanding as before as each finds many opportunities to make the other aware of their love. Lucy, although appearing coy and just a little shy glories in the attention, and from her limited experience, assumes it to be love. She has never had anyone want her for just being herself and basks in the sensations such behavior gives her.

The cabin progresses well. All concerned learn of the arrangement and many of the Atwood and Wilson families have visited the homestead to assist with the work.

It's July when, after a bout of frequent nausea, she announces, "Evans, I'm pregnant."

"Yeah, I know."

"You know?"

"Certainly I know. I have a mother and sisters. Are you unhappy about it?"

"Of course I'm happy to be carrying your baby." The fearful question comes, "Are you going to leave me now?"

He's quiet for a few moments, takes a deep breath, audibly lets it out, and answers, "How can you think that of me? There's only one thing to do."

"And what is that?"

"We will get married." She melts into his arms and it makes him smile thinking of her complete surrender.

Lucy Jane knows the truth of her emotion. It is a release of months of tension. Her plan for "better" is moving along, better and better. She smiles as she says, "Good."

The cabin is finished by October as planned, but not without the help of family and friends; even Buck. The happy, growing couple takes up life with all the vigor of the young. They improve their home, even to the extent of a wood floor, and both are happy. It's a nice home. Lucy has never had one and "better" is always in her thinking.

Evans and Lucy Jane are married Sunday, November 6, 1859.

Martha Jane Atwood is born April 3, 1860 and is healthy and beautiful; a perfect blending of both parents. All is well and all are happy; things are getting better and better with each passing month.

Evans has friends, family, a home and promise. He's contemplating higher education and is happy to be teaching school, working the farm plot of their homestead, and loving Lucy every chance he gets. He's happy but the spirit of adventure still burns in his young heart.

Lucy is pregnant again when the world catches up to them. War is upon the land and will turn their world and her plans upside down.

11) Lucy Jane
Saturday, May 30, 1863

The man riding the trail toward the house does not look like trouble. A bush whacker would not be so bold, but Lucy can't be sure. She stays in the house peering out the loophole cut in the door. There are several around the cabin that allow her to see in all directions. Even if the shutters are closed over the four windows, she can see who is approaching and defend herself. The loopholes have plugs that fit into "T" shaped slots and are beveled so they cannot be extracted from outside the cabin and latched so that they can't be pushed in. They're cut large enough to accommodate the shot gun or the rifle Evans provided for her.

As the man nears, his features became identifiable. It's no bushwhacker, but she wouldn't put it past him. The crusted black hat covers filthy, long, black hair over an ugly face with a perpetual five day growth of black beard under a drooping, filthy mustache. The man is Gavin Tate; a sometimes hireling of the postmaster to deliver mail, member of the Home Guard, and full time scoundrel and drunk.

The Home Guard, the local militia charged with defending the area from Yankee incursion, and with rounding up deserters from the Confederate Army, is his primary endeavor. There are few deserters in the anti-secession area of northwest Arkansas, but those that there are, are worth more money apiece than Gavin Tate will see in three months of mail delivery.

He is merciless in his pursuit of them. Willingness to apply any and all means no matter how cowardly or low is his strength. In Benton County he kidnapped one man's wife and children and held them in the squalor of a pig sty until the man surrendered. Tate's laziness has allowed him to develop extraordinary skills of deviousness and patience.

Lucy Jane hates Gavin Tate. He gets his shine whiskey from her step father so knows of her past. His lewd suggestions hint that she can do for him what she has done before. Such comments are sufficient for her to know that her stepfather has spoken of her and her uses.

He's Home Guard which gives him almost unbridled authority to search for deserters and always asks after the whereabouts and actions of her husband, Buck, and Martin Wilson. He wants to line his pockets with their reward money, especially Evans who, being an officer brings a larger bounty.

Her strongest reason for hating Gavin Tate is that he wants her. With Evans absent, she is, in his mind, and the minds of others, available. Women left alone are becoming fair game to those who have not aligned with the cause and have stayed home. Only Evans honor and reputation as well as that of his family and Buck protect her. Anyone taking advantage of Lucy will have a lot of decent, hard men to answer to.

Lucy steps onto the front porch with the shot gun cradled in her arms while Gavin's still fifty yards off. She does not look at the filthy man approaching, but scans the surrounding woods for any company he might have recruited. She's already checked the rear approach to the house.

She walks to each end of the porch scrutinizing the woods and sides, never looking at Tate who is watching her as a fox watches a chicken. He's looking for weakness in the small, pretty woman, but she won't show him one.

"Good morning," bellows Tate, still riding toward her.

Lucy does not respond, but stands in the center of the porch, in front of the doorway where the two babies play. For the first time she looks at Gavin Tate.

Unfazed by Lucy's ignoring him, Tate continues, "It's a beautiful day ain't it Miss Lucy?"

Lucy speaks in the coldest, most unwelcoming way she can, "That's Mrs. Atwood to you Gavin Tate, and I expect you to address me as such."

"Oh, that's right! You're married to an *officer* ain't 'ya? I near forgot what with you being your pa's who..., 'gal', I mean. Haven't seen your soldier boy around these parts have you?" Gavin's voice is as sweet as new birch syrup, but the bite of sarcasm and his disdain for her rejection of him is clear.

"The whereabouts and doing's of my husband ain't none of your concern. Now, Mr. Tate, do you have business here, or are you trespassing? Being a lone woman, I deal with trespassers quick and hard." She moves the shotgun from across her body to a more threatening frontal position and gestures toward him with a slight elevation of the barrel.

"You go easy with that there scatter gun Mrs. Atwood; you don't know what that can do!"

Lucy laughs at the consternation on the face of the coward Tate, and his underestimation of her skill with fire arms. To emphasis the latter, she, still smiling, looks to the end of the porch where hanging in the shade, are three squirrels, still in their skins with their heads missing, a dressed deer, and a turkey, headless as well.

Gavin follows her gaze and seeing the animals hanging to season says, "I guess you're pretty good with that thing after all."

"Oh no, the shot gun is for close in work. I took those with the rifle." Then with a chill in her speech, "What brings you to my home? State your business and be on your way."

Tate looks at Lucy Jane with one eye squinted closed, chewing on his wad of tobacco, wondering if she is lying, or has made all those shots. He gives up wondering, and says smiling, "I've got a letter for yoooou." He draws out the last word in a sing song voice that he thinks will sway her to girlish glee and she'll drop her guard.

"Ride forward, drop it on the porch, and be gone."

He's surprised, but tries to not let it show. He fails as he stammers, "Well, don't you want to know, I mean, aren't you excite..., It's from...", and as he gets his wits back, "You owe me postage due."

Lucy laughs again, "Tate, don't insult me. I'm sure it's from Evans and with him in the army, mail is delivered free. Now, put the letter on the porch and get!" She says as she would to a dog and punctuates the words by the stomp of her right foot and a wave of the shot gun.

Tate starts to protest, "Well, you owe..."

"No, I don't owe you a tip, or delivery fee, or anything else. And no, I will not invite you in for coffee; now leave the letter and go!"

The disgusting man rides forward, loosens the buttons on his jacket, and takes out a letter. Lucy can smell him as he draws near and shakes her head in disgust. Tate drops the letter on the porch, gives Lucy a look that tells of his humiliation and his desire for revenge, but cannot hide his longing. He tries a softer approach, "Mrs. Atwood, how long do you think you can keep this place up and them babies," nodding to the two playing around the porch, "up and safe? Why don't you let me take care of you? You need a man; a woman as pretty as you has needs."

Lucy laughs; this time in disgust, "Tate, I will keep this place up as long as I need to, and the babies are safe. If you ever hint at a threat against them, or lay a hand on them for any reason, or even look at them, I'll blow a hole in you," gesturing with the shot gun right at Tate's middle, "wide enough to walk through and not get my skirts bloody! Do you understand me?" Before he can answer, "As for having a man around, neither you nor any of the rest of the no goods can begin to measure to the man Evans is even when he's not here."

"You're going to regret those words woman! You ain't as safe as you think! There's talk, and I'm of a mind..."

Boom! Lucy fires the shot gun into the ground next to Tate's horse, causing it to rear up and throw him. He scrambles to his feet, gasping for air, swearing at Lucy. He reaches for his horse, mounts, and says, "Your day's coming woman! You ain't as good as you think you are, or as safe. I'm gonna have you and those pretty children..." The rest is lost, covered by the sound of the horse's hooves beating against the hard packed trail as its rider retreats.

Lucy lowers the shotgun. Martha Jane and baby James stare at her. Lucy sees the concern on their faces and says, "Never you mind about that man. He's the worst of the lot, but he's afraid."

Martha Jane, who looks more like Lucy every day, asks, "Mama, why do these men come around?"

"Honey," she kneels and takes both children in her arms, "they think they can replace your Pa."

"Are you going to let 'em?"

"No baby; no one can replace your Pa."

"When's Pa coming home?"

"I don't know Martha Jane. Maybe this letter is from him. Let's see." Their attention turns to the letter lying on the porch. Lucy reaches for it, gets a whiff of Tate's stink, waves it in the air to freshen it and settles herself on the steps, puts a child on each knee, opens the sealed letter and reads…

Monday evening, May 11th, 1863
North bound on the Mississippi River

My dearest, most precious Lucy Jane,

How I long for your embrace, your tender reassurance that all is well, or will be soon. My heart aches for the words, "I love you," from your sweet lips. I know you do, but to once again hear them pass from you to me is a yearning that for now will have to go unrequited.

As this finds you, and only God knows if it will, or how long it will take, or the conditions you are in when it does, I am now a prisoner of those who would oppress our freedom; those who would crush our right to choose as we may. I am now subject to tyranny that I never knew existed. Oh, the irony of it! I have sacrificed so much to assure our freedom, and am now in the very hands of those who would tyrannize us. Buck and I were captured May 1st at Port Gibson, Mississippi as we fought General Grant's invasion. Space and time require that I spare you the details, but Buck was wounded and I was forced to leave him at the hospital. Please pray that he was able to escape and still lives.

Our lads, Martin Wilson in particular, fought brave and well, but our resistance was futile. There were just too many of the invaders to repel.

Today, about 4:00 in the afternoon, our flotilla of troop ship and guarding gun boats passed the mouth of our precious White River; the very one that flows past our haven, our home. It pulled hard at my heart to be so close to home, but we might as well have been on the moon. As I passed, I shed tears into the water. I long so to be home. I would have jumped and swam for the shore if guards had not been vigilant. I chose rather to survive to once again fight; to once again be in the bosom of my family.

This news must come as a terrible blow to you, but I also know you have the strength to endure. This war is stretching on longer than anyone foresaw, but dearest wife, it will end and when we have achieved victory, peace and freedom will be ours in a free land where we can raise our babies in harmony and rest.

Plead with the Lord as I do for the quick resolution of this conflict and my incarceration, but only with honor. Please pray for all of us.

Buck, if he survives, is going to assist a cousin who has fallen under the iron, tyrannical fist of the Federal government. She has been banished from her home in St. Louis and deposited without purse or means in Arkansas. She is the wife of a fine man of medicine whom I have had the pleasure of calling my friend. Once Buck has her established in his home, I have asked him to care for you in whatever way is possible.

Show my family this letter. I am pleading for their support of not only you and our children, but of me, for supporting one is supporting the other. I know they will never let me down, nor will they abandon my wife and children.

When I look back to boyhood years, I remember the many bright paths that were presented to me. In this "choosing of one" to follow through life, my eyes were too dim to see the obstacles that would be thrown across it. Little did I think that a penitentiary wall would ever take me to its charge, or confine me within its limits as a criminal or prisoner. But it has, and in after life, when peace shall predominate over our now distracted land, and I have returned to enjoy the fruits of our present toils and sufferings, one gloomy thought will rise up saying, "I was once an inmate of Alton Penitentiary," but I shall also have the pleasing reflection that the crime for which I was incarcerated was none other than my assisting in the advancement of my country's cause, and I trust that cause, our new country, has a bright future that, though now in embryo, will 'ere long be ushered into life; ripe with all that goes to make a nation wise and powerful.

I implore you to stand with me, with the cause and look to a bright future together. I cannot know your struggle, but please think on mine and pray for me as I pray for you. We can overcome. Do not lose the faith. We will triumph and do so with honor. In the mean time, I fear it is my duty to be subjected to the oppression of those who we so staunchly oppose.

Your loving husband,
Evans

"What's it mean Mama? What's a prisoner?"

Lucy fights tears and anger. She deflects the question as she explains, "It means that your Pa will not be coming home for a long time."

"How long?"

"I don't know baby, I don't know." She stops herself from adding, "maybe never". It would not serve to burden a baby with such a prospect. Martha Jane is growing up fast and is wise beyond her years. She's developing the sense of survival that her mother has.

"Are we going to be alright?"

"Yes, of course baby. Mama can take care of us, and we will be alright; I promise."

"What about the men coming around Mama; are they going to hurt us?"

"No, Martha Jane, they will not hurt us. They will die first."

James Calvin squirms off her lap to investigate a bug crawling in the yard. He navigates the steps backwards and has lost interest in the letter, but Martha Jane is concerned.

"Mama, I'm scared. Can we go to Grandpa's?"

"Yes my darling girl, we will go to church and Grandma's and Grandpa's tomorrow. Now hop down and go play. We've got a lot to do before this day is done."

Martha Jane follows her brother down the steps into the yard. Lucy watches as they move about, playing and exploring.

She rereads the letter and lets her anger out. "Your honor can go to hell, Evans Atwood; what about me? What about what I need?" She says out loud, wiping tears. She and the children will go to see the Atwoods tomorrow, and relate the letter and Evan's plea for their help. They won't let them suffer. She knows this, but there is something deeper in her that she's letting surface.

What of her plans? She had sought a better life and was willing to postpone that for the duration of her man's adventure into soldiering. It was supposed to be over long ago, and she had been, along with many other wives, lovers, and betrothed, patient, but do the others face such an uncertain future? Do they have to face a prolonged absence of their spouse or lover? Her question is, "What of my plans?" She set the trap and married Evans to provide a better life for herself. Is there something better yet? Lucy thinks to herself as she folds the letter and puts it into her apron, "We'll see what we can do to make tomorrow better."

12) Alton

"My God, how can this happen; please protect us all."

"Amen," I add to someone's prayer.

"Amen," says the supplicant.

The voice sounds familiar, "George, is that you?"

"Evans! I heard you were dead!" George Paul, 1st Lieutenant of Company B is making his way toward me in the throng of over two hundred men. Our Yankee captors have us packed so close together, it is hard to move. They have brought us to prison in the dark to keep us confused, disoriented, and frightened thinking we'll be easier to control. It's working, we are terrified, but do our best to not show it. We have taken their verbal jabs as well as their frequent physical ones, but they are becoming more numerous and brutal as we get closer to the walls of the prison. George, in all this confusion is a welcome comfort. He reaches for my hand and shakes it, "Not dead," he says with a smile and a whisper. "What happened; how did you get here?"

I tell him how we had been forced to fall back and were cut off, and how Buck and I were captured. I ask, "What's your story?"

"My capture came around noon. We were forced back and back. The men stood valiant, but it was not enough. The blue coats were like a swarm of locusts. We were forced to cross the Little Bayou Pierre's only bridge. I was taken there, me and about twenty others. Several of our boys were shot or drowned as they tried to get across. It wasn't deep, but they couldn't move through the mud."

"Did you see any of my men?"

"The only one I saw was Wilson. He was searching for Steven Wayne so I followed him until we found him directing our withdrawal. Wilson told him of your capture and how you and Buck were both covered in blood, and you were going to the hospital. I guess that's how the rumor of your death got started."

"Part of that's true, but it was Buck who was wounded. I stayed at the hospital to assist Doctor McPheeters as long as I could. I tried to slip away, but the prisoner chaser was a tenacious bulldog. He never gave up and stayed well into the evening. I wonder if he ever found his unit." We laugh, which brings attention from one of the guards who slaps George in the face. I brace for my blow, but it doesn't come. We stare straight ahead.

After the guard leaves, Lieutenant Paul asks in a low, quiet voice, "Have you seen any of the others?"

"A couple of the enlisted men; I don't even know their names. I've just seen 'em around and know they're from Arkansas."

"Home," George says, "do you think we'll ever see it again?"

"Of course we will. I'm going to make it, aren't you?"

He hesitates; when he does answer, he says, "I'm afraid. Battle I can stand; I'm armed, but here at the will of armed men not fit for battle, I fear for my life. I am so thankful I have found someone as strong as you"

I am surprised at George Paul's frankness. He is an excellent leader and officer. I have admired his way with the men even though he is a Missourian. He's from Greenfield in Dade County; about a hundred miles north of the Arkansas border. In truth, he is voicing my own fears, "George, hold to your faith. We *will* make this, and as long as they allow us, I will not desert you, but you may not like where I take you."

George cannot reply as the guards are moving us forward and are pressing in close on all sides, shouting, pushing, and calling us names. There are a few of us who are struck, but dare not strike back.

The dark makes it all the more terrible as the gates open. We are marching into the mouth of hell. I am tired, hungry, disoriented, and angry. George clings to me like a child and I have to push him away to maintain my balance. He is so distraught that he cries out, but I cannot help him. It's every man for his self as we are hurried along into who knows what. The fear of the unknown is a great fear, and what lies inside these gates is unknown, and being at the mercy of armed men who hate you, makes it terrifying.

We burst through the gates into the yard of the prison as dark as the inside of a cold stove. We are a milling, disorientated mob, afraid to move forward, backward, or stand still. Our predicament is amusing to the guards. Cattle have more dignity than we at this moment. The gates close, making the yard even darker. It is the most terrifying moment of my life. There are shouts from our group as fear gives way to panic.

A commanding voice in a deep baritone calls out, "Men of the South, fall into ranks, on me!" Someone is taking charge, but in the dark yard, and with our night vision lessened as torches are lit and waved in our faces, the order to form ranks is difficult to carry out. We get arms length apart and fall in.

We must be a sight. Two hundred men trying to comply with an order from an unseen speaker; some are facing one way, others another. The unseen guards light torches faster than I thought possible, and harangue our mob, not wanting us to organize. With the light we are able to form ranks.

"Fall in, fall in," orders the booming baritone.

The Union guards are countermanding with, "Stand where you are!"

Standing in ranks gives us a sense of order and control. The fear of confusion is gone. In the torch light I can make out George standing five from me and two ranks back.

The baritone commander orders, "Officers to the front, enlisted to the rear!" We obey to the consternation of the confused guards. Shots are fired into the air, but to our credit, no one flinches. It's with pride that we come to attention, facing a line of torches, ready for instruction.

George moves next to me when we reorganize and says with a new found confidence, "Good evening Lieutenant; fine night isn't it. I do love the Spring!" Before I can reply, the guards shout random, unintelligible orders to us. No one moves. It is a defiant and a defining moment.

"Order in the yard!" Is shouted from outside the circle of torches, and is not directed at us. We in formation, are exactly still at the position of attention. The Federals guarding us are now the mob and their commanding officer is trying to control them. "Enough of this," he says in disgust as he steps in front of the torches, and nods to a sergeant standing more or less at the position of attention. The sergeant's feeble attempt at military decorum does nothing to change the look of disgust on the commander's face. It's laughable to us, and there are sniggers heard from the enlisted ranks. Minutes ago, we were a terrified herd; we are now an example of correctness to our captors.

The commander speaks, "I am Captain H. W. Freedley, 3rd Infantry; commander of Alton Prison." He waits before he goes on, "You will take orders from no one here but me, and the officers, and guards under my command." More chuckles come from our ranks.

"He's only a captain," Paul says, "another Stevie Wayne." He doesn't have to say more; I am thinking, "This is the best they've got?"

Captain Freedley continues, "There are only four rules for this camp; we try to keep it simple for you boys from the south," he says with a smile. It's an attempt at humor but is wasted on us, and only a few of the Union troops offer a courtesy laugh that makes the moment more awkward. "The first rule is, 'Do not cross the 'dead line'. If you have any question about what the 'dead line' is do not go near the boundaries of the prison. Should you not heed this advice, you will be going to either the cemetery or the hospital, depending on the marksmanship of the guard enforcing the 'dead line' rule. I suggest you stay away from the walls. The rest of the rules you will find out over time. Are there any questions?"

Silence from our ranks; shuffling from the Union troops. I wonder if the guards know the rules, or do they make them up as they go along. I wonder if Freedley knows the rules.

"Sergeant, take charge of the prisoners!" Captain Freedley turns on his heel and moves into the dark.

"All right you traitorous bastards! You will do as I say without question, or we will shoot you down as the scum dogs you are! No more fancy talk; you are prisoners, enemies of the United States of America and traitors against the same and as such, have lost any claim to mercy. If we don't like you, we'll shoot you, and I can tell you right now, we don't like you."

There's a slight stirring in the ranks as the realization that we are in hell sinks in, but we maintain our composure. I feel fear again and sense it among the others.

"You are the second lot of maggots we've received this week. We've had to fit one of you scum in ball and chain already. We will do it to any and all if necessary. Let me remind you dense, stupid, southern boys, we do not like you, and we do shoot those we do not like. In other words, give me an excuse!"

We are silent. They're not going to get the satisfaction of seeing our fear, but it's there. My mind wanders wondering how they would do in a Southern prison. How is Buck faring? Where is he?

"You will fall in by rank; officers to enlisted, NOW!"

We don't move; we're already in ranks, by rank.

"Alright, you smart assed sons of southern maggots, move!"

No one does. Then the baritone voice booms, "Sergeant, the men are arranged by rank in rank. Do you have any further orders?" The man is an officer, but in the faint light, I cannot make out his rank, and I don't care. He's in command because we follow his orders and he is willing to step forward and bear the brunt of the Union sergeant's wrath.

"Are you in charge of these son's of maggots?"

"No sergeant, I am not, but I do seem to be speaking for this group of fine southern gentlemen who are displaying far better manners than you. Of course, such things are of value in a southern home and are taught from an early age even in the poorest household. We would never disparage the parentage of guests in our homes, as you have done."

"This ain't a home, this is a prison you impudent son of a maggot! This is your hell on earth boy, and you can expect no 'manners' from me, you Johnny Reb piece of filth! Who the hell do you think you are; what's your name you southern fried piece of dung?"

"Since you have asked so colorfully, I am Major Washington B. Traweek, 15th Alabama Regulars." Lowering his voice, and being cordial he says, "My friends call me 'Wash', but you sergeant, may feel free to call me Major Traweek, or simply 'sir'."

The sergeant rushes at the major putting his face inches away and shouts, spraying spittle about, "Why you arrogant piss pot puss on a sore! Who do you think you are talking to?"

Before the enraged Yankee can go on, the major replies, "Sergeant, I will give you high marks in your ignorance. That is the most colorful use of adjectives I have heard in a long time, but I think we've been over this; I am Major Washington B. Traweek..."

"Shut the hell up! I've heard enough from you!" The sergeant is bouncing up and down in front of the major like a terrier defending a bone. Major Traweek does not move or react in any way.

Maintaining decorum and control, the major says, "Sergeant, it is late, and these men are tired. If you have no further instructions or orders, I respectfully request we be shown to our quarters."

The sergeant looks at Major Traweek as if he is species never before seen. He turns and looks at his men, back to the major, then back to his men. It is obvious to Yankee and Rebel alike, the major has trumped the sergeant and the latter has no wit to recover.

Captain Freedley calls from the dark, "Sergeant is there a problem?"

Not wanting to show his commanding officer that he has lost control of the situation, the sergeant answers, "No sir, no problem."

"Then why are these men still standing there, and why are you haranguing this prisoner?" The captain approaches Major Traweek and the sergeant saying, "This man has organized his men, and is doing all he can to cooperate with you. Move them along now."

"Yes sir, right away sir." Turning back to our ranks he bellows, "Officers will follow me in ranks of two. Enlisted will follow this man," gesturing to another sergeant, "to the enlisted barracks."

There is some shouting by the other guards, but we give no heed. We peel off into twos behind Major Traweek, George stands with me, and we move out.

There is a large, three story building that fills the length of the yard. It's impossible to see details, but there appears to be a stone wall enclosing part of the compound that has additional buildings within. We file around the far end of the large barracks into an area hidden from the light.

We are guided into a long hallway that is lighted by oil lanterns. There are solid doors about every six feet on both sides of the hall. The doors have a locked, barred window large enough for a man to put his head through and an iron latch with a steel rod running through it, securing the door. We halt and hear the rods scraping against their guides as they are removed. Guards open the doors to the cells. We cannot see inside, but the smell of unwashed bodies and un-emptied slop buckets overwhelms us. This is hell; or at least the portal to it.

We are shoved into the cells. My best guess is that there are four of us, but it could be more. We stumble over each other, but no one says a word. We stand shoulder to shoulder, hoping to maintain orientation while we adjust to the dark. The doors are slammed shut, cutting out what light there is. We hear the rods being re-inserted, and we are locked in; prisoners of war.

The fear rages in the total blackness of our cell. It is crippling; no one says a word. I hear the rapid breathing of my cell mates. I have to do something, or die of fright, so I say, "Gentlemen, count off," I lead with, "One".

"Two," I recognize George's voice.

"Three."

"Four." Then silence. Names are exchanged and forgotten in the fog of fatigue and fear.

Doing my best to hide the quiver in my voice, I say, "Gentlemen, I suggest we find places to sleep and get as much rest as we can. We are safe for the night." I don't feel as confident as I sound, but it's better than breaking down crying, which is my alternative. We stumble past each other in the tiny cell finding bunks and blankets. I lay on a hard bunk with my coat for a pillow and a stinking blanket over me. I think of Lucy, my children, my parents, Buck and a thousand others as they parade through my mind. Tears come to my eyes. Is it worth it? Is freedom this valuable that I have to sacrifice my own for the sake of others? How selfish I am, "For man hath no greater love…," and with that, and the sniffles of my companions, I drift off to sleep…a prisoner.

13) POW Alton, Ill.

Monday, May 18th, 1863

A Prisoner of War

A prisoner of what? A prisoner of war! What is war; a difference of opinion; politically, religiously, or otherwise, which brings about the too frequent necessity of engaging in desperation and inhuman barbarities; man taking the life of his fellowman in mortal combat.

When the battle is over, if you are captured, your life is spared you thorough the mercies of your captors, only. How humiliating the hour! How humiliating the scene! These who, but a few moments past were engaged in using all the means that their wily thoughts could suggest to bring down their antagonist, now meet, perhaps take each other by the hand, calling to mind, recollections of former friendship and peaceful associations that they have enjoyed in bygone days. These are now enemies, must be treated as such, must now lead a life of confinement, a life of retirement, and perhaps of seclusion, removed from the society and associations of friends; shut out, as it were from the world and its charms.

Confinement, it is true gives us opportunities for study and reflection, and if proper means be afforded us, we can educate, and enlighten our minds, and if those means are denied us, memory will bring up pleasures, and scenes, of former years on which our minds can feast, and expand, and will then fall back upon the present and search with untiring energy through all its recesses, for joys, for pleasures, and peaceful enjoyments, though it is confined in prison walls; but reflection reminds us of the associations of other days, then our hearts are sad! We then impatiently look forward to a time when those lost enjoyments shall be again resurrected to former greatness. Pleasing melancholy takes possession of our breast and we become more resigned to our fate.

In prison, like other places where a multitude are gathered from promiscuous points, there are vices of almost the deepest dye, apparently gathering strength and influence daily, haunting, even the borders of religious assembly, though engaged in Divine Worship. "How degraded man is becoming in these latter days."

Dawn, filtered by the windows in our cell, moves its gray grace over our confinement to reveal the world in which we now live. We are four to this cell which appears to my waking eye to be no more than four feet by seven. Four grown men confined in twenty-eight square feet! I shift onto my back and lay looking at the small window opposite our door. It's open to the elements, but barred. This will, I think, prove to be a blessing and a curse as the days wear on.

The others stir as I move putting away my journal in my coat and all of us jump onto our feet as the door to the outside of our building slams open. In the corner closest to the door is a second opening near the floor. It is large enough to accommodate entry and exit of the two buckets in the cell; one slop, the other water. I splash some of the water over my face and head. I tuck my journal into the inside pocket of my uniform jacket and hope that I am able to conceal it.

The scraping sound of metal on metal announces the opening of the doors. Ours is slammed opened with the command of, "Out". We move into the passage way to join others in the long hallway.

The voice of Major Traweek reverberates as he calls, "Officers and gentlemen of the South form two ranks facing me!"

An angry voice countermands Traweek's order, "Stand down from that! I give the orders here!" It's too late; we doing as ordered by Traweek. "I'll thank you Major Tra-week, to refrain from giving any orders. I am in charge here!"

"Very well ser-geant," the major mocks, "what orders do you have for us?"

He blusters, and resorts to a string of obscenities in an attempt to intimidate us, but they serve only to make him smaller in our eyes and a subject of humor.

He spews and fumes until Major Traweek says, "Assembled thus sergeant, is there somewhere you would like us to go?"

Red in the face, our sergeant bellows, "You pigs are to follow the guards out the far door and to mess; now, move!"

No one does. We are facing the wrong way.

"Move you maggots!"

Nothing happens. A first year private could see that we await the order to "about face", but the sergeant is so flustered that the command eludes him.

"Sergeant, if I may suggest…"

"You may not you ignorant maggot; I'm in command here!"

"…that you give the command to 'about face'? I think you will find the results most satisfactory."

The sergeant says through clinched teeth, spraying spittle as he does, "Major, you had better watch your smart-assed self. I'll have your guts for garters!"

The major, with a stare and glare that would quell the devil, says, "Sergeant, I do not think that even possible, but if it gives you some small measure of satisfaction, go ahead and dream; in the mean time; 'about face'?"

Not moving an inch from the face of the taller major, the sergeant bellows, "About face!"

We stand rigid at attention and do nothing.

"Perhaps, I should try?" Not waiting for a response from the furious, red faced sergeant, the major speaks the words, "about face!"

Our response is immediate. One of the guards commands "Forward march!" We move out. I cannot see the major or the sergeant and can only imagine the end result of the confrontation. I need to know Major Traweek. In a difficult situation, he has helped us maintain our dignity.

I look around as we go outside. It is a little after dawn as I take in our prison; our home. In the light, our building is larger than I imagined. It's about six hundred yards long, and using the size of our cell, quick math leads me to guess that there are two hundred and fifty or more cells. That, times four prisoners per cell, makes one thousand prisoners.

There is a line forming outside a building where there is a great deal of noise and commotion with many men standing, milling about, all with tin plates and spoons in hand. Major Traweek's voice comes from the back of our formation commanding us to "Halt", which we do. We left face, and await further orders.

The red faced sergeant says, "You will fall out and into line for chow. You will be given plates as you go through the door, which you will use along with a spoon. These will be returned and counted before you leave the area. If one is found missing, you all will be stripped and searched. You have just learned another rule; 'You will enter and leave the mess area empty handed'."

"Men, fall out and into line for mess."

George walks beside me toward the mess hall. "Doesn't look too bad does it?"

I look at him as if I have been bitten by my own dog. "What do you mean it 'doesn't look too bad'? It looks horrible!"

"It could be a lot worse."

We're about to enter the mess, I whisper to George, "Don't be so quick to accept your fate. Never stop fighting, never!"

George looks at me. There's no fight left in him. He's beaten and will be content to sit in the prison and rot until the end of the war.

We step in line to be served. We're given gruel that is more water than grain, two pieces of salt pork or beef. I can't tell which until I'm able to cut into them.

At the end of the line, a half cup of water's poured for us. I gesture to the Confederate soldier ladling it out of a big tub that I want more. He laughs,

"You're new here, ain't you?" Asks a Union Sergeant standing at the back of the serving line.

"Yes I am."

"We don't have any water inside the walls. It has to be hauled from the river. Unless you want to volunteer for that detail, that's all the water you are going to get. Take it and be glad of it."

"I do believe I'll volunteer for that detail. How do I get assigned to it?"

"What's your name boy?"

"Lieutenant Atwood, 15th Arkansas Infantry, and yours?"

"I'm Staff Sergeant Zachary. I'm in charge of the water. I'll find you boy, I'll find you."

When we step outside, I say, "Let's find Major Traweek. I want to meet this man."

We walk the compound carrying our food. I spot the major in a building adjacent to the mess hall with other field officers, none under his rank.

We stand at a distance until recognized by a General of slight build, but commanding presence. He's smoking a cigar and sharing quips with Major Traweek when he notices us. He has a twinkle in his brown eyes and a smile on his face as he waves us over.

I step up and say, "I do believe I have the honor of addressing General M. Jeff Thompson, the 'Swamp Rat of the Confederacy'! Am I correct sir?"

His smile intensifies with the recognition and my usage of his nickname. He has a shock of neat, wavy, brown hair. His moustache is of the same color and well trimmed. "You flatter me Lieutenant, but you have me at a disadvantage; I do not know whom I have the pleasure; please, introduce yourself."

There are introductions all around. General Thompson speaks to the gathering, "Gentlemen, make room for our fellows here," then to us, "brother officers, please join us."

As Lieutenant Paul and I sit, I say to the man who I came to meet, "Major, I wish to thank you for your courage in taking command yesterday evening. Your voice was a beacon in the darkness, a guiding horn in the fog."

The general smiles and asks, "What of this Major? Do you care to expound on the compliment of the lieutenant?"

"It was really no matter sir; I simply took command and restored order to the chaos created by our Federal captors," the major demurs.

General Thompson looks at me then at the major and asks, "Did you now?"

I answer for the major, "Yes sir. It was a bad time, and the major's voice in the dark established order, and gave us the upper hand."

"It was due general, to the fact that I had officers willing to set an example for the enlisted. We were able to stand as a body, not a mob."

I interject, "It is most appreciated sir."

"Yes, indeed," adds George, "a real comfort. I don't mind admitting, I was frightened." There are agreeing nods and mumbled assurances around the table.

I look at what passes for my food. The salt pork has more fat than lean meat and the gruel has as much water as my cup. "Could any of you gentlemen shed light on the water situation? I hear there is a detail that goes to the river to get water, but nothing more."

A major down the table says, "We have a well in the yard, but it is not fit to drink. What water there is has dissolved minerals and contamination from the latrines. It has limited usefulness for washing clothes and such if it doesn't smell too bad, but do not put any of it in your mouth."

"As for the detail; three times a day, there is a group that goes out the gates, under guard with a wagon and barrels to the river. Ten to twenty men and an officer bucket the water from the river into the barrels and it is brought into the compound. After the blue bellies have taken what they need, we get the rest. There is never enough water, so we ration it as much as we can. In the coming summer, it'll be worse."

The Swamp Rat, a name given by the press to General Thompson when he was in command of Missouri troops in the southeast part of the state, adds, "Lieutenant, we have a health problem; small pox is rumored to be about, so we keep as clean as we can. It seems to keep the disease at bay, but it will get worse. The Yankees are setting up a hospital on an island in the river as a quarantine facility. The townsfolk of Alton are worried about the disease being so close. What is your interest in the water situation?"

I explain to him about the sergeant in charge of the detail and that I am available. "I thought that being outside the walls might be of value."

Major Traweek says, "I think I know what you mean lieutenant. A man on the outside seeing how the land lies could be most valuable. I encourage you to pursue this opportunity," turning to General Thompson, "with your permission of course general."

General Thompson nods his agreement. "Lieutenant, I want you to observe gun emplacements, guard cycles, blind spots, or any other weaknesses, and report daily."

"Yes sir, anything to further the cause sir."

Major Traweek asks, "And what cause might that be Lieutenant Atwood?"

"Freedom, and liberty, sir, the right to choose. That is what you mean isn't it major?" I am answered with smiles from both officers. The men at this gathering have no intention of staying in Alton Prison a minute longer than necessary. I get the feeling that there are plans at work.

The general ends the discussion, "Gentlemen, shall we adjourn to the yard for a stroll and some fresh air. I find there are too many blue ears in this facility. Atwood, you and Paul join us."

"Yes sir." The general stands to leave, we follow.

As we move into the warming sun of this northern May day, Major Traweek falls back to walk with us and in a voice loud enough for the assembly to hear, says, "Lieutenants, please tell us of the nature of your being here, any news of the war, or home, were you captured at the same time?"

I relate as much detail as I think appropriate, including my relationship to Buck and Dr. McPheeters. George's recounting of the events surrounding his coming to be a prisoner is brief.

General Thompson asks, "In your opinion Lieutenant, how goes the war? Can the north be stopped?"

"Sir, the Union landed an overwhelming force under General Grant; about twenty thousand to our eight or less. There is a vicious bastard, a southern hater by the name of Sherman who vows to burn the South from the Mississippi River, to the Atlantic when Vicksburg falls. If it does, the south is open."

"In your opinion, lieutenant, will Vicksburg fall?"

"Sir, General Bowen is fighting to withdraw to Vicksburg, but the losses are heavy. If he can get to Vicksburg, there is a chance, but we do not have the men to withstand a prolonged engagement."

It's quiet among the group. General Thompson, looking at me, "That's a somber portrayal Lieutenant."

"I do not disparage our men in battle. They are giving better than they are taking, but the numbers are awful. Our only hope is that Vicksburg can stand and that Grant will make some blunder that our generals can take advantage of. We can win, but it is now a protracted campaign."

"Yes, indeed it is." The general looks up past me and says, "Gentlemen I believe we are about to have company."

Conversation ceases as the Union sergeant in charge of the water detail gets closer. We are like dogs on the porch watching the approach of a stranger. He stops, looks at me, and asks, "You the one who wants the water detail?"

"Yes sergeant Zachery, I would find the duty refreshing."

He laughs, "Oh, you'll be refreshed alright; you'll be soaking wet before we get back. Come on." He walks away.

"Gentlemen, duty calls." I step away and glance at George. "I'll see you later George. Why don't you see if these gentlemen can tell you the ends and outs of this place? You can fill me in later."

"Stick with me lieutenant," said Major Traweek, "I will have need of your assistance, I am sure, and we can both learn of the prison's workings."

I trail after the sergeant. As we are clear of the officers, he stops and waits for me. I make up the distance as he says, "Pretty tall company you're keeping boy."

"I just met them today. They seem friendly enough for field officers." I hesitate, trying to read the sergeant. He is staring at the group of officers. "In case you have forgotten, I'm Lieutenant Evans Atwood of Arkansas."

He turns his attention to me, smiles and says, "This is a shit detail Atwood. They put the charged prisoners, the lowest of the low, scum, on this detail. These are the ones who've broken rules, or committed crimes, but you seem like a hearty sort, so I am going to give you a try. These men hate officers, and you'll be the only one on the detail. It'll be your job to get the men to work and fill the barrels quick. Some, those in ball and chain won't be able to move fast, and you have to keep them away from the water. Some of the other boys want to throw them in. One is particular bad; his name is Justice McHenry."

"Never a lower man to be born of woman."

"You know him?"

"We've had run-ins. We enlisted the same day, he was bad from the moment he made his 'X'; picking fights and finding ways to get out of work two minutes later. He deserted and no one missed him, but the Home Guard got him and brought him back. By then, I had been elected an officer. Justice couldn't accept it. He's been looking to take a bite out of me for a long time; this may be his chance."

Sergeant Zachery sizes me up, before he says, "You just might be the one to handle him. Everyone else is afraid of him, even us guards."

"Can he be taken out of the ball and chain? You know, so Justice can be served."

Zachery laughs, "I like you boy; it shall be done. This is going to be fun. I'll be standing by with a pistol if you need help."

"I won't need any help with that coward. Unless he has men to back him, he's as yellow as they come. He won't make a move if he thinks he has no support."

"I don't know Atwood; that's a mighty big boy there. He's hurt some people. That's why he's ball and chained. Do you think you can handle him?"

"I hope we don't have to find out."

"Let's go; we've got water to haul."

The detail is at the gate waiting for us. There are hoots and hollers about the new boy, and derision from the Yankee troops to Sergeant Zachery for being late.

The detail is comprised of twenty men aligned behind a wagon, ten to a side. The wagon has ten barrels per side and is pulled by four mules.

"The boy lieutenant!" A voice from among the prisoners declares. "We're going to have us some fun today! There is justice for Justice! Thank you Lord for answering my prayers!"

Sergeant Zachery steps up to McHenry and stares up at him. McHenry doesn't move. Zachery reaches around his back causing Justice to jump back, ready to fend off a blow. Zachery smiles as he holds a ring of keys in the face of McHenry. "Justice, today is your lucky day. I'm taking you out of your extra forty pounds."

McHenry recovers and declares, "Two prayers in the same day Lord! How can it be?" He claps his hands, laughing as Sergeant Zachery unlocks his manacles. His eyes never leave mine.

Zachery tells him, "The only prayer ever answered for you will be from the devil himself." McHenry doesn't hear, but our eyes are locked; this is the day.

Sergeant Zachery climbs up onto the seat and bellows "Open the gates." They let us out and are closed again.

It is grand to be outside. I imagine the day when I am on the outside with freedom and liberty. I have faith, it will come. It may be sooner than later.

The prison is situated on a bluff overlooking the Mississippi River. There's a wharf, and a road that passes it. The road is long as it winds down to the river. There is a lot of weight to be hauled up this hill, the more gradual the slope, the better for the mules.

There are no guns or guards looking our way. There's no need; we have four of our own. The guards in the towers cannot see us because they're set more into the yard than along to wall. They aren't thinking of an assault from the river or anywhere outside the prison compound. Their focus is on the prisoners.

I'm walking beside the men on the right side of the wagon, next to Sergeant Zachery. "He's sizing you up; there's going to be trouble."

"He's sized me up before. We've never come to blows, but he wants it bad. I won't fight if I can avoid it, but if it happens, let me handle it. It won't take long."

"I've seen him fight. He'll kill you if he can."

"He won't touch me. It won't last that long."

"That's cocky talk from a man your size."

"I can handle him."

I wish Buck was here to see this, or participate. He would love to kick McHenry's ass.

We halt and move out of the way as the wagon turns to face back up the hill. It backs as close to the water's edge as it can without getting into the mud. Several prisoners, including Justice climb up on the wagon and reach into the barrels and come out with two buckets from each. We start the work of walking twenty yards down the slope, wading into the river, filling the buckets, carrying them up the slope, handing them one at a time to men at the barrels who empty the buckets, hand them back down, and the process starts over.

I see need for improvement and step to the line and say, "All right men, we will rotate positions every ten minutes. Those in the wagons will rotate down to haul, and the haulers will take their places."

"We've done that before brain boy. We know what we're doing," says Justice, "you just stand there and watch real men work."

"It's going to be different this time," I continue, "every ten minutes there will be a man resting. I'll be taking my turn along with you."

There are hoots and hollers of, "I can't believe an officer will work," and "I've got to see this," and others, but work I do and it goes well for the first hour or so. As we're returning to the river for another haul, Justice McHenry makes his move.

"Who the hell do you think you are?"

I turn to the group of men I am leading and ask, "What did you say?"

"You think you're better than us, don't you?"

I stare at McHenry. He's a mountain of a man in more ways than the obvious. He is big, but he moves like a mountain, which is to say, not at all. The only time he seems motivated is when he's in a fight, and that's whenever he can be.

"Justice, why don't you just shut up and work like the rest of us?"

"Lieutenant Boy; we've got some unfinished business, you and me do."

"We've got no business. I'm not going to fight you," I say, smiling, "we've been through this before; you're just not worth the effort. Besides, like I told you, I don't fight men that are weaker than me". I turn my back and start to the river.

It takes awhile for the insult to process through McHenry's rock like brain, or maybe he's waiting to get further from the wagon; "Atwood, you're a chicken shit, son of a bitch!"

I stop, set down the two buckets, turn, not smiling, but with my hands open, and at my side, and say in a soft, calm voice, "There are two things you don't call me Justice; a liar, and a son of a bitch. You don't know my mother, and you cross a line when you speak of her so". I turn again to walk away...

"You're a lying, chicken shit, son of a bitch!"

I keep walking.

"Coward!"

I guess there are three things you don't call me. I set the buckets down again, this time knowing I'm going to fight. My assets against the much larger man are my speed, strength, and intelligence. I know I have to stay up and keep my feet. If Justice gets hold of me, or gets me on the ground, it's all over.

I turn around and walk toward McHenry. My hands are still at my sides, but my eyes are moving. I see Justice shift his stance, putting his left foot forward, "Right handed," I think to myself. I walk in close, knowing Justice won't try to grab me; he wants to beat me with his fists.

"I'm gonna beat you to a bloody pulp, boy".

Yep, he wants to beat me. I keep coming, hands still at my sides, eyes moving. I get within McHenry's range and see the round house right coming before Justice even moves. I step to my right causing Justice to shuffle back with his left foot, throwing him off balance for a split second. I duck the swing, and come up hard with both hands clasped together into one fist into the big man's gut.

Hearing and feeling the foul wind rush from deep within McHenry, I know he'll double over, and step back to give him room. He bends hard and fast, which only serves to multiply the force of my still doubled fists as I swing up and into Justice's face. I feel the bones in his nose give and my fists hit teeth as the force lifts him up, off his feet, and onto his back where he lies motionless; fight over.

"Don't ever call me a liar, a son of a bitch, *or* a coward. Next time, you won't get up". I turn, pick up my buckets, and move on to the river. The men follow, leaving Justice to roll in the dirt, spitting teeth and blood. No one makes a comment that I can hear, but there is low mumbling among the men.

He's still laying there when we trudge back up the hill. Sergeant Zachery meets my eye and smiles as he says, "That was quick."

"I told you it would be."

"Yeah, I guess you do know a thing or two," he surveys the situation, the men working without complaint, and McHenry trying to get to his feet, "and not only about fighting. You're a damned fine leader Lieutenant Atwood."

"Thank you sergeant; it has always been my pleasure to work. I thank you for the opportunity." I turn to Justice, now on his feet, but unsteady, "McHenry!"

He staggers a bit, and says to everyone's surprise while wiping his mouth, "Sir."

I hear the sergeant laugh behind me as I tell Justice, "Pick up your buckets and move to the wagon. Take your ten minute break."

"Yes sir," is the weak reply. No one is more surprised than me. Justice McHenry is beaten.

We finish the work in good time. The sergeant is pleased with the detail. We trudge back into the prison walls, wet, but satisfied with our morning's work. Zachery asks me, as we are dismissed, "We do this in the afternoon and evenings too; you up for that?"

"Yes sergeant, I'll look forward to it." I go to report what I've seen. It's been an interesting first morning.

14) Steven Wayne Culpepper

May 18-19, 1863

"Sergeant Wilson!" Steven Wayne calls for one of the few soldiers left under his command. The company is much bloodied and decimated since the battle at Port Gibson. The retreat to meet with General Pemberton, and the battles for Champion Hill, the city of Jackson, and the just concluded debacle at Big Black River Bridge, left the units of the regiment disorganized, absorbed, or nonexistent.

Evans Atwood's platoon has remained intact since his and Buchannan's capture. Martin Wilson has proven his ability time and again and the men follow him. Atwood's absence is cause for mixed emotions in Steven Wayne. He misses the lieutenant because he was level headed and dependable, but is glad of his absence because the men look to him now for leadership.

Steven Wayne is proud of his accomplishments in the Army. He didn't know he possessed leadership skills, and didn't discover them until he was tested in battle. He loved the test. Something takes over his thinking in combat that he does not have before or after. It's a shame to both Colonel Reynolds, the regimental commander, and Culpepper that the skill seems to be only available during battle. When it comes to the everyday running of a company, Steven Wayne is below average.

"Yes sir," answers Sergeant Wilson, winded from running to see what his commanding officer wants. Wilson is more amazed than the rest of the company that he's a sergeant. Less than three weeks ago he was a private. So much has happened. Evans and Buck were captured; he had to witness that, and now he's thrust into a leadership position because the others don't know what to do.

The men will elect him their officer if Steven Wayne ever calls for the election. They've been fighting for their lives since Grand Gulf, and there hasn't been time for such things.

"Sergeant," Steven Wayne hesitates as he looks into the grim, tired eyes of a man with a boy's face. The eyes tell of experiences no man should endure. Martin Wilson will never know innocence again, "I want the men ready to move in thirty minutes. Make certain they have water and have eaten something. Check the ammo available and distribute it evenly. There will be no more until we get to Vicksburg." Wilson stares at him. "Are those orders clear to you sergeant?"

"Yes sir."

"Well, what are you waiting for?"

"Sir, all that's done; I was waiting for anything you might add."

"No, sergeant; that will be all; you're dismissed."

"Yes sir."

Steven Wayne watches him go; a young man enduring defeat, looking for an anchor in the storm, and knowing that he could not offer that anchor. "It'll be over soon," he mumbles to himself, saying out loud what everyone knows; the war in this part of the south is lost. Vicksburg is lost; it's just a matter of time.

The thought of an end to the killing, the deprivation, the fatigue, brightens Steven Wayne's thoughts, and just as quick, they cloud again. Both reactions are caused by Patricia Ann Robinson whom he has heard nothing of in over six weeks. His hope brightened when he thought of going home to her, and dimmed when the prospect of her having moved on rises in his thinking. He sighs. Whatever is happening back home is out of his control. He has more pressing matters at hand. He has to get his men to Vicksburg, and that, he hopes will keep his mind occupied.

The day wears on. It's hot for May as the reduced, battle weary regiment marches to Vicksburg. They're tired, hungry, and thirsty, but not yet defeated. Hope is renewed as troops from Pemberton's army meet and mingle with them sharing stories of baths, liquor, real food; plenty of it, and every soldier's wish, women. The mood brightens even more as the word spreads that there's mail waiting.

Steven Wayne tries not to let his hopes get too high, but is unsuccessful. He's desperate to hear from his beloved. He expects the worse, but clings to hope. It's all he has. He envisions letters bundled together, emitting the sweet fragrance of expensive French perfume that her father first, and Steven Wayne have lavished on her. He smiles at the thought of the joking and joshing he will get from his fellow officers and his men. He envisions himself stepping forth at mail call to the hoots and hollers of his comrades. He refuses to allow contrary thoughts to play in his mind; they are too painful. He focuses on hope, but lurking in the back of his mind is the faint possibility that maybe... No, that couldn't be; Patsy declared her love for him over and over; no, it just cannot be.

Steven Wayne is astride his worn black stallion. The men and the horses are all exhausted from the continuous cycle of battle; fall back, battle, retreat, meals on the run, if there is food at all, water from streams, or worse yet, ditches, no baths, but the worst of all, no rest. It's taking its toll.

The road is congested with civilian traffic moving into and out of Vicksburg. The troops are cheered as they pass crowds of people who wave flags and banners. They and the troops occupying Vicksburg are fresh and full of hope. They either do not see the suggestion of defeat in the eyes of the arriving, battle worn soldiers, or they ignore it.

The men watch, almost laughing as a very pretty young woman approaches Steven Wayne with a bundle in hand. His extraordinary prowess with the fairer sex shows; he has been singled out by the prettiest. He raises up to his full height, hoping that he does not look too trail worn. It frustrates him to not be able to think of a way to bring his wound into play while on horseback. The old, but still unhealed wound is always good for sympathy and compassion, and he wants the lovely lady to know that whatever she has in the package is going to a true hero of the Confederacy. He smiles, tips his hat and says, "Ma'am."

The young lady's countenance shines as she approaches the handsome officer on the black stallion, the very symbol of virility, and meets his gaze unabashed as she smiles up at him and says in a voice as sweet and slow as honey dripping off a spoon, "Welcome gallant warrior to 'The Gibraltar of the Confederacy', Vicksburg, Mississippi," and hands up the bundle which smells of baked ham and sweet potatoes. He takes it and smiles while nodding his thanks. She falls in stride to walk with Steven Wayne beside the horse and asks, "Sir, you will not, of course allow these northern invaders to plunder our fair city will you? Why, my very virtue is at stake! Surely you will not allow us to fall!" She continues beside him, imploring him with her blue eyes.

He looks at her more closely and is surprised at her beauty. She looks a great deal like Evans Atwood's wife, Lucy Jane. He half expects her to answer as such when he thanks her and asks, "To whom do I have the honor of addressing?"

"My name sir is Rilla Mae Gadston, *Miss* Rilla Mae Gadston, and yours sir?"

He identifies himself, and asks, "Miss Gadston, would you permit me to call on you, perhaps this evening after I have settled my men and availed myself of a bath and clean clothes?" He sees hesitation in her eyes and adds before she speaks, "I am betrothed to a fine lady, much like you, at my home in Arkansas. I assure you ma'am that my intentions are honorable. It is just that after having been in the field so long, and being deprived of the finer things in life, and Miss Gadston, you are certain to be one of the finest things in all Mississippi," his smile is dazzling, "it would be a luxury to sit in your presence."

"Yes, Captain Culpepper, it would be an honor for myself and my family to receive you. My brother is away in the service of our cause as well; I am sure my parents entertain the hopes that he would be treated the same where he is."

"And where might he be serving?"

"He is very nautical and is serving on a blockade runner on the river. It is dangerous duty to be sure, and I know he does not get to shore much, but when he does, I am certain he would long for company as do you sir." They had walked a goodly way from her carriage where a very tall, stout, and concerned Negro driver is standing in the seat, looking after his charge. Miss Gadston notices him and parts with instructions, "Ask for the home of Beau Gadston; anyone can give you directions; even the darkies," and with that she's gone. Steven Wayne watches, still smiling as silly as a school boy.

Laughter from the men redirects his attention. Having been so taken with the beautiful belle of Mississippi, he has ridden off the road. As he makes his way back, to his great consternation, he finds himself riding adjacent to Colonel Reynolds.

The colonel is smiling at the embarrassed captain as he asks, "Making inroads with the indigenous personnel?"

"Just visiting with a young well wisher sir, nothing more." Steven Wayne blushes under the growth of beard and grime that cover his handsome face.

"Well, I see you have done well," nodding to the bundle, "do you intend to share out the bounty with your men?"

"Oh, yes sir, always sir. I always share the fruits of such labors."

"So I have heard. Please enjoy some for me." He spurs his horse to move ahead, and adds, "I will need to see you as soon as you are settled for a staff meeting. Say sixteen hundred hours? That should still give you plenty of time to call on the lady with my and the regiment's compliments."

"Yes sir; thank you sir!"

The colonel rides away, Steven Wayne calls, "Sergeant Wilson!"

"Yes sir!" Martin Wilson arrives next to the riding captain, "How can I assist the dashing defender of southern virtue sir?" A roar of laughter bursts from the company and Steven Wayne reddens more.

"Sergeant," tossing the package to Wilson, "serve this out among the men, but not before you prepare me a plate," an action that brings applause and shouts of approval for the now proud captain. He rides a little taller in the saddle as they wend their way up the road to the bluff where the city of Vicksburg sits overlooking the Mississippi, and where fortifications loom. "There lies our last hope," Steven Wayne says aloud.

The approach to Vicksburg is gradual but constant as it climbs to near a thousand feet above the Big Muddy. The north and south approaches to the city are defended by swamps and marshes as Grant is well aware. Earlier in the year, in campaigns known as the Bayou Expeditions, he tried to dig a canal around the fortifications but failed. It was laughable at the time, but Grant is relentless and knows how to fight. He, unlike his counter parts in the eastern theater, is not afraid to lose men to accomplish his orders, and his orders are to take Vicksburg. His second attempt was a naval assault from the river, but the town with its advantage of elevation blew the Federal Navy out of the water.

The only approach open to him is from the east, where the retreating army of Pemberton and Bowen is moving from. Grant is massing for what everyone in the city expects to be an assault in the morning, or the day after.

Company A is assigned an area near the center of the fortifications facing east. For once, they are not the vanguard, but are placed to be able to reinforce any of the forward positions. Troops from Alabama, Texas, Mississippi, and Louisiana, have been here for months and have done an amazing job of fortifying the city. The question everyone is asking is, "Can the depleted Confederate forces hold against the overwhelming numbers of Grant's army?" Tomorrow, or maybe the next day, will tell, but now it doesn't matter, it is time for mail call.

Steven Wayne is grinning ear to ear when his name is called; at last, word from his love. He strolls with confidence from the back of the gathering with visions of the bundle of pink enveloped, perfumed letters. He nears the front and is confused at what he sees; there on the table waiting for him, while the post master continues to call names and soldiers make their way forward, lies a single letter. He recognizes the hand writing of his father. "There must be a mistake," he blurts. No one has noticed him before now; he was anonymous while men were paying attention to hear their names called, or were sharing letters and news from home. Now, all eyes are on him. "There are more aren't there?"

The post master, embarrassed, says, "Sir, that's the only letter for you. I have been through the mail for two days now, and that's all."

"But it can't be! I should have six or more, one for every week!" Steven Wayne's voice rises. "She writes me every week and has since..." He stops; realizing the spectacle he is making of himself. He is the man all admire for the way he has with the ladies, fuming over the one he is engaged to marry. Her unfaithfulness is evident to all. He regains his composure, picks up his letter and says, "Thank you post master; please carry on." The man nods and resumes the calling of names, as Steven Wayne, red faced leaves under the knowing gaze of his men.

His tent is set up in the shade of several oaks where his gear is being cleaned by the servants and Negros assigned to the duty. He finds a comfortable place behind a large oak and opens the letter. In the strong hand of his father he reads...

April 30th, 1863
Shiloh, Arkansas

My dear son,

It is your mother's and my most sincere prayer that this finds you well. We have not heard good things about the war in Mississippi, and we know that is where you are. We fear that you are in the thick of things.

We received word via the Atwood family that you are doing well in your role as an infantry captain. Evans related to them that you are an excellent leader in battle. We are very pleased and proud of your success.

There is no easy way to tell you the news here. Your mother has seen Patsy in the company of young men and confronted her. Patricia was on the arm of Thaddeus Yeller, youngest son of the congressman from Chicot County. Your mother noticed that Patricia was not wearing your ring, and that it had been replaced by a gaudy bauble, and asked her about it. Patricia was charming, but rude, informing your mother that the betrothal between you and she was off and that she was now engaged to be married to the young Yeller. They have picked July 4th for the date. It will be a big celebration and a political opportunity for Thaddeus' father who has aspirations greater than congressman when the war is over.

Mother asked her if she had had the decency to write you and explain, or to return the ring. She said the ring was hers, and if your mother wanted to, she could inform you. Mother is devastated because of Patricia's awful indiscretion and callousness, and refused to write you with such news.

Son, I am sorry, but it is best that you find out Patricia's true nature now rather than spend a life of misery with an unfaithful woman. I do not know her motivation, but she has always appeared to me to be a very selfish young woman. It was our hope that she would outgrow that tendency, but it seems that it is not the case.

I know you can overcome this. I implore you to not stoop to Patricia's level of inhumanity, but to stay above the fray, serve your country honorably, and come home to us whole. Please let it pass and seek what happiness you can where you are.
Our love and prayers are always with you…

Steven Wayne does not finish the letter. There is no point, the news has been told, and nothing can lift him, or sink him deeper into the remorse he is in. He is lost, cuckolded, made a fool of by a woman. He crumples the letter and throws it behind him into the fire. He watches it burn as his anger matches the intensity of the flame. "Fair thee well Patricia Ann," he says with the hiss and venom of a rattler, "you've ruined me, made me a laughing stock; now it's my turn. I will unleash hell for you." He did not heed his father's words and from that moment on, vengeance would be his reason to live.

15) Portal of Hell

May 22nd, 1863

I have learned much in my few days here. There is hell on earth. Before being imprisoned, I thought war the greatest evil on earth; man at his worst; Lucifer at his best, but I was wrong. Being a prisoner and subject to another is man at his lowest. How depraved, cruel, and horrible men can be to one another! When one has total control over his enemy without restraint, the horrors of hell show forth.

Being imprisoned would be horrible enough in times of peace. Civilian incarceration pales by comparison to what a man is willing to subject his brother to in times of war. When two factions declare themselves enemies, hatred knows no bounds. The controlling party dreams of ways to make the incarceration of the subjected more horrible. Such men are here, working in the name of a government. If this place, and all those like it, is not hell, they are the portals to it. Evil rules here.

I think that the biblical hell of fire and brimstone is fantasy; something conceived of by those without experience. Hell is here. I have learned hell will be a place of filth, degradation, and want; there will never be enough; never enough food, enough water, warmth, medical care, clothes, companionship, trust, safety, books, paper, wholesome communication, and more.

What there is, is filthy, or made so by the way one must obtain it. The small amount of food is infested with maggots, weevils, and all manner of filth our captors see fit to stir into the pot. I have become willing to stoop to the unpardonable to survive.

Hell will be full of rumors. There is constant rumor of exchange and freedom. It is a source of great pain as our hopes are raised by rumor only to be dashed time and again. There has been an exchange system in effect for over a year now, but it does not function because of politics on both sides. When the war broke out, no one thought it would last, so there was no system for prisoners, now there has to be, and it, like the prisons, is a debacle. There are some officers that are exchanged, but very few enlisted. We do have hope of exchange in June and it is discussed every day, all day.

I have learned that hell will be boring to the point of insanity. There are singing groups, thespian groups, men who carve, men who forage, men who haggle, but all are nothing more than diversions as is this journal. Many write poetry as I have, but it is not what we want to do, and those who have nothing, lose everything. Deep boredom brings a loss of hope and I have seen men who have lost it and quit living.

I thank God for Sergeant Zachery and the water detail. It gives me opportunity to clean myself and my clothes. I have even been taking clothes of some of the others for a quick rinse in the river. It does not rid us of lice, but it helps, and takes away some of the odor.

Small pox is here. Three hundred have died since last August and are buried in the Alton cemetery as well as a makeshift one on the island. With warm weather, we are out of doors more, and the sickness has abated.

I have been offered parole. In exchange for my freedom, I must sign an oath of loyalty to the United States and pledge to not take up arms against that country. All but a few have rejected the offer. It is not an honest parole when an oath of allegiance to the enemy is attached. I feel it would be a betrayal to my country and to freedom itself to accept such an offer even though it would relieve me of much suffering and allow me to go home to my Lucy and children.

Oh, how I long for home, but not without honor and liberty! The only way we can fight, imprisoned as we are, is with our loyalty to our oath as officers, to our country, and to the cause of freedom and justice. We encourage each other daily to remain strong in our cause, which is just, but it is hard. Yet, this is the only avenue available to us to resist the tyranny of the north. God help us in our cause.

I am sitting in the late May sun on a cloudless day. We've finished the water detail for the morning, and with nothing else to do, I am writing in my journal. It does me good to be away from the constant rhetoric about the cause and parole, and let my thoughts go home. I have learned to let my mind transport me outside these prison walls. If I dwell on the conditions here, and the hopelessness of this place, I will go insane as many have.

George Paul ambles toward me. He has clung to me like a shadow since we walked into this place. It's been hard to find breathing room away from him. His presence would not be so bad, if he didn't feel like he had to talk the whole time.

I miss Buck. He and I can sit or ride for hours and never say a word; secure in the fact we're together, and whatever's around the next bend, we can count on each other. That's all we need. I hope he is well.

George sits down on the stool opposite me.

"Howdy Evans."

I look up from my journal, "George," and lower my head, looking at the page.

"Evans, I've been thinking…,"

"Always a good thing."

"I've been thinking," he continues as if nothing else has been said, "that I might take the parole."

"Figured you might."

"Why; why did you figure I would take it?" He is tense and defensive.

"George, before you go off half cocked, I didn't mean anything by it. I'm not judging you. I don't know what you're thinking, but…"

"You surely do not! You have no idea what I'm going through!"

"I just might; we're all going through it. We're all afraid George; you're just having a harder time dealing with it than the rest of us."

"I'm not the only one taking the parole, you know," quieter now, but still defensive, "there's plenty others. I think it's a good idea. The war's lost anyway…"

"And how do you know that George? How do you know the war is lost? Is it because you're lost? I don't know why you joined the army, but don't tell me what I believe in is a lost cause! If you want to quit and go home, quit and go home, but don't try to justify your actions to me. I will ask you this George, win or lose, where does your allegiance lie?"

He looks at me hard then looks away across the yard. "I thought you were my friend."

"I am your friend George. Be honest with yourself. Don't take the parole because others are doing it, or because you think the Confederacy is a lost cause. Take it because it's what you need. Don't try and get me to agree with you, because I won't. I want to go home too; I've got a lot waiting for me there, maybe more than you."

He's quiet. I wonder if he heard me, when he says, "I'm just tired," he pauses, "and afraid; tired of being afraid, tired of no water, lousy food, and most of all tired of being locked up." There's life in his eyes. "You don't know what happens to me when they lock that door at night. I can't stand it. I don't sleep; I lay there and tremble. I can't handle it; I don't want to handle it. I'm not strong enough to do this. I can fight, hell, I can die, but I can't be locked up. I gotta get out, and if the parole will do that for me, then I'm going to take it. I am Evans; I'm going to take it right now."

He stands, and I with him. He offers me his hand and smiles. I can see relief in his eyes. I can feel it in his grip. "Do you have money? Do you know how you will get home?"

"I've got some sewed away in my trousers; I'll manage."

"I know you will George; you'll be in my prayers. Are you going straight to Arkansas?"

"No, the folks went to Missouri before I left. With any luck, I can get there in two or three weeks."

"Be careful of the Home Guard; they'll be looking for deserters…"

"But I'll have papers."

"Papers can be stolen, lost, or just ignored. Be careful. You'll be in danger from anyone who wants ten dollars to turn you in as a deserter."

"I'll be careful. Would you like me to call on your missus if I can get down there; maybe take her a letter or something?"

"I don't have a letter written. When do you think you will be going?"

"I don't know, just as soon as I can. I can't stand another night in that cell."

"I understand. I'll scribble out a quick note for you to carry if you don't mind."

"I would consider it an honor and a privilege. You've been good to me. I wouldn't have lasted this long without you."

"Go on and sign your parole," I say with a smile, "get out of here before I get weak and go with you."

"You'd be a welcome companion."

"No, my duty's here."

George looks off toward the administration building where he has to go to sign and with a wistful look on his face says, "It'd be hard to explain to a woman," then walks away.

I go in search of Major Traweek and to find a piece of paper to write a note to Lucy. Traweek and other officers are gathered under an oak tree in the yard. I am waved forward as I approach. "Evans, come join us; we have information that may interest you."

"Thank you major," nodding to the others, "gentlemen."

"What news do you bring us lieutenant?"

"Sir, Lieutenant Paul is taking the oath and parole as we speak." There are looks between the men, some ambivalent, a couple surprised, most with a knowing expression. Traweek speaks, "Good."

"Good sir?" It surprises me.

"Lieutenant, there are things afoot that Lieutenant Paul would have had to be excluded from. It is best that he leave us."

"What things?"

"Sit close here Atwood." He pulls a stool next to him. After I am seated, he continues, "We have all been offered parole."

"Yes sir."

"Some have accepted while we," gesturing to the group, "and others, have not, do you know why?"

"Yes sir, because we reject the idea of swearing an oath of allegiance to the Union, which would be tantamount to swearing that home is the enemy."

"Well said lieutenant, but there are new things that need our consideration."

"Which are?"

"There are two things that are going to happen that will cause positive change in our imprisonment." He pauses; seeing my rapt attention, he continues, "We officers are going to be offered limited parole for access to the city and all its wonders," he pauses, waiting for comment.

"Sounds like a gracious gesture; what do the Yankees want in return?"

"They want us to give up more freedom."

"I don't follow sir. What other freedom can we give up?"

"They want us to give our parole that we will make *no* attempt to escape, or aid those who do make such an attempt."

"I see."

"Do you?"

"Yes, they're trying to circumvent our duty to fight the enemy in all ways, wherever possible. If we swear to not escape, we have more freedoms but we are eliminated on our honor from fighting the enemy. We are sworn to not escape even if such an opportunity arises. The Yankees do not have to be as vigilant guarding us, knowing we have sworn such an oath."

"Very good lieutenant."

"But I don't fully understand the significance. Escape through the gates seems impossible. An assault from the river would stand a chance. It would be a daring, desperate, well coordinated, and risky expedition. Such an assault would be counterproductive; we would lose as many or more soldiers than could be rescued. It would serve no purpose. With the war going badly in Mississippi, the rescue of us cannot be a priority."

"Again lieutenant; your reasoning is sound. What then do you propose as the next most viable alternative to acquire our freedom and re-enter the conflict?"

"Escape sir," I say with a smile of realization. These men are organizing an escape! It will have to be well organized and able to release sufficient of our numbers to make a difference, but how? "You must have a plan sir otherwise you would not be, pardon the expression, so 'smug' sir. Please, share."

Major Traweek laughs and says, "Keep it under control lieutenant. I want you to reason with me here." I shift on my stool, anxious to hear the plan. "Are you aware of General Thomas's occupation, how he made his living before the war?"

"I do believe he is a civil engineer sir."

"And what to civil engineers do lieutenant?"

"Sir, I believe the general worked for the railroads, draining swamps, building bridges, digging...,'' my face brightens as I realized our avenue of escape.

"Yes lieutenant, please continue; digging what?"

"Tunnels sir, he built tunnels."

"That is correct Evans; he dug tunnels of all sorts."

"But how..."

"Remember I told you there were two things happening tomorrow," he interrupts. I nod; he continues, "We officers are being granted the convenience of having our cells unlocked at night as well as during the day. We can gather, plan, and dig."

"We will have to have some of our officers take the local parole. The Yankees will be lulled into a sense of security, and the operation can begin."

"When sir?"

"It began weeks ago when General Thomas was captured. He's been about this yard taking measurements of every sort. He has a plan, and will be ready to implement it soon."

"It will be an honor to serve in any way you deem appropriate."

"Good lieutenant, I know we can count on you. For now, remain on the water detail and bring back as much information as you can about the river bank and road to town. We will soon have others doing the same in town." With that he laughed, "We're in for a good ole time now boys; we'll be back in this thing before you know it!"

All smile and nod to each other and the conversation turns to mundane, everyday topics. I look up and see Sergeant Zachery walking across the compound and say, "Gentlemen, if you would please excuse me; I have to write a quick letter to my wife for Lieutenant Paul to carry home."

Voices mingle in agreement and compliments to Lucy as I rise to leave. I run to catch Sergeant Zachery.

"Hello sergeant."

"Atwood," he says with a nod.

"Sergeant, my friend George Paul is taking parole today and has offered to carry a letter home to my wife. Would you by any chance have some paper?"

"I think I can rustle you up some, come with me." We continue to walk. "You're getting pretty friendly with that group."

"Nothing wrong with friends in the higher ranks is there Zachery? They're just fellow officers passing the time as best as they can. You know, telling stories, sharing out a joke; that sort of thing. Is there something wrong?"

"No, not yet," he says looking back over his shoulder at the group.

I let the remark go, but know I will have to watch him, as I know he is going to be watching me, but for now, I have a letter to write.

16) Lucy Jane

Sunday, May 31st 1863

My dearest husband,

I received your letter dated May 11 and am sick at the news of your capture. I know you have suffered. I am thankful to know you are alive. It gives me hope.

I took the children to church today and to your parent's home for dinner. It was a long and tiring day, but a happy one. Everyone was relieved to hear you are alive. It was hardest on your mother to know you are a prisoner.

Your family is helping us. I explained the situation, and your brothers have agreed to come out and work on our place when I need it. Your father even offered for us to live at their place. I thanked them, but for us to leave our home and go to live with your family, things would have to get a lot worse.

Prison is hard for you, but we're having it hard too. We are in danger. There are men making advances and some threats. The pressure to go with one of them and be "taken care of" grows daily. It's so hard without you. It is difficult for a woman alone with so many men who have not gone to fight. I am afraid and lonely.

The children are well. Martha Jane is a help with James Calvin who is walking, and into everything.

I am glad you taught me to shoot. I have managed to keep meat on the table all spring. We have eaten well and have planted a garden which is showing promise. Our little ones are a help with it; Martha Jane especially. James' health has shown improvement since warm weather is with us, but he still seems frail. Your mother is worried for him.

Evans, I am hearing talk of the Union offering parole. Is it something you can do? Folks here abouts are saying you should take parole and come home. I know they are trying to put doubt in my mind about you, but it is so hard alone. I don't know how much longer I can hold out. If you come home, it would mean the world to us. If they offer you parole, whatever it is, will you please take it? I am desperate to have you here and to get on with our life.

We have so many plans, so many things that I want us to do. I want a better life for us. I want you to become someone, be somebody. You can't do that in prison! I hate this war! It has cost us so much, and now there is no end in sight and you are locked away. I don't even know if you will get this. Will I ever see you again? What will I do if you don't survive? This is not what I agreed to; you promised only a few months and this winter it will be two years, and now I don't know if you will ever get out. Please think of us; please think of what we need.

Oh Evans, what am I to do? You are locked away in hell, and I am a prisoner here; my life cannot go forward without you. Please come home.

Your loving and loyal wife,
Lucy Jane Atwood

Lucy Jane looks at the letter while it dries. It's late, and it's been an exhausting day. The children are asleep and have been since they rode the horse home at dusk.

It feels good to write Evans. She feels more connected, and it's a relief to know he's alive. She hasn't told him half of what she's feeling or thinking.

With the added assistance coming from Evans family, she feels more secure. It's their nature to aid those in need. She loathes being in need. It is so powerless, and Lucy Jane wants the power and freedom of independence.

The power and independence she understands is secured by having a man who can make her life better. She wants better; always better. She deserves better; no one deserves better more than she does. She wants it now.

She busies herself about the house with getting ready to go to bed. She checks the doors to see that they are locked. The windows will provide ventilation with the heat of the coming summer. She does not feel secure with the doors left open as she would if Evans were here. She checks the powder and prime on the shot gun, and rifle, and makes certain of their positions should she need them in the night. Now that Gavin Tate has threatened her, she makes doubly sure of each fire arms' condition. She extinguishes her lamp and sits in the dark.

It's near a full moon, and since the weather on the last day of May is warm the windows to the cabin are open allowing for a nice cross draft along with the beauty of soft moon light. She looks about her and marvels at all she has. The house, the children, the land all fill her with a warm glow, a feeling of achievement, but the thought fades as the facts of her current condition force themselves into her awareness. The feeling of satisfaction is replaced with one of fear, confusion, dread, and desperation.

What is she going to do? "Oh Evans," she says out loud, "if you were only here, you would know what to do. Of course," she now thought, "if you were here, this wouldn't be happening."

She goes to get ready for bed; strips to her bare skin and stands in the moonlit room, feeling the breeze blow across her. It's a relief from the anxiety and concerns of the day. She folds her dress and under garments, opens her trunk, and puts them away. Takes her cotton night gown from the same trunk, closes the lid and slips the gown over her head. The soft swishing noise of it sliding over her head, past her ears masks the first soft foot falls outside the cabin, but as the gown settles over her, the next steps are clear.

17) Steven Wayne

The siege of Vicksburg, May 22-June 1863

"Stop it! Stop it! Stop it!" Steven Wayne screams into his coat that serves as a pillow. It would make no difference if he screamed from the tallest spire in Vicksburg; no one would hear him. Such insane screams are common throughout the garrison and the city. It is the sixteenth day of the siege and the bombardment of Vicksburg has been incessant. The garrison has been receiving and returning fire every day, every night, all day, and all night. The only time the guns are silent is when they need service, to be aimed, or cooled.

For an infantry battalion, there is little to do but endure. There have been two assaults on the city; one on the 19th and again, on the 22nd, both of which were repulsed at great loss to the Federal forces. The joy of victory was short lived as Grant began the siege. There are water details to the river to load barrels, but they are too infrequent to break the monotony of the constant noise and concussion. Earthworks are always in need of repair and that helps, but that too is not enough. The problem is not so much the boredom, nor the constant threat of death from the falling, exploding shells; the real demon is the noise.

It stops, but for brief seconds; sometimes almost a minute. The lulls tease and heighten tension as each wonders, "Is this it, is it over?" All know full well that it isn't. The quiet moments are heaven sent.

Men who have them, pull bee's wax plugs from their ears, untie rags from around their heads, both of which reduce the concussion, but not the noise, and stand with their mouths open looking idiotic. The mouth open, slack jawed look is formed of habit. It is necessary to equalize pressure against the ear drum during the concussion of exploding ordinance or cannon fire. If they close their mouths, ear drums will burst with the concussive forces. It is common to see men with blood running from their ears.

In quiet periods, the soldiers shout from habit or impaired hearing. Their eyes are glazed but there is a flicker of hope that vanishes when the bombardment resumes. As it does, their eyes dull and they resume what has become normal; the open mouth, shouting to communicate, and the dull pounding felt throughout their exhausted bodies. Steven Wayne wonders if it will ever end as he fades in and out of caring. He is certain he is going insane.

He lies with his face buried in his coat, his hands over his ears, screaming. He cannot hear Colonel Reynolds calling him from outside his cave. He, like all the other men have abandoned tents and taken to caves dug into hill sides or battlements. Someone is kicking his feet which are extended beyond the mouth of his dug out. He has enough room to turn around, and after he does, sticks his head out and into the gathering dark and shouts, "What!" It takes him a moment to realize who is interrupting his misery, and when he does, he rises, comes to attention, but barely, salutes as sloppy as he looks, and without apology shouts "Sir?" Lieutenant Colonel Reynolds looks at him with disgust and concern.

"Captain, you look terrible, are you ill?" Steven Wayne understands very few of the shouted words over the combined noise of the bursting shells and outgoing artillery. He has learned to lip read and is able to discern what the colonel is saying.

"Yes sir, no sir," Steven Wayne shouts, not answering the statement or the question. He's suffering. His love life is a shambles. He can't get over Patricia Ann's breaking off the engagement, and still hopes for her letters if they ever get mail again. Even the distraction of Rilla Mae Gadston, has not served to lift his spirits. He's living in a cave, filthy, exhausted, delirious from lack of sleep, and hungry. The garrison has been on half rations for so long, he cannot remember when he was full. He's suffering from intestinal problems from drinking the river water; has constant ringing in his ears, and knows he is losing his mind. He dreams of charging the Yankee positions and ending it all. At least combat is something he understands. "Who knows, I just might kill General Grant and end the war."

"Captain, you are not fit for duty." Steven Wayne starts to protest, but is too numb and tired to do so. The bombardment requires too much effort to talk, and he is thankful when the colonel cuts him off, "clean yourself up and report to the Gadston family. They have requested an officer to come stay with them in their dug-out quarters at Sky Parlor. I do believe you have been there?"

"Yes sir, I know the place," he shouts, "but what am I to do there?" Most of the question is lost in an explosion, but Colonel Reynolds too has become proficient at lip reading.

"Damned if I know captain. Mr. Gadston is prominent in the city, and he wants his daughter and wife protected from the incursions of the lesser ranks, or should the Union troops break through. It's become status to have an officer to protect them."

"Sir, what can one man do? And my men sir, what will they…"

"Captain, I am ordering you to attend the Gadston family until relieved. Do you understand that order?" The colonel shouts. He is afraid for and of Captain Culpepper. It is easy to see that a drastic change has occurred; Steven Wayne's mind has snapped. If he doesn't get some rest, the colonel is certain that Steven Wayne will hurt someone.

"Yes sir, I understand," and repeats it back to the colonel.

"As for your men, I will take care of their needs." There is silence, real silence, but the colonel continues to shout, "Speaking of needs, I do believe that Atwood's platoon has gone without an officer long enough don't you?" Steven Wayne fishes wax plugs from his ears. They are a treasured possession. The first time he used them, he did not get all the honey out of the wax, and ants crawled into his ears. It was frightening and disgusting, but now he doesn't care.

"Yes sir, I guess so." Atwood is not coming back. He thinks, "What of his poor wife?" That's all he can muster. Maybe he'll think on it later.

"Good, in your absence, I am going to hold an election...," the bombing resumes and shouting too, "... and see what young Wilson can do with the troops. He's leading them now isn't he?"

"Yes sir, he is." Then thinks to himself, "Let me get away from here."

"Very well captain, you are dismissed to attend to your new duties." With a sly smile, the colonel adds, "I believe you have a relationship with the Gadston woman, am I correct?"

"Yes sir, but I will not let her distract me from my duty sir."

"Captain, she is your duty!" He smiles even more as he turns to leave.

Vicksburg hangs on a hill overlooking the Mississippi River. The northern part of the city is a gentle slope of that hill which is called "Sky Parlor". As Grant's forces, months ago had tried to take the city from the river, the populace gathered there to watch the display of pyrotechnics of the shore batteries versus the Union navy; one trying to annihilate the other. Blankets and picnic baskets were laid about as the citizenry enjoyed the spectacle and eventual victory.

The mood at Sky Parlor is no longer festive, nor the view spectacular. The city is fair game to the guns of siege, and has suffered greatly. There are very few if any buildings that have not been damaged. The streets are a pockmarked no man's land, not suitable for transportation or any other use. The churches have sustained so much damage that services have been suspended as has most honest commerce. Life is on hold as the siege continues, and as of now, it seems interminable.

Sky Parlor's gentle, rolling, hill is still used as a gathering for the citizens of Vicksburg, but the occasion and cause are much different. The hill is now itself an embattlement, filled with the citizens of the city. Its soil is light and friable, and yet sufficiently stiff to answer the purpose of excavation. Wherever the passage of a street leaves the face of the hill exposed, into it and under it, the people burrow; making long ranges and systems of chambers and arches within which the women and young take shelter. In the caves all the offices of life are discharged. Cooking stoves stand near the entrance, opportunity to perform upon it being seized and improved when the shelling is diverted to other quarters. Sometimes the eaves are strengthened by pillars and wooden joists, and beds and furniture are crowded in. Whether they are effective against the largest shells dropped directly from above, no one knows. Stories are told, more than once during the siege, of people who have been buried alive by the collapse of caves; but no one seems to be able to verify this. This is where Steven Wayne is bound.

The Gadston's quarters are along the most prominent avenue of Sky Parlor. Steven Wayne observes that the higher one goes up the hill, the lower the class of people. "Everything is backwards in this war," he says out loud, but with the bombing, no one hears him, "this is the only time in this city that the poor can shit on the heads of the rich." He laughs as he observes chamber pots being emptied out the doors, which, with the help of rain and gravity will descend on the more prominent families below.

The noise is less here, but the earth still shakes with every impact, and the concussive force still pounds in his head. There are men standing and sitting about who give him a hearty hail. It's rather a point of honor among men not to abide in the caves, which are reserved for the women and children.

The men are engaged in various games of chance, drinking what beverages are available as they anticipate the evening meal. There are a few bottles of spirits being passed around and are offered to Steven Wayne. He declines, much to the relief of the men. Since the city water is supplied by cisterns, he consumes all offers of water which, in its ability to satisfy, far surpass those of the spirits. Wherever he stops he is bombarded with questions concerning the siege; when will it end, do we stand a chance, is the city in danger of being overrun, should they try and get out, and on, and on.

He notices that not one person asks after the troops and how they're faring. He has begun to conclude each conversation with something to the effect of, "Yes the troops are enduring, but have no water, are on half rations, and are forced to sally forth under the cover of darkness to butcher felled horses and mules to be able to have meat."

He becomes more sullen and is surprised that he is being so forceful. It must show. He is greeted less, and asked fewer questions as he goes.

The cave dwelling of the Gadston's is lavish if caves can be such. The Gadston fortune is a result of shipping, mostly between Memphis and

New Orleans, and mercantile outlets in the city. The labor is accomplished by a few white overseers, and many slaves.

Being at war has not altered Steven Wayne's ambivalence to slavery, although his distaste for the institution has grown. As the war goes against the South, the Negro population is not showing as much deference to him as previous, and in some cases, bold hostility.

Not seeing the elder Gadston about, he asks one of the Negros sitting in front of their dwelling, "Boy, is your master about?" The young Negro ignores him.

The boy is sitting with several other black men and all their eyes are looking between Steven Wayne and the young man, then back to Steven Wayne who moves closer to make certain there is no mistake as to who is addressing whom and says with some anger, "Buck, I asked you a question." The black young man stirs the fire.

"Ruff," pleads one of his companions, "answer the man." There's no response. The other warns by inquiry, "Are you looking for more stripes on your nigger back?"

"Don't you call me that, don't *YOU* ever call me that!" Ruff lashes at the other young Negro.

"What, nigger; you's don't wan's to be called 'nigger'? You thinks you's better'n the res of us? Why boy, you's worse than a nigger; least wise we ans'r a polite gentlemen's asking us a querstion! Nigger, you gonna get us all whipped!"

Ruff explodes at his protagonist who backs away, but not before Ruff has him by the throat and is raising a fist.

"Stop!" Bellows an authoritative voice from the dark. "Stop, both of you!" Beau Gadston steps into the light of the fire. He is an imposing figure standing over six feet tall. With him is a burly man with a whip and a Colt on his hip. Steven Wayne steps back and watches. He rests the butt of his Springfield rifle on the toe of his right boot.

"Captain Culpepper, I apologize for the behavior of this boy. Instruction concerning manners is wasted on him since the Union invaded and Lincoln signed that damnable proclamation. He thinks he'll be free, which may or may not be true, but he forgets one salient point captain; do you know what that point might be?"

Steven Wayne is too tired to care and doesn't like being recruited into the confrontation between slave and master. He looks at the two Negros standing, one humble and terrified, the other defiant. The overseer, who the other man accompanying Gadston must be, is untying the whip from its thong on his hip. Steven Wayne answers, "No, Mr. Gadston, I do not know what this man knows or does not know, or what he may have forgotten."

Not hearing, or ignoring Steven Wayne, Gadston continues, "He's forgotten his station in life." Turning to Ruff, he asks, "Haven't you boy?" Ruff does not respond, but stares hard at Mr. Gadston and the overseer.

"Callahan," he says to the overseer who steps forward with his whip free and ready in his right hand; "give ole' Ruff here a lesson in manners - unless you have an objection captain." He's leering, enjoying the moment and the opportunity to show his power and importance.

"Thank you for asking sir, I do object."

Mr. Gadston had expected enthusiastic support for the beating from the insulted captain, so it is with incredulity that he blurts, "What? Are you a nigger lover? Are you not a man for the South?"

Steven Wayne surprises himself and Gadston with his anger as he shouts over yet another fusillade, "You ask me what kind of man I am? I'm a man who is bone tired of fighting for a cause that you equate to slavery and I equate to freedom. I'm a man who is tired of human suffering, white or black. I'm tired of blood and the screams of wounded men. So, Mr. Gadston, if you want to beat this man, please do so outside my presence; and before you go off on me sir," spoken in response to Mr. Gadstons' raised and pointed finger, "I want to remind you that you did ask if I had an objection."

Gadston looks at Steven Wayne, as does Ruff. Callahan is slapping his leg with the whip. Steven Wayne is on familiar ground now, this is combat. Not what the last several weeks have brought, but it is confrontation and dangerous. When danger is imminent, Steven Wayne is at his best.

He moves his rifle to his left hand so his right hand will have free access to a Walker Dragoon pistol hanging on his hip. The sight of it brings a halt to the whip slapping against Callahan's leg. Steven Wayne breaks the silence, "Mr. Gadston, let me make something clear; I have come here on orders from my commanding officer to assist you. I have come, I believe, at your request. I will offer you and your family all the protection I can as a single soldier, but I will not sir, stand to have any man beaten in my presence. If that is not satisfactory, I will return to my troops with your compliments, I am sure, to Colonel Reynolds." He looks between Gadston and Callahan, waiting for a response.

Gadston raises himself up, squares his shoulders and says, "You can't talk to me that way, why I'm..."

"Sir, I am fully aware of who you are, and by the moment, it is becoming clear to me what you are. Now, enough of this bluster; am I to be of service to you or not?"

There is silence as Gadston mulls his options. He looks at Steven Wayne who cannot see what Gadston sees or he might be frightened too, because Gadston is staring into the cold, hard, vicious eyes of a killer. Something has risen up in Steven Wayne that is frightening to behold. "Ruff," says Mr. Gadston with force.

"Yes sur?" Ruff is not willing to push Mr. Gadston any further.

"Go clean the slop jars and chamber pots."

"But…"

"Now!" He cursed the boy for all he was worth, but neither he nor Callahan raised a hand to him. As Ruff leaves the fire ring, he passes Steven Wayne who is still glaring at Mr. Gadston and Callahan, and cowers away from the fierce young captain. Steven Wayne does not notice.

Gadston smiles and says, "Now Captain Culpepper, what are we to do with you?"

"Do with me sir? I don't believe you will do anything with me." The fierceness of his gaze has not diminished, "The question sir is what I am going to do with you?"

"Son, we are two to your one! You need to relax, have a drink," He nudges Callahan who obliges the direction of his master and holds out a bottle of whiskey, "go on now, take it, we mean no harm."

The transformation of Steven Wayne's countenance frightens the men. He has switched from killer to being as placid as a puppy and says as he takes the bottle, "Don't mind if I do," raising it to his lips and chugging the whisky. "Oh, that's good."

Handing the bottle back, he says, "Much obliged; now, what can the Army of the Confederate States do for one of its most prominent citizens? I understand you requested me personally?"

Confused, and uncertain of the stability of the captain, Gadston says, "Rilla Mae wants you here."

"And she is a fine example of a southern womanhood if there ever was one. Now gentlemen, shall we not keep the lady?"

Gadston glares at Steven Wayne. This is not settled. Affable and smiling, he says, "Let's call on Rilla Mae, shall we?"

"At your service sir; please show the way." Steven Wayne follows Gadston bewildered by his mind. It is going, and with it, there is a new, fierce persona that frightens and intrigues him. He knows he can kill anyone, uniform or not. A new Captain Culpepper has emerged from the confrontation, and he is not wholly displeased with what he's learned. He smiles as he goes to enjoy the sweetness of his southern belle.

18) Evans

Tuesday, June the 2ⁿᵈ, 1863

Alton Prison, Ill.

Exchange! How glorious the word! A synonym for "freedom", and Haw to Dixie! There has been talk since we arrived of an exchange of prisoners. It is a burden to feed and house so many of an enemy to the detriment of your own forces.

There have been rumors of exchange every day. I suspect the guards are the source of such cruelty. Our hopes are raised with each utterance, and dashed with the next, but today, names were called, mine among them. We are told to fall out tomorrow morning to sign the paper work and be exchanged.

There is a non-combatant oath to be signed. It is the same for their troops we are releasing, but it is different from the hated parole. We do not have to swear allegiance to the Union, only that we will not bear arms against it. There is a warning that should the person thus pledged be captured again, they are to be hanged. I do not fear this, nor would any soldier.

Much has changed since my last entry. I dare not write of it. I fear that we will be searched again, and this journal confiscated.
Each time new prisoners are brought in; we are stripped and searched along with them. The Yankee bastards have already stolen everything we had of worth and anything that we get from home to ease our hardship is declared contraband and confiscated.

Friday, June the 5ᵗʰ, 1863
Alton Prison

The Confederate prisoners subject to exchange were called upon to sign a parole, preparatory to starting to City Point, the place of exchange. For the first time, there is the shine of hope in the eyes of my fellow soldiers. Tomorrow is to be the day of the beginning of our deliverance.

The day of our liberation, our Independence Day, Saturday, June 6ᵗʰ, dawns as bright and clear as our smiles. It isn't hard to spot those whose names are on the list; we're the ones grinning like kids at the circus. I am thinking about George Paul when Major Traweek walks up to me and says, "Evans," he has never called me by my given name before; I didn't even know he knew it, "it won't be long now."

"No sir, it won't. I'm so excited, I'm about to wet my pants. I can't wait to be out of here!"

"Don't get your hopes up, there are still rumors, but you know how rumors are. We can never tell."

"Yes sir, you're right, but I have to admit, my hopes can't get any higher." I'm smiling ear to ear and Major Traweek is too.

"What're you gonna do Atwood when we are released, what are your plans?"

"I'm going home sir. My wife is having trouble with some of the local men who think she's fair game because I'm a prisoner of war. They think of me as good as dead, but when I get back, it will be resurrection day!" We both laugh. "What of you major; what are your plans?"

"Much the same as yours, except me being from Alabama, I will be called upon to lead more men to their tedious and onerous deaths."

We're quiet, him smoking a cigar, and me staring at the gates. Major Traweek breaks the stillness by reaching into his tunic and withdrawing a book, and says, "Here lieutenant, write your address in my copy book. Should both of us find ourselves in need of more duty, I would like to be able to correspond."

"And I too major." I exchange books with him.

We write our respective addresses, he asks me, "Do you wonder of Lieutenant Paul, Evans?"

"Yes sir, I do; as a matter of fact, I was just thinking of him before you walked up. I was thinking how if he had been able to endure just three more weeks, how much safer and easier his journey home would have been."

"Do you think he's there yet?"

"He should be; I hope so. He's carrying a letter to my wife."

"Lovely woman, your wife."

"I've showed you the picture have I?" I ask with a smile, knowing I had. When he opened my journal, he had to see it. I have it mounted in the front.

"Yes, many times; many, many times." We're called to fall in by rank. "Good luck to you lieutenant; I'm sure we'll see each other in the depot, if not before."

"Thank you sir. Good luck to you."

He raises his hand and waves without looking back. It's starting; we're going to be exchanged!

We're marched out of the prison gates and into the sunshine of freedom; on through the city to the railroad station and assigned cars. They're the stock cars used to transport prisoners, but this time we don't have to suffer the indignity of being strip searched. We're leaving, and besides, there's nothing left to steal.

The cars have very little ventilation, and only a bucket of water and a bucket for slop. I crowd to a side where the boards are loose and set about removing them for more air and light.

It's about 4:00 PM when the shrill whistle blows and we roll out of the station. A great cheer erupts from the several cars, that I am certain can be heard all the way back at the prison. We are under way to our homes, freedom, and a more southern clime.

We roll through the night without a stop, and on Sunday, we are allowed off the train in Indianapolis, Indiana. As we shuffle off, tired, hungry and in need of a latrine, we find ourselves being ordered into ranks and marched into town. By now I have begun to wonder about our destination, and our exchange. We are marched past town to another prison called Camp Morton.

It's a dismal place which, when compared to Alton, even with its small pox, is better than here. We are not assigned barracks or tents, but told to make do on the ground. Some of us complain of hunger and are told to, "Shut our Dixie loving mouths." This does not bode well for release.

I find Major Traweek holding council with the other officers of our loose affiliation. He notices me and signals me to join them. I arrive as a lieutenant colonel whose name I can't remember is asking of the group, "... so what do you think is going on?"

Not wanting to interrupt or ask to be caught up, I stand and listen.

"We've traveled east colonel, not south. We're not going to be released," says a morose captain.

General Thompson seems un-fazed by the conversation as he sits back and smokes. "Gentlemen," all grow quiet, "may I speak?"

There is a consensus that he should, and he says, "We have every reason to believe we are to be exchanged don't we?"

There are muttered words and phrases of agreement among those gathered, so the general continues, "We have signed the exchange papers, we have complied with all our captor's wishes, and there is nothing more that we can do. I suggest we relax, enjoy the evening. I am told by the commanding officer, that we will not continue our journey until Monday, it being Sunday, and maybe not until Tuesday."

"Sir, did you ask him concerning the exchange?" A voice in the dark asks.

"Yes, I did. He is no more enlightened about the situation than we are. He seemed taken by surprise at our arrival. We will just have to wait gentlemen and see what tomorrow holds. I suggest we have as comfortable a night as possible." With that, we are dismissed.

It's a difficult evening with the specter of the exchange being a ruse, but it passes with the distraction of some Quakers in camp having for distribution quite a number of testaments, tracts and such which were thankfully received by us prisoners. For most of us, it was the first reading literature we have been able to acquire other than days old newspapers since captivity. It is a welcome relief as a sermon is delivered by one of the Friends as they call themselves. There are quite a few of we Dixieans assembled, many through curiosity more than any good discourse we might hear, myself included, because it is the first opportunity that we have had to listen to a religious discourse from the lips of a Quaker minister. It is good to hear the Word preached again.

Early the next morning, we are marched to the depot, loaded on stock cars; these being much more ventilated, and travel yet east.

It takes us two days to reach Pittsburg; arriving in the evening. We're well treated and marched into the city and quartered in a large, official looking room. We are allowed access to latrines without the benefit of guards and are fed bread and beans in large quantities. The room is large enough for twice as many men, and we are certain that this is where the exchange will take place.

There is a great deal of banter, good natured ribbing, and laughter. We are minutes away from freedom. Major Traweek is sitting near the front of the room with General Thompson. Due to their rank and station, I did not expect levity, but at least smiles; however, that is not the case.

"Gentlemen, it's almost over!"

My glee is dampened by their dour countenances. I stand silent and am met with the same. I wait for a response from the group.

Major Traweek says, "Lieutenant Atwood, sit please." Others in the gathering make room on the facing benches and after I have taken my place, Major Traweek says with a kind smile, "Evans, don't get your hopes up."

"Why is that sir; are we not being exchanged?"

Looking at the general, he gets the slightest nod, before continuing, "It is rumored that the exchange system has collapsed."

"Sir, I'm not trying to be dense, but I don't understand."

"We don't know anything more than that. We were just told by the apparent officer in charge that ...," his explanation is interrupted by the opening of the main door near where we are seated. A Union colonel, a major, and a captain enter and fan out in front of the door and wait for silence. "That's the man," he gestures to the colonel, "I fear, Atwood, that this is not good news," whispers Traweek. He has no sooner spoken when the other doors into the room open and in file armed troops who take up positions around the room, standing at attention.

The Yankee major wearing the braided cord of an adjutant, hands the colonel a portfolio while at the same time the captain, cries in a strained voice, "Prisoners," the word cuts deep, "attention to orders!"

The colonel steps forward, opens the portfolio and says, "I am Colonel William Williams sent by General Hallick, commander of the exchange cartel. These are your orders; "Whereas the government of the rebellious states has declared by unlawful assembly of their governing body to wit: 'Any black soldiers taken as prisoner will be treated as escaped slaves, not subject to the agreed upon exchange cartel. Furthermore, any white officer taken as a prisoner leading Negro troops will be charged with inciting a slave insurrection and will be subject to capital punishment.' In light of this declaration by your government leaders, the United States will no longer honor the terms outlined in the signed cartel and hereby suspends all prisoner exchanges."

There's a burst of angry shouts from the four hundred or more officers who are affected, mingled with cries of anguish, and in some cases tears. I lower my head to hide my disappointment. I am shocked and stupefied. A thousand thoughts charge through my mind, "What of Lucy and the children, what will they do? What of Buck; did he find Dr. McPheeter's wife, did they make it home? What of my family?" For a moment, I wish I had signed the parole and would be home now; to hell with honor, but I come to my senses. I have sworn an oath, and I will honor it, but this is so hard to take, so hard...

I look around at the others in our group hoping that someone will take the initiative and order a charge against our captors. We can overwhelm them, but then what? It is a forlorn hope.

"Silence!" The captain shouts above the din. "Silence, or I shall have the guards clear the room." The chaotic voices and noise began to subside when the captain once again yells, "Silence!" A strained quiet along with the pall of defeat settle over us.

The announcement is worse than being captured. I am so angry, and the longer I ponder the words I just heard, the more resolved I become to the cause I have pledged my allegiance to so many months and battles ago. This tyranny must be defeated!

The tension and the anger in the silent room are palpable. The Union soldiers fidget at their posts, ready for action. The colonel continues, "Your orders: 'Due to the suspension of the exchange cartel, you are hereby ordered to be incarcerated at Johnson Island, Illinois in an 'officers only' facility for the duration of the war, or when exchanges can once again be resumed.' This order is signed, Henry W. Hallick, General, Commanding, USA."

The colonel continues, "You will be loaded onto the train and taken to Johnson Island; fall into ranks by rank and the guards are to take charge of the prisoners."

We move with slow and deliberate steps into ranks until the melodic baritone of Major Traweek, booms out, "Gentlemen of the South do not give these blue swine the benefit of seeing you forlorn, stand tall, this is but a small moment before they are subject unto us. Let's hear a 'Hurrah!' for Old Dixie and the South!"

We raise that roof with our shout. The blue bellies are nervous now! As we fall into ranks, we are once again an army; a captive one to be sure, but we march into the night as soldiers standing for freedom, not defeated men.

19) Lucy Jane

Were those footsteps? Could it be? Her heart is racing at the possibilities. Her first thought is, "Gavin Tate; would he be this bold? No, he's stupid, but not stupid enough to make such obvious footfalls. Gavin would come on horseback. He's too lazy to walk where he can ride."

She grabs the shot gun leaning against the wall by the door. "It could be one of Evan's brothers," she thinks, "but they would have come earlier and would have hailed from the yard regardless of the hour." She checks the gun's loads and snaps the receiver shut.

The noise of a gun's mechanism working is a death knell to anyone familiar with weapons, and the steps halt short of the porch. Silence.

Lucy starts to shake. She takes a deep breath and forces herself to be calm. She's prepared for this, and has expected it, but now that it's here, she's unclear what to do. She checks that the gun's additional loads are right where she put them. She feels for the pistol hanging on the peg on the wall and it too is as she left it.

The windows! She's forgotten to close the windows! "How stupid of me!" She thinks as she knocks out the prop rods holding them open allowing them to bang shut. She doesn't care if she makes a racket; maybe whoever's out there will leave. She goes to the loopholes cut in the walls, removes the plug from the one at the back of the house looking toward the river. The footsteps came from the front, but they might be a diversion.

The light from the moon is so bright that it casts shadows of the leafed tree limbs. If anyone is out back, they're well hidden. She replaces the plug and moves to the front of the house. Evans and Buck taught her that if a fight is inevitable, strike first, and fast. While they're back on their heels, you can take the next move too. "Once you're the aggressor, you keep moving; never let 'em regroup," and that's what she does.

She bangs the plug from the door and looks out at a man standing in front of the porch with his hands held far out from his sides. Lucy says in as calm a voice as she can muster, "Stop right there, or I'll blow your head off!" It sounds more forceful than she thought it would. She glances to the kids who are sitting up in bed. She points to the table and the rug next to it. Martha Jane moves James Calvin across the room, crawls under the table, and sits down. Should people get onto the porch, Martha Jane and Calvin know to move the rug, open the trap door cut there and squeeze through under the house. It's small, just big enough for the children and Lucy. If intruders get into the house, the children are to run to the barn. Lucy shoves the shot gun through the loophole of the door and looks out.

Her antagonist chuckles before saying, "I'm already stopped. I stopped when I heard you slamming the windows. I mean you no harm ma'am. Are you Mrs. Atwood; Mrs. Evans Atwood?" The voice is calm and does not sound threatening.

The man is smiling, dressed in traveling clothes. He is wearing an officer's hat, and has a light beard like Evans. She can't help herself, "Evans?"

"No ma'am, I'm afraid not, but I do have news of him…"

"Who are you? Where did you come from? What of my husband?" It all gushes from her as she struggles to maintain her composure. Why is this man here in the middle of the night? "Well, speak damn you!"

He smiles again, and says, "Please be calm Mrs. Atwood, don't go off with that shot gun; I have a letter."

"A letter, from Evans?"

"Yes ma'am, I…"

"Who are you?"

"May I lower my hands please?" The rattle of the gun in the loophole gives him his answer, "I'm Lieutenant George Paul, late commander of Company B, 15th Arkansas Infantry."

"What do you mean 'late commander'?"

"I was taken prisoner at the Battle of Port Gibson, so I am no longer their commanding officer."

"Prisoner, were you in prison with Evans? Is he coming home? Is he alright? What about the letter?"

"Mrs. Atwood, I can answer only one question at a time. I know you're excited about news of your husband, but if you would just let me put my hands down…"

"No! You keep 'em up and where I can see 'em. If you so much as move one hand lower than the other, I'll open you up like a ripe melon in the hot sun, do you understand me?"

"Yes ma'am, I do!" He says with another chuckle, "Please, ask your questions."

"Are you alone?"

"Yes ma'am, I'm alone. I've traveled the last three days alone; no one's seen me, stopped me, or asked me anything."

"Are you armed?"

"Yes ma'am, I've got an old Colt tucked in my back pants waist. It's only got one round left."

"Take it out with two fingers."

"Okay, I'm moving now," he starts to lower his right hand.

"Stop! Use your other hand."

George smiles, "Yes ma'am." He removes the gun with his left hand and holds it out. He likes this woman. "She's smart to know that a man's going to use his familiar hand. She has gotten me to use my off hand. I wonder if she's as pretty as her picture?" He gestures with the gun toward the porch, seeking permission to lay the gun down. With a wave of the shotgun barrel, she motions him forward.

"Why are you alone?"

"Can I lower my hands? My arms are getting awful tire..."

"No, you don't! If you can't hold your hands up, I'll just as soon shoot you! What, are you some weak old man; are you hurt?"

"No ma'am, I'm just plum wore out. I ain't eaten in three days and I walked most the way from Missouri. I tell 'ya Mrs. Atwood, I ain't had an easy time of it, but I did bring you a letter from your husband. I'm hoping that the delivery is at least worth a little food, maybe a night's sleep in the barn?" Lucy Jane says nothing.

"Ain't you got no family to go to?"

"No ma'am." Sensing her softening, he presses the issue, "I won't be here but as long as you say. I can help with things that need fixin' and such, but as soon as you say 'go', I'm gone."

"We'll see about that; let me see the letter."

George reaches for the letter in his coat pocket. "Whoa! Left hand, two fingers, real slow."

He's shaking. This man's scared, or sick; most likely, both. He manages to get the letter out of his jacket and holds it in the moon light for her to see.

"Bring it real slow to the porch, both hands up high, lay it on the porch."

He does as he's instructed, and stands looking up at the T shaped slit in the door.

"Turn around," he does, "walk ten paces from the porch facing the road," he complies. Lucy sees his legs shaking now with his wavering arms. "Stop! Get on your knees," he almost falls, "lay down on your belly, and don't move. If you do, I'll kill you."

Lucy looks at the children on the floor. "How ya'll doing over there?"

"We're good Mama, James's asleep."

"Can you carry him back to bed? I don't think we're in any danger from this man."

"Yes ma'am, I can, and I ain't scared neither."

"Good baby. I'm not scared either. Go on to bed."

Martha Jane struggles to her feet with the sleeping little boy and stumbles to bed.

Lucy looks out the loophole, George hasn't moved. She can hear soft snoring. She closes the loophole, unlatches the door, and steps onto the porch. She goes to either end checking for any danger. George is alone. She looks back to him. He twitches, and she brings the gun to bear on his back, but he's sound asleep. She shakes her head in pity.

She goes inside and lights a lamp, and carries it to the porch. She sits on the steps near the Colt and the letter, checks the pistol; it's unloaded. "The poor man's carrying an unloaded weapon." She picks up the letter, and looks at it.

It is in Evans hand. She trembles. Her eyes roam the darkness. Not seeing anything that's a threat, she leans the shot gun on the step, holding the letter. A gentle sigh of wind blows across her, stirring the light of the lantern and forming the cotton gown to her curves. It feels good as it filters to her skin. She squeezes her legs together, tucks the hem of the gown under her and opens the letter. It reads...

May 23rd, 1863
Alton Prison, Ill.

My dearest wife,

I love and miss you so much. If you have received this, you have done so at the hands of Lieutenant George Paul, a fellow officer and prisoner with me, at least for today. George's circumstances are such that he needs to take the parole and sign the pledge to the Union. His reasons are his, but they are not mine.

I know you are going to be upset when this finds you. You are going to ask, "Why didn't you take the parole?" Please don't be angry. I have told you before, that I am sworn to the Confederacy and cannot break that oath. How can a man swear an oath to two nations? He cannot; he must choose one. I have chosen the country that promises us freedom and liberty; not oppression and fear.

I have lived under the tyranny of the Union. Imprisonment has served to convince me of the worthiness of our cause and the sacred nature of the freedom for which you and I are asked to sacrifice so much. I cannot turn my back on my country and my fellow officers. We are indeed, in our darkest hour.

Lucy, my love, please bear with me. Please catch the vision, our suffering will be but a small moment, then we have the rest of our lives to build the better things for which you so long. They will come my love, but for the moment, I implore you to endure to the end.

Please afford Lieutenant Paul every courtesy of our home. He is in a bad way. He has had a hard time dealing with things here and I do not think he is stable in the head. Your service to him will be paid back by others along the road when I am able to travel to you.

I have to get this to George now, so I must close. He is leaving this hellish place this afternoon. The thought of you and our home and children weakens me so. I am so tempted to sign and be done, but the disgrace I would have to live with every day of my life is too much. Pray, as I do for the end of this war and my time in hell.

I love you; kiss the children for me. I seal this with my kisses and tears.

Your devoted husband,

Evans Atwood

Lucy folds the letter and holds it. She curses Evans, the war, and life in general, but she smiles as she does so. "I, dear husband, will be delighted to 'extend *every* courtesy of our home' to your wayward, and in your opinion cowardly friend; 'every courtesy' indeed." George Paul snores in his sleep on the cold ground. Lucy smiles again and says aloud, "Every courtesy indeed."

20) Steven Wayne

Siege, the Final Days

Beau Gadston and Steven Wayne have exchanged very few words since Steven Wayne's arrival, and those were spoken only in the presence of the women and out of necessity. None have been cordial. Steven Wayne is no longer the affable bumbler that the men make fun of for his flowering, and windy speech; he is precise, to the point, and almost cruel. He was, pre-war, given to naïve innocence and sentimentality, but combat, siege, and Patricia Ann Robinson's betrayal has robbed him of his gentle nature.

He has become an intolerant, confident, focused officer…when sane. As a result, his presence at the Gadston's cave system is no longer desired. He has been pleasant, charming, and there have been no outward displays of violence, but within Steven Wayne the animal seethes below the surface. It can be sensed, and it is fearful.

The Gadstons are relieved on the morning of July 3rd, after three weeks, that Steven Wayne is ordered to return to his troops without delay. Second Lieutenant Martin Wilson has brought the messenger.

"I'm so sorry to see you go," declares Rilla Mae who is the reason for Steven Wayne's being at the Gadston's dwelling. She extends her hand to the rested, rejuvenated officer who smiles, charming her again, gathers her in his arms and kisses her deeply to the discomfort of her mother, father, servants, and Lieutenant Wilson. She breaks away and declares, "Why sir! I've never…, How dare you?"

"Oh, yes you have Rilla Mae, many times, and how dare I? Your invitation to me is always open, you said so yourself!" He stands looking at them, exuding charm, but the animal is lurking just out of sight. None are charmed, most are embarrassed, Beau Gadston is angry, Steven Wayne smiles.

Lieutenant Wilson declares, "I'll wait outside," and leaves, not knowing what to make of his captain's behavior.

Beau Gadston blusters, "Now see here sir!" He's quelled when the animal stare of the feared and fierce Steven Wayne settles on him.

"You have something you wish to say sir?"

"I'm going to report this despicable behavior to your commanding officer!"

Steven Wayne laughs. "You do that sir! I'm certain he'll be most entertained! As a matter of fact, I'll save you the trouble; I'll tell him myself. I'm sure he and the troops will enjoy stories of my time here."

He smiles; the animal has retreated; he bows and says, "Thank you all for your hospitality. It has been a wonderful interlude to death and destruction."

He gathers his gear as the animal surfaces again. He glares at Gadston, and in a fierce deep throated voice inquires, "Do you sir, wish to continue our conversation outside? I do believe we have some unfinished business from my first night here." Gadston is silent. Steven Wayne steps to inches from his face and says so no one else can hear, "If I hear so much as a rumor that you have beaten that boy, I will find you and do what you have done to him ten times over." Mr. Gadston makes no reply.

As quick as the animal was out, it is gone. Steven Wayne, nodding to all, and with a smile says, "Thank you again," turns and leaves.

He steps into the late afternoon sunshine, hefts his gear, and sees two unfamiliar bundles with his. "Lieutenant Wilson, are these your bags?" He shouts to make himself heard. It is much quieter in the caves than outdoors.

When he arrived at Sky Parlor, he was a shell-shocked, and empty man. He spent days inside resting and enjoying the charms of Rilla Mae. Men made fun of him being inside, but Steven Wayne did not care. They had not been, seen, nor done what he had. They were free to think what they may. He needed rest, food, and the soft affections of a beautiful woman, and he had all three in abundance. To hell with all their posturing; if they wished to gauge their manhood against his, they were welcome to put on a Gray coat and stand a post.

"No sir, a slave boy left them, saying they were for you."

"Ruff," Steven Wayne says. The name is lost in the concussion of the ceaseless bombardment. Wilson steps closer to his commanding officer and shouts,

"What sir? I didn't hear you."

Steven Wayne, waves off the question. Gesturing to the bags, he asks, "What are they?"

Wilson, tired of shouting too, does not answer, but stoops to open the bags and reveal their contents. They are filled with food taken from the Gadston larder, enough for a feast for many men.

Stephen Wayne gestures to Martin to secure the bags and carry them. Wilson nods, re-ties, hefts them, and falls in alongside Steven Wayne. "I see you still have the charm for the ladies sir," he shouts.

Steven Wayne nods without comment. It's too much effort. Instead he yells, "Congratulations on your promotion lieutenant; it is well deserved."

Newly elected 2nd Lieutenant Martin Wilson touches his hand to his hat and mouths, "Thank you sir." Steven Wayne nods and returns the casual salute. They walk down the road off the hill and back to the garrison.

The regimental area is worse than it was before Steven Wayne left, and his company is in terrible shape with the exception of Lieutenant Wilson's command. His troops are well organized, neat, and ready to fight in spite of being bombarded for over a month. They come to attention around their fire when he approaches.

Steven Wayne is embarrassed. While spending three weeks in luxury, his men were on short rations, with little water. They are dirty, lice ridden, and exhausted. Yet, they show the proper courtesy.

He is further surprised to have forgotten their names! The faces are familiar, but the names are gone. He shakes his head as if to jar them loose. "What are their names?" He tries to remember, but it won't come. "Men," he nods as they slide around the fire to make room for him. There are nondescript pieces of meat on a spit over the fire. "What's cooking?"

The men look at each other. Something is different about their company commander. "Sir," says one of the men who Steven Wayne thinks might be named Briggs, "them there chunks are the last of the horse we were able to butcher the other day, and the other two critters are rats sir."

"Rats! We're reduced to eating rats? My God, have things gotten that bad?"

"Sir, we've been eating rats for weeks. Are you alright sir?" Asks a man who Steven Wayne recognizes but through a fog.

"Who are you?"

The man looks puzzled. The others stare into the fire and are silent; uncomfortable, not knowing how to handle the situation. Wilson saves the captain by saying, "Moss," to the man, "the captain's worked his charms on another lady, and she's gifted us with vittles to last a long while if we don't eat them all tonight!" He holds the two bags of food out and adds, "Let's hear it for the captain!" He leads them in a chorus of "Huzzahs".

Corporal Moss is relieved and sets to the task of sorting and cooking. It doesn't take long for men from other units to gather. Moss divides the rations into four, one each for the platoons under Captain Culpepper's command.

Steven Wayne is feeling strange. As the pounding of the incoming shells increases, backed by the percussion of outgoing artillery, he becomes more and more disoriented. He's holding on to the log he is sitting on.

Wilson notices and asks, "Captain Culpepper, are you alright sir? Can I get you something?"

Steven Wayne shakes his head, and stares at the fire.

Colonel Reynolds, when the odors of the cooking greens, ham, and beans reach him, is lured to the fire. He sees Steven Wayne, "Captain Culpepper," the colonel hails, "it is good to see you back! How are you?"

Steven Wayne does not respond. He is transfixed by the fire; looking at something no one else sees. It's clear that his mind is elsewhere. The men are uncomfortable for their captain. Lieutenant Wilson, standing near him, nudges Steven Wayne to call him back from wherever he's gone. Steven Wayne doesn't notice. Martin knees his commander again.

Steven Wayne leaps to his feet, grabs Martin by the throat with his left hand while his right whips out his pistol which is cocked and shoved under Martin's chin in an instant, and screams, "Don't you ever kick me again! Do you hear me? Never, never again!" Lieutenant Wilson is reaching for his pistol when Colonel Reynolds steps in; grabs Culpepper around the waist and shouts, "Captain, cease this behavior at once!" He lifts and swings him around clear of the fire and onto the ground.

Culpepper bolts to his feet, charges the colonel, when Wilson meets him with his pistol as well.

Steven Wayne draws up short, smiles, and says, "What's this?" No one speaks. The men puzzle at the transformation Steven Wayne has made from demon to angel.

"Colonel, I am so sorry for my behavior. It's going to take me some time to adjust to the noise and conditions. I have to admit sir, being back is a bit of a shock. Please accept my sincerest apologies sir."

"And if it had been one of the men; what would you have done?"

"I, uh, I…, I'm not sure what I…," Steven Wayne stammers.

"Captain, report to the command bunker. I need to brief you with regard to your command, and the requirements of the regiment."

"Sir, I am so…"

"Captain Culpepper that order is to be acted on now sir, without hesitation!"

"Yes sir, I'm sor…"

"Not another word! Do you understand your orders sir?"

"Yes sir!"

"Then I suggest you execute them!"

"Yes sir," salutes Steven Wayne, and leaves without his gear.

"Private Johnson," calls Lieutenant Wilson.

"Sir."

"Take the captain's gear to the command bunker. Set it outside and come back."

"Yes sir," says Johnson, who salutes and gathers the gear.

"Don't dally none boy," said Moss, "it's vittles before long!"

The colonel looks at Wilson and asks, "You don't want him back in your area lieutenant?"

"It's not that sir; the captain will be a mite embarrassed facing us. He's welcome back, we all make mistakes, and he's as tired as the rest of us, but if he ain't comfortable coming back; well, I just thought it would be easier on him."

"Good thinking lieutenant. You're a good officer."

Wilson's glad for the bright sun so that the men won't see his face redden, "Thank you sir. He's a good man."

The colonel smiles, braces himself to attention, and says, "Very well lieutenant; carry on."

Wilson and the men spring to attention and salute the colonel as Lieutenant Wilson says, "Yes sir, thank you sir."

The salute is returned, "As you were men," and turns away.

"Sir," Wilson calls, "may I get one of the men to bring a plate of food for you?"

"That's thoughtful lieutenant, you may; the smell is about to kill me," he smiles and walks away. The colonel looks worried. The men think it's the altercation with their captain, but it is much more.

After he's out of ear shot, someone asks, "Lieutenant, what the hell's wrong with Captain Culpepper? He seems like he's a wild animal one minute and good ole Stevie Wayne the next. He scared the hell out of me sir!"

There are murmurs of agreement. Wilson says, "I don't know men; he ain't the same man who led us here that's for sure. He's different."

"Time on that hill did something to him," says someone else.

"No, I think whatever happened was before he left. I think he's lost." Martin Wilson says as he looks in the direction of the command bunker. "I'm glad I'm not in that bunker," he thinks, then out loud, "Is it ready yet Moss, I'm starving."

Steven Wayne is waiting outside for the arrival of Colonel Reynolds. He had gone in and was greeted by the other officers. They were pleasant, kidded him about his recent duty, and his dalliance with the local lady, but there was tension that made him uncomfortable, so he excused himself, preferring his own company. He's certain he is losing his mind, and it frightens him. He stands in the sunlight and wonders, "Am I crazy, or is everyone else?"

Colonel Reynolds approaches; Steven Wayne leaps to his feet and salutes him. The colonel returns the salute, and brusquely says, "Come in captain."

Steven Wayne follows the colonel into the bunker. As they enter the main chamber, Colonel Reynolds says to the other officers, "Gentlemen, please excuse us."

There's a chorus of, "Yes sirs," as they make their way past the colonel and Steven Wayne.

When the chamber is vacant the sound and shaking of the bombardment is less pronounced and the silence is eerie. Dread hangs heavy here. Steven Wayne looks around the lamp lit room.

The ceiling has been shored up with timbers and is inches from his head. There several desks trenched into the walls for work stations, and another chamber further back that serves as the colonel's quarters. The usual office accoutrements are visible, pens, ink wells, and papers which seem to be everywhere with no semblance of order. It appears to be a place under siege; a place where war is the subject of all conversation.

Steven Wayne stands in front of the colonel's field desk and awaits his fate. The colonel is studying a map of the fortifications. He picks up a sheaf of papers and thumbs through them; finds the one he wants, pulls it out, and turns to Steven Wayne. "Captain, we're in a helluva situation here."

"Sir, I'm sorry; it will never happen again, I…"

"Captain, I don't give two hoots in hell about your boorish behavior in front of your men. They still respect you," nodding and gesturing to a private who is standing at the door to the bunker with two steaming plates of the best food either man has seen in months. He brings the plates in and sets them down, leaving as quickly as he came, "as is evidenced here by their generosity." Before Steven Wayne can speak, he continues, "They respect you as a combat leader, but that all is a moot point now." He pauses, looking at the floor.

"Sir, I don't understand."

A long silence causes Steven Wayne to struggle to hold still. He feels as if he's being held prisoner. The silence stretches as the colonel continues to look at the paper. Steven Wayne fidgets.

"It's all moot now captain," repeats Colonel Reynolds, more to himself than to Steven Wayne.

The colonel raises his head and looks at Steven Wayne. There were tears, on his face. Colonel Reynolds is a defeated man. "Negotiations for surrender are to begin this afternoon at 1500 hours between General Grant and General Pemberton. Generals Montgomery and Bowen met this morning under a flag of truce to make the initial arrangements. Pemberton will hold out for favorable terms, but we are in no position to bargain. We have killed many Yankees, but our supplies are depleted, and our forces are diminished. We bury too many every day. We're beaten. It's over; probably tomorrow."

"Sir, I can't believe it!" Steven Wayne hopes that his words do not betray his joy. To cover the possibility, he asks, "What terms sir, do we know?"

"We are to surrender the fortifications and the city, and in exchange for our arms and colors, we are to be paroled and sent home. We will have to sign an oath to not take up arms, but there will be no oath of allegiance. We will be able to serve the Confederacy in other ways, but for here, we are done, defeated. It has cost us much." The colonel shakes his head.

Steven Wayne fights to keep a proper air about him, but is struggling to not smile. "So, we'll be surrendered tomorrow sir, the 4th of July?"

"Yes captain; ironic isn't it?"

"Yes sir, ironic, that is just what I was thinking," which is not true. He is thinking that he's being paroled on the day of Patricia Ann's wedding, and the irony has nothing to do with losing a war, but independence from the army. He'll be free; he'll be going home! He will see Patricia Anne, and won't that be a scene?

"Captain, you are dismissed to prepare your men." Steven Wayne makes no response. "Captain, did you hear me?"

Steven Wayne snaps from his dreams of humiliation for Patricia Anne, and starts, "Oh, sorry sir, I'm shocked by the news. I can't believe it's over."

"We're all shocked and angry. This is going to be hard on the men. They will be looking to you for leadership. Are you capable of it captain?"

"Yes sir, I am. I feel sorry for you and all the field officers who have given so much to this cause. I am just sad, shocked and sad; I am sorry sir."

"It's to be understood captain, now go, enjoy your meal, and prepare your men. Tell them and help them to be ready to go out with dignity. We may be beaten, but we are proud of our country and our cause. Tell them that for me captain, will you please?"

"Yes sir, I will. Will there be anything else sir?"

"No captain, that will be all; you're dismissed."

Steven Wayne salutes, turns, eager to get out of the cave and into the sunlight. He takes his plate and hurries out.

"Captain, will you please send in the rest of the staff?"

Not turning back, and with a mouth full of ham, "Yes sir, with pleasure." What a pleasure it will be! In less than a day, no more than two, he will be headed home. He is preparing for a war of another sort; a battle he will win because he has right on his side, and revenge in his heart.

21) Patricia Anne Robinson and Horatio Thaddeus Yeller

Sarah Anne, and Hubert Rodney Robinson

Of Spring Dale, Shiloh, Arkansas

Do cordially invite you to the wedding of their daughter

Patricia Anne Robinson

to

Horatio Thaddeus Yeller

Son of the Honorable Congressman

Clifford Wade, and Lola Bye Yeller

To be held at Spring Dale, Shiloh, Arkansas

On

Saturday, July the 4th, 1863

At 4:00 o'clock in the afternoon

The continued honor of your presence

Is requested at a reception to be held

Immediately after the ceremony

The Reverend Samuel Leroy Claiborne of

The Friendship Baptist Church, Shiloh, Arkansas

Is to officiate

Patricia Anne Robinson is ecstatic on her wedding day - almost. If she can only get through the morning without being sick again she will be able to enjoy the festivities, "I mean it is *my* day isn't it? I should not have to deal with this hateful sickness."

Although it has occurred to her that Horatio Thaddeus Yeller may be the cause of her daily nausea of the past two weeks, she refuses to accept it. It must be nerves and stress of the wedding and feast for the one hundred plus guests that has caused her malady.

Her mother, Sarah Anne, does not approve of the union, or the circumstances surrounding it, and has taken to her bed and bottle. If not for the slaves on the house staff, nothing would have been accomplished at all. Their motivation is that Rodney Robinson will put them to field work if the wedding comes off in any way less than perfect.

The house is crowded with guests. Many have traveled from all over the state and beyond, which, in the midst of a war, is no mean feat. The most notable attendee is, of course, the Honorable Clifford Wade Yeller, former member of the U.S. Congress, and now a member of the Confederate Congress from which he is absent at this critical time. Lee is massing the forces of Virginia for a war ending push in the east and is at a place called Gettysburg in Pennsylvania, while the Army of Tennessee is besieged at Vicksburg. It is a time that could decide the fate of the south, and he is not in place to assist. He and Mrs. Yeller pleaded with their prospective daughter-in-law to postpone the nuptials until a more appropriate time. The bride-to-be would hear nothing of it and let it be known that she would take it as a personal insult if the congressman did not attend, or was even late.

Such behavior does not faze Congressman Yeller; he has dealt with pouting, tantrum throwing politicians, but it does not settle well with Lola Bye Yeller who is not accustomed to being ordered about and made demands of by a mere girl, and a selfish one at that. Neither parent can resist the pleadings of Thaddeus who was in a state of panic when they suggested that the betrothed couple should put off the wedding. He is also furious that his parents have spoken to him of the common way Patricia Anne dealt with Steven Wayne Culpepper, the son of the banker who oversees the Yeller holdings in Washington County, and hence, a necessary friend.

Thaddeus, well coached, defends all objections concerning his bride-to-be to his family who think she is not much better than a common… well, a common woman. Thaddeus having heard of the siege of Vicksburg, and knowing the Arkansas 15th to be there, declares that Steven Wayne is probably dead, and if not, will to be taken prisoner when Vicksburg falls.

The congressman reminds him of the cause of the Confederacy and that his brothers are defending the ideals and principles that have made the Yeller family for three generations one of the wealthiest in the state if not the nation.

Thaddeus rants against the Confederacy, "I don't give two hoots in hell about slavery, ideals, or principles. I want Patricia Anne, and I want her now, and we will make no concession to this stupid war."

The Yellers, not wanting to lose their youngest son, since the older ones may be dead, shake their heads and relent.

Patricia Anne has been careful to school her boy/man in what to say. She has spent many a night drilling it into him when there is sufficient blood in his brain to absorb such details, and the all important question to ask, "When will the trust be available?"

Mr. and Mrs. Yeller smile. With the war raging and banking funds depreciating and at risk, they have liquated all trusts and converted the funds to gold which are now secure overseas awaiting the outcome of the war when they will be redistributed. "The trust is available as soon as all the stipulations are met."

This satisfies the not too bright Thad and will appease and calm Patsy Anne. Mr. Yeller is guilty of a sin of omission. There are no funds and the trust stipulates that there must be. He will have to deal with the consequences at a later date, but in the mean time, the congressman has leverage over his son and his bride, and he's satisfied. It will do Thad good to learn to dso for himself and it will test Patricia Anne's devotion. Mr. and Mrs. Yeller have a pretty good idea which will get the most attention.

July 4th dawns beautiful and bright. It is a perfect day for a wedding. The South no longer celebrates this day as one of independence; that is now reserved for either March 4th, the date the original seven states seceded, or May 6th, the day Arkansas joined the Confederacy. The invitees are accustomed to a celebration on this day so it is fitting for a wedding.

Spring Dale is located on a hill that allows for an ever present breeze which today is cooling the guests through the large, open doors and windows. The house, normally magnificent, today is regal.

To come into the massive main entrance is a breathtaking experience. The doors are carved native oak with glass stained and leaded so that at night, the windows from the inside appeared to be made of gold. The entry and foyer are Italian marble, cut so that it appears to be one slab. The foyer is large enough to accommodate the honored guests seated in rows of red velvet and gold trimmed chairs. The lesser rank of souls will have to do with attending on the front veranda which is covered and cooler than being in the house but is less desirable for viewing of the ceremony. The veranda's primary advantage is that it is nearer the reception area which is down the fourteen steps onto the front lawn.

There, under the lane of oaks in the shade are set white canvas tents with every form of southern cuisine spread on numerous white clothed tables. Other tents are set with tables and chairs for the guests to sit and enjoy their food and beverage which is legion. Each table is attended by one or more slaves tutored by threat of stripes on their black backs to serve and clear as is proper. There is no joy on their faces as they wait for the ceremonies to commence, but will be all aglow when the wealthy white faces descend on the reception area.

Acquiring the food cost a small fortune, but the money paid for alcohol rivals the gross national product of the Confederacy. With the war, all potent potables are extravagant, valued as gold, and Rodney wants to see them flow. Such extravagance is a testament to the Robinson wealth and ability to overcome the inconvenience of a war economy.

Spring Dale's dominate feature is arguably the most gorgeous staircase ever built. It is in fact, two staircases, one right, one left, connected by an balcony that spans the width of the entry. The cases make sweeping turns as they descend into the wide and spacious foyer below.

Each banister, and there are four of them, is a work of art, being made of rich, native oak, inlaid with darker imported mahogany which is in turn inlaid with mother of pearl. The banisters are barely visible as pink ribbons entwine the right staircase, and blue for the left. Both are covered with Magnolia blossoms procured that morning and are intertwined with laurels of gardenia. The perfume of the room is exquisite.

Soft music is flowing from behind a wall under the center of the balcony where an orchestra pit is hidden. The music ramps to something sounding very similar to "Ruffles and Flourishes" as Hubert Rodney Robinson dressed in a gray suit cut in the style of the uniform of the CSA, but without rank, descends the blue ribbon bedecked stair case while Sarah Anne Robinson in a camellia pink, full length gown with a bodice designed to display her still marvelous and abundant features, simultaneously descends the opposite pink stair case to a polite ripple of applause from the gathered guest. As their left feet strike the floor of the foyer turned gallery, the seated guest turn their attention to Congressman and Mrs. Yeller as they begin their choreographed descent of the gender specific staircases.

The congressman is wearing a true uniform befitting his rank as a full colonel and a member of the congress of the Confederate States of America, while Mrs. Yeller is wearing a full length, flowing gown of the palest yellow, recently brought from France. It has a light, matching shawl draped over her arms. The applause is louder, more polite, and longer for the congressman and his bride, but if Rodney and Sarah Anne notice, they do not betray the fact as the two families greet each other with embraces and handshakes to the rising crescendo of applause.

Over the noise, Congressman Yeller, with his best "I'm running for office" smile, says, "Robinson, you've done yourself proud today! The house and settings are as near perfect as a mortal could ask," bowing to Sarah Anne, "ma'am I cannot imagine the genius that it took to orchestrate such a happening. Why, you must be exhausted!"

"Sir, you do flatter me," Sarah Anne says as she performs a deep curtsey to the congressman, "it was nothing at all."

"Oh, nonsense dear," blusters Lola Bye Yeller, "you must be near losing your mind from all this work. Why, I do admire you so!" Mrs. Yeller then takes Mrs. Robinson by the hands and kisses her on the cheek followed by another embrace. Mrs. Yeller wonders at the perfume of Mrs. Robinson; it smells strangely of bourbon.

"You just have no idea," gushes Sarah Anne. The two couples, long associated through their slave arrangement, shake hands and hug once again, then part to assume their seats on the respective bride or groom side of the isle.

A processional march by Pachelbel, Canon in D major, begins to play as the bride's maids and groomsmen begin to descend their appropriate staircases. The ladies ranging from well founded to skinny as a rail are all dressed in the same camellia pink as the bride's mother. The gentlemen are dressed similar to Mr. Robinson and the congressman. They file off left and right to their traditional locations. A drum roll, then a martial cadence announces the groom dressed in confederate gray which he loathes, but would have dressed in a pink pinafore if Patricia Anne had so ordered. He steps to the top of the stairs and makes his descent, assuming his place at the altar.

The Reverend Samuel Claiborne bedecked in his finest robes, steps from around the staircase where the orchestra is playing and takes his position with his hands piously folded over his testament held at his breast. He assumes a pose looking skyward as if the Lord Jesus himself will descend any moment as an invited guest. The reverend is so intense that not a few attendees follow his gaze hoping to see what he sees. Reverend Claiborne is perspiring profusely and seems on the verge of faint. All assume he is having a personal spiritual moment, a communion with deity as he sways gently back and forth.

Somewhere in the procession, pomp, and ceremony, Rodney Robinson, the beaming father of the bride, has slipped out the back and up the stairs to now stand with his daughter at the exact center of the balcony. There is a ripple of applause at the appearance of the bride who is garbed in pure white to be sure. Her gown is the one her mother wore on her wedding day and her mother before her. It is old, and although the seamstress who fitted it to Patricia Anne did a wonderful job, she only had so much to work with since Patricia Anne did not receive the bosom endowment of her mother. She is radiant none the less with at least a thousand *faux* pearls sewn or attached in some way to the dress. She displays a smile to match the pearls and looks every bit the virginal bride.

Not all eyes are on her; many are exchanging knowing looks and whispers concerning her recent antics in divesting herself of Steven Wayne for Thaddeus Yeller. No amount of white applied in any manner can remove the stains to one's reputation that have been so callously applied by one's own hand.

The father and his radiant daughter move to the right, pink draped staircase and began their descent as the *Wedding March* by Wagner begins to play. The guests rise to their feet with "oohs, and ahhs"; moved by the flowing, graceful entry. With a fifteen foot train, the bride seems to float on a cloud. The music and aroma from the flowers filling the gallery seem to lift and carry her along.

Thaddeus cannot take his eyes off her. He steps to the front of the altar, still facing his bride who is aglow from the heat, the champagne, and the moment.

Mr. Robinson turns with the bride to face Thaddeus who extends his eager hands and the father places those of his daughter into Thad's in the gesture of giving away the bride. He turns and takes his seat next to the bride's mother.

Patricia Anne and Horatio Thaddeus stand for long moments looking into each other's eyes as if for the first time. They both beam with joy. If you did not know the circumstances of their union, and the wiliness and cunning of the bride, you could not have kept from issuing a tear or two. It is a wonderful, touching moment.

The couple turns to face Reverend Claiborne who is not there. In the grandeur of the bride's entry, and with the heat of the afternoon, and no doubt being unaccustomed to champagne in any quantity much less being exposed to the effervescent wine in such generous amounts, the right reverend has, vestments and all, slumped to the floor behind the altar unconscious. His visionary experience having been alcohol induced.

The orchestra, unable to see around the wall separating them from the gallery, has stopped playing on signal as the bride and groom take their places. The guests are seated, but when the ceremony does not start, an impatient murmur can be heard. Questions of, "What's happened", and "What's going on" from the guests on the veranda who cannot see Samuel Leroy Claiborne reposed on the floor; overwhelm the now general, low toned remarks from the guests seated closer.

The slave attendants are desperate. They know that they will bear the brunt of reprisal for the good reverend's indiscretion. The leader, a woman of no small size known as Miss Bessie, shouts to the orchestra leader in a stage whisper that can be heard at least ten rows back in the gallery, "Play something!"

The poor conductor is screened from the proceedings and is without a clue as to what is happening on the other side of the wall. As one does in emergency situations, he falls back on what he knows; what his training and experience have taught him. He taps on the music stand with his wand; the members of the orchestra give him their full attention and as his hand falls, burst forth with *Nearer My God to Thee.* It is, of course, the poorest choice the conductor could have made from his vast repertoire of music.

No one seems to know what to do with the solemn, slumbering man of God. The wedding party, twittering with laughter, stands in confusion looking from one to another, and at the passed out drunk on the floor still staring heavenward. Patricia Anne, fearing all will be lost, and not wanting to lose her moment in the sun, takes action. Being closest to the reverend, she steps around the altar and begins to kick the reposed saint, shouting, "Get up you lush; you're not going to ruin my wedding!"

Whether coincidence, or on purpose, or intervention of the gods, Miss Bessie who had directed the conductor, and can see what is happening whereas the poor man responsible cannot, is beside herself with the poor choice of music, and declares in a shout, "No, you idiot; something else!"

Without any more direction than that, and not being able to see, but can hear the rising noise of riot, the man again falls back on his training, and decides that since the *Star Spangled Banner* is no longer appropriate to be played to calm disruptive situations, he will play the popular southern anthem, *Dixie*, which he does.

Dixie is a fine tune, arousing feelings for the new country, but for the current circumstances playing out on the floor of the foyer on the other side of the wall out of the view of the poor conductor, it is far too rousing, and most inappropriate.

Patricia Anne is just starting her assault when the first strains of *Dixie* burst forth and serve to increase her vigor. All who have remained in their seats as the commotion began, leap to their feet in patriotic fervor, singing their hearts out and better to view Patsy's kicks as the martial beat increases.

There are few who do not take joy in the comic spectacle of Patricia as she flails away with both feet, skirts of her gown held above her knees, train yet extending down the aisle, cursing like a field hand at the unconscious man of God curled in sweet repose on the cool marble floor.

Thaddeus, being the next closest to the scene, and much to his credit, does not, "kick the living shit out of the bastard", as his lovely, tender, bride directs; instead moves to restrain her. "Now, now, my sweet," he says in a calm, reassuring voice, "all is not lost," as he places his hands on Patsy's upper arms, near her shoulders, and attempts to restrain her and move her away from her victim. He pulls, attempting to guide the now red faced bride, when she thrashes her shoulders back and forth to free herself from Thad's grip, causing his hands to jerk down her arms while still resting on the sleeves of the gown.

Patricia Anne is not as well endowed as her mother, and the bodice of the dress, holds her, but just. As Thad's hands pull down the sleeves, the dress follows, penning her arms to her sides but with the additional result of slipping over her inadequate bosom, exposing her charms which swing in time with her well placed kicks as the resounding strains of *Dixie* reach the refrain, "…look away, look away…", which, of course, no one does.

Patricia Anne begins to make efforts to raise the front of the gown to cover her exposed features, but with her arms pinned, her struggles only exacerbate the situation and cause her to thrash even more. As she tries to free herself from her well intentioned groom, she manages to knock him off balance and down he goes with his right hand tangled in the sleeve of her gown which he, by instinct, grabs to break his fall. The result is a shower of pearls exploding off the dress and scattering about the marble floor where Thad now lays with the reverend. Patricia Anne, to her credit, does not miss a beat as she now alternates kicking the reverend and then her betrothed, one foot dedicated to each.

The double assault is short lived. As the red faced, exposed, cursing bride grows more furious with the deteriorating situation, her kicks became more vigorous, and as she lifts her feet to kick, pearls roll into the vacated spots on the floor where she intends to step down and as she plants one foot to swing with the other, she too joins the now writhing heap on the floor.

Thaddeus, scrambling to regain his feet, cannot for the scattering of pearls, and Patricia is unable to do anything with her arms penned to her side, but lay there and scream curses that the servers on the front lawn hear. Mrs. Yeller saves the day as she whips off the yellow accessory shawl and sweeps the floor in front of her enabling her to move to the rescue of her was-to-be-daughter-in-law, cover her, and help her to her feet.

Mr. Robinson, and Congressman Yeller, following in the clearing wake of Mrs. Yeller, go to the aid of their children. The congressman assists his son to his feet, but Mr. Robinson's aim is not to assist his daughter in rising, but to staunch the flow of profanity issuing from her. He clasps his right hand over Patricia Anne's mouth which results in an even more violent thrashing of the girl's shoulders and the subsequent entry of her father's fingers between her teeth as she bites down hard.

The resulting cry of, "You bitch! You bit me," could be heard, it was declared later, all the way to Benton County.

All the while, the guests are in a state of shock not knowing what to do, or what to say, or how to do, or say it. There is bedlam and turmoil throughout the house as servants run, guests gasp and shout, family curses and wrestles, and the band plays on, "Oh, I wish I were in the land o' cotton...".

Mrs. Robinson, who now has a glass of champagne from who knows where, is hysterical with laughter, as are several guests who know the true nature of the bride. Laughter is said to be cruel, and so it is this day. None laugh harder or longer than Steven Wayne Culpepper II, the father of the jilted suitor who is at this very moment being issued his parole after the fall of Vicksburg. Steven Wayne's mother refused to attend, and senior has done so only out of obligation to his two clients. He rejoices in the shame of Patricia Anne. He wishes that his son could be here to witness this but even so, what a story he will have to tell when he does arrive!

22) Evans

Johnson Island, Illinois

July 20th, 1863

Johnson Island, Illinois Prisoner of War Camp

We have been here for over a month, and this is the first time I have had my journal. It was confiscated the day we arrived. We were kept on the wharf at Sandusky, Ohio, on Lake Erie with a good view of Johnson's Island a mile off the coast where the prison is sitting in a calm blue ocean, but it's all fresh water. We marveled at the sight.

We loaded on the *Little Eastern* and made the slow journey to our new prison. The gates of the stockade are a few yards from the Lake, so we pulled in close and waded ashore since the wharf was still under construction. In the winter we are told, you can walk to town over the ice. None here look forward to the cold, but the frozen lake will be a sight.

We came ashore and were strip-searched again. I told the guard, "There's nothing left to steal; the boys at Alton got it all five 'inspections' ago." It made him mad so he confiscated my journal, and my filthy underwear, the only possessions I have of any value. I don't know why he took the underwear, but I hope he gets lice.

He brought my journal back after a few days and said the commandant was through with it. I was glad to have not written some things in it. General Thompson asked me about its contents and I was able to tell him that it contained nothing about activities, or names other than the autograph pages.

All in all this is a first rate place compared to where we were. We have blankets, bunks with straw mattresses, only six to a room. The prison was built as a prison, so it's new, but poorly built. The buildings are constructed with green, knotty boards nailed to uprights and are shrinking as they cure, leaving gaps in the walls. Those who survived the past winter thank God it was a mild one, but they are already dreading the coming season.

The rations are better here. There are not as many of us, but I fear that is to change. As the war goes on, there will be more prisoners.

There is a hospital, but no small pox; thank God. The island is wooded, so fuel is not a problem if they let us cut it. Our ration of fuel will have to increase if we are to survive the winter.

I miss the water detail. We have wells that serve, but are inadequate to allow for washing of bodies or clothes. We are becoming vermin infested. I miss getting clean in the river. I also am bored. The water detail was a diversion which I do not have here. I have nothing to do, nor anything to read.

"I see you're writing in your journal again."

There is no mistaking that voice. I look up for Major Traweek, "Yes sir, and how are you today?"

"I am doing well lieutenant for a man denied his freedom and the right to choose; how are you?"

"Sharing the same sentiments sir; trying to take my mind off things back home."

"Bad?"

"No sir, well, yes sir; no one has died, it's that things are so hard on my family. They're having a tough time of it."

"You got a letter?"

"Yes sir, yesterday," I pull it out of my pants pocket. It's growing hot in Illinois and wearing of uniform jackets has been suspended, if we have one to wear. "She wants me to take the pledge and come home."

"I don't blame her. It must be hard for a woman to be alone with, how many little ones?"

"Two sir."

"Yes, two," he continues, "and have to provide for, and support them alone, but we are all called upon to sacrifice for the cause of our country. What are your feelings about her request?"

"I understand her concerns for her safety. She's a beautiful woman, living alone in the cabin in an area that is anti-secession so there are many men who would love to have her, and are scheming to do just that."

"I see; what do you propose to do?"

"Escape."

"Oh?"

"I cannot accept parole and I can't sit here while my family suffers. Since the exchange has collapsed, the only avenue that answers is escape."

"I see, but how do you expect to accomplish this? You can't tunnel to the mainland. Once you get out of the compound, you'll have to have a boat, unless you think you can swim to shore."

"No, I'm not that good a swimmer, but I have the beginning of a plan."

Major Traweek nods, indicating me to continue.

"The *Little Eastern* is here two and sometimes three times a day. I've been thinking of commandeering the vessel and escaping with as many as it will hold."

Traweek twirled an unlit cigar; deep in thought. "Lieutenant, General Thompson wants to gather the officers this afternoon. I suggest you broach the subject with him at that time. What do you think?"

"I look forward to it sir, thank you for including me."

"That's why I sought you out. The general requested you."

"I'm flattered sir."

The major smiles and ambles off singing a song popular on the western front, *Short Rations*. I smile at the words. I would rather be on half rations than locked up and full. Maybe that time will come soon.

I approach the officers gathered around a table between buildings. They notice me and wave a welcome. I move about the group, greeting old acquaintances, and making new ones. I am the most junior officer present, and feel honored to be so. There are senior officers I have not seen before; several colonels, and a new group of generals.

Major Traweek makes the introductions, "General Trimble, may I present 2nd Lieutenant Evans Atwood of the 15th Arkansas?"

Major General Isaac Trimble is honored and revered by some and loathed by others. Since his first wound, he has not been in command and was at Gettysburg as a volunteer on General Ewell's staff when he confronted his superior pleading with him to move forward while the Yankees were on the run and take the higher ground of Cemetery Hill, but Ewell had just looked at him without response. When Trimble had begged for a unit to take the hill, Ewell had ignored him. He, Trimble, then stated that, "...a blind man could see..." the necessity of taking the hill and once again pled for a regiment and he would do it. Ewell is quoted as saying, "When I need advice from a junior officer, I'll ask for it," at which time Trimble threw his sword at Ewell's feet and left. Ewell later admitted his temerity had cost the campaign and apologized to Lee. It was the most significant decision of the campaign. He was captured when he was wounded in the left leg, which had to be amputated. He's older, close to sixty, and in poor health. "I hear good things about you; that you were valuable in gathering intelligence at Alton Prison; do you think you can do the same here?"

"Yes sir, I can do more than that."

"Oh?"

"Lieutenant Atwood has an idea Gentlemen," interjects Major Traweek, "but with your permission general, allow me to introduce the rest of our gathering."

"By all means major; excuse my anxiousness, please continue."

I am already looking at the other general officers present.

"Lieutenant, this is Brigadier General James Archer..."

General Archer I have heard of. He is called the "Little Gamecock" for his small size but fierce attitude in battle. He has a full black beard that comes to a point at his mid-chest. He served with General A.P. Hill's cavalry and was captured at Gettysburg due to being left behind for ill health, becoming the first general captured.

"...Brigadier General William Jones..."

I nod at the handsome, young man. His face is almost overwhelmed with a sweeping, thick, brown moustache that engulfs his mouth, but I can see he is smiling.

"Lieutenant, I believe you were a private when I commanded the Arkansas troops at Corinth, Mississippi. I am anxious to hear of your battles, wounds, and capture."

"Thank you sir, it's very good to see you again; I only wish the circumstances were better."

"Yes, indeed."

"...John R. Jones..."

Traweek did not introduce Jones by rank. General Jones has been accused twice of cowardice. He has an angry expression as if he hates everyone. He glares at me.

"...and of course, you already know General Jeff Thompson."

General Thompson stands and offers his hand which I take. "Here we are again Atwood."

"Yes sir, we are."

General Thompson is a general only in the Missouri militia. He has campaigned to have the rank honored by the Confederacy. He picks up where General Trimble left off by asking, "Tell us Lieutenant of your idea that Major Traweek referred to."

"Yes sir," I address the body of officers, "Gentlemen, my idea is simple. We outnumber the garrison ten to one. The guards are lax because they know if we manage to get out the gate, or over the walls, we will have nowhere to go but into the woods of the island."

"We have all observed this, what of it?" Jones grumbles. "Do you have a plan or not?"

"Yes sir, I'm trying to make certain that all are aware of what we are facing so we can all participate in the decision." There is mumbled ascent, so I continue, "My scheme will require much planning, perfect timing, and courage." Jones responds with an angry snort.

"The steam ship *Little Eastern* makes two to three trips a day from Sandusky. Two trips a day are for personnel transfers, bringing new prisoners, and a change of guards in the barracks. When she makes three trips, the third is at noon, and is a supply run. It is the most confusing time of the day. The guards are occupied with transfers, shift changes, loading and unloading. We prisoners mill about the yard and are not closely watched. That gentlemen, is the ideal time to strike."

"To what end?" General Jones asks with impatience.

"John, please, let's hear the man out," says General Trimble.

Jones falls silent and I continue, "That's when the guards and the prison are most vulnerable. If we are organized into commands with say, fifty men per, each directed by one of the general staff, we could overwhelm the gate, move to the wharf, commandeer the *Little Eastern* and make our escape with few or no causalities."

The generals look at each other nodding and there is a murmur of approval from the other officers. "I like it," says General Thompson. As a cavalry leader, the idea of a charge strikes a chord; he's all smiles, "but Atwood, once we have two hundred and fifty to three hundred men on that vessel, where do we go?

"Yes sir that is the tricky part..."

"Lieutenant," I face General Beall, "once we have commandeered this boat, what will we do then? We are all ground soldiers with no knowledge of the nautical."

"Yes sir that will be no problem..."

"Oh and how is that?"

"I worked on the steam boat *Dardanelle* on the White and Mississippi rivers, and stood my share of watches. I believe I can handle that part sir."

"And should you fall?" Trimble asks.

A colonel with blond hair says, "I too have river boat experience; I'm your back up lieutenant." There are hands raised and comments made about various abilities. We have a crew.

"Once underway and clear of the island, we cross into Canada. We have to plan that the *Little Eastern* will not have sufficient fuel on board for us to cross Lake Erie to the Canadian border. I suggest that we, when work details are dispatched to cut fire wood, stack cords close to the lake for ease of moving in the coming winter months. When we are aboard, it will be a simple matter to put into the island and load sufficient fuel."

"How do we keep such a plan secret?" General Beall asks.

"The key gentlemen," spoke up General Thompson, "as we did at Alton, is to pick the men we can trust and who are willing to swear an oath of secrecy."

"What kind of plan were you working on at Alton general?" General Beall asks.

"We were building a tunnel sir. For security, we will have a diversionary project that we can sacrifice if necessary."

Jones spoke, "What are we to do when we get to Canada?"

"There are many southern sympathizers who aid Confederate escapees. I have heard of one route going through New York to Halifax, Nova Scotia, sailing to Bermuda and south. There are a good number of contingencies after we get out. It will be impossible to plan for them all. I suggest we focus on the escape and worry about the details later. The priority is to get out, and away. After that, we break into smaller groups and go our separate ways."

There was a long silence before General Trimble says, "Gentlemen, we have been given a lot to think about, but I for one, think the plan has a reasonable chance of success. General Thompson, I think our diversion should be another tunnel. With your engineering background, would you be willing to head up that part of the plan?"

"Yes sir, it would be my pleasure."

Turning to me, he said, "Please move forward with whatever information gathering you think we need, and let General Thompson and Major Traweek know what you find out. Speak of this to no one outside this gathering until you are instructed to do so by one of the general staff. Is that understood by all?"

There are mumbles of agreement, and nods of acceptance.

"Is there anything else?" The general asks the group; silence. "You are dismissed, but leave the area in singles or groups of twos not to arouse unwarranted interest."

I am one of the first to file out. Major Traweek hails me.

"Well done Atwood. The old man bought into it pretty quick. How do you feel about it?"

I smile bigger than I have since I last saw Lucy and say, "Major, I'm going home."

23) Lucy Jane and Buck

Down the hill, across the valley, along the river, miles away from Spring Dale, the Fourth goes unobserved at the Evans Atwood homestead. Lucy Jane despises Patricia Anne Robinson for how she handled the breaking of her engagement. She feels her circumstances are different, therefore her behavior is warranted.

George Paul has stayed on, but has been a disappointment. She had hoped that Evans' assessment of George was not accurate, but with each passing day, her hope diminishes. He works, but not hard, he provides, but not enough, he loves, but not well, and she is worried that he will not be able to protect, and that is the reason Lucy has allowed him to stay. There's no fight in him; no fire, no ambition. He is like raising a third child. She tells him what to do, how to do it, and when. After it's done, there's no more, no initiative. Whatever is required is enough. He wants no more than what the day holds.

He's awkward with the children, and they do not know what to do with him. He is Mr. Paul, not "papa", or "uncle" and never will be. Lucy wonders if he will be more than "George" to her. The little ones ask about their papa, and Lucy explained that Mr. Paul served with their father, and has come to help mama with what she needs.

"What do you need, Mama?" Martha Jane asks.

Lucy answers with a smile but no explanation.

Martha Jane wonders, "Mama why is Mr. Paul here?"

Lucy Jane takes her daughter in her arms and tells her, "Mr. Paul is here to protect us."

Martha Jane looks into her mother's eyes and sees no truth there. Mr. Paul is incapable of protecting even himself. Lucy Jane's lie, the first to her child, is the beginning of a hell for Martha Jane. She knows something is not as it should be, and feels the fear of the unknown.

It is into this situation, that Buck rides. He has completed his family obligation to Dr. McPheeters and has rescued not only his cousin, Sallie Buchannan McPheeters, the wife of the doctor and their three children, but Olivia Lacey who was banished from Missouri with Sallie. With that done, Buck, who was ever mindful of Evans saving him in battle and his sacrifice of his own freedom for the sake of Buck and family, has now come to return the favor by seeing what aid he can offer Lucy Jane.

He yells from the yard, far enough out to not be an easy target, but close enough to be recognized. "Hello the house! Is anyone home?" The day is waning, but there is light to see. No reply; Buck looks around.

The place is not the same. Somehow he expected it to be. This is the spot where he and Evans left to go to war "for a few months". Buck laughs at his naivety and wonders at how he has changed and the things that have happened. Innocence has passed from even a weathered warrior.

The Atwood place has grown. The garden is well tended and nearing harvest for the tomatoes and corn, there are animals freshly killed hanging from the end rafters of the porch. The smoke house is giving off an aroma that makes Buck salivate. The place is in good condition and eases his mind.

He hails again, "Lucy, its Buck. Come on out; welcome me home darlin'!" He rides slowly closer.

"Oh my God; it's Buck!" Lucy whispers as her hand goes to her mouth. "I never thought..."

"Buck who?" George asks.

"Oh my God; it's Buck," she repeats, "I wonder if that means Evans..." She stands trembling at the window of the cabin.

"Evans is in prison. Is that Buck Buchannan?" George asks.

Lucy looks at George, surprised to find him there. In the late afternoon, early evening, a visitor is not a threat, but with the situation at the cabin what it is, all visitors are unwelcome.

"Mama, why are you so scared; is Buck one of the bad men?" Martha Jane has a vague remembrance of the name.

George, in a rare show of courage and caring, steps around Lucy and says, "I'll handle this man." He has never commanded Buck, but knows of his reputation and thinks that his officer status will be sufficient to handle him.

"No you won't!" Lucy shoves him back away from the door. "I'll handle this. You stay out of sight. Kids come with me." She opens the door and steps onto the porch with the children toddling behind her. They feel the tension from their mama and it scares them. "Buck," Lucy acknowledges as neutral as she can sound.

Buck rides closer. "Buck'? That's all I get is 'Buck'? No, 'how ya doin' Buck', or 'I'm so glad to see ya Buck'; or maybe, 'How's Evans, Buck'; I get 'Buck'?"

"I'm sorry; I'm surprised to see you. I didn't expect you. Evans wrote of your capture and wounds. Are you alright? What are you doing here?"

"You sound a bit confused; not too welcoming darlin'. Everything alright here?" Buck asks as he moves his jacket to the side to get to Evan's LeMat pistol which Dr. McPheeters recognized in the possession of the wounded Lieutenant Sykes and took from him and gave to Buck the day after Evans left for the rear under guard. He rides to the foot of the steps, looking about. He does not dismount and loosens the shot gun in its scabbard under his left leg. Martha Jane is peeking at him from around her mother. "Hi Martha Jane, you little sweetheart" he says, "Do you remember me?"

Martha Jane nods her blond head as her thumb comes to her mouth. A habit she has developed since the appearance of George Paul.

Buck laughs and smiles at the little girl, "Honey, I most sure remember you; my, how you've grown!" Looking up at Lucy, he says, "It seems like another lifetime don't it?"

"It was Buck; it ain't like we left it. I've moved on."

James Calvin toddles from behind his mother and looks at Buck.

"My goodness boy; you weren't more n' a handful when I last saw you, and look at you now; walking and all! Gracious, your pa would be proud to see you! You're the spittin' image of him!" Then to Lucy with a cold edge to his voice and stare to match, "I notice you ain't asked about Evans."

"Figured you wouldn't have any news, him being in prison in Illinois, why waste breath asking?" Her tone is hard and cold to match Buck's accusation.

"Sounds like you know more n' me darlin; a lot more. Tell me the news."

She stares, wondering how to resolve the situation, and decides to be blunt. "Buck, he ain't coming home; least ways not for a long time if ever. I've moved on, I got to take care of myself."

"What do you mean, 'moved on' girl; that's twice you've said that. What have you done here?"

George Paul steps onto the porch. He stands looking down at Sergeant Buchannan, "Sergeant," he says.

Lucy shakes her head at George's ill timed show of bravado.

"Lieutenant," Buck replies with a look that freezes Paul even in the July heat. "What are you doing here?"

"Don't question me sergeant. I outrank you, and you will address me as 'sir'."

"What are you doing here?"

"I don't have to answer you sergeant!" Lieutenant Paul's voice rises.

Buck sees the fear, can smell it. "You've changed."

The quiet of Buck's judgment puts Paul off guard and he thinks that this might end friendly, "We've all changed; we're all different. War does that." He smiles.

"When did it become too hard for you; when did you become a coward?"

"When I was in…," George starts, but realizes the second part of the question is the real one and screams, "I'm not a coward!"

Martha Jane begins to cry and then James Calvin starts because Martha Jane did.

Paul shouts, "I'm not a coward!" Lucy stoops to comfort her children, but Martha Jane breaks free and runs to Buck who swings down from his horse and scoops her up.

"Lucy," Buck's voice is sorrowful, "what have you done here?"

"Don't answer him Lucy, I outrank him," George Paul bellows, "It's none of his business!" He finishes in a screech that confirms Buck's assessment of him and shatters Lucy's hope. The children cry louder.

Lucy steps in front of George who is red faced, spitting, and fuming. She pushes him in the chest toward the house saying, "George, go in the house."

"But this man…"

Lucy Jane shoves him again, "George, go in the house, get the buckets and go fetch water; it's time to make supper."

"But…"

"George, do what I say…"

George sees the ferocity on her face and goes into the cabin. He does not look at Buck. Lucy stands with her back to him while he holds Martha Jane who has stopped crying. James is distracted by something in the yard and is climbing down the steps to investigate.

"Martha Jane?"

"Yes, mama?"

"Go with your brother and play for awhile; I need to talk to Mr. Buchannan."

Martha Jane looks to Buck with questioning eyes. They have the same piercing blue as her mother's. He says, "It's okay darlin'; go on now; let your mother and I talk."

"Will you go away?"

"Not right now; not before I come to get a big hug from you." He squeezes her tight before putting her down.

"Promise?"

"Yes, sweetheart, I promise." Martha Jane goes after her brother.

To Lucy's still turned back, Buck asks, "Lucy, what have you done here?"

Not turning, she answers, "Buck, it's just too hard." She turns, "I had to do something; the men in town are threatening me, I had to do something! I've been so afraid."

Buck knows what kind of men are around, and what they want, and how they'll take it if she doesn't give in. He knows the price she will pay for protection. "And you're not afraid now?"

Lucy knows what Buck is implying, that she's little better off with George Paul here than alone. Her position may be worse since he'll be worthless in a fight. She hopes that when it happens, and she no longer hopes that it won't; that the raiders will be placated that she has taken up with a man. She hopes he doesn't have to show his mettle, for it does not exist. "Yeah Buck, I'm afraid. I know they're coming and I know I'll have to protect George, not the other way around, but what am I to do?"

"Lucy, I'm here. I'm here to help my friend, and you are part of my friend. I'll help."

"You're a good friend to us both."

"But you have to get rid of him," Buck gestures with a nod of his head in the general direction of the house, "it ain't right; you're someone else's."

"I know, and I am grateful that you are here, but you can't stay can you?"

Buck is silent as his mind wanders to Sallie, the kids, and Olivia. He has been thinking a lot about Olivia since he left. He will have to leave sooner than later, and Lucy will be unprotected again. Does he have a right to ask that of her? "You can go to the Atwood's; they'll have you."

"Buck, this here," she looks about as she spreads her arms, "is mine. I helped build it; I made it come out of the ground. My children were born here," she pauses, then continues, "I've never had anything. You know how I come up, and I ain't going back like that by letting some scum, Home Guard, worthless no good like Gavin Tate take anything from me. I'll die first."

Buck knows she has worked hard to get where she is and have what she has even if her methods are questionable. She is Evans' wife, and a good friend to him. "Gavin Tate huh?"

"Him and others, but he's the worst. He's made threats; comes to the cabin at night, wanders around. I've put the kids under the house so many times they think it's normal." She looks down at Buck from the porch. "It ain't been bad since George took up here. I can sleep at night even if there's no fight in him."

"It's a high price you're paying to be able to sleep."

The double meaning is not wasted on her, "It's better to pay on my own terms than have it taken from me."

Buck can find no flaw with her argument. "You're my friend's wife. He took care of me; I'm going to take care of you. I'll stay," he pauses wondering what he is getting himself into, "at least as long as it takes to handle Gavin Tate, but Lucy, I love you, and I understand the needs of a man and a woman, but him being here ain't right. He has to go."

"And you'll stay?"

"Yes, I will."

Lucy nods, comes down the steps to the yard and stands before Buck. "Thank you Buck; I know you'll do what you say, but I can't just kick George out; he ain't got nowhere to go. What'll he do?"

"I don't know, but he has to go. It ain't right him being here with the babies and all."

"I know, but...,"

"He has to go Lucy."

"...I just can't kick him out. He has done a lot of work here, and..."

"You've paid him for it."

"...yes, but... Buck I need a few days to break it to him. He'll go, he said he would when I told him to, but I need to be gentle about it. He ain't strong in the head. Buck, it's my place, and my situation. I've got to take care of it my way."

"Okay Lucy, do it your way, but he goes, do you agree?"

"Yes Buck, I do."

"Good, let's round up these little ones and get supper cooking; I'm starved. Is it okay if I sleep in the barn?"

"Yeah, when he leaves, you can come into the house."

"No, I won't do that. The animals will take to my smell easier than you and the kids."

Lucy laughs; she hasn't felt this happy and safe in months. "You know where the river is. Why don't you get settled in the barn, wash up and let me get supper going. I'll have the kids bring you a plate."

"What about him?" Buck asks, looking at George watching them.

Lucy looks around and makes a shooing motion with her hand and says, "Go on now; start getting the fire going for supper." She looks back at Buck, "I'll tell him you're staying on to help out. He'll figure it out and move on, but I ain't going to kick him out. I'll help him leave gentle like. You go on now, get cleaned up." She pats him on the chest, and hugs him. "Thanks for coming."

"You're welcome," he held her for a moment and feels the fear in her. "My God," he thinks, "how long has she had to live this way?"

She breaks the embrace, turns, and as she goes she calls, "Kids, come on and help with supper!" They run past Buck, each slapping him on the leg as they go laughing to their chores.

"It's good to be home," he thinks, "I just need to get Evans here."

He leads his horse to the barn and finds fodder and hay. In the fading light, he gathers straw in an empty stall, spreads his blankets, and arranges his gear. Satisfied, he walks down the trail to the river.

He strips and washes in the sun-warmed waters. His shirt and underwear are washed and he spreads them over the low hanging branches of the willows and oaks, pulls on his trousers and boots and makes his way to the barn.

He expects to see the little ones waiting for him with his food, but is surprised to see Lucy there with a lantern set on the tail of the wagon waiting for him.

"What's for supper?" Buck hollers, never looking at the house, but knowing he is being watched.

"Squirrel and dumplin's, with beans and cornbread. The cornbread is this morning's, and that there's the last of it, but it should be fit to eat. There's some peppers from the garden if you want to season it up a mite," she says, "it's all we got today."

"It looks and smells great. This here's a feast!"

Lucy smiles. Buck likes her being near. Without his shirt, she sees his scars and asks, "Are you hurt real bad?"

"Evans'll tell you different, but it ain't no big thing."

"Tell me; I want to hear it all, every detail. I want to know what he said, and what he thought, and what he did; don't spare me." She sounds like a girl around the camp fire asking for a scary story; not wanting to hear one, but not able to resist.

As he eats, he tells her; all of it, sparing nothing, no pain, smell, or fear. After he finishes supper, he extinguishes the light and continues the telling. He can hear her sob, or sniffle sometimes. He tells her of Cousin Sallie and the children, William, JoAnne, Christiana, and of Olivia.

Lucy Jane listens. It breaks her heart to hear of the loss of the women, but gives her joy as Buck speaks of Olivia. She wonders at the miracle of Buck falling in love. It brings a smile to her face as she says, "God damn war."

"Lucy, don't you go talking like that! Why, if Evans heard you say that he'd give you a whipping."

She laughs, and says, "I wish he was here to try. No Buck, it ain't a curse; it's a prayer."

He thinks on that. "You have a right to it. I say 'amen'," then after a moment, "yes God, damn all war."

They sit in the dark for a long time. Lucy takes Buck's hand. "Thanks for coming Buck," she says real quiet, "thanks for understanding."

Buck squeezes her hand in reply. They sit that way.

The sound of boots on boards causes them to turn and look. Neither can see George, but both know he's there.

To Buck's unasked question, she says, "Maybe he'll see the obvious and just go away."

"Do you really think he will?"

"No."

"He'll want to fight first. When a man's been called a coward, he's got to fight. Even if it means he has to die, he'll fight. If he's a man, or wants to be, he has to prove it." There's quiet between them as they both think.

"Buck, in the fights, are you ever scared?"

"Every time, until it starts, then you don't have time to be scared."

"But you've never been a coward?"

"Not yet; but you never know. It's different every time."

"Don't it get easier?"

"No, every time's different and you can't think too much about what you've done before. You have to go through the fear every time, and sometimes it gets to a fellow and he can't do anything, he can't fight."

"It's never happened to you?"

"No, I don't think on it. The fellers who think on it are the ones that go crazy."

"You think that's what's happened to George?"

"I don't know; all I know is that when he came out earlier, I could smell fear on him. Something happened to make him have that much fear. Maybe in prison; he didn't act like that in battle."

They grew silent again. Lucy Jane took her hand away. "I wish Evans was here; I've wished it a million times."

"I know."

"But tonight I wish he was here to tell me what happened to George. I don't think he'll make it without help."

"Maybe, but it's help you can't give."

Lucy Jane gets up, gathers the plates and lantern.

"Thanks for supper, it was delicious; and Lucy," she turns, "thanks for letting me do the right thing here."

She doesn't say anything and walks away.

Buck needs sleep. It's been a long ride. "Things'll look better in the morning," he tells himself as he goes to the barn.

He wakes with a start. Did he hear it, or sense it? He knows the feeling; he has had it a many times on many nights; danger's near.

He listens. There it is again; foot falls. He lays still, sorting out noises. His horse is agitated. There it is again; clearer; a horse, or more. Buck's horse whinnies. There's the noise again; a horse shuffling on the other side of the barn wall at his back. It's the wall opposite the house.

He can see out the open door into the yard, and the front of the house. There's a gibbous moon, waxing, almost full, and it's clear. Under a moon like this one, three months ago, he was in a plowed field in Mississippi with his friend in command. Tonight, he may have to defend that friend's home and family. He hears the creak and strain of leather under a load. There's a man in the saddle.

Buck reaches for his weapons. He sits up. The man on the other side of the wall dismounts; Buck hears the weight shift and feels the foot falls through the ground. They are light. The stranger's horse catches the scent of Buck's mare, snorts and neighs. Buck hears the man shuffle and quiet the animal. As the rider is distracted, Buck gets up, pulls on his boots, raises his suspenders, and without a sound, moves to the door.

The yard is empty and quiet. Buck waits and watches in the shadows. Is it a lone rider, or is he part of a group? For some reason, Buck knows it's a group, and he suspects it's the Home Guard who heard about a Confederate officer staying with the Atwood woman, but why in the middle of the night? An officer is worth ten dollars, but wouldn't it be easier in the day? Buck looks at the moon and figures it to be mid-night or after.

He looks around the yard. There, in the woods behind the garden, is another rider still mounted. As he wonders at these two, he hears horses coming up the lane, two, maybe three; that would make five. He does not turn his head. He's watching the cabin. It looks quiet, but Buck senses Lucy's watching. He knows he has the drop on the men riding in, and the one behind the barn, but the man across the yard is a problem.

The riders appear. Buck sees another man moving up the trail from the river. "Cocky," thinks Buck, "they think they can handle a woman and one man. That fool's walking in the moonlight like a Sunday stroll."

The riders come in at a trot, two of them, not sneaking. That makes five; not good odds, but he has the element of surprise and whatever Lucy has in the cabin. They rein up right in front of the steps, an easy target for anyone inside. The windows slam shut, then the interior shutters. Lucy's ready.

He sees movement beneath the house; Lucy's escape plan. "I wonder if it includes her." No, she'll be the diversion as the kids run, but to where?

His gut tightens as he realizes where they will run; to the barn. They'll never get past the riders, and prays they'll stay put. Has Lucy coached them to run when the shooting starts, or wait until it's quiet again? He has no way of knowing.

Buck hears a loophole being opened in the door. A shotgun barrel appears. Lucy Jane's voice rings clear, "Get off my property Gavin Tate, or I will open you up like a can of beans, now get!" There is no fear in her voice.

Tate spins his horse at Lucy's challenge, looking about the yard seeing if the riders are in place. Buck has never met Tate, but knows of him. He's uglier than an outhouse on a summer's day, and smells just as bad. The man is a snake and a coward.

From inside the barn, Buck can do little. He'll have to go into the yard to shoot. Running scenarios through his head; he'll take the one by the barn first with a shot from the LeMat, then the two off the horses in the front yard by blasting away with both barrels of the shotgun as he moves forward. "Please God, don't let the little ones be running at the same time."

Satisfied that the backup riders are in place, Tate replies, "I'm here on official business Mrs. Atwood; you come out now and let's get this straightened out."

"What kind of official business can you have in the middle of the night with a woman and her children you pathetic weasel?"

"Good," thinks Buck, "she's the aggressor. Keep it up darlin'."

"We know you ain't in there alone Mrs. Atwood, you'se got's a man in there…"

"What if I do? What business is it of yours you disgusting bug?"

"…word is that he's a deserter," pausing for effect, an *officer*; he's worth a lot of money."

"Ain't no one here worth anything to you Tate, now get before I start shooting."

Lucy Jane is not backing down; "Keep at him Lucy, he's confused."

"If you're harboring a deserter Miss Lucy…"

"The thing I'm harboring Tate is a lot of ill will toward you and your men around the cabin. Now, if you ain't turned and moving off this land by the count of ten, I'm going to start shooting, and you know I'll do it, and you know I can shoot, you've seen it. Do you want to guess who goes first? Now, one…"

Buck decides to let Lucy handle it unless it goes bad.

"Two…"

"Lucy Jane…," Tate tries to sound firm and threatening.

"It's 'Mrs. Atwood', you walking outhouse; three…"

"Mrs. Atwood, if you're harboring a deserter, we can take you too, and be within the law…"

"You can try you loathsome worm; four…"

"Mrs. Atwood you can settle this by letting us search…"

"Over my dead body; five…"

"That can be arranged you bitch!"

"You're not man enough, you phony; six…"

"Woman, there's four of us here waiting to have you!"

"You liar, there's five of you, and what are you going to use, you eunuch; seven…"

"Mrs. Atwood, this is getting out of hand!" There's panic in his voice. "If you'll just…"

"Eight…"

"…let us search the place, we'll go on and leave you alone; please!" Tate starts to back away from the door.

"You're doing great darlin'; you've got 'em on the defensive," Buck thinks.

"Nine…"

Buck hears the double click as Lucy pulls the hammers back on the shotgun. Tate gives more ground, and the others look around in confusion. Lucy is about to pull it off; it's almost over. Buck hears the squeak of leather as the man outside the barn mounts up; he's leaving. Buck can't see across the yard, but hears a horse thrashing and feels sure he's leaving too. The man behind the cabin moves up to see what's happening.

Lucy has the upper hand then it comes unraveled. Buck hears Lucy start to say "Ten", but it turns into, "George, don't!" There's a scuffle as the door burst open and George Paul, dressed only in his trousers, screaming his best Rebel Yell, comes out with his revolver blazing. The rider in front goes over backwards before George turns his attention to Tate who's backing and turning, squealing, "Stop, Stop!"

The man around the side of the house steps to the front and takes a bead on George as Lucy Jane shouts, "George, you fool, NO!" The man opens up with his pistol and fires three shots in rapid succession. Buck hears the "thwack" of at least two rounds, and two grunts from George, as he drops.

Tate dismounts and starts up the steps. He's met with a blast from the shot gun and is blown off the porch to never move again.

The man beside the barn dismounts and moves into the yard, forcing Buck to act. He waits till the man is moving across the yard, steps behind him with the shot gun raised high, butt first and brings it down onto the man's head. The rider slumps to the ground making no more noise than a breeze.

The gunman that shot George is climbing onto the porch as Buck continues across the yard. The gunman's raising his pistol to fire at Lucy when the kids burst from under the house and start to run to the barn. They might have made it uninterrupted, had they not seen Buck standing poised to shoot. They stop in their tracks and scream. The man on the porch turns with his gun coming to bear as Buck shouts, "Martha Jane, down!"

She either obeys, or stumbles, but she goes down in front of James Calvin who falls over her. The man on the porch fires at Buck. The round goes wide, and Buck fires one barrel of his 10 gauge. The man takes the load in the face and chest, the force slamming him against the wall of the cabin, and slides down to the porch.

The children are up and running for the barn. Martha Jane is dragging her brother as he stumbles to keep up. Pounding hooves on hard packed ground redirects Buck's attention to see the rider from the woods charging him, firing away.

Buck's in combat mode. Everything is in slow motion. He sees two rounds hit in front of him, and hears one crack past his head. The man is firing wild from horseback and Buck has plenty of time. He turns sideways to offer a lower profile target, raises the pistol, sights, and squeezes off a round. The .44 slug hits the man in the chest where Buck sees a puff of dust explode off him. He falls in slow motion and slides dead at Buck's feet.

On the porch, Lucy Jane is standing over George, holding the smoking shotgun. She doesn't stoop to see if he's alive. Buck sees a cold, hard look on her face and it chills him. Lucy Jane has crossed the line; she has killed a man.

She looks at him. "Put away the scatter gun darlin'; it's over." She moves to the house as he calls after her, "I'll find the kids."

They're hidden under Buck's blankets. As he goes to comfort them, Martha Jane says, "Mama?"

"She's fine." Buck sees another question forming, but before she can ask, he says, "Ya'll rest easy here. Let me and your Mama clean things up. Ya'll be safe here. It's all over." Then to reassure them, "Ain't nobody gonna mess with your Mama and you again." She lies back on the bedding and holds her brother. Buck covers them, then finds a piece of rope and goes into the yard.

The man Buck knocked out is starting to move, holding his head where Buck hit him. He rolls the man over onto his stomach and brings his hands behind his back and ties them. He ties the legs bent at the knees to the hands and leaves him on the ground.

Lucy Jane is on the porch with her hands folded in front of her as prim and neat as a girl just home from church. She looks frail and vulnerable, not the cold blooded combatant from minutes before. He makes his way to the porch, checks the first rider, then Tate. George's and Lucy's aim was true, they're dead. Lucy asks, "The kids okay?"

"Yes ma'am, they're fine; they're asleep in the barn."

"Asleep?"

"Yeah, cuddled up under my blankets."

Buck checks the victim of his shotgun blast. He's as dead as the others. George Paul is lying on the porch on his back with his arms flung out; his lifeless eyes staring, his mouth open in mid yell. His legs are bent making him look like a large, loosely put together doll.

"Why did he do it do you think?" Lucy Jane asks; "Why did he charge like that?"

"I don't rightly know. Maybe it's because I called him a coward. Maybe he was tired of living and saw this as a way to go, defending your honor and all. Who knows?"

"You've seen it before?"

Buck nods.

"I didn't love him you know?"

Buck says nothing.

"It didn't make any difference did it? Having him here only made it worse. God, if he had only stayed in the house; I had 'em backing down; it was almost over. Why did he do that?" She stands for a minute looking around. "If it hadn't been for you, me and the kids would be dead or worse. Thank you Buck; it is God's blessing you came when you did."

"I just did what needed doing, ain't no more reason than that."

"Yes there is; you did it because you love Evans."

"Yes, that's true, and he loves you, so I love you too."

They stand a few moments more.

"What do we do now?"

"First light I'll ride for the sheriff. He'll want to see this. We'll turn that 'un over to him. He'll tell what happened. No body's gonna mess with you again."

Lucy Jane nods and starts to the barn. Buck looks at her as she passes in the moonlight. She's not the same woman.

"She's right; God damn all war. What else can it rob us of?"

24) Evans

I received the following letter from Buck on August 23rd, 1863 at Johnson Island, Ohio:

July 12th, 1863

Shiloh, Arkansas

Evans,

It is late Sunday here at your folk's place. Nothing much has changed; the food was abundant, and delicious. Your Ma is sitting across the room writing to you. Hers will have more family news.

I found Sallie McPheeters in Plum Cove as I thought. We had some adventures and a near miss, but got home to my place safe and none too worse for the wear. Traveling with two women and three children is not as easy as traveling with you.

I suppose you caught the part there about two women. I rescued another woman in Plum Cove who had been banished. She'd lost her man and kids. She hates Yankees; her children either thrown, or fell overboard on the river trip. She hitched up with us and is with Sallie at my place. Her name is Olivia, and you may be seeing a lot more of her. She is going to stay on until we get definite word about her husband. His name is Daniel Lacey. He rode with Jeff Thompson's Swamp Rats, so if you hear anything, write and let us know.

Evans, I wish that we were face to face for me to give you this news, but we ain't, so I have to put it in this letter. There is great sadness over your family tonight; Lucy and the children would not come with me to your folks. Things are bad at your place.

Lucy wrote and told you about Gavin Tate, the local Home Guard who had been threatening her, well, the problem is solved. It is too much to go into detail here, but I got to your place July 4th, and he showed up in the middle of the night with four other riders. Lucy shot Tate, killed him; I killed two others, and captured one. The captured boy spilled his guts to the sheriff who said Lucy was in her rights.

Lucy Jane was scared being on the place by herself because of the threats she's been getting, so she let George Paul stay on to help. He was killed as he charged the riders killing the fifth one.

I am sorry to be the one to tell you, but it ain't good, and you need to know. The killing changed her. She's a lot harder now; like steel with a sharp edge and just as dangerous.

I stayed on for a few days to help, but with word of the killing, no one's going to mess with her. There wasn't much I could do, so we agreed I could go. I'm on my way home now.

The kids are fine. Martha Jane is a wonderful help to Lucy Jane, and James Calvin is the spittin' image of you; skinny ass and all.

I understand you've got to do what you've got to do. I know the honor and oath you took, but Evans, from the word I get, it looks like we're losing the war. Vicksburg fell on the fourth. If we'd been with the unit, we would be paroled and on our way home. I expect to see the boys coming in any day now.

There's a place called Gettysburg where Lee lost the "battle of the war", they're calling it. Some of the southern papers are saying we're done.

I know you can't just leave, but Lucy ain't going to stay loyal to you. Being alone and desperate is hard on the woman. She wants it all now; she ain't going to wait.

I can't guess how this must hurt you, and it surely will drive you crazy not being able to do anything about it, but I had to tell you. We're praying for you and keep a light in the window. Keep the faith; all things pass.

Your friend,
Buck

"Damn, damn, damn," I curse as I fold the letter after having read it three times, "what else can I lose to this war? How many lives lost; how many lives ruined?" I put the letter in the cover of my journal after having copied it as I have all the letters I've gotten, and all the letters I've sent.

"Thank God I have a plan; I wish I could write Lucy Jane and tell her to hang in there just a little longer without giving away what's going on here," I think to myself.

Plans for the escape are going well. I am assigned to wood cutting crews that go out every day for felled trees. We stack the wood in cords to be able to cure and be ready for winter. Come winter with the lake frozen we can use sleds and pull it over the ice. That's the ploy. None of us plan to be here for that. The wood we stack is for the *Little Eastern*.

All the participants have been assigned to crews. We are stealing as many blue uniforms as we can from the supply barracks. General Thompson has built a tunnel up into the building. Most of us have secreted our Federal uniform inside our mattress.

I am more anxious than ever. We should have gone last week, but General Jones' unit was not ready. No one is surprised. The stories of his cowardice have made him a pariah. I have no patience with his ineptitude.

I go in search of Major Traweek; walking too fast, but I'm anxious, angry, and ready to move. I'm hailed from the window of one of the mess halls. "Come on in here laddie, you're looking a might anxious." It's Traweek; we've all picked up a few of the Irish phrases from the Yankee guards. They speak a rich brogue which we mimic.

The last thing I want to do is call attention to me or our operation, so I slow down and go in. Traweek's sitting with some other officers, but I cannot remember their names. I hurry to their table, but Traweek slows me with, "Stand at ease Lieutenant," he says with a calming smile. "Come," he gestures to the bench next to him, "sit and enjoy the heat of this building."

The group laughs as they swelter in the heat of an August afternoon. "Gentlemen," I say, nodding to the gathering.

"What do you have for us Evans?"

"Sir, there is nothing unusual to report. The guard schedules are the same. You can set your watch by them if you have a watch; otherwise, they're good to tell time by."

There's a smattering of laughter. "Anything else?"

"The wood piles are in place and should take no more than a few minutes to load. We should be off the wharf and underway in less than ten minutes."

"Ten minutes; that's all you think it will take to load the better part of two hundred soldiers?" One of the other officers asked.

I turned to him, but addressed Major Traweek, "Sir, this ain't going to be a Sunday stroll; we had best be moving fast. It won't take long for the Yankees in the city to see what's happening and launch troops."

"Speaking of Sunday," Major Traweek interrupted, "we're going next Sunday," he announces with joy.

I am stunned and the major sees it. He asks, "Is that not good news lieutenant?"

"No sir, it's not. Why so long; isn't Jones ready yet? Damn!" I slam my fist on the table, "The longer we wait sir, the more likely is our being discovered. We need to go."

Major Traweek looks at me with undisguised anger. He cuts me with, "Bad news from home Evans?"

"Yes; real bad news. My home was raided by Home Guard and my wife and my friend Buck were forced to kill four."

There are grumbles, Major Traweek says, "That is terrible Evans, but that word will spread fast and no one will bother her now. Is there more?"

"Yes sir," I slip the letter out of my coat and hand it to him.

He opens it and reads, raising his eyebrows at the part about of George Paul. He finishes and says, "I see," and pauses. "Sunday lieutenant; those are General Trimble's orders. I will make your concerns known, but I doubt he will change the time table for one man. On Sunday, as you have noted, there is a laxity among the guards and more are on shore than in the compound, so it will be next Sunday. At this point, what will one more week matter?"

I fight to control my anger, "I could be one week closer to home. Will that be all?"

"Yes lieutenant, you are dismissed, but do not let your hot head jeopardize the rest of us. We all have loved ones struggling back home. It is frustrating for all at this table to not be able to provide for our families." There are nods around the table and words of understanding, but an order is an order, and being a sworn officer, I must obey, but damn, I want to go home.

I take my leave, forcing myself to walk out of the building and around the yard until I am under control. I walk until the sun sets, and the stars are rising. Looking up at the freedom they represent, I say, "Lucy, Lucy, what have you done?"

The week passes with agonizing slowness. Everyone has to work hard to not arouse suspicions. We all remind each other to, "act normal". Preparations are ready on Wednesday, and I urge the General Staff to move the date up. It is to no avail. The date is set in stone, Sunday it will be, but I fear treachery in the ranks.

I wonder as I walk what we will do for four more days, when I am hailed, "Lieutenant Atwood!"

I turn to see General Thompson waving to me. "Yes sir," I respond and start back to him.

He nods as I salute. He is smoking a cheroot and blows a cloud of smoke, "Do you have reason to feel that we are betrayed?"

"No reason sir, but I have a feeling. I'm concerned that the longer we wait, the higher the chances are that we will be discovered. You know better than I general, this is a military operation; we can count on something going wrong."

He smiles and nods in agreement before asking, "What else can happen lieutenant? Please, brain storm for a moment."

"I have no feel for specifics, the longer we wait, the higher the risk of someone ordering an inventory of uniforms in the warehouse. What if the tunnel is discovered? I do not see the advantage of waiting." I pause for a response. When none is forth coming, I add, "If there is treachery among us sir, the way I see to combat it is to go now so the traitor doesn't have time to warn his cohorts."

He stands for a few moments longer, deep in thought, then says, "That will be all Atwood. Thank you for your candor."

"Yes sir," and I turn to go, but something occurs to me, "Sir?"

"Yes lieutenant?"

"Sir did you have a man by the name of Lacey under your command in Missouri?"

"Yes, I did, Daniel Lacey, a fine officer. Why do you ask?"

"I've gotten a letter from my sergeant who met Lacey's wife on the trail home. It appears she was banished from Missouri for not signing the loyalty oath. She does not know the whereabouts or condition of her husband. Can you assist her, sir?"

"Yes, of course; I fear it is not good news. I personally attended services for Mr. Lacey. He was killed in action. I have the dates and place written in my journal if you would like to have them to forward to your sergeant. As a matter of fact, please let me write a letter of condolence to the widow. She must have not gotten the first."

"Yes sir, please sir; I'm certain it would be a great comfort to her."

I salute and he returns it saying, "Let's get together tomorrow. I will have the letter written by then."

"Yes sir." Something isn't right; but what is it?

Thursday dawns bright, hot, and clear. I hope for rain by Sunday. Rain will give us cover. I am anxious to go. The longer we wait...

"Evans...Evans...!"

I look around to find who is shouting to me across the yard. Every guard is looking at the other lieutenant, Bowen; I think his name is, as he runs toward me.

He gets near, and I chastise, "Every guard in the prison's looking at you! What the hell's the matter with you?"

"It don't matter anymore; come see." He grabs my sleeve to drag me with him.

I go, fearful at the, 'it don't matter anymore' comment.

The gate is wide open in the middle of the day for the work details coming and going. The guards smirk at us and make no effort to stop us as we go out.

I see the *Little Eastern* tied at the wharf. Bowen keeps pulling me to the shore and pointing out into the lake. We move closer to the water. I'm getting more and more anxious. The guards are looking out into the lake toward the town. I shake loose from Lieutenant Bowen and move to the edge of the water. I see, heaving into view, a sloop of war with her gun ports open and the guns run out, elevated and trained on the prison yard. As she passes, I see her name; *USS Michigan.* She sails past the island, comes about on the ten knot wind, and sails back the way she came; Old Glory flapping in the breeze behind her. It would have been a beautiful sight except for what she means to us; the escape will be impossible now; we're done, finished. She would be on us in moments if she does not open fire before we leave the wharf.

I watch as she moves around the island, the crew working her sails to perfection. She's glorious in her strength and defiance. We have been found out. We have been betrayed.

This is a dark moment. I leave men watching the passing of the *Michigan* and turn to reenter the prison. I walk by the guard station and look up. The guards are leering with satisfied looks on their faces, "Won't be taking the *Little Eastern* for a spin on Sunday now will you boy-o?" I glare at the Irish bastard. He laughs, "You be telling your commanders to spread the word; none of you southern lads are to cross the dead line. We've orders to shoot to kill starting as soon as the word passes to you traitors." Then, for good measure, "Ain't that something now; the traitors are betrayed?" He laughs long and hard; my heart is about to break.

I find Major Traweek and tell him the news. He, in turn, drags me to General Trimble who goes white when told. "Major, find the others, bring them at once, and don't dally, we've not a moment to lose."

"A moment to lose for what?" I wonder.

I wait as the general staff gathers, and when called upon to give my report, I do and am then dismissed. I walk out disgusted, and no longer caring about the group's plan. If I'm going to leave Johnson Island any time soon, it will have to be on my own. I have a plan just for this circumstance. It will take time, but I have that. "Hang on Lucy Jane; I'm coming."

August 28th, 1863
Friday

Johnson Island, Ohio

My dearest family,

I hope this finds you well. The conditions here have worsened with the continued influx of prisoners. As you have heard, things do not go well for our Confederacy, but we are hearing more news of victory, so hope is still with us.

I received a letter from Buck explaining your situation. Nothing has happened that we cannot work out. I long to be with you and it will be but a <u>short moment</u> compared to the rest of our lives before I am. Please endure with me until I can once again rest in the love of your arms, and you, in the security of mine.

I must live a life with honor. Please do not ask me to betray my oath and country. Once again, it will be but a <u>short moment</u> before I return.

Your loving husband,

Evans

"I hope she is able to read between the lines." I seal the letter and hope against hope.

25) Steven Wayne...

...arrives in Shiloh the middle of August. He does not go home. He has other plans. The peace and coddling of home can wait. Being off the road is enough for now.

When the conquered Confederate army was released on parole with the oath to not take up arms against the Union, they were free, but in terrible shape. They were given very little to eat, and very little aid with transportation. Most had to make their own way and that meant walking. Steven Wayne was allowed to keep his horse which had survived without being blown to pieces or eaten.

Steven Wayne traveled north out of Mississippi, and took his time. He traveled alone by choice, but with so many moving north, alone was rare. He was appalled to see the wounded; men who were walking in twos and threes, leaning on each other, or carrying a man in the center. There was very little food, but wherever Steven Wayne stopped, if there was a woman home, he ate and shared what he had with others.

He carried no visible scars from Vicksburg. His were deeper, but just as horrible. Steven Wayne had lost his mind. No matter how he fought, he knew he would lose. Watching the soldiers on the road confirmed his diagnosis.

Some would beg him for assistance and he would ride on in silence. Some he helped. Once, he took a frail, emaciated man on his horse riding behind. The man leaned against Steven Wayne and went to sleep. It wasn't comfortable, but he tolerated it. After a while, the man began to slide off the horse. He had died. Steven Wayne dumped him on the side of the road. "Let his friends bury him," he said to himself, and rode on. Even Steven Wayne did not know which of him would emerge in any circumstance; the compassionate one, or the monster.

"What have you done?"

Steven Wayne looked around as he rode. There was no one in sight. The voice was strange. It sounded like him, but... "I put the dead man down," he said aloud. His voice sounded strange too.

"Why?"

"He was dead." This time the voice was heavy, dark, cold, and was familiar. The other voice was quiet. The one had dismissed the other.

He thought on it and realized it was one of the voices that spoke to him in the night. It was the monster's voice. It was the voice that gave him power, and frightened him. Steven Wayne was afraid because the enemy was himself.

The men of his command answer to Lieutenant Wilson now. Most of them want nothing to do with Steven Wayne, which suits him. He needs to take care of himself. He's taken care of others too long.

He is confused. He becomes more comfortable with who and whatever he is becoming and accepts the fact that he is no longer who he was. He has no control when the monster comes, but is learning.

He rides up the hill through the gates of Spring Dale. The voices are silent. He has no plan; he just knows this is where he has to go. He knows this will be an end for him, and a beginning.

He believes that Patricia Anne is married. He doesn't know if she's home or if she will see him, and if she does, what the reception will be. He doesn't care. He knows if he presents himself, and she is home, she'll see him; she has to, or he'd...

He rides at a walk, and stops in front of the house, remembering simple, innocent times. He wonders what happened to the adventurous boy who sat astride this same horse on this spot three years ago anxious to go to war.

Dismounting, he stretches, feeling the pain from the battles of the last two years, and is overtaken by fatigue. He wants to lie down and sleep. "It's almost over," he says to himself, "just this to do." He ties the horse to a hitching post as he has done many times before and approaches the entry.

Steven Wayne has changed into his best uniform and it not much more than a rag. He remembers the day he got it from the tailor, and laughs. The uniform shows wear, but so does he. He is unshaven which reveals more than a lack of hygiene. The last time he stood here, he was just shaving, now he has the beard of a man. When he sees his reflection, he is amazed and frightened; especially when the monster is out.

Steven Wayne's eyes are still light brown, the color of creamed coffee, but when It takes over, they turn dark, almost black. He has lovely eyes, and knows it; they are part of his seductive charm. As he walks up the walk, he knows they are light, bright, and soft.

His hair is long, almost to his collar, and darker brown. He wears a kepi cap having abandoned the Stetson for the versatile and nearly indestructible utility cap of both armies. It is dirty gray, but the gold braid and crossed swords denoting an officer have survived, but don't shine. He wears the sword his father says was passed down from the Revolutionary War; he no longer believes it. He adjusts it so as he climbs the stairs, it doesn't clash against the stairs. It is considered uncouth, and shows no respect for the weapon. "To hell with all weapons," he says out loud.

He stops on the veranda and stares at the door. He knocks and hears steps inside. The door opens. He looks into the face Miss Bessie, the house slave. She knows all there is to know about the workings of Spring Dale and everyone in it. She is just the person he needs to talk too.

Miss Bessie does not recognize the worn officer standing on the steps. Making recognition more difficult, Miss Bessie's eye sight is failing. Steven Wayne wonders how old she is, or if she even knows. "Miss Bessie," he speaks.

"Steven Wayne; is that you child?"

"Yes ma'am, it is."

"Lord child, that devil in the war done worked hold of you! My God boy, but you's not a boy anymore are you?" She reaches out and touches his chest. Steven Wayne sees the fear on her face, but he smiles and it goes away.

"Is she here?" Steven Wayne asks.

"Yes sur, she is," replies Miss Bessie, formal and business like.

"Would you be so kind as to tell her that there is a gentleman calling?" Steven Wayne asks with a lazy, easy smile.

"You's ain't gonna hurt her are you Mr. Steven? I won't cotton to no hurtin her."

"If you mean physically, the answer is no, but if you mean will she be hurt at my refusal of her affections if such are offered, well, we'll see."

"I guess she's got it comin'," she pauses, shakes her head, and says, "poor child; she brought it on herself."

"Yes ma'am, she has, and I'm powerful sorry for her, but I need to see her."

"Yes sur, but I'm sorry; real sorry." She stands aside and allows Steven Wayne into the foyer where the wedding had taken place, then led him into the parlor.

"Before I's goes to get's her, there's something you's should know if you's don'ts already."

"What is that?"

"Have you heard about the wedding?"

"No ma'am. This is the first place I have stopped."

Miss Bessie cannot resist a broad, gap toothed grin, "Honey, I's gots a story for you!" And she told it.

As the saga unwound, Steven Wayne's countenance lightened considerable. He was enjoying Bessie's vivid description and as she wove her tale, he closed his eyes and was almost there. "So, she's not married?"

"Lord no honey! But she needs to be!"

"What do you mean?"

"Honey, ole Miss Bessie's been around a long time and I's knows some things, and what's I's don'ts knows, I can figger; Miss Patsy's carrying Mr. Thad's baby!"

Steven Wayne smiles as he asks, "Will you go fetch her please ma'am?"

"Yes sur, I's will," and with a smile, she goes to do just that.

He watches her trudge up the steps and imagines her trying to subdue the chaos in the foyer as the band played, a half naked Patricia Anne flaying away at anyone in range, people trying to get their footing as they stepped on the pearls on the marble floor, the cursing, and screaming; he laughs.

He turns as he hears the rustle of petty coats coming down the stairs and rises as Patricia Anne comes into the parlor. She gasps in disbelief and says, "Steven Wayne, is it you?"

He nods. She is showing the ravages of her stress and pregnancy. Her face is bloated and her belly has a bulge. She was never petite, but is now more than pleasantly plump.

She does not hesitate a moment as she runs to him, throws her arms around his neck, hugging herself to him and declaring to the astonishment of both Steven Wayne and Miss Bessie, "Oh, Steven Wayne, my darling, you've come home to me at last! Oh, thank God for your safe return! I've prayed for this moment every minute of every day since you left. I'm so thankful, so thankful!"

Steven Wayne pushes her away and holds her at arm's length. She's wide eyed and innocent as if he had been gone a week and nothing had happened between.

"Didn't you get my letters? I wrote you every week," she says with such conviction that Steven Wayne almost believes her.

He smiles while still holding her away from him and says, "Patricia Anne, have you forgotten a wedding that happened here a few weeks back."

"A wedding?" Patricia Anne asks with a confused look on her face. She begins to pull away from him and turn to the still present Miss Bessie, "Did you tell? I'll have you beaten…"

Steven Wayne shakes her; not hard, but firm enough so that she faces him, "My father wrote me. He was invited."

"Well, of course…," she says before she realizes the trap. The innocence is gone as she looks at him with loathing. Her face red as she says through clinched teeth, "…and he laughed at me; now, let me go!" He does. She is furious, but is quick to recover.

She lowers her head, and folds her hands across her belly; a movement that does not escape notice and says, "It was all a big mistake. I can see that now; I'm sorry..."

"And selfish," he interrupts.

The fury flames again, just a flicker. This opportunity, Steven Wayne here, is unexpected and she is not going to let it pass without a fight. This is a chance to recover her dignity, and have the man she originally intended. This is no time to be combative; that can come later. She says, "Yes, I was very selfish."

"You couldn't wait for me so you chose to move on, why?"

"I thought you would die..."

Interrupting, he laughs, "But I didn't!" It wants out to show this sniveling, lying girl, it wants to do things to her, to the baby. "Down!" He shouts in his brain, and looks around fearful he had said it out loud, but neither Patsy nor Bessie show any sign of notice. He smiles, and says again, "I didn't; I lived, and now I'm here."

"Yes, and I am so glad!" She tries to force an embrace, but he holds her off.

"And you want to pick up where we left off?" He takes her hands in his and moves his thumbs over the fingers of her hands.

"Oh yes, can we please? That would be so wonderful!"

"Why?"

"Why? Well, uh, because, uh, it's right," she pauses, tosses her head and continues, "yes, it's right. I made a mistake. I realize that now, I want to make it right."

"Did you write me to explain all this?"

"Of course! I felt so foolish that night after the wedding, I wrote you immediately. Didn't you get it?"

"You wrote me to say you were wrong, and you were sorry?"

"Yes, so sorry! I've made a terrible mistake! I've hurt you and I am so sorry!"

"And you said in this letter that you wanted to get back together; wanted to resume our betrothal, wanted to be mine forever?"

"Yes, oh yes, yes, yes! That is exactly what I said! You must have gotten the letter, those are my exact words!"

"Wonderful! Now, my sweet," as he holds her hands, "one more question."

"Yes dearest?"

He applies pressure, not hurtful, but firm with his right thumb on her left ring finger as he let a little of the monster out, "Yes," he thought, "just a little, just enough for her to see what she has done." Cold eyes grab her and she gasps as he asks in a fierce, but sweet voice, "Then dearest, where is the ring by which we are betrothed?" He applies just enough pressure to the pudgy digit so that she cries out more in surprise than pain.

She shakes her hands free, and says, "Who are you? I don't know you," and backs away.

Miss Bessie, who has been standing outside the door and has seen the transformation come over Steven Wayne, steps in and asks, "Mr. Steven, are you alright?"

He does not answer, but takes a step closer to Patricia Anne, letting a little more of It out and says in a voice as cold as his gaze, "No Patricia, you never intended to get back with me. You never wrote; you never felt the slightest remorse other than for yourself. No one else has ever mattered to you, and never will. No, I think not Patsy; I think being back with you would be a travesty. No, I think you are not the right woman for me."

"But why?"

"In all this conversation, have you ever felt for me?"

"Of course darling, why...," at a loss for words, she stammers.

"You were going to say that you love me?"

"Yes, of course I do."

"No you don't; all the love you have is reserved for you and only you. I doubt you love that baby you're carrying. I feel so sorry for that innocent soul."

"Why, you bastard!" She shouts at him.

"No Patsy, that's what you are growing in your belly; a bastard."

"How dare you?" She shrieks and rushes him with her fists raised. He grabs her by the wrists and twisting his hands down and behind his back, brings her into him. He can feel her heaving against him. "Let me go! You're hurting me!"

Calm, smiling, he holds her, and asks, "Hurting you? You have no idea what hurt is." She struggles, he continues, "Patsy, I pity you. You have only you, and at this moment, you must loathe yourself. You have nothing, and never will until you realize there are others who have needs too, and you are willing to fill those needs, but darling, I don't think you can do that." He releases her with a little shove to get her away from him, "so goodbye Patsy. I am done with you. Thank you for showing your true self before you ruined my life along with the baby's"

She steps toward him bringing her right arm back to slap him, he sees it coming, catches her by the wrist, and spins her around by her own force and pushes her toward Miss Bessie.

Steven Wayne walks toward them. Miss Bessie moves Patricia Anne to one side. Steven Wayne takes the old, large, black woman into his arms and holds her tight. She returns the embrace, as he snuggles her head under his chin and says audible only to her, "Thank you for your healing goodness." Steven Wayne releases her, steps back, and looks at them. He smiles his sweetest, most charming smile, puts his cap on, and walks out of the Robinson house and into his future.

26) The Wilson Home

September 13th, 1863

"...and Lord, we thank thee for the safe return of our son, brother, and friend, Martin. Let his heart be at peace in the bosom of his family and may he not be called to war again. Lord, we ask thy blessing upon this bounty of which we are about to partake and give Thee great thanks for it, in the Holy name of Jesus, Amen."

The chorus of "Amen" is louder than usual following Reverend Claiborne's blessing. All present have much to be thankful for this Sabbath day.

The Reverend has survived his personal debacle at the Robinson house because Patricia Anne is more worthy of comment. He is viewed as a victim and somehow has become more endeared to his congregation and the community for having suffered humiliation at the hands of such a crass family as the Robinsons, being slave owners and all. It escapes the critics and gossips that the Robinson enterprises feed about a third of the families in the valley. The rich and powerful seldom stumble, but when they do, there is no mercy.

The story has grown in its telling. At the last recounting, Patricia Anne, stripped naked by those trying to hold her had assaulted the reverend with a brass candle stick and if not for the intervention of Congressman Yeller, the poor preacher would have been beaten to death by the screaming banshee.

It does not matter that there were no candle sticks in the house in the middle of the day in July. Such an inclusion adds to the story to the point that even those in attendance see its value and thus it lives in the re-telling.

Reverend Claiborne, for his drunkenness, expected condemnation. To his astonishment, his reported crushed skull, fractured ribs, and broken leg all healed the week after and are considered a manifestation of God's power and the reverend's close association with Him. The reverend capitalized on his *faux* miracle by holding a revival that broke records for attendance and offerings, bearing testimony that people will believe what they want.

The reverend waxed eloquent for three nights and twice on Sunday about the evils of demon rum. He had never preached with such fire and passion. Most assumed he was in reference to the drinking of the assailant, and none suspected that the depths of his passion sprung from the well of self reprisal. His repentance being a personal matter between himself and the Lord, he was not about to set them straight. Moonshine sales plummeted, but the local moonshiners blamed their woes on Patricia Anne Robinson, not the dear reverend.

Claiborne's presence at the Atwood/Wilson Sunday gatherings is as a revered guest, not just a man of the cloth looking for a free feed. The community considers it an honor to have him grace their homes. Today, he beatifically sits at the table, taking dainty bites of his meat and beans as he thinks an angel or a saint would. Every so often, he stops eating and looks heavenward with the same countenance that amazed onlookers at the cursed wedding as if he were communicating with heaven. He sighs, and continues to sustain his mortal existence with the earthly necessity of eating.

The Wilson clan, suffering for the loss of John Wesley in February, is buoyed by the return of 2nd Lieutenant Martin Wilson. "Son, please eat all you want," pleads Rebecca Wilson, the relieved, and proud mother of the hero. Then to herself, "he looks so thin, and so old."

His brothers respect the change in him. Even the older ones with families of their own, now defer to his commanding presence. The younger children treat him as if he's a returned crusader; none with more deference than Susan Wilson.

"Martin," she says within hearing of Eliza Atwood, Evans' mother, "tell us of Evans' capture, please."

Martin is uncomfortable at the request, but the gathering expects it, and he relents. He tells them in detail. As he finishes, tears run down his cheeks as he says, "He could have escaped, but he would not leave Buck even though it's the order of battle; we were to leave the wounded for the hospital corps to take care of, Evans would not leave his friend, and now is a prisoner."

"May God protect him!" Declares the Reverend, and is joined by another chorus of "Amen".

"Yes," Susan Wilson says, "please God, protect him."

"What are you going to do Martin?" One of the Atwood brothers asks.

Martin smiles, "I'm going to stay here and look after Ma, and see what I can do to help Lucy Jane, and hope that I'm not called back for duty."

"Do you think that'll happen? Solomon Wilson, the oldest of the brothers asks.

"The 15th regiment is not being reorganized, and I do not know if I would go if called. If the cause needs me, I will serve in some capacity, but I won't go to battle."

Rebecca Wilson squeezes the hand of her son, and says, "Martin, anwer the call if you must, but it is so good to have you here."

"Yes Ma; it's good to be here."

She looks at him, now twenty years old. He was a boy when he left, barely seventeen; he's a man now. There is flint hardness about his eyes. He's different in other ways too. He does not handle his rifle and weapons as things of joy anymore. He respects and cares for them, but they are tools, nothing more. His brothers asked on the third day back, "Martin, do you want to go hunting?"

Martin stopped reading and asks his mother, "Do we need the meat?"

Rebecca was surprised. In the past, it would not have mattered if they needed it or not. It would be smoked, and eaten later, but the question of need had not risen before. "No son, we don't need it."

To his brothers, "We don't need to be killing just because we can." That was the end of the discussion. They felt he would come around, be his old self, but they did not understand that the old self was left piece by piece on the battlefields where killing brought him no joy.

The gathering begins to break up, the dishes are cleared, and cleaned; goodbyes are said, and Martin wanders to the back of the yard to watch the sun set over the Ozarks. Susan goes with him and stands near. She reaches and rests her hand on his back. He sighs and puts his arm around her, pulling her close. She rests her head on his shoulder and asks, "How was he? Was he happy?"

"He was wonderful; an excellent leader; we all loved him and Buck and would follow them right into hell; did on more than one occasion."

"Was it terrible?"

"Yes, words can't describe it."

"Will you try? I mean, to describe it?"

"No; there aren't words. Poets and people who write and talk prettier than me have tried, and they've all failed. You have to be there, but you don't want to," he pauses cradling his sister, "it's the smell; you have to experience the smell. The smell is the horror of it; you can't describe a smell or a taste." He pauses, "Can you tell me what salt tastes like?"

She raises her head and twists to look at him; she smiles as she says, "My goodness listen to you; my baby brother so wise and thoughtful."

He stares at the sunset, "Evans tried to get us all to think like that. Some got it. The ones who loved him got it. He taught everyone to read some; it was important to him for all of us to be better."

"And you love him?"

"Yes, he's the greatest man I know. There isn't anything I wouldn't do for him." They stand for a long time looking at nothing, and everything. "Susan, I'm sorry, I tried to take care of him, and did once or twice, but in the end, he wouldn't let me. He ordered me away." He waited a moment as if trying to decide something then told her, "I tried Susan, I tried; I'm so sorry, I know you love him."

"Yes, I do. Are you going to help Lucy Jane?"

"Yes, if she'll let me."

"Why wouldn't she?"

"I don't know. I feel something's wrong there. I've got to go see Buck first."

"When?"

"Tomorrow; I think I have to go tomorrow."

"Please be careful."

"Do you feel it too?"

"Yes, there's danger around Lucy."

They watched the sun dip below the horizon and the dark creep out of hiding. All soldiers dread it; it's when the nightmares come.

27) Buck's Place

It's cool in the higher country in mid-September. The colors in the Ozarks are changing foretelling an early winter. Martin rides with his brother Ben and Bill Atwood who are anxious to see Buck and Olivia again.

The three are happy as they ride in the crisp clean air. They speak of anything and everything. The boys tell Martin of Buck and Olivia; about Cousin Sallie, and the children. They're anxious to get there, but for different reasons; the boys, to hear more tales; Martin, to see his former comrade in arms and to know of Lucy Jane.

She's his friend's wife, but the situation is delicate with the strong feelings that Susan has for Evans. He knows that his sister harbors no ill will toward Lucy Jane, but doubts it is reciprocated. He feels a duty to help Lucy Jane, and when he does, he will be helping Evans.

They arrive at Buck's place in the middle of a sunlit afternoon. Buck walks onto the porch in shirt sleeves; no jacket, no gun belt. It's the first time the three have seen him without weapons. He greets them with a big smile and, "Hello boys!" Ben and Bill lead the way up the path. Martin holds back. He says it's because he wants to surprise Buck, but the truth is he's nervous meeting up with the man he abandoned on the battle field.

"Who's that with you?"

Both boys smile, but neither speaks. Martin is now between them.

He gets near the steps, raises his head, and says, "Hello sergeant."

"Martin! Oh my God, it's Martin! Olivia, Sallie, come see here; it's Martin!" Buck ambles down the steps as Martin dismounts. Buck meets him before his feet touch the ground and takes him in a bear hug as he twirls the young man around like a child.

"Buck," says Ben, "I don't know it for a fact, but I don't think you're supposed to be hugging officers!"

Buck sets Martin down and looks into his face, and sees a man where a boy was the last time they saw each other. The shock of the change shows on Buck, but he recovers and says, "An officer; they made you and officer?"

"Yes, they did. We were in Vicksburg during the siege. Colonel Reynolds called an election, and they picked me."

"You're the youngest of the bunch!"

"Yeah, I know. It was awkward, and I took a lot of ribbin' but everyone did as I said, and we were the best of the company in no time."

"You are a good leader; I always knew it. I'm happy and proud for you." Buck comes to his best position of attention and salutes.

Martin, as natural as if he's born to it, returns the salute and says, "As you were sergeant."

Buck says in a mock, officious tone, "Yes sir," cuts away his salute and gathers Martin in another bear hug.

Martin says in a whisper, "I'm sorry I left you that day; I'm so sorry."

Buck returns the whisper, "You were ordered away by your commanding officer, and you disobeyed anyway."

"You saw me?"

"Every step of the way, right up until the time we were captured. I had to close my eyes and fake being unconscious. Then when we were going to the hospital, there you were, hiding, going tree to tree."

"How did you..."

"That was dumb boy; you could have been captured too, but it's obvious you weren't."

"No, I wasn't dumb. Sometimes I wish I had been captured to keep my oath to Susan to watch out for Evans."

"Oh yeah..."

"...but I didn't, did I?"

"Yes you did; you did your best, that's all anyone can ask. Susan don't blame you none, does she?"

"No, and she has great faith in his return; a faith I wish I shared."

"You don't think he'll make it?" Martin doesn't answer and looks away. "Let me tell you something Martin, Evans is a fighter. He'll find a way to make it. I half expect him to walk up that path any day now."

"Have you heard from him?"

"Yep, just the other day; I'll let you read the letter. Right now, there's some people I want you to meet."

The women and children gathered and were greeting Ben and Bill. Buck releases Martin and makes the introductions closing with, "this is Martin Wilson; we served together." It sounds both sad and strange to both men.

There is a change in Buck's tone as he says, "Martin, may I present Olivia Lacey." It's simple, but the affection is unmistakable.

"It is a pleasure to meet you all," replies Martin to all the greetings, continuing with, "and I'm glad to be here; real glad."

The formalities done, they talk about various subjects as folks who haven't seen each other in a while do. It's a mixture of catching up and making everyone feel welcome, it is light banter. They talk of such as the fall colors, the right time to slaughter hogs, winter garden of root crops, and more.

Ben and Bill, with William along, go to "hunt up something for supper". The girls turn to play, while the women go to take care of the cooking, leaving Martin and Buck on the porch in chairs Buck has crafted from river willow. They're quiet, enjoying the day, the sounds, and smells of Fall. Martin breaks the silence, "You mentioned a letter."

"Yeah, I did. I'll get it." Buck pushes himself up, stretches, and declares, "I'm getting old."

"You've been old; now you're getting ancient."

Buck gives Martin a playful cuff on the side of his head and goes into the house. In a few minutes he comes out and hands Martin the letter. "You read it. I'm going to walk around some."

August 25th, 1863
Johnson Island, Ill.

Buck,

Thank you for your letter. It was hard to take, and made harder by the circumstances of not being at liberty to fend for my own. Should you see my sweet Lucy Jane, please do all you can to assure her of my devotion and love.

Conditions here are worse. Rations are cut again, we no longer get newspapers, and buying such things as paper have been severelly limited as word has spread north concerning the conditions of Yankee prisoners being held at a place called Andersonville in Georgia. I do not know the place, but the stories told to us by the guards are, I hope, hateful exaggerations. I doubt this place is much different. We are beginning to be desperate.

The men who guard us are not combat soldiers and are a source of comedic relief. They spend a great deal of time playing with their rifles as if they were toys. The other day, two were doing a mock battle and shot each other.

They are allowing darkies to guard us. They are the worst. Their cruelty knows no bounds, but is usually short lived. They are still intimidated by whites and don't know how to act other than as bullies. In one of the barracks the other night, a guard thrust his rifle through one of the cracks in the wall and fired, seriously wounding a captain from Virginia.

Please tell Mrs. Lacey that I am friends here with General M. Jeff Thompson. He sends his best wishes and condolences to Mrs. Lacey and regrets to inform her of the demise of her husband, in Missouri. He is sending a letter with details under separate post. Please extend my love and best wishes to the widow. I hope this news brings peace to you both and you can move forward. It is a brave, honorable, and selfless thing you are doing.

There is no chance of my leaving this place. With the Andersonville revelations, the Yankees have suspended any kind of parole. I wonder at George's choice. Was it the right one, or in death, does he regret it? I must not think such thoughts. I am doing the right and honorable thing. I am sorry that it is hard on Lucy and the children, now you.

Thank you for standing by me. Keep the faith, and hope there is a way out. There is a way off this island, but we must endure a little while longer.

Your friend and brother in arms,

Evans Atwood
2nd Lieutenant, CSA

Martin folded the letter and held it in his lap. "Buck, I feel like I need to go see Lucy Jane. I don't know why, maybe it's because I need to tell her what I know about the capture and all, but I feel that I have to go."

"Is that why you came up here?"

"That's one reason. What do you think?"

"I don't think she's gonna want to see you because of you being Susan's brother." He pauses for a moment, thinking. "Maybe it'd be worth the trip over. You want me to go with you?"

"Yes, I do, but aren't you needed here with Olivia?"

"You mean about her husband?"

"Yeah, how'd she take the news?"

"She'd been 'specting it. She pretty much knew he was dead, but the news is never easy. It was hard at first, and when she got General Thompson's letter, she just read it, walked into the woods for awhile, and came back quiet, but no tears this time. She and Sallie been talking a lot. It's good." They are called for supper and it gives them a chance to move away from unpleasant thoughts.

The meal is a joyful event with eight people around the table; lots of smiles, talk, and laughter. Buck watches, smiling for no reason other than he's happy. Olivia is watching him, and as their eyes meet, she's smiling too. She winks at Buck, and he laughs. She puts her lips together in a pucker and makes a kissing motion to him. He turns red under his black beard, and laughs louder. Olivia says for only him, "Thank you".

He replies, with a deep, satisfied smile knowing that Olivia is not ever going to leave this cabin. She's home and knows it. He's home, and it's full, and he's happy. "Please dear God, if you're there, don't let war touch this group and the families here," but he knows what he prays for is not ready to be answered. As long as Evans is in prison, William McPheeters is still with the army, and Lucy Jane is doing whatever she's doing, the prayer's answer will take time.

Sallie sees the exchange between Buck and Olivia, and smiles more than usual. There's joy for her too, but as long William is God knows where, there will be no peace. To see Buck and Olivia together gladdens her soul.

As if reading her mind, Buck shakes his shaggy head, and to no one in particular he says, "Will there ever be peace again?"

There is a sudden silence. Sallie breaks it by saying, "Yes, there will be peace, if you mean no war, yes, it will come. If you mean peace in the families affected by the war, there will be some, but none of us will ever be like before." She's quiet for a minute. All know she's not finished. "We're going to have to help each other, stand-up for each other for there to ever be peace as you mean it. You boys," looking at Buck and Martin, "you've got to go do what needs doing."

The next morning found them gone.

28) Lucy Jane and...

The fall chills Lucy Jane and the children, but is invigorating. There's energy in the air. Everything in nature senses the change and is preparing for the winter to come.

It's a busy time. Crops have to be harvested and put up, hogs butchered, meat smoked, animals hunted, wood cut, and countless other chores in the day-to-day effort of protecting and feeding herself and two little ones, but today is different. The small family has made a journey to town.

The attractive blonde threesome walks the hard packed dirt streets of Shiloh and the town's people stare. Lucy is a killer, and an adulterer. Even those who understand her plight judge harshly.

Lucy Jane and the children go about their business. People are courteous, but not friendly. Lucy Jane is accustomed to the shunning that a narrow minded populace can impose. She suffered such pains before marrying Evans. He would not tolerate innuendo or snide remarks from the town gossips, and she had been happy to come to town. Now, she hates it.

They are loading the wagon with their stores when an acquaintance from the church whose name she cannot remember approaches. "Maybe she'll walk on by and not notice me," she thinks, "Oh, what is that woman's name?"

"Lucy Jane? Lucy Jane Atwood; is that you?"

She turns, smiling at the lady and makes eye contact which has its desired effect; it always does. The woman's countenance shows a little fright.

"Honey, how have you been?" The woman gushes.

"We're fine, thank you, and you; how's your family?"

"Wonderful, we've been having a time of it like all, but we're well; praise the Lord."

"Indeed, praise the Lord," Lucy Jane replies half hearted as she works to load the wagon, "excuse me, these are heavy."

"Oh, of course dear, never mind me."

The woman moves to the side; there's no offer to help. Lucy busies herself with her purchases and the children, and as she turns to get another load, she is surprised to find the woman standing near, smiling. "It was so nice to see you. Maybe we'll see you in church."

"I do hope so dear. Those tiny children need the Lord in their lives don't they? We haven't seen you much lately."

"Yes, they do, and no, we have been busy at the place."

202 David Wilson Atwood

"Yes, I imagine it's hard to run a place by yourself and handle two children. How is Evans? Have you heard from him in that awful prison?"

"Yes, we have, and he's doing tolerable well."

"I know you miss him and all the things a man can do…"

"Here it comes," thinks Lucy Jane.

"…with all the chores, and at night, alone out there, it must be hard."

"It's coming," she thinks.

"I heard you had some trouble out there awhile back."

"There it is," to herself, then answers, "Yes ma'am; it wasn't nothing I couldn't handle."

"Dear girl, that's not what I heard. I heard you were attacked by a small army and if it hadn't been for a man on your place, you might have been killed or worse."

Lucy Jane has experienced "worse" and prefers it to being killed, but she's not going to debate the point with this gossip, so answers, "Yes, Evans' good friend Buck Buchannan helped out when things went bad."

"Buck, isn't he that awful mountain man who won't set foot in church? I can't imagine allowing him on my place!"

"That's a shame for you," Lucy locks her piercing, angry eyes on the woman, "his Christian act of selfless protection is the reason me and the children are able to stand and talk to you. Otherwise we would be dead, or worse, although, for the life of me, I can't imagine anything worse than my babies being dead. What could be worse than that I wonder?"

"Nothing, of course," the flustered woman replies, "I only meant…"

"I really have to be going. We have a long trip back before dark catches us. The light goes so much earlier these days…"

"I understand there was another man there that night," the woman interrupts, insistent.

"There were many there that night; they're all dead now thanks to Buck. Now, please excuse me," as she loads the children onto the wagon. "Have a good day." She climbs up to the wagon seat.

The woman presses on, "I heard there was one of Mr. Atwood's comrades in arms, even a fellow prisoner of war present that night."

Lucy Jane manages to be civil, "I would love to stay and chat, but I really must go."

The woman is desperate to garner more fodder for her gossip mill, "Mrs. Atwood don't you think that having a man on your place, not your husband is…"

"…most fortuitous," a masculine voice from behind the woman finishes the sentence. "Yes, I think that's a wonderful blessing and most timely to have a man visit that very night. The Lord is looking out for you Mrs. Atwood," the man says as he steps forward.

"Well, Steven Wayne Culpepper, good afternoon sir! I heard you were back from the war, paroled and home safe; how wonderful to see you!"

"Thank you Mrs. Clarke," then to Lucy Jane, "How are you Mrs. Atwood; well I hope?" Steven Wayne is dressed in a suit and tie, polished boots, and is clean shaved and barbered. He looks calm, and at peace.

"I am well sir. Congratulations on your parole. I am so glad you do not have to be a prisoner like Evans."

"Yes, that is ironic isn't it? If your husband had not been captured in Mississippi, he would be home too."

Lucy Jane does not like Steven Wayne's tone, and doesn't know what to make of it. She stays silent, glaring at him from the wagon seat. He stares back, his smile never wavering.

"I need to run along," interjected Mrs. Clarke into the uneasy stillness, "it's nice to see you both. Lucy Jane I hope to see you in church."

Lucy looks from Steven Wayne to Mrs. Clarke, who has felt the heat of the exchange between Steven Wayne and Lucy as one would from a hot stove. "Thank you for stopping to chat; I know you got nothing from it, so I wish you a better day."

"Good day Mrs. Clarke; give our regards to Jimmy when you write him." She nods and walks away. Steven Wayne comments, "Horrid woman; the only reason she talks to anyone is to get information for gossip." Silence hangs in the cool, Fall air. Steven Wayne is still smiling. "I do hope you will forgive my not calling on you sooner to pay my respects. Your husband was a wonderful officer."

"'Is', Mr. Culpepper, 'is' a wonderful officer. He's not dead."

"Of course not; I didn't mean to imply anything of the sort."

Lucy Jane smiles her prettiest, lets Steven Wayne swim for a moment in the cool, inviting pools of her eyes and takes up the reins to leave. "Good day to you sir."

"Have you eaten?"

"Sir?"

"Have you and the children eaten? It is near noon, and if you can spare an hour, I would be delighted to buy dinner for you. I was on my way to the café when I saw you."

"Yes, well, thank you, but we must be going."

"Mrs. Atwood," Steven Wayne persists, "please allow me the honor of doing you this service for the service of your husband; to honor him and you as well for your sacrifice." Steven Wayne can charm just as effectively as Lucy Jane. His teeth are immaculate and white. His brown hair and eyes are soft and shining. It's hard to say "no".

It's Lucy's turn. Her voice loses its hard edge. Her eyes are a seductive magnet. "In honor of Evans, we accept. Will you assist me?" She offers her hand as she steps down from the wagon. She holds his hand a moment longer than is necessary after she is down. It does not go unnoticed.

After he helps the children down, he says, "Shall we go?" He offers his arm to Lucy Jane.

She takes it, and says, "Come children, take my hand."

Heads turn and talk stirs at the sight of Lucy Jane Atwood in town, but with her on the arm of the dashing war hero, folks stop and watch as the two with the gorgeous children walk to the café.

They enter and are seated, place their orders and are left alone. The talk is strained at first. The weather, the war, the children are made a fuss over, and finally, "Mrs. Atwood, I don't…"

"Please, call me Lucy Jane."

"Thank you and I would consider it an honor if you would call me Steven Wayne."

She smiled. "You were saying…"

"I don't mean to pry, but what did transpire at your place the other night?"

"Evans' and my place don't you mean?"

"I hope he rots there," thinks the monster in Steven Wayne, but says, "I used the word 'your' in the plural, of course."

"Thank you."

"So, what did happen?"

"Steven Wayne, I do not want to discuss it with the children present, but it was awful. If it hadn't been for Buck, it would have been much worse."

"Buck, Buck Buchanan? He's here?" Steven Wayne asks, startled.

"Why, yes he is. After he was wounded and Evans was captured assisting him to the hospital, he was furloughed, but since the fall of Vicksburg, and the 15th not being reorganized, he, like you, is waiting. He had a difficult trip from Mississippi." Steven Wayne is looking out the window of the café as if he expects Buck to walk up at any moment. Lucy's wondering why Steven Wayne seems concerned with Buck. "Steven Wayne?"

"Yes," he says as he directs his attention to Lucy.

"Is there something wrong?"

"Buck is a good man; the best sergeant under my command. I need to look him up, wish him well. I suppose he is fit for duty if he aided you the other night."

Lucy Jane senses danger in Steven Wayne and wonders at it. "Why is he so interested in Buck?" To redirect the conversation, she asks, "Isn't your enlistment and obligation fulfilled?"

"That's right, but they could form a new unit and require our service."

"So, he's as free as you are?"

"Yes."

"Good, he has been a good friend, and is Evans' particular friend. I would hate for him to go back to the army. We've had enough of that haven't we?"

Steven Wayne's tension eases, "Yes Lucy Jane, we have; more than any of us should be called to bear." After a pause, "How are you faring out there alone?"

"We get by."

"From what I hear, you can handle it."

"Yes."

"Lucy Jane, rumor has it that George Paul was on your place that night and was killed. Is that true?"

"George was there," she answers, and before Steven Wayne can ask more, she adds, "he was delivering a letter from Evans. They were in prison together. He took the parole and could not find his family in Missouri, so came to fulfill his obligation to Evans."

"That's not all he fulfilled," thinks Steven Wayne. "I'm certain it was a terrible time," he says aloud.

Wanting to re-direct the conversation, Lucy says, "I cannot imagine the ordeal you suffered at the siege."

"Yes," he says with more force than he intended, but his pain and the monster are just below the surface. "It was horrible," he says softer. "I won't go back," harder again.

"Good," she said, "you've done enough."

"Do you have anyone to help around your place?"

"Yes, Buck comes, but he lives in Benton County, so it's not often. Evans' brothers and neighbors come by. The church people assist, but not as much as before..." She leaves the thought hanging.

"Lucy, would you mind if I came to call?" He sees her shock and is quick to add, "Just to help out? I would consider it an honor to be able to assist the family of a fellow officer of my command. I would appreciate the honor to serve him as well as you. Would you allow that?"

She softens, smiles her most seductive smile and says, "Steven Wayne, of course you can call. I look forward to it."

Lucy too wants information, but not knowing how to extract it without being blunt, she is. "Didn't you suffer a great loss at the hands of Patricia Anne Robinson?" She can tell by the way his face goes cold and hard that she has been too bold. Something terrifying shows for a flash, then it's gone, but she saw it.

Steven Wayne's charm comes back in an instant as he says with sadness, "Yes, but that's all over. We've met and there is to be no reconciliation. It was terrible, but it's behind me. We must look forward from our losses, don't you agree?"

"Oh yes, I do. I wish I could turn my back on it and move on. I want something better than this, don't you?"

"Yes, I want better; something much better."

Their food is served, and the kids wolf down so much that Lucy Jane has to share her food with them. Steven Wayne smiles and says, "It looks like they're eating for two!"

Lucy Jane smiles at him and thinks, "No, they aren't, but I am Steven Wayne. You are so welcome to come help us. I'm sure that together, we can make it all better."

29) Johnson Island

October 11th, 1863

Sunday

Johnson Island, Ohio

Today we had preaching. Several came from Sandusky to offer services. I have been attending the various denominations with a great deal of interest.

The conditions here are worsening. We are overcrowded. Since the collapse of the exchange cartel, there are 2,500 here in a place built for 1,500. There is little water, and our rations have been cut to bare subsistence. I am hungry all the time. Our meager rations are met with glee. We are given brown bread, small amounts of beef, and water. Rice soup is occasionally substituted for the meat. Any who have money, or things to barter can buy extra food from the gardens of some of the guards. Those who have been here for awhile, "dry cod" they call us, have been stripped of all valuables and have to suffer through on what we have.

Sanitation is horrible. The sinks or latrines at the back of the barracks are dug eighteen feet long, five feet wide, and five feet deep with a shed over them. These were adequate and not too unpleasant, but as more and more prisoners use them, they fill up, necessitating new ones. The problem is that eight feet below the surface, the island is a bed of rock which allows for poor drainage so even when the sinks are filled and covered over, they remain a filthy bog. To complicate this, many men won't make the trip across the yard to use the filthy facility and have taken to easing themselves where they may, making the entire yard filthy.

The sinks breed numerous rats which the catching of has become a necessity and a sport. Some of the fellows have devised rakes as they call them which are similar to their namesake with sharpened tines that can impale five and six rats at a time. These are cleaned and sold to offset the meager rations. It's a growing business. I have eaten them, and although not a fare I would chose, hunger lowers our social resistance to many of the atrocities we see here.

The "dead house" is seeing increased use. The dead from the night before are laid outside the barracks and left until a detail can go out and dig the graves for them. Since I have been here, we have seen almost two hundred receive their permanent parole. Cholera is the prime killer, although dysentery or the "Ohio High Step" is taking more than it would if we had enough water and food to care for our sick and wounded.

There have been some who can no longer tolerate living in these conditions who have stepped over the dead line and dared the guards to shoot them. I watched one poor soul crying as he crossed the yard with his friend pleading with him to "not do it", but to no avail. He stepped across the line, raised his shirt and dared the guards to "do your duty". He was warned, and the guard did his duty. The load of buckshot took the poor fellow's jaw off and part of his neck. He died later that night.

I sometimes think George did the right thing leaving, but he is dead and I am alive, and as long as I am alive, I have hope and where there is hope, there is life and I will survive.

"Atwood!" Bellows a Union sergeant coming toward me, beckoning.

I put away my journal and pen and holler back, "Sergeant, what can I do for you?" He is a good sort; respects those of us who have stood in battle and provides our mess with extra rations when he can.

"Are you up to leading a wood cutting party boy-o?"

"Yes sergeant, I am, if it will get me out of the yard for awhile."

"It'll do that and more," he says with a wink.

I know he will give our mess extra food for my work, and there are some who are growing weak who can use the nourishment. I have remained in good health when compared with others. I have lost weight, and the loss has diminished my strength, but work like this alleviates the boredom and makes things better for some of the men. "Then, I'm your man," I reply smiling.

"When you get done with the detail, the doctor wants to see you in the hospital."

"What for?"

"I don't know laddie, but it seems to be a good thing. I wouldn't worry none about it if I was you."

But I do. The wood cutting detail, instead of providing a happy relief from the tedium of the yard is something I want to end, so I push the men. They are angry and call me turncoat saying I work harder for the Yankees than for my own.

The day drags by. By mid-afternoon, we are done; wood stacked, axes put away, guards dispersed, and we are left to ourselves. I make my way to the hospital near the main gate, away from the barracks and sinks.

I go in and wait at the entry. There's a desk to one side for a clerk. Behind that desk, through a door, there is another desk in what I assume is the doctor's office. There are anatomy charts on the wall, a human skull sitting on the corner of the desk with letters in its mouth which must annoy the postal clerk.

My laughter gets the attention of a Union corporal that I can see through a double door leading to the hospital ward. He stops his work and comes asking, "What do you want Reb?"

"I was sent here. I'm told the doctor wants to see me."

"What's your name?"

"Who are you?"

"I'm the one asking you questions traitor, now what's your name?"

I turn to go; whatever the Union doctor wants with me will have to wait; I may be a prisoner and subject to their whims and abuse, but this man rubs me the wrong way and I am not willing to put up with it.

"Hey, where are you going?"

I don't answer, open the door and step out. It is much cooler as the sun dips toward the horizon.

"I'm talking to you!"

I don't care and keep walking.

"Is your name Atwood?"

I stop and look back. The clerk is standing on the top step, and behind him, through the open door stands a tall, dark haired man of about forty, maybe younger, in a white, full length coat that is splattered with blood. He's wearing a shirt, open at the collar, and has a bemused look on his thin, bearded face. "Yes, I'm Lieutenant Atwood, and who might you be?"

"I'm Corporal Mather," he says, a little more pleasant.

"That's better corporal; now, what can I do for you?"

"The doctor wants to see you."

"I believe I told you that when I was inside while you were being ill mannered."

"You'd better get inside; you don't want to make the doctor mad."

"I'm sure you don't Corporal Mather, but I don't care; however, I will come inside if you invite me." I can see the man's face, who I assume to be the doctor, break into a big smile.

"Invite you; what do you mean invite you?"

"You know corporal, manners; like, 'come right in sir, I'll tell the doctor you're waiting? They do teach manners in the North?"

The corporal is frustrated and angry, but he doesn't want to get on the doctor's bad side. "Come on in, will you? I don't want doc finding me out here arguing with rebel scum."

"Corporal the only scum out here being argumentative is you. Please give the doctor my compliments, and I leave it to you to explain why I was here and left." I turn and walk away.

"Wait…"

I stop and turn back.

"…will you please come inside, the doctor would like to see you."

"Certainly," I say and start to the door. As I pass the corporal at the top of the steps, I say, "Now that wasn't so hard was it Mather?"

He turns to follow me and is about to rip into me verbally when he sees the man who has been standing behind him and says, "Oh, doctor, sir; I didn't know you were there. Sir, the rebel Atwood is here."

The tall, thin man has happy blue eyes and a black beard and hair. His nose is as thin as he is, but not as long as it needs to be. It is out of proportion to the rest of his face. As I get closer, I can see that there is a scar under his right eye running to his nose which is misshapen. The doctor has been wounded. "I'm Dr. Allison," he says extending his hand.

I take it, and complete the introduction.

"Won't you come in lieutenant? I've been expecting you."

His words cause me to wonder; "Expecting me; what is he expecting me for?"

We pass the corporal who falls into step and follows us in. We go to the office and Dr. Allison says, "Please come in." Turning to close the door as I walk past him, he says, "that will be all corporal; I'll call you if I need you." He turns back to me with, "I apologize for Corporal Mather, he hates rebels. He lost his father and a brother at Bull Run, or Manassas as you boys from the South call it. I think he wishes he was killed there too. He was wounded and near death, but survived and has been bitter and unhappy since."

"It looks to me sir, that he was not the only one wounded," as I touch my nose to mirror the doctor's injury, "did you receive yours at Manassas?"

"I did; shrapnel in the face. I was fortunate to not lose more than my beauty."

"We all carry scars from this war sir, and perhaps Corporal Mather has an excuse for rudeness, but I would suggest sir, that it is not a reason."

"I agree; perhaps you can teach him some manners and change his attitude about southerners as you work with him."

"Work with him sir?"

"Yes lieutenant, he and I, if you agree to be my assistant."

"Your assistant? Sir, I don't understand."

"No, I didn't think you would," he smiles and chuckles, "I am playing light with you lieutenant, but I do find it ironic, how the world turns and we find ourselves crossing paths with people in the strangest circumstances, don't you?"

"I beg your pardon sir, but I do not follow?"

"Do you believe in coincidence Mr. Atwood, or do you believe that all things happen for a purpose?"

"I believe that we are all in the hand of God and he provides us with what we need, or allows us to help others."

"Ah, I too believe in God and His providence, and He has shined on both of us."

"How so sir?"

"I have a colleague, who I was privileged to work with in St. Louis. I believe you know him; Dr. William McPheeters?"

"Yes sir, I have had the honor of assisting Dr. McPheeters twice. The last time he patched me up just before I became a prisoner."

"So he said; and he also says that you were a tireless assistant, and a quick study in medicine. He indicated that with the proper training, you might make a fine doctor someday."

"I am flattered sir. How did you learn this?"

"From a letter asking if I might make inquiries as to your location and see if I could effect a transfer for you to here. As bad as this place may seem, the other prisons are far worse. When I searched, I found you here, no doubt the hand of providence, and would like to ask you to be my assistant in the hospital aiding your southern brethren. Would that interest you?"

"Yes sir; it would be an honor sir."

"Good, I'll make the arrangements, and expect you here at first light. You will be taking meals with us as I cannot wait for you to get your rations, eat and come here. It would be too late in the day. You can take any leftovers to your mess mates, so they will not think you are consorting with the enemy. You will rotate with Corporal Mather staying on the ward at night. It is rough duty, you will be doing all the dirty work of a hospital all night, and then the next day without rest, but it is rewarding, and it will break the monotony of looking for some way to pass the day."

"Thank you sir, you are an answer to prayers. I will be here first thing in the morning. Will that be all sir?"

"No lieutenant, I will ask Corporal Mather to show you around then you are dismissed until tomorrow morning, but first, Dr. McPheeters would like any news you may have concerning his wife and family. I understand your sergeant discovered that he and Dr. McPheeters' wife are cousins; another example of the Lord's provident hand, and that he was to try and locate William's wife and secure she and the children's safety. Do you have any news?"

"Yes sir I do. I received a letter last month from Sergeant Buchannan and he reports that he located Sallie, that's Dr. McPheeters' wife's name..."

"Yes, I know; as I told you, we were colleagues."

"...oh, yes sir; Mrs. McPheeters and the children are at Sergeant Buchannan's home in Benton County, Arkansas safe and sound. They had some adventures, but no mishaps, I am happy to report."

Dr. Allison beams and says, "Thank God for some good news in this awful conflict. It brightens my heart to hear of this. I will write him with the news."

"Sir, I would also like to write the doctor and thank him for thinking of me and being an answer to my prayers."

"Of course; as soon as Corporal Mather and you finish your orientation, you may use the desk in the outer office to write your letter, and I will post it along with my own."

"Thank you sir; not only for the opportunity to serve, but for your friendship to Dr. McPheeters; I admire him."

"You are welcome lieutenant. You are an answer to my prayers too. I have needed an assistant. Now, go find Corporal Mather and tell him to come see me. I don't think he will take the news of your position well coming from you."

"No sir, I don't believe he would."

Dr. Allison offers his hand again, saying, "Welcome aboard Mr. Atwood; I look forward to working with you."

I am smiling so big it hurts. I have an opportunity to continue to serve my country, my fellow prisoners, and to provide for their health better than anyone else in camp. I know that working with Dr. Allison will provide me more access to the outside and advance my other agenda. There are many things I need for my plan to work; now I have them at my finger tips.

Working with Corporal Mather will be a diversion as well.

30) The Atwood Homestead

Martin and Buck ride into the yard of the Atwood Homestead in the mid-morning brightness of a late October day. The leaves of the maples, poplars, pecans, and cottonwoods are in their full Fall colors and are gorgeous to behold in red, green, and gold hues.

It has been a casual journey south into Washington County. The two veterans, separate by age and experience, see the war different and exchange ideas about war, life, and God. It was enlightening for both of them as they develop a different friendship.

Laughing, and joking, talking loud and happy, they arrive. Lucy Jane is in the garden, watching them with her right hand shading her eyes. She does not recognize the visitors and Buck is surprised that there is no challenge.

Lucy has no weapon at hand. If she had, she would have reached for it with strangers approaching. Since Martin's father had fallen victim to bushwhackers and with the shooting here, he thinks Lucy would be more vigilant. He wonders why she isn't.

They ride within hailing distance, when Martha Jane recognizes Buck and runs to greet him hollering "Uncle Buck, it's Uncle Buck Mama." James is doing his best to keep up and mimics his sister with "Uncky Uck!" Buck swings to the ground and scoops up the little ones. He is their savior, and he will always be special to them.

Lucy Jane remains silent. Both men have dismounted and walk toward the garden. She puts down her hoe and starts toward them. Buck and Martin are too occupied with the children to read the look on her face. It takes only a glance to see that they are not welcome.

"Lucy Jane," Buck says with a nod of his head and a questioning look.

"Buck," she replies without a smile.

"This here's Martin Wilson who came with Evans and me to the 15th. He's now Lieutenant Wilson," Buck says with pride.

"How nice for you Martin; you've grown considerable since I saw you last," before Martin can respond, Lucy Jane continues, "What brings you here Buck?" The question is frosty and challenging.

"We've come to see if we can help out with the harvest and such," gesturing to the garden.

"Do you really know my pa?" Martha Jane asks of Martin.

"Yes ma'am, I know your pa well. He was my commander before he was captured."

"Oh," Martha Jane says, "do you know Mr. Culpepper?"

Martin looks at Buck, and Buck looks at Lucy Jane, who looks toward the cabin. "Yes, I know Captain Culpepper; how do you know him?"

"I know him," said the little girl, "because, he's here."

Martin looks, and sees Buck staring at Lucy while Lucy Jane is focused on something over Buck's shoulder.

He and Buck turn as a familiar voice declares, "I sure am here; aren't I Martha Jane?" Meeting the gaze of Buck and Martin, he continues, "Sergeant," to Buck, "Lieutenant," to Martin. The charm is working, his smile is glistening, but both see that Steven Wayne has changed. There's something sinister in his look.

His hair is darker, almost black from the brown of a few months ago, and although clean shaven, there's a dark shadow over his jaw. He has grown too, but the change does not give Buck the same comfort that Martin's transformation has.

The men nod, touching their hats, saying almost in unison, "Captain."

"What brings you boys over this way?"

"We've come to see if we can be of help to Lucy Jane. And you, what brings you here?"

"Same; seems Lieutenant Atwood has a lot of loyal brothers from the unit." He smiles at Lucy Jane who's not smiling at anyone.

"I see you survived Vicksburg," Buck says noticing the captain's thinner than usual physique, "Martin told me about it."

"Indeed; and what exactly did he tell you?"

"All about it; every last horror; it's a wonder anyone came out of it sane."

"Sane?" Steven Wayne challenges, then softer, "yes, sane. It is a wonder." He says to Lucy Jane, "I got a nice buck hung bleedin' out down near the river. We'll have fresh venison tonight."

"That'll be good," Lucy Jane replies without emotion.

Buck says, "I didn't hear no shootin' as we were riding," looking at Martin, he asks, "did you?"

"No, I didn't."

"I can run you both down," says Steven Wayne in a guttural voice with a glazed look in his eye. The faraway, animal sound frightens Buck and Martin.

"Is that how you got that deer? You ran it down?" Buck jokes.

Steven Wayne, isn't joking as he replies, "No, didn't need to. I jumped him from a tree." There is a maniacal leer on his face.

Buck notices blood on Steven Wayne's clothes. "You take him with a knife?"

Steven Wayne raises his hands with his fingers spread, showing the backs of them, flexes his fingers and the powerful muscles in his hands and forearms bulge showing strength not visible before. He laughs a strange, foreign laugh and a look of wild glee comes over his face as he says, "No I used the..."

"That'll do Steven Wayne," Lucy Jane interjects in a commanding voice, "why don't you go down and clean the buck and bring it up here?"

Steven Wayne looks at her for a few moments as if he does not know she's there. A peaceful look settles on him like changing a costume and he says, "Yes ma'am, I'll surely do that very thing," and turns without a look or a word as if the two men weren't there.

When he was out of ear shot, Lucy Jane demands, "What are you doing here?"

Buck's meets the glare of Lucy Jane while saying, "Girl, like I said, we've come to help get you ready for winter, or has Stevie Wayne done everything?"

"It's none of your business what Steven Wayne has done, or is doing here. I don't need rescuing Buck."

"There's no need to be hostile girl. Like I said, we're here as friends." Buck doesn't like where this is going, but presses the point "Has he taken George Paul's place?"

"What if he has; what's it to you?" She plunges on, "He's done a lot of work that needed a man to do. People round about are afraid of him. He keeps it safe; ain't nobody been around or making advances. I like it; he treats me good."

"You have a husband who treats you real good..."

"He ain't here!" She shouts, then softer, "and ain't going to be for a long time if ever; and I've got to look out for myself. I want better than loneliness and fear."

"Lucy Jane, you're the wife of my best friend, so I'm gonna speak my mind," She tries to interrupt, but Buck cuts her off, "I can almost understand George Paul being here, and Evans wanting you to aid him, but since Gavin Tate is dead, you're safe, and I can't abide Stevie Wayne being here; it just ain't right no matter how you dress it up."

"You don't have to like it."

"You've got family to help you, and we're here, what more do you want?" Lucy Jane's gaze meets Buck and is unflinching. Buck knows what she wants, and that she has moved on. In her mind, Evans is not coming back. Lucy Jane has crossed a bridge and burned it.

"He makes me feel safe; he takes care of me," she says with conviction, then softer, "he's got money."

"Lucy Jane, I've lived with the man for almost three years; he's changed..."

"So have you and Martin."

"True, and so have you, but Steven Wayne's change is different. He don't seem right somehow."

"He ain't, he's wounded deep in places you can't see."

"You've gotten that close?"

"Yeah, we're close. He tells me things; he's got plans for a better life. He's talking about going to Nebraska and starting up there."

"Just like you; always looking for better."

"And what's wrong with that? Don't I have a right to a better life?"

"Yes, but a better life is something you build, not something you grab onto on a whim; it takes time and hard work; that's what makes it better."

Lucy Jane is silent. Her look, unwavering and hard, tells the story; she's not willing to wait. She wants it now. She breaks the uncomfortable silence by saying, "If you boys want to stay for supper, you're welcome, and you can bed down in the barn, but I want you gone in the morning." She gestures for them to follow her as she starts to the cabin. They take up the reins of their horses and start to walk with her. "You've heard from Evans? What's he say?"

"The first thing he says is how much he loves you and the children. He tells about conditions there in Ohio, and how they have suspended the parole, but he thinks there's a way out. It's kind of confusing there."

"Can I see the letter?"

Buck opens his saddle bags, takes it out and hands it to her, "Read this; me and Martin will tend to the animals at the barn then we'll come up."

She takes the letter and goes up the steps to the cabin. Buck and Martin move to the barn. "What do you think?" Martin asks. "Do you think she's taken up with Stevie Wayne? Is he that big a snake? I thought he was engaged to Patricia Anne Robinson."

"Boy, I guess you ain't heard that story yet."

"What story?"

"About Patricia Anne's wedding."

"You mean Steven Wayne's married?"

"No, far from it. Come on in here," gesturing to the barn, "I got a story to tell you."

After the tale is told, Martin smiling, chuckles, trying not to laugh at another's misfortune, but before long both he and Buck are roaring with laughter at the imagined sight of the wedding.

When they are able to converse without gasping for breath, Martin says, "You know, it's kind of sad, but in a way, pompous little Stevie Wayne got his comeuppance, I mean, the way he was always strutting around all self important, using flowery language that none of us could understand. Buck, did you see his eyes when he was telling about that deer? It was like there was someone else talking."

"You said something happened to him at Vicksburg."

"It sure 'nuf did; that man's scary. There's a lot of us that Vicksburg happened to, but Steven Wayne kind of lost his mind."

"Let's go see Lucy Jane."

The door to the cabin is open. "Come on in boys, have a seat," Lucy Jane calls to them.

They make their way inside and see Lucy Jane sitting at the table with the letter spread out before her. There's a sad look on her face.

"Buck, Martin, he ain't here, he's there; I can't help him, and he can't help me. I've got to move on, and I've got to survive."

"You forgot about a 'better life'," Buck says with a sarcastic scowl.

Lucy Jane reddens but manages, "Yeah, a better life; I can't wait forever for it, and he may never be here again."

"So, you're 'moving on' with Steven Wayne."

"I could do worse, a lot worse, and he's going places."

"And where's that?" Buck asks, barely able to control his temper.

"Better."

"It don't matter to you how you get there; how many folks you have to step on, or lies you have to tell, or schemes to trap people?"

Lucy is silent.

"Martin and me'll be moving on. We don't want to interfere with your doin's here, but we are Evans' friends, and we are going to help him, and if that involves helping you, we're willing."

"I don't want your help, but you're welcome to stay for supper and sleep in the barn, but I want you out of here at first light." It is not said cold, hard, or hateful; it's just facts; deal with them. Nothing's going to stop Lucy Jane.

"What about Evans' babies? He ain't going to cotton to another man raising them. He'll come after his babies."

"Let him come; he can have 'em. I ain't gonna fight him over them."

"You don't care about them?"

Lucy glares at Buck with fierceness that he has never seen from her. He glares right back.

"Come on Buck, let's go to the barn," encourages Martin.

"Yeah, but we ain't stayin'."

"Sorry to hear that Buck," says Lucy.

"If you ever come to your senses, send word; you're still my friend's wife, and until he tells me otherwise, I'm gonna look out for you." He puts the letter in his pocket so she would not see his hand tremble with anger. "Come on Martin, let's get outa here."

"Sorry you feel that way Buck."

He turns and walks out the door, down the steps with Martin tagging along. Martin catches up, falls into step beside him, looks at Buck and decides to keep quiet.

When they get to the barn, Steven Wayne is standing by their gear. His arms are resting over the top of a stall, looking at them. "You boys ain't thinkin' of stayin' for supper are you?"

"Yeah, and spending the night too," Buck replies cheerily.

"Not a good idea," says Steven Wayne in a dead pan, flat voice.

"Why's that?"

"You boys ain't welcome here."

"Her husband who owns the place asked me to look after her, and told me I was welcome here anytime."

"You boys ain't welcome here."

"It ain't for you to decide Stevie Wayne."

"That's Captain Culpepper to you sergeant, and I will decide where you go, and where you don't. You're still under my command."

"You gave up your command when you signed that parole boy. Don't you go around ordering me like you mean something. You don't outrank what the pigs leave."

Steven Wayne starts to move from around the side of the stall, but Martin is quicker. "Hold up there Captain, we're leaving right now. There's been too much killing here and elsewhere. We got no call to be killin each other."

"Let him come Martin; I can solve at least one of Evans' problems right here and now," says Buck.

Steven Wayne's eyes have gone flat and black again, and his voice is a deep, flat, bass as he speaks, "You'd best leave now Sergeant Buchannan, before I unleash all hell on you."

"As the lieutenant says, we're fixin' to leave, but let me tell you a couple of things Stevie Wayne. Lucy Jane is a fellow officer's wife, who *was* a friend of yours, the second thing is that if I hear of you lifting a hand to her or the children, I'm coming to fix it. Do you understand me boy?"

"Don't you be threatening me Buck, I'll…"

"You ain't going to do nothing except walk out of this barn before you get yourself killed, and we ain't gonna' do nothing 'cept ride out of here, and good riddance to you and you're doings, but mark my words *Captain* Culpepper; you'd better do right by this woman."

Martin stands between them and does not relish being there. Buck's hand is in his jacket over the butt of the LeMat pistol, and Martin knows this cannot end well. He reaches for the halter of his horse and pulls him around in Steven Wayne's direction, forcing Steven Wayne to step back. "Get your horse Buck. I ain't gonna let you get into it." To Steven Wayne, "Captain I would be obliged if you'd walk away so we can leave in peace. We don't want no trouble. It'll end bad and we all know it." There's no response from Steven Wayne, "Captain!" Martin shouts.

Culpepper snaps at Martin's voice as if he has been asleep, and says, "What lieutenant? What do you want?"

"Sir, I want you to leave now, so we can saddle up. Would you oblige me that sir?"

"Yes, of course lieutenant. Please see that the sergeant leaves with you. I believe he's under your command anyway."

"Yes sir, he is, and we are leaving as soon as we can saddle up."

"Very well," and with that, Steven Wayne walks out of the barn in a daze.

"What in heaven's name was that all about?" Buck wonders aloud.

"I don't know Buck, but let's get out of here while we can, before that monster comes back. I think the siege vexed Steven Wayne in the head."

"Amen to that."

They saddle and walk their horses out into the yard. There's no one to see them leave. It seems to Buck the place is dead. They're happy to be leaving.

31) Evans

November the 5th, 1863

Benton Co., Arkansas

My friend Evans,

I read in some of the papers, that Lincoln has declared a national day of Thanksgiving the end of this month. I bet you'd like to compare thankfulness with him. You're loved and missed here by friends and family. That's worth something, I hope.

I got your letter of August last, and we was all glad to receive it. Olivia, sends her compliments and thanks for the sure knowledge of her husband's death.

Martin was made lieutenant at Vicksburg before the surrender and has been paroled. He has grown to a fine man. He ain't got the need to roam and adventure around like you and me. He worries about you and will do anything for you. He still feels beholden to Susan for his promise to take care of you. We're waiting the reorganization of the 15th which none of us believe will happen. None of us wants to get back to fighting.

Steven Wayne is back home too. He is showing an interest in Lucy Jane and is spending a lot of time at your place with her. When Martin and me went to your place to see if we could help Lucy Jane, he was there and was hostile. Something happened to him at Vicksburg; he's changed. To tell you the truth, he's not in control of himself at times.

The kids have grown. Martha Jane has become a little lady. She has seen too much for her age. James Calvin is well, but seems frail. Lucy Jane is worried for him this winter.

So far the weather has not been too bad. It's cold, and we've had snow up high, but nothing real hard yet. It's been good hunting, and a good harvest. Everyone's got lots put by for the winter including Lucy Jane, so you don't worry about that.

Your friend,
Buck

"Steven Wayne," I say to myself, "I never did trust him."

"Bad news from home?" Corporal Mather asks.

"Don't sound so gleeful Mather; I don't think the Lord would approve of your taking joy in another's suffering."

"The Lord never had to deal with rebels."

"As a matter of fact he did. You do err in not knowing your scriptures. Aren't we told in the book of Revelation that Satan rebelled against God, and a third of the host of heaven followed him?"

"I don't know; you're the one who reads them fairy tales."

It has become sport for me to needle Mather. He is so full of hate, and is so bad at it. He says he does not believe in God, but he's not telling the truth. He's angry at God for the war taking his father and brother and causing his mother, who is home in Pennsylvania to have to be taken in by friends. I have tried to tell him that God does not allow evil to reign; that that is the purview of man. If man would stand against evil, the devil would have no power, but we are weak.

I say, "Walter," that's his first name; he won't call me by mine, nor lieutenant, nor Atwood; the only thing he calls me is 'Reb' or worse, "when are you gonna stop blaming God for your loss? He didn't kill your Pa and brother."

"He didn't stop it neither did he?"

"No, he didn't, and he didn't stop me from being taken prisoner, but it ain't His fault, and besides, he has a purpose in all of it."

"What possible purpose could all this suffering serve?" He gestures with a sweep of his arm to the hospital ward where there are men of both nations clinging to hope, and dying for the lack of it.

"Well," I begin, "we've learned the difference between good and evil."

"Hell, I already knew that! Why did I have to lose my Pa and all; what good did it do?"

Walter is getting worked up, and I don't want him to go into a full blown tantrum. Still smiling, I say, "Walter, if this war hadn't happened, you would have never met me, and we would never have had such wonderful conversations!"

Walter, a big man, awkward in stance and bearing, ranges closer to where I am sitting and scowling at me from under black, heavy eye brows says, "See, another curse from God. He hates me, and I hate him."

"No you don't. You can't even say it with conviction. Every time you declare hatred for God, your voice softens. You don't hate Him, you're mad at Him, but you don't have it in you to hate."

"Yes, I do! I hate Him, and I'm sick of you talking about Him!"

"Nope, sorry; that's not very convincing hatred. You're going to have to work on that if you are going to be a real hater, but you don't have what it takes."

Walter swears at me. He's bad at that too. He can't accept that he's a good and gentle person. "I'm going to take care of my patients," he declares and storms from our shared office. He pushes through the doors to the ward with such force that they stay open.

I watch as he goes about his rounds, and then begin to write...

Journal Entry
Sunday, November 22nd, 1863

Corporal Walter Mather, for all his bluster, is as kind and gentle as a man can be. He loves his work, and I have learned from him in the few months I have been at the hospital. He still has a way to go with his gentleness for the Confederate prisoners, but when they are patients, he becomes color blind; there is no blue or gray. Watching him makes me smile.

I will follow him into the ward in a few minutes and tend the more serious cases. Walter has a hard time dealing with those that are beyond hope. They are almost always the result of a lack of nutrition and hygiene, but there is little I can do about either.

The diseases that kill here are chronic diarrhea, scurvy, and pneumonia. Those with the diarrhea are by far the most difficult to tend to. They pull at your heart, because there's little we can do.

My life in the hospital is a good one if there is such a thing as a good life in prison. At least I am able to aid my fellow soldiers, and further the cause. I am not subject to the tedious boredom that affects so many. I witness many who give up hope and die, as is recorded in our official records, of "home sickness".

The work is hardest when I have the night duty and then have to work all the next day. When I am off, I go to my quarters and sleep for hours without notice of any activity around me. I am still on the prisoner roles and receive rations even though I do not mess with my group. They divide my rations among themselves; the most to the sick. No one has accused me of aiding the enemy. They think that the Confederate prisoners would not receive the same treatment at the hands of the Yankees, which is not true.

Dr. Allison is a wonderful man and cares for all he treats. He has been able to arrange furloughs for the sicker patients to go home and recuperate.

I have loved Lucy Jane with my whole heart, but she has abandoned me. My misery lies not in that she has taken up with another man, although that hurts worse than any wound I could receive, the deeper pain is that I can do nothing about it.

I have pleaded with her in letters, and she has not replied. I now know why. If I can get out of here, I can salvage what I have left. It may not be Lucy Jane, but my children, home, and land are not hers for the taking.

A few years ago I was at home, a child. My brothers and sisters were there, sharing with me the pleasures of childhood; fond parents looked upon us with the hope of seeing us grow up to riper years endowed with those graces that would be a blessing to us, and a comfort to them in their declining years. They expected our associations and aid in later years, but alas, how changed the scene now appears. A brother has been called away; a sister has also gone to that place from whence no traveler returns, except in angel form, to watch over us. Friends murdered, loves lost, wife's treachery, and not knowing, never knowing.

War has marched her minions through our once happy country. Another sister has moved to Indiana, the wife of a **former** friend, and now a political enemy, while I am here on this "Second Patmos"; a prisoner.

A wife, children, father, mother, and sister; perhaps a brother at home in Arkansas; not knowing that I am alive. Three years have almost passed since I saw them, and war is yet moving onward, recruiting for death; marching her thousands to the grave. How long will times thus go on? When shall the Angel of Death stay his arm of revenge, and wing his flight to other realms; and mercy, the angel of peace shall revisit us with the olive branch entwined around her radiant brow, saying "Peace, be still." Then shall the "weary" soldier return to his friend and home of former days. Many instead of homes will find ashes and graves of those whom they loved and whose memory is dear to them.

I put away the journal as Dr. Allison walks into the hospital. He is tired and drawn, "Good morning sir; rest well?"

He forces as smile and a nod, "Good morning Atwood. How did it go last night?"

"No real problems sir. No one passed, but I fear that that will not be the case tomorrow morning. Some are going fast. I tried to make them comfortable, but…"

"Yes, it is hard when there is so little we can do."

"I wrote a few letters for them. That always makes me very tired. It reminds me to much of my home."

Noticing the letter laying on the desk, he asks, "News from home?"

"Yes sir, and I am afraid it's not good."

He stops, sits across from me and says, "Care to tell me about it?"

I did. I told him the whole sordid tale finishing with, "If I can get out of here, I know I can salvage it."

"Will you take the parole if it is offered again?"

"No sir, I cannot do that. I cannot dishonor my country and my oath by signing that parole."

He smiles at me and says, "I understand, and admire your commitment, but lieutenant, family comes first."

"I agree sir, but in my thinking, when Lucy Jane and I said, 'for better or for worse', we made a commitment of loyalty, a covenant, an oath. I have not broken mine, and I expect her to honor hers'."

"In a way, you have broken yours. You swore to provide for her, but you have not, and now she is desperate and hopeless as far as you are concerned."

"Sir, let me ask you a question," the doctor nods his assent, "when this war started, did you think it would go on for three years?"

"No, I did not."

"Another question if you please," again, a nod, "has your wife stood by you?"

"Yes, she has, but our situations are different. She has family close, and she has my pay coming to her. I dare say that your Lucy does not."

I nod my agreement.

"Then she has chosen to take the only path available to her. You cannot fault her for it."

I don't feel like explaining about Susan Wilson and the beginning of Lucy Jane's and my relationship, so I do not answer for a moment and let the silence be construed as my acknowledgement.

I have, over the period of my posting to the hospital, pushed my plan forward. I have secreted a full uniform for a captain in the medical corps complete with insignia to aid me in my escape. I have learned enough medicine to be able to pass for a doctor. The problem will be in getting to the mainland without arousing suspicion or sounding the general alarm. My plan calls for scaling the wall of the compound at night in winter, walking across the ice and catching a train south. I will not have orders, so if stopped and questioned, I will be doomed.

I turn to look out the window, "Look sir, it's snowing!"

"Yes, the lake will freeze solid soon."

"Yes sir it will. We'll be able to walk to town." I smile. Walking is easier than getting a boat.

32) Susan Wilson

"Honey," begins Susan's mother, "just because your Pa's dead don't mean you have to stay around here and take care of me and this house. I may be forty-five, but I ain't dead. I can fend for myself."

Susan smiles as she darns the socks of her brother Martin who is tending the animals.

"Did you hear me girl?"

"Yes Mama, I hear you."

"Well, what you got to say for yourself?"

"Nothing Mama; do I have to say something?"

"Girl, I love you, and love having you here, but it hurts my heart to see you unhappy moping around here."

"I'm not moping; and I'm not unhappy. Besides, where do I have to go?"

Rebecca Wilson looks at her daughter. Susan is right; she has no place to go. She turned twenty-four the past July, but to Rebecca, she's wasting away. Since Evans chose Lucy Jane over her, Susan seems to have stopped living her life.

She's kind, works hard, and does it all as smooth as ever, but the blow Evans dealt her has hurt deeper than she had ever knew was possible. She hurts at the thought of him and the pain is intensified to agony at the mention of his name. She never shows it, but Mama knows; mothers do. She sighs and asks in a resigned voice, "When are you going to let go and give him up?"

"Give up who Mama?"

"You know damned well who!" Rebecca shouts at her daughter.

Susan drops her darning and looks at her mother dumbfounded. She has never heard her curse before, and has heard her rarely shout; but to have her curse and shout at the same time is something that has never happened. She stares at her mother. This is serious.

"Say something girl!"

"Mama?"

"Oh, for heaven's sake; is that all you can say? Let him go honey; he's caused all of us enough pain!"

"I can't Mama."

"Why not? He's not coming back, and if he does, he's got that tramp Lucy Jane to deal with. I've heard she's allowed that Culpepper boy to take up with her at her place, and I've heard he ain't right in the head anymore."

"Oh, Mama, that's talk. People talk all the time. You do remember what they were saying about me when Evans married Lucy Jane? I didn't give two hoots about what was said then, and I don't give two hoots now."

"Baby, let him go."

"No," Susan says with firm resolve to close the matter.

Rebecca is not deterred, "Why not?"

"Because I love him Mama; I always have, and probably always will. When he comes back, and Mama, he is coming back, I will be here. If he goes back to Lucy Jane, so be it, but I don't think I will ever stop loving him."

"Oh, Susan, it breaks my heart to see you hurting so."

"I know Mama, but it has to be this way. I knew he was the man for me when they first moved here and we were little children, and in spite of what he's done, he knows it too."

"And your just gonna take him back; just like nothing ever happened?"

"Oh no! He's going to have to do some serious penance, and make some serious promises to me before I'll even talk to him. He thinks prison is hell; wait till he has to deal with me."

"And if he doesn't?"

"He will, but if not, I'll have to look elsewhere for a husband, but it has to be Evans. It has to be, and he knows it too, deep down. He's being a little boy now, but when he gets back, he'll be a man. He'll know what to do when he gets back. Mark my words Mama; mark my words." She smiles at her mother and goes back to darning her brother's socks.

"Honey, I pray he does, but if he doesn't, I'm sure he will be in a hell worse than even Samuel Claiborne can conjure up."

"He will Mama. It's all about the faith; we've got to keep the faith. Besides, if he doesn't come back; I'm pretty sure Martin will go after him and bring him back at the end of a rifle."

They both laugh as Susan rises to tend the fire. It's cold and snowing in the winter of 1863-64.

33) Winter, Arkansas, 1863-64

It's a hard, harsh winter. Cold grips the area with a fist of purpose. There is much snow and constant cold. Very few days are above freezing. It's as if the valley and mountains are cursed. Folks wonder if it's the hand of God coming on them for secession.

In barber shops, saloons, restaurants, and anywhere else people gather, the cold is the topic of conversation. It has become the basis for sermons by area preachers, but none more powerful than those of Reverend Claiborne. He is certain that the burning of hell referred to in the Holy Scriptures is not going to be from fire and brimstone, but the intense burning one feels from extreme cold. There are few who will argue otherwise this year.

There are repentant sinners that come forward every Sabbath. These are extreme times, and when a soul is in need of declaring repentance, he does. Church attendance is up; the offering plate is full, and Samuel Claiborne is happy.

Across the valley, along the White River at the Atwood homestead there is no joy or festivities of the season. It isn't that Lucy Jane and the children are unhappy, or wanting; they have the things necessary for their temporal comfort. There is spiritual lacking that Lucy Jane fails to recognize as the reason the cold will not recede from their home.

She does not consider that the gloom and despair around the house are caused by her and her bad decisions. She thinks it is due to her condition making her feel out of sorts. Lucy Jane is expecting and has been since August. She thinks the baby is George Paul's, but maybe, by a stretch Steven Wayne's. It does not matter to her as long as Steven Wayne thinks it's his, and he has no reason to believe otherwise.

Steven Wayne is not incapable of rudimentary math, nor is he ignorant of George Paul's presence at the home preceding his arrival. He simply does not care. He's happy that Lucy Jane is pregnant. It's a witness to him that life will go on. There is light represented by the new life in Lucy Jane, and if he can just focus on that, he might survive.

He and Lucy Jane speak of Nebraska and little else. They do not speak of the children, the homestead, or of loves past. Martha Jane asks about her Pa, but she's ignored and soon views such efforts as fruitless. The last time she brought up her Pa, Steven Wayne's gaze had such malevolence in it, that she was scared. She cannot articulate it, but she knows something is wrong with Steven Wayne and from that day, she avoids him.

James Calvin has become Martha Jane's charge and spends less and less time with his mother. His health has declined with the deepening of winter but Lucy and Martha Jane can do little about it. They keep the little fellow warm at night and make sure he eats, but there is something missing which Martha cannot explain.

The children, though not abused, are ignored. There are times when Martha Jane is busy about the cabin that Lucy Jane will look at her and her brother as if she doesn't know who they are. Martha Jane knows this, but does not understand it. She does not know that she and James Calvin serve as reminders of Evans, and her mother has moved on from him and anything associated with him. It's as if the children are forgotten; some bad memory that surfaces uninvited at odd moments.

Lucy Jane's quest for a better life has taken her down a path that grows darker with every step. She does not see it and speaks of Nebraska as the Promised Land, flowing with the biblical milk and honey and of her longed for dream. She is so blinded by the brilliance of her hope that she does not recognize the fulfillment of her life's wish as she walks past it and leaves it further and further in dark history.

Steven Wayne clings to Lucy Jane with desperation born of madness, and can see no better the darkness of the future than she. He's willing to be led as long as she allows him to anchor his hope with her. He does not care where they go, but has heard so much of the new territory, that he's determined to settle there.

Lucy Jane wants to be gone from Arkansas by spring or summer. She will be ready to travel then. The baby will be born in May, or June, or for that matter, April. She does not care as long as it's born and she can move on with her life.

Despair cloaks the Atwood homestead. Its residents cannot see or understand it with the exception of the smallest ones, and they are powerless to stop it. Winter creeps on.

34) Winter 1863-'64, Johnson Island, Ohio

December 12th, 1863

Dear Evans,

We have not had the pleasure of meeting, but I am anxious to do so. I am Olivia Lacey who you were kind enough to find information for concerning my late husband. Thank you very much for your help. Please extend my compliments and thanks to General Thompson.

The reason I am writing is not to be morbid concerning my loss, but to celebrate with you my gain. Buck and I are to be married the 31st of this month. What a wonderful way to start a New Year, with a new marriage. We regret deeply that you will not be able to attend, but your family and friends will assemble and we will hold a prayer vigil for you.

I know it must be a powerless and dark time for you in the winter in the north with so much happening at home. My heart goes out to you. Your name is mentioned every day, several times a day and always concerning your honor, your courage, and your love. You are missed here. We are all extending you wishes for a Merry Christmas and a Happy New Year. I know it will be difficult away from family and home, but you are a brave and resourceful fellow and will make the best of it.

Buck has some things he wants to write…

Evans, Lucy Jane has taken in Steven Wayne. It is worse than we feared, but you need to know. Lucy Jane is pregnant and is a good ways along. The baby is due in the spring and she and Steven Wayne are planning to leave as soon as she is able to travel.

We worry for the children. We can't take them from their mother, but we will do all we can within the law to delay their leaving. A letter from you that we can take to a judge asking that the children not be taken out of state may help, but only as a delaying action. We hope our combined prayers for the war to end are answered and your plans to come home work out. We love and pray for you.

Buck, and Olivia Buchannan (soon to be!)

"Damn it all to hell, but I hate this war!" I cannot say this aloud in the confines of the hospital, but I shout it to the tops of the mountains and the depths of the sea in my soul. What a miserable letter! I know Olivia and Buck mean well, but how it hurts to not be able to attend such blessed events, to be with family and friends at this time of year.

I hate being a prisoner! This is worse than combat; at least in battle, I can do something. I am impotent here, I can do nothing! My family moves away from me and I am powerless to stop it. My children and their benefactors may be powerless, but they have no idea of the limits on me! This letter changes things; I must act sooner than later. I have no idea how long it will take to travel south, but I HAVE to do it.

"Dr. Allison?" I call to him from the outer office desk.

"Yes lieutenant, what can I do for you?"

I step to the door and look in on him as he sits puffing his pipe that he has taken up of late, reading a medical journal. "I'm sorry to interrupt sir, but I have a letter from home with information for General Thompson concerning the wife of one of his former command."

"Not bad news I hope?"

"No," I lied, "it is good news for her and him. I would like to be able to take a few minutes this morning and go find General Thompson to relay the message."

"Is Corporal Mather on the ward?"

"Yes sir, he is. I won't be gone more than an hour sir."

"Go ahead lieutenant. You've been spending a great deal of time here. A break will do you good. As a matter of fact, don't come back until noon then you can relieve Mather and me for a break. How will that be?"

"Wonderful sir; that is most generous of you; thank you very much."

Dr. Allison smiles. That is the only thing that I regret about my escape plans; I hate to betray someone who has been so generous and helpful to me. I don't know how I could have survived without the doctor and Mather. I'm going to miss them, and sooner than I had planned.

I leave the hospital and go in search of General Thompson and Major Traweek. The yard is packed so hard the snow covered ground is almost ice. A fresh, light covering of snow has fallen overnight, and I can hear the crunch of it as I make my way across the yard.

The prison has run down a great deal over the winter. The barracks are frigid except around the stoves which are only lit intermittently. When they are not, the prisoners gather in tight groups huddling as close as possible to keep each other warm. It's a vain effort.

The cold weather has caused the wells to freeze and men are detailed to go out of the compound and chop holes in the lake ice which is at least three feet thick and haul water into the compound. The men are allowed out individually to fill canteens. With such a shortage, there is no bathing, and has not been for months.

Lice are becoming epidemic. We all have them, I to a lesser degree, but handling the patients, I cannot help but carry away some of them with me. I have access to a more sanitary environment than do my fellows, but I am filthy all the time. It will require a great deal of effort on my part when I escape to get clean enough to travel without arousing suspicion generated by my appearance and odor.

I find General Thompson's quarters. Many officers are crowded into the day room of the barracks. As I push open the door, I am assaulted with the odor of unwashed bodies pressed together. The foul breath of the men who are sick, mixed with the choking smoke of those who have tobacco are almost more than I can handle. I thank God for the blessing of my hospital work.

Major Traweek is sitting with his back to the far wall and sees me making my way into the room. He hails me with his familiar and comforting baritone, "Dr. Atwood, how kind of you to grace us with your presence," he says with a chiding leer, "what brings you to the depths of hell?"

"Sir," I address Major Traweek, "I am looking for General Thompson with a message."

"You can deliver it to me lieutenant; there are no secrets here, as you have learned."

"Is General Thompson not available sir?"

"No, he isn't, he is attending to duties in the compound. Is this bad news that you bear here at the Christmas season?"

"No sir, it is good news, but of a personal nature. Perhaps I can beg your indulgence sir to direct me to the General. I come on orders from Dr. Allison." The last is a stretch of the truth but should serve to extract Major Traweek from the room.

"I could use some air and a walk although it is almighty cold out. Has the wind died at all?"

The winds off Lake Erie are incessant and cutting, but on this particular day, the sun is out, and the air is calm. "Yes sir, it is actually quite pleasant out today. It would be an honor to accompany you on a walk."

"Let us do so lieutenant."

We make our way through the crowd of bodies and into the blessed fresh air. It has been all I can do to not vomit from the stench. Once we are several paces from the building heading I do not know where he asks, "What is this news you have?"

"It is nothing of consequence for the General, but of dire importance to me."

"Oh? Do explain."

I did so in detail finishing with a question, "Are there any plans for an escape by any group. I have to get out of here now, if not sooner. I feel I can salvage my family if I can get back."

232 David Wilson Atwood

"And what of your duties in the hospital that aid our cause so greatly?"

"There will be another to take my place sir, but at this point, I need to take care of my family first."

He looks at me in a disapproving way before he answers, "There is nothing organized. The men are too weak and cold to survive out there, but this is the time to go if one is to go. The guards are not vigilant as they stay in their shacks rather than patrol. The ice is thick enough to march a regiment across, and the town is all in doors at night. So, if a man wants to go, all he has to do is survive this sub-zero cold, move into Canada, but you've already thought of all this haven't you lieutenant?"

I smile at the major and ask, "Has anyone made it?"

"I suppose there have been a few. At least we have not heard from them again. That could mean they are dead. Most are caught, or freeze to death. Some, as you have seen, have come back on their own with bad frostbite. I believe you've assisted in some of the amputations haven't you?" He stops walking and I with him. He turns to look me and asks, "Is it worth the risk Atwood?"

"Thank you for your time Major," I offer my hand, "it has been a pleasure to serve with you."

He smiles a wistful smile and takes my hand and shakes it, "Go with God lieutenant. You are a fine man and I will do nothing to interfere with your plans."

"Thank you sir, and please, when you see General Thompson, tell him that Olivia Lacey is to be married to my sergeant and best friend the last day of this year. That should be good news for him."

"Yes indeed, and when you see your sergeant give my best regards to them both, as well as your family."

"If there is any family left, I will do just that sir."

He smiles at me, I step back and salute, he returns it, and walks away. After a few steps, he turns and says, "Oh, by the way Atwood, General Thompson has raised an army and is challenging the army of General Trimble to a snow ball fight the end of this week. They are organizing into regiments and battalions and it should be a real battle. If you are on duty, you will be seeing some unusual injuries at the hospital. You're welcome to participate if you are available."

"Thank you sir, I would like that very much." With that we part, and it is a bitter sweet moment. Major Washington Traweek has become a good friend and a solid rock I can depend on. From the first moment of my incarceration, he has been a comfort to me. It will be hard to leave men like him, but leave I must, and soon; very, very soon.

35) Escape

Journal entry (addendum)

December 22nd, 1863

   This entry is sewn into my clothes as a loose page. I hope at some time in the future, I will be able to put it in its proper place. I cannot risk putting these words in my journal and they being discovered by a search. I have addressed it to home in case I am discovered, or worse, killed.

   The time is near; it has been long in coming. I am going to leave Johnson Island tomorrow. I am excited and terrified. There is a measure of security to this place. Although my chances of survival are low here with disease, cold, and malnutrition, they aren't better with escape, but I will be free and it will be my choice. Out there, I have not only the cold and hunger to deal with, but I will be a fugitive and will know no security. I regret leaving those I serve in the hospital. I hate to abandon my post, but I must, my family's future depends on it.

   I did not answer Major Traweek's questions this morning because I do not want anyone to know my plan. I do not want repercussions to befall anyone here, Yankee, or Confederate. If no one knows where I am going or what I am doing, they cannot reveal it to the enemy willingly or otherwise.

   On the eve of my escape, I am not sure what I am going to do. There is an Underground Railroad system of Confederate sympathizers who aid soldier's return to the south. The travel is East and dangerous. The route is to Rouse Point, New York then into Canada. I dare not write too many details if this paper is captured.

   My disguise as a Union Medical Officer will serve me well, but for how long? The odds are that at some point, I will be asked for my orders, and although I have managed to forge orders with Dr. Allison's signature, how long will it be before my name and description are known? Will they pursue with a vengeance; do I merit such energy? I think not, but I will still be vulnerable. Maybe they will not discover my having taken a uniform, much less the insignia, but I must plan for the worst, and hope for the best.

   I have little money. I will steal from Dr. Allison or the hospital funds. I hate to do it, he has been so good to me, but I have no other source. He will understand. I hope that tomorrow's snowball war will provide the distraction I need to take the money that I must have. He is still the enemy, and this is still war.

> Everything is ready. My clothes and coat are in the supply room hidden in a box of blankets. I have the all night duty tomorrow, and it is forecasted to be cold and windy. The cold is good; it will keep the guards in. I need to sleep tonight, but doubt I can. This will be my last sleep in this place, and my last journal entry. My hopes have been raised and dashed so many times I am fearful of what tomorrow holds.

The morning of the 23rd dawns sunny, cold, and windless, and I am there to greet it. Scudding clouds from the northwest indicate a change is coming. Before I reach the hospital, the winds are moving in faint gusts cutting like knives.

Men are in the yard making and piling snowballs at various strategic locations. The battle field is being readied. A projectile misses me by fractions of an inch. I smile, but do not turn around. I want to participate, but it will have to be later. I have duty now.

I go to the hospital early to make a tour of the ward before breakfast. I get a feel for the day, and Mather, Allison, and I can discuss any pressing cases. The doctor can then give us treatment instructions. In the last months, Mather and I have seen most there is to see, and know the treatments ourselves.

Knowing my desire to continue medicine after the war, Dr. Allison allows me to diagnose and recommend treatment in these discussion. Mather most often broods. Dr. Allison and I cannot bring our selves to dislike the young man, but his anger is tedious.

Our consult over our breakfast of oatmeal and milk has gone into a lull. It makes me nervous and I try to refrain from appearing anxious. Dr. Allison saves me with, "I hear there is to be a battle in the yard today. Do you know anything about it Atwood?"

"Yes sir, I spoke with Major Traweek of Alabama who informed me that Generals Thompson, and Trimble have organized armies. I was nearly hit by an errant missile on the way here this morning."

"It sounds like a great diversion."

"Sounds like Reb stupidity to me," interjects Mather.

"I guess we all deal with incarceration differently; we of the south choose to have a snowball fight to end all snowball fights, you on the other hand choose to deal with it by being bitter and hateful."

"I'm not a prisoner! How dare you make me equal to you traitor scum?"

"You are in prison, but of your own making. You are so bitter, you cannot see the joy of the season, the fun of a massive snowball war, or the brightness of hope you give as you aid and comfort the patients."

"Don't talk to me like that you traitor!"

Before I can respond, "Corporal Mather, calm down! I am not of the disposition to accommodate your dark moods today. If you cannot say something pleasant, please, for once, keep your mouth shut," insists Dr. Allison, then, "I'm sorry Mather, but you are getting too morose by far. You need to look on the positive side of things and let God work in your life."

"He doesn't care...," starts Mather, but is cut off by a raised hand, palm forward by Dr. Allison. Mather sullenly goes back to his oats.

I say nothing. I am so keyed up I am afraid that if I open my mouth I will blurt out something I should not.

"Are you planning to participate in the snowball war, lieutenant?"

"That would depend on you sir. If my duties are complete and I am not needed, I might participate if both of you don't mind. I suspect it will be a long and drawn out affair with injuries that may require our attention."

"I don't care if you go," says Mather, "I'll come get you if things get busy here."

"That is very generous of you Corporal. Besides, it would be fun to see how many times you're hit as you try to find me." Mather smiles and continues to eat. He would like to participate too. "Thank you Mather."

Dr. Allison smiles and nods at both of us.

After breakfast, I go about my duties, but my mind and heart are elsewhere. I muddle through until noon then leave for the snowball fight.

The yard is a blizzard of flying snow. I work my way to General Thompson's army. He's standing on a huge pile of snow that is being whittled away one snowball at a time. He is directing troop movements as if our lives depend on it

With a bull horn made of heavy paper he is shouting orders, "Major Traweek," pointing for my benefit, "move around to flank that unit whose attention is being held by Major Ruik!" His face is red, and his eyes are aglow from the excitement of battle. His black cavalry hat has a heavy dusting of snow and his hands are as red as his face from packing snowballs when he is not commanding. "Helluva fight we're in here Atwood," as he smiles down at me, "but I feel we will carry the day! My kingdom for ten men who know how to ride and ten horses; we would seal the victory post haste!" His cavalry officer's zeal is running unbridled. I stand smiling at the base of the snow hill being jostled by soldiers from the various units reporting to the general, and securing more ammunition. Some have serious cuts on their faces and heads. It's obvious that the snowballs are not pure snow.

One such is a 2nd lieutenant who runs up with a report for General Thompson. His mouth is a bloody mess. His lips are split and teeth are missing, but he's smiling ear to ear. He sees me and declares, "Damn fine fight; wonderful, glorious fight!" Then turning to General Thompson, he comes to attention and reports, "General Thompson, Major Traweek sends his compliments and ask your permission to attack that flank!"

"Yes, of course, by all means, attack, attack, attack! He shouts above the fray.

The young lieutenant, blood running down the front of his tunic, turns to me and says, "We are advancing as soon as I get back. Do you care to join us?"

"Yes, of course," then looking at the Swamp Fox, "with your permission general!"

"Of course, go, bring us victory!"

The other lieutenant and I run to Major Traweek's position. My companion says, "Run low, but be prepared to be hit. These boys are loading the balls with rocks," smiling his bloody smile, he says, "the snow don't soften the blow much."

We arrive to find Major Traweek in the final stages of organizing an assault on a fortification opposite our position. The troops in the fort are busy repelling an attack on the opposite flank, and are unaware of our presence. Major Traweek smiles in greeting, displaying a very large, very red, going to purple, circle on his face where he has been hit, slaps me on the back and orders, "You and Lieutenant Carlson," my companion, "are to be ammo bearers for this attack. See that tarp there?" He is pointing to a large square of canvas on the ground with snowballs being heaped on it.

"Yes sir," we shout.

"Get two others and follow the attack. Drag it over the snow. All the troops are carrying five shots apiece in their hats or whatever, and will be falling back after they fire to reload. You are the ammo dump! The enemy will try to flank us to acquire our armament; you must defend it with your very life! Do you understand these orders?"

"Yes sir!"

"Good, as soon as you are in place I will lead the attack. Do not be far behind. Now, go!"

We find two others already in place. We each pick up a corner of the canvas as the cry comes from the major whose baritone carries over the battle field, "Charge!"

We move forward in mass, hurling missiles as fast as we can. Aim is not as important with this attack as is overwhelming firepower. A solid wall of snow is being hurled toward our enemies. We watch from the ammo dump as the first fusillade hits home. The results are astonishing;

so many snowballs have been thrown that the fortification is no longer there, it's buried as are the bodies of our enemy. Our troops are falling back for more ammo and keep up the barrage, never allowing the attack to falter until the position is ours.

Carlson and I are so engrossed in the attack, that we are not ready for the attempt to take our ammunition. I am hit hard in the right side of my head. I have moments to recover as the attack reaches us. We are fortunate that their attack is not well organized. Our troops are falling back for more ammo and we are able to repulse the enemy and defend our movable ammo dump.

We have overrun the enemy fortification and are taking prisoners, moving them to the neutral area where they are held and cannot reenter the fray until an exchange is arranged. In other words, until they escape. There's not a frown on any face. That's a first for this place.

As the battle winds down, a voice from behind says close to my ear, "Your about to be hit with a snowball on my command," it is the out of breath voice of Major Traweek. I start to turn, but his hands on my shoulders prevent it. "Fall down and pretend to be out. I will see that you are taken to the rear. I need to speak with you, it's urgent."

No sooner than he releases me, I am hit with what feels like a cannon ball. Falling down requires no acting on my part, but staying conscious is an effort. I try my legs, but they won't work. I slump down to the snow and feel strong hands lift me and part carry, part drag me away. I'm in a fog and left to lie on the snow to recover. I, being rendered senseless, am deemed by rule to be dead. I cannot reenter the war, by rule or ability.

In a few moments, as I lay recovering my senses, Major Traweek kneels next to me and says, "Lie still. Can you hear me?"

I nod but otherwise do not stir. My head is beginning to pound. "You cannot go tonight." I start to rise in alarm. His hand pushes and holds me down as he continues, "A plot to storm the garrison and free us all has been discovered." I once again try to get up, and he once again holds me down. "Lieutenant, I am ordering you to hold still. I have reason to believe that they suspect you. The best thing you can do is to act as if nothing has happened and postpone your escape; do you understand?"

I nod, and hold still as I whisper, "What's happened?"

"Do you remember Charles Cole?"

"Yes sir, he's the captain from Nathan Forest's cavalry isn't he?"

"Yes, as you will recall, he disappeared several months ago."

"Yes sir, no one knows what happened to him."

"He escaped," I stiffen but Traweek's hand steadies me, "and made it to Canada where he was able to get drawings of our prison to Richmond."

I make no reply. "The authorities have sent Captain John Yates Beall; the south's naval master here to work with Cole to commandeer the *Michigan,* turn its guns on headquarters and demand surrender of the island."

"But the lake's frozen; the *Michigan* can't get over here till spring. Why attack now?"

"They weren't; there are fifty-four Copperhead, northerners sympathetic to the south, here or on their way to meet Captain Cole who was to get them jobs in the area until spring. The Yankees have found out who they are and are going to capture the lot tonight. Unfortunately, we will once again be graced with the presence of the captain."

"How did this get found out?"

"Who knows? But you need to be careful; word has it they're looking at you real close." I open my eyes, astonished. Traweek's looking at me. "Have you said anything to anyone, done anything to arouse suspicion?"

"No sir, I haven't even told Dr. Allison about the situation at home that I got in the last letter. I don't understand how I could be under suspicion."

"The only thing that matters is that you're being watched. Probably because of your position; the freedoms you have."

"What do I do sir?"

"Get up, and go to the hospital under the guise of being injured, and resume your duties as soon as you can. If you're questioned, you don't know anything, and you really don't, but I will keep you informed if you need to know. Do you understand what I'm telling you?"

"No sir; I need to go."

"Atwood, don't make me have to order you to stay. Do I have your word you won't try in the immediate future?"

"It seems I have no choice sir."

"No, you don't, but neither do any of us. We were all certain we would be out of here before spring." I sit up and Traweek stays with me for a moment longer then helps me to my feet. He smiles and says, "I'm sorry Atwood, but I needed to stop you before you got taken with the rest of them. You could be hanged. Can you make it to the hospital on your own?"

"Yes sir."

"Good, I've a battle to win!" With that, he smiles, turns bellowing orders that can be heard across the lake in Sandusky where I had planned on being tonight.

I make my way to the hospital, my head throbs. I don't know if it's because of the blow I have taken to the head, or because of the blow I have taken to my heart.

It seems to take hours to get to there. I stagger in. "Reb!" Mather exclaims, shocked at my appearance, "you look awful. Are you hit; is it bad?"

"Worse than you can imagine." I move to our desk and take off my soaked and cold jacket. I look up at Dr. Allison, who is watching me with a whimsical look on his face. "Does he know? Is he the one?" I wonder to myself.

Dr. Allison says, "I'm sorry Atwood."

"For what?" I ask him, surprised.

"For your loss."

He knows - but had he told, or like Traweek, he knows that someone is suspicious? I am quick to recover, "We didn't lose sir, our army won!" His looks surprised; he does know! In pure innocence, I say, "You should have seen our attack on a fortification sir! It was amazing; a complete slaughter!"

He looks quizzical, unsure of what he thinks he knows. Good, I can still use him although it will take awhile to regain his trust. I am down and hurt, but I will bounce back. I will get home, but when? Will this ever end?

36) Johnson Island, February, 1864

Number and Rank of Officers on Johnson's Island, Feb. 9th, 1864 as prisoners of war:

Maj. Generals	1
Brigadier Generals	5
Colonels	51
Lieut. Colonels	44
Majors	57
Captains	623
Lieutenants	1712
Chaplains	2

Also there are :

Privates	45
Citizens	72
Negros	3

Total No. officers	2495
Privates, Citizens, and Negros	120
Aggregate	2615

That I Live For

I live for those who love me,

For those who know me true;

For the Heaven that smiles above me,

And awaits my Spirit too.

For the cause that lacks assistance,

For the wrong that needs resistance;

For the future in the distance,

And the good I can do.

Lieutenant Evans Atwood

Johnson Island, Ill.

February 29th, 1864

Today is Monday and there is great excitement about the removal of two hundred officers to Sandusky for exchange. The officers to be exchanged will be determined by drawing.
March 2nd
The excitement is still up, but the number to be exchanged is much smaller than we were first told. I am not among the few to go. They will leave tonight with the sick and invalid from the hospital. God speed.

37) Johnson Island, April, 1864

Officer's Camp, April 1st, 1864

I have been a prisoner eleven months today. The time has moved wearily by, many strange things have passed; war is yet promenading our land, and furloughing many to be borne from whence no traveler returns.

Let us hope that such things will not continue long, that the tomahawk will soon be buried; then shall the prisoner be released from his home and be returned to his own country to his own home and family. What a day of joy that will be; the long confined prisoner free to roam over the fields, where in childhood, he played with a heart as free from the present troubles, as from those that have been forgotten in the past.

Sometimes I become weary of such a life; sometimes my heart is filled with joy, when a little billet from "a distant land" speaks all things will I know that I have anxious friends whose thoughts daily visit this lonely prison. They are listening daily to hear of my release from this bondage and my arrival in the "Sunny South". I hope the time will soon roll around, for I long to be free again, and enjoy the Society of Friends and mingle again in the struggle for Liberty and Freedom.

I received the following today, April 1st, 1864

Monday, March 14th, 1864

Shiloh, Washington Co., Arkansas

My dearest son Evans,

It is with much sadness and a heavy heart that I sit to write. Your son, James Calvin passed to the eternities to be with our Lord Jesus last Friday, March 11th, 1864. The winter had been hard on him. Lucy said he had a cold, but had been doing much better, then did not wake up that morning.

We held his service yesterday after Sunday services. Everyone stayed and helped. It was a chilled, but clear day as we laid your babe to rest. He is buried in our cemetery at the Friendship Baptist Church. Reverend Claiborne delivered a beautiful eulogy.

We were able to get word to Buck and he and Olivia came to be with us. Buck is very upset at the loss. He loves you and is a dear friend to us all. He almost lost control after the graveside service when Steven Wayne was smirking at him while he held Lucy Jane tight. Buck wanted to defend your honor, but Papa and the boys restrained him. Lucy Jane and he left then. They left Martha Jane with us for awhile. I fear for her and the situation.

Lucy Jane is with child to be born this month or in April. No one is sure who the father is. There is still talk about the killings at your place where that Paul feller was killed; he might be the father.

The rest of the family is fine. We are thawing out and look forward to a good planting and growing season. With all the snow, we have lots of water in the soil, so the seeds should jump up quick. There is the usual argument as to when to plant. I think most folks don't trust there won't be another freeze and are waiting till April.

I am so sorry to bring you such bad news. I know you are in a living hell, and this can only make it worse, but you had to be told.

Lucy Jane said she would write and pleaded for you to come home, but to what? Evans, we've done all we can for that girl as has your sister Harriett. She has turned her back on us and has taken up with another. I will take care of Martha Jane as long as they let me.

God bless you Evans. We pray for you. You are loved and missed. I hope you survive this challenge. There is a bright future in store for you if you can just wait and live.

Love,

Your Mother and Father

Sadness rests upon me like a grave stone; heavy and cold. How much longer can I hold up? I can't even be there for the death and burial of my son! I want to scream, but there is no where that I can. There is no privacy with almost two thousand souls here. I will seek solace in the supply room tonight as I have the duty.

I get up from the desk and move like a walking dead man to the ward. As I go through the doors, Dr. Allison sees me, "Are you all right lieutenant?"

I suppose I look as dead as I feel. There is no sense in lying, "No sir." I keep moving.

"What's wrong; can I help?"

"Not unless you can raise the dead; my son died last month." I hear my voice, but it sounds like it belongs to someone else. I keep moving.

"Atwood, I am so sorry. How can I help?"

Anger rises in me and bursts out, "You can let me out of this hell hole!" My voice rises and I feel my face flush. "I can't even be there to bury my child!" I scream at the innocent man. Saving my grief for the supply room later is not going to happen; I am letting it out now. I walk to Dr. Allison, patients are watching me. The grief must come out. "Because of you and all like you," I gesture with my hand still clutching the hateful letter to include the entire Yankee contingent, and the whole north, "I am kept here while my family is destroyed, and I can't do a damned thing about it!" My cries escalate as the frustration of a year's imprisonment and a dying family all rush out as tears come with sobs of the deepest grief I have ever felt.

The doctor moves back as I continue toward him. "I know how you must feel."

"Do you; do you have any idea what it's like to be locked up, to not be able to rescue all you have worked for, or even to attempt to save it. Do you know what it's like to lose all you have to another man while you are locked up with no choice but to endure?" My face is near his, spraying him with spittle as I continue my tirade, "Well, do you? Come on doctor let me hear how I must endure to the end, how I must rise above all this, how I should act like a man! I can't act like a man! I'm locked up in hell, and you hold the key you son of a bitch! YOU SON OF A BITCH!" I hate those words but they erupt from me like a geyser. I loathe myself as they spew from me. My burden is too hateful to bear!

I am fuming, but spent; out on my feet. Mather and Allison guide me off the ward to our office. I doubt I could have moved otherwise.

"I know what you are going through," restates Dr. Allison.

"Me too," joins Corporal Mather.

I look at Mather and the doctor.

He smiles and says, "I lost a son at the beginning of the war, before Bull Run."

"Were you able to go home?"

"Not for the funeral. I got there the next day."

"And you Mather, with the loss of your brother and father, were you able to go home and assist your mother?"

"No, I was wounded, but got home."

"Then neither of you knows what I am going through. I cannot go home on furlough or parole. I cannot even support my wife and daughter. You cannot know what I am going through. You don't know the frustration. Just look at this scene; the only consolation and comfort I can receive is at the hands of my enemy? How painful do you think that is?"

Neither speaks for a long moment. The doctor says, "You take the rest of the day; rest; walk the yard. It'll do you good."

"No sir, I would prefer to stay here; write and think, and then go back to work. I won't have to answer as many questions."

"Come on Mather, let's get back to the work. You go to the ward, and I'll be along in a few minutes." Mather leaves, and Allison and I sit alone. After a long silence, he says, "I am truly sorry Atwood," pats my shoulder, rises and goes into his office.

I am alone.

The Departed Babe

You said that he had left this vale;
His Spirit home had fled;
And that his lovely form you laid,
Among the silent dead.

His stay with us on earth was sweet,
His presence here our joy,
But, He, who watches now his dust,
Called home our angel boy.

He never trod the walks of sin;
He'er knew how much of woe,
Hangs around the gloomy path of life.
Which mortals tread below.

Bright forms unseen – Sweet Messenger –
When the last tie was riv'n –
Did pinion him with angel wings,
And flew with him to Heav'n.

No more will he come back to Earth,
Except in angel form;
To cheer our hearts, and calm our fears,
Through life's tempestuous storm.

Long since; he's learned those notes of praise,
Sung by the heavenly band;
And strayed with loved ones through the bowers
Of that Elysian Land.

Then why should we grieve for that form
Beneath the old churchyard;
Since God, and heavenly angels too,
That sleeping dust will guard.

> When Earth, and skies shall flee away,
> And time shall be no more;
> We'll meet him in that Paradise
> Beyond this mundane shore.

April 14th, 1864, Evans Atwood

The following I received April 18th, 1864:

March 27th, 1864 Shiloh, Washington Co., Arkansas

Evans,

By now, I am sure you have received the news of James Calvin's death. He was so thin and sickly. He had been sick most of the winter, and succumbed to what Dr. Black says is the pneumonia. I am so sorry to have lost him.

I do not know what is happening to me. Nothing is as it should be. Nothing is as we planned. Oh Evans, how I hate this war! I agreed for you to go. If you wanted to sacrifice yourself to such a cause as the Confederacy, then you could make that choice, but what right do you have to drag me, your wife and our children down that road? What right do you have to destroy our lives as well as your own? This war is the ruination of all we hold good and love together. Why did you go?

You are gone, I have had to fight for my life and kill a man, I am afraid all the time, your family has shunned me, our baby is dead; what am I to do? I have had to fend for myself as well as I can, have done terrible things, but I and Martha have survived.

Martha has taken over much of the house work that I am no longer able to do, and has grown distant from me. Another lost soul to this war. Will you not at least come home to save her?

I plead with you to come home by whatever means and help me. Can we turn back? Can we ever live in the peace and passion of our youth? I feel so old; this war and you have robbed me of my youth and beauty.

There is insanity around me. It is dark here even in the spring. Please come rescue me from this hell. Please take the parole. All this so that you can honor your oath to this new country? What if the war is lost; where will your honor have gotten us?

Evans, the very walls are crumbling down around me. Please help. You rescued me once before; do you not remember? Can you not do it again? Can we not revive the passion and joy of those days?

What are your answers? I wait, not knowing even if tomorrow will dawn.

Lucy Jane

38) Home, May, 1864

"Mama, there's a man riding up the trail!" Breathless, and aglow with excitement, Martha Jane bursts into the open front door of the cabin.

"Shhh," Lucy hushed, "you'll wake your baby brother."

Martha Jane, a month past her fourth birthday, is old for her years. Circumstances have required it. She acknowledges her new brother, but ignores him. She refuses to do like she did for James Calvin, and does not call the new arrival by his name.

She is not cruel, hurtful, or hateful. He isn't hers. She has been ignored while her mother and Steven Wayne have wallowed in their individual and collective self-pity. "Why don't they just be happy?" She wonders.

She is hurt and sad for the passing of James Calvin, but she listens to Grandma Atwood and knows that he is happier where he is. Grandma is speaking church talk, but Martha Jane knows he is better off.

It was a warm day in late April when the boy decided to come just before dawn. The mid-wife rode in to assist. Steven Wayne and Martha were both shooed out of the cabin. Steven Wayne headed to the river. Martha Jane watched from her secret place.

She stayed there for most of the day. No one came looking for her. She played all day with friends she alone could see. Pa is one of them.

He is difficult for her to remember, so she makes up the details. She has taken his picture to her secret place. Mama never asked about it. He might be dead. She wonders often about that.

The day of birth wore on, and she began to get hungry. She was afraid to go to the house. The one biscuit she had brought with her in the early morning was eaten long ago. She had water from the river. She had spent hours there wondering where it came from and where it went, and did it go to her Pa?

Just before dark, Steven Wayne came onto the porch and called her. She ignored him for a long time until he said, "Martha Jane, come see your new brother!" She could not resist and burst from her hiding place not caring if it was discovered; she could always find another, but doubted Stevie Wayne cared enough to notice where she came from.

She ran to the cabin past Steven Wayne and inside to her mother's bed, and there, bundled next to mother's breast was a little boy who looked like…she didn't know, but he didn't look like her family. He was a stranger.

"Do you want to hold him Martha?"

Martha Jane nodded her head, but fear crept into her.

"What's wrong honey, you scared to hold the little baby?"

She shook her head and held out her arms. Lucy Jane eased her nipple from the sleeping little mouth, and handed the baby to Martha.

The little girl held the boy for a moment then looked at her mother and said, "Mama…"

"What's a matter Martha; are you sick?"

Martha felt the blood drain from her face and the sick of her stomach rose up. Blackness began to close around her. She had no idea what was happening, but managed to put the baby back in her mother's arms before she sank to the floor in a faint.

When she came to, she was in her bed which she no longer shared and felt cold and sick. Lucy Jane was standing over her, wiping her face with a cool cloth.

"Are you okay baby?" She asked.

Martha Jane nodded, but lay still.

"Are you hungry?"

Martha remembered being hungry, but did not feel so now, yet she knew that she had to eat and nodded to her mother. "Water?" She asked.

"Sure baby, let me get you a slice of cornbread and jam with a cold glass of water. That'll fix you right up!"

That was the last time she had ever held the baby and from that day, she ignored him. Lucy and Steven Wayne attribute her behavior to the loss of her brother and all the things she has witnessed in the past few months. "She'll grow out of it," they think.

She never will. He is not her brother, and she knows it. There is also something else she knows; she's not going to Nebraska. Conversations overheard between her mother and Steven Wayne discussing leaving have convinced the little girl that it will not, as her mother has said, "…be better when we get to Nebraska." From the first time she heard it, she knew she would never go. It's not a scary thing to her; it's as natural as eating and drinking; you just do it, and she isn't going to go.

"What's got you so excited?" Lucy Jane asks after she shushed the little girl. "What brings you running into the house?"

"Mama, there's a man riding up the trail, and he looks like the man who carries letters like Mr. Tate did before you killed him!"

Lucy is taken aback. "What does this child know?" She asks herself and looks at Martha.

"Maybe it's from Papa! Come on Mama, let's go see!"

They go onto the porch as the man rides up at the hitching post. "Got a letter for you Mrs. …uh, Lucy Jane." No one is sure what to call Lucy Jane. She's still married, but has not acted like it for a long time. Most just call her Lucy Jane if they speak to her at all. The man dismounts, reaches into his saddle bag and takes out a bundle of letters. He takes the first one off the top and walks to the steps. Without mounting them, he holds his hand out, looking up without a smile.

Lucy Jane steps down to reach the letter. The man mounts his horse, and turns to leave. Before he does, he tips his hat to Martha Jane. She watches him ride away quick; slow enough to not show fear, but fast enough to get away from the place.

"What is it Mama?"

"It's a letter from your Pa."

"Will you read it to me, please," she pleads.

"Let me read through it first, then I'll read it to you if I can, or at least the parts about you. How will that be?" Martha nods her assent and sits on the porch steps and pats a place next to her indicating for Lucy Jane to sit. Lucy joins her, breaks the seal on the letter and reads…

April 20th 1864

Dear Lucy:

Your letter of the March 27th ultimately came to hand. I was glad to learn that you and Martha are well, but sorry to hear that your sorrows and troubles are fast overcoming you; that the afflictions of earth are wasting the life of one so worthy of a better fate.

Lucy, these are truly "the days that try men's souls." I would be delighted almost beyond measure could I but forget the present and so arrange the future as to meet you in that little cottage so dear to me called home.

Since receipt of your letter, ten thousand thoughts have wearied my mind, my soul, my very life, and Lucy, after calm, sober, and serious meditation, I have weighed, pondered, and reexamined your request, and excuse me for saying so, I must follow the path of duty to my country for which I am now a prisoner.

I have gone through many dangers; have passed often by the very gates of Death; heard often, the unearthly howls of the "Dogs of War", but amid all this, I ever thought that your prayers, your sympathy, and your love followed me, but now, what must I say? What must I do?

I must not disgrace friends, character, and more than all, kindred wife, and child! No, Lucy, I do not think you desire this. Let me stay in prison until released honorably; let me; let me discharge my duty; then, when peace shall silence the instruments of Death; if I survive, happy will be our future. If I do not, you will have but lost one more friend.

My thoughts are often with you. I see you in dreamland as of yore, but what would be thoughts, or dreams, to the blissful reality of seeing you face to face!

Lucy, I must soon close. I hope, <u>soon</u>, to be in my lovely "Dixie". Write to me; and when the persecutions of life shall hedge in your path, look to Heaven for succor. Pray for me through your Pilgrimage.

I remain your true and ever faithful friend and husband,
Lt. Evans Atwood

Lucy Jane folds the letter and drops it in her lap. Her face is ashen.
"What does it say Mama? Is Papa coming home?"
"No Martha, your Pa ain't coming home."
"Ever?"
"No, never," Lucy Jane lies…again.
Martha does not believe her mother, and asks, "Will you read it to me?"
"No honey, it's too old for you."
She looked into her Mama's eyes, those pools that have intrigued so many, then she knew; Papa is coming home, and Mama's afraid.

39) Johnson Island to Point Lookout, Maryland

May 1st, 1864

I was captured by the Federal forces under General Grant just one year ago, today; and I am yet a prisoner. Many battles have been fought, many victories have been won; many have died; many, a great many, have met their fate upon the battlefield since my capture.

Still the tide of battle is ebbing and flowing. The destruction that wastes at noonday is vigilantly prosecuting its mission, and none, but the eye of Him that never sleeps, can see the end of these things.

The present campaign is opening with desperate vigor by both parties. Armies, rested and recruited during the past winter, will meet and are meeting to try again with force and power of arms and numbers upon the field of carnage.

I hope that before another year shall pass, I shall be restored to my Country and my country liberated and free; its enemies driven back to their own soil, and peace and quiet reigning supreme. I am truly tired of prison life; shut out from the busy world by a prison wall and guards with musket in hand upon that wall! Who would not rather be in his own element, free from such?

"Mr. Atwood," called Dr. Allison as he sat at his desk, "come in here please."

I stop my journal entry and go to the door, "Yes sir?"

"Come in; have a seat."

This is odd. I have never been invited to sit; not even from the first day I was here.

The doctor is staring at a handful of papers that have the look of officialdom. He glances up from his reading and says, "As you well know, our camp is overcrowded." He pauses.

"Yes sir," I say aloud, and then to myself, "What's this all about? Why the serious tone?"

"The War Department has built more prisons. The newest is at Point Lookout, Maryland."

"Yes sir," I say; still no closer to understanding.

"Your name is on the list lieutenant; you are to be transferred to Point Lookout, Maryland with two hundred others."

"Yes sir." There are no immediate emotions, but I feel I must say something. "I will miss our association sir; you've been most kind and generous with me personally and professionally. I shall remember you always, and with great fondness."

"And I as well Mr. Atwood; this comes as a surprise to you I would guess?"

"Of course sir." With that, the emotions rise. "I will miss the hospital. I will miss the men, the patients most I think. Perhaps you can write a letter of introduction to the medical staff at, where did you say I'm going?"

"Point Lookout, Maryland."

"Yes," I say, "the name sounds nice enough. Anyway, if you can recommend me to the hospital there, I would appreciate it. I would like to continue to learn medicine. I feel strange about leaving here."

"Yes, I can understand that; and of course, I'll be happy to write you a letter. As for the place, I know nothing more than that it is on the Maryland coast on the Chesapeake Bay where the Potomac River joins it. It will be nice in the summer except for the insects, but I fear you will suffer from the cold and wet of winter." I say nothing as I sense more coming. "I understand that it is a very large prison and has grown to almost twenty thousand, and I've been told that prisoners are confined without walls, and live in tents. It should be an interesting experience."

"Yes sir," I say as dull and flat as I feel. The one thing I feel relief for is that I will no longer feel obligated to stay and serve here in the hospital; I am being transferred and therefore relieved of duty. Then it hits me.

Fate has laid a gift at my feet. A way is shown where so many others have been closed. With a signed letter of introduction coupled with forged orders, and my medical Union uniform, now is the perfect time to escape. I speak to suppress my enthusiasm, "May I see the list of those being transferred?"

"Yes, of course," as he hands me the order.

I scan. It's arranged by rank so the first name I am looking for will be near the top, and there it is; "General; M. Jeff Thompson". The Swamp Fox is going. I look for Major Traweek's name and find it near the bottom of the "majors" column. My friends and confidants are both going with me. I hand the list back to the doctor without comment, but a question, "When do we leave?"

"This afternoon."

"This afternoon!" In a more controlled voice, I laugh and say, "That's quick." I panic for a moment. How to get my uniform and such out of the building? Providence shines again.

"Atwood, there's an old rucksack with a red cross on it in the supply room. Why don't you take that with some medical supplies? I will supply you with an arm band to designate you as a corpsman. That way, what you carry won't be stolen by the guards on the other end or along the way."

He knows! He even knows what's in the rucksack! I fight to control my surprise and do not know if I am successful. He is smiling at me. "Thank you again sir," I manage to say, "it seems I am once again in your debt." What a debt it is!

"You've been a wonderful assistant. I will miss you and our conversations. You'd better get moving. You have much to do before they call muster."

"Yes sir, thank you again. It has been an honor and privilege to work with you. I hope that after the war is ended, we can continue our friendship."

"Yes, I would like that very much. After the war, I will be taking a position at the Medical College of Louisville, Kentucky. If you would like to continue your education, please look me up."

"Yes sir that would be good. I look forward to doing that very thing." I rise to leave, "Will that be all sir?"

"Yes, lieutenant; I will write that letter for you now. You can pick it up after you get your things from the storage room."

I turn to go with a cold lump in my belly. Does he know it all?

He adds, "Don't let anyone inspect that medical aid pack. It would be damaging to your effort."

I want to ask how and for how long he has known, but knowing that he knows and has not betrayed me is sufficient to hold him in my highest esteem. I manage a smile in reply.

He cannot resist one more barb, "I hope it works out at home."

"Thank you again sir, for everything."

I make my way through the ward to the supply room. I am folding the uniform as tight as I can into the bottom of the rucksack, and hiding it under supplies when the door opens. I shove the bag behind some boxes into its hiding place and see Walter Mather watching me. "I'm done for," I think, this man hates me and all that I stand for. I'll be punished and held here, but the worst part is that Dr. Allison might be caught up in my scheme as well. "What are you doing Mather?"

He's standing by the door with his hands deep in his pockets and his shoulders hunched forward looking sheepish. He lowers his eyes to the floor, then raises them as he says, "I came to say good-bye." After a pause, and still not looking up, he moves to me, pulling his right hand out of his pocket.

I step back into a defensive posture, not knowing what to expect. "He's discovered me; my plan's ruined. Is that not enough; does he want to hurt me too?"

254 David Wilson Atwood

"Here, take this," he says as he opens his hand to show a roll of Union dollars, "it ain't much, but where you're headed, you'll need it."

I'm flabbergasted, "Walter, I can't take your money. Your mother needs it, you need it."

"Yeah, that's true, but you need it the most. Here, go on, take it," he thrusts it at me, "before I change my mind."

I reach my hand to accept the roll. There must be twenty dollars here, maybe more. "Walter, I don't know what to say; you've overwhelmed me."

"Reb, I ain't giving it to you; it's a loan. My address in on the paper in the roll; I expect you to pay it back, and none of that Confederate script neither. I want Yankee dollars!" I smile, his bluster has returned; making demands and calling me names. He continues, "Evans, you've been real good to me. I've given you a hard time, and you've never even raised your voice to me. I've tried to make your life miserable and all you did was make mine better. Sometimes I hated you, but you're right, I need to be more positive."

"Are you going to do it?"

"Hell no," he says and we both laugh.

"You called me by my name."

"Did not!"

"Yeah, you did, you said 'Evans'."

"No!"

"That's okay; I'm not going to make you call me sir!"

"Why you traitor trash, I ought to take that money back," and extends his hand. I take his hand with mine and shake it, but that's not good enough, he pulls me to him and hugs me tight. "Good luck lieutenant; you're a good man; I'll pray for you," and before I can register my astonishment, he releases me and walks away, but not before I see a tear in his eye. I'm glad he's gone; he can't see the tears in mine. There are good people everywhere, even if they do wear blue.

Muster is called for noon. I step out of the barracks dressed in my Confederate gray with my black cavalry hat; the sun feels warm and different. It feels almost like freedom. "Almost," I think, "almost."

This transfer is a blessing. If I can get a break, a faint opening, a diversion, I will escape. It is dangerous, and may cost me my life, but I have to take the chance; I have to get home.

I assemble with other lieutenants at the end of the line opposite the general, staff, and field officers. I am anxious to go, and do not speak to anyone for fear of giving myself and my plans away.

I see General Thompson and Major Traweek coming down the line as if inspecting the troops. The major has a board in his hand with a list attached to it, checking off names as they come. "Look who we have here major; our old friend Lieutenant Atwood," then to me, "How have you been lieutenant?"

"Very well sir, it is good to see you again, and you as well major."

"We've missed you Atwood," says Major Traweek, "but I understand how the medical field takes your time. Are you happy with medicine?"

"Yes sir, I am able to do good and serve my country by serving its soldiers sir."

General Thompson notices the bag at my feet which is very conspicuous since the majority of soldiers in the formation do not have anything with them that cannot be carried in a pocket, and asks, as he moves it with his foot, "Medical supplies?"

"Yes sir, Dr. Allison was generous with supplies so that I can treat any illness in route. I hope to be able to continue as a medical assistant where we are going. The doctor has written me a letter of introduction to the medical staff."

"Indeed? May I see that letter?" General Thompson asks.

This makes me nervous, but I say, "Yes sir," as I reach into my jacket and extract the letter being careful not to expose the forged orders and hand it to General Thompson who in turn hands it to Major Traweek.

After a few moments of reading, the major hands the letter back to the general and asks me, "Have you read that letter Atwood?"

"No sir. I had wanted to, but had so much to do at the hospital to get ready that I have not taken the time."

General Thompson says, "You should," handing the letter back to me, "it looks and reads more like orders than an introduction. That could be very useful," he says with a knowing look. "Good luck lieutenant if we don't see you before you leave; it has been a pleasure serving with you."

"We're going by train on stock cars again," says Major Traweek, "and will change trains twice; the first time in Mansfield, the second in Pittsburg. I recommend that you make your attempt at one of those places. The further east we travel the harder it will be to get back south. If you miss the chance in Pittsburg, I recommend you make your run into Canada. It will be slower to home, but safer."

I am amazed at the general knowledge of my plan. Does everyone know; even the Yankees? "Sir," I ask, "how do you know?"

It's General Thompson who speaks up, "Your Dr. Allison asked me to make sure you have every opportunity to make your break. He seems to be quite fond of you and sympathetic to your predicament. He says you are a fine medical officer." Almost as an afterthought, he adds, "But traveling in the ranks, your bag and plans are both in jeopardy. Get your bag and come with us. The title of 'Medical Officer' carries enough weight to allow you to travel with the general and staff officers. That way, I can protect your supplies with orders of my own. Even Union troops are intimidated by a general officer."

"Yes sir," I say as I pick up the bag and start with them.

"You signal us when you are to make your break, and we'll create some kind of diversion to cover you." He turns away, but then back to add, "When you set up medical practice, please let me know. Missouri is not that far from Arkansas should my family and I ever need care," says the general.

"Sir, it would be an honor, but I have a colleague in St. Louis who I highly recommend."

He laughs, and says to Major Traweek, "See major, he's been a medical officer less than five minutes and is already making referrals!" We laugh and make our way to the front of the formation. I will miss these two men.

40) En route

When we step out of the gates of Johnson Island prison, and onto the wharf, every one of us looks back with a smile. We are not free, but we are not in a prison, and there is a difference. We are carried across the lake to Sandusky. It is one o'clock.

We board the cars and move out. A cheer rises as we pull away from the station. We don't know what lies ahead, but it doesn't matter. As a prisoner you learn to live one day at a time. Not a bad way to go through life. It is sufficient for the day that we are not locked up.

I am riding in the first car with General Thompson. Many of the men did not have time to gather rations before we left Johnson Island, but that's not the case in this car. There is food and good water.

Conversation abounds although I do not participate much. I don't want to call attention to myself. When I'm gone, if I'm gone, I don't want be missed.

I am alone in the group. I have no friend or companion until I get back to Arkansas. I can't trust anyone with the possible exception of Major Traweek, and General Thompson. They seem to be on my side and supportive, but I do not allow myself any feeling of security. I know that if they have to sacrifice me for the good of the whole, they will without a moment's hesitation. It is the way of war and those who wage it.

Our stop in Mansfield, Ohio will be my first opportunity to escape; the sooner, the better. We arrive about 5:00 p.m. We are to change trains here. As soon as I step out of the car, I see that I will have no chance to make a break.

We are taken off in squads, directed to the woods behind the station where we are allowed to relieve ourselves, then still under guard are herded onto other cars waiting for us. They smell horrible. As we approach the cars, there are bails of straw which we toss in and scatter over the filth before we climb aboard. This leg will be overnight without a stop.

As the sun sets, so does the music and the shows the various choral and thespian groups have been putting on since we left. We are all getting tired and hungry. Nerves from the crowded and uncomfortable conditions are becoming frayed, yet we are freer than the others back on the island.

Sometime in the night I am awakened by Major Traweek who asks, "What are your plans?"

"I don't have any plans," I tell him, "I did not plan for this, so I am going to have to dance to the music played."

"If you did have plans, would you tell them to me?"

I do not hesitate with my reply, "No sir, I would not."

"That is wise of you lieutenant. That's what I came to tell you; trust no one, friend or foe, not even me." He lays his head back to rest against the side of the rail car, pulls his hat over his face and goes to sleep.

I do the same, hoping as I doze that when we got to Pittsburg or before that he will move away from me. He has grown too friendly, and it makes me nervous. Is he supportive, or destructive? Does he want to know my plans because he has one working himself that mine might interfere with? I doze, but I do not rest. I, as he advised, trust no one.

It is late afternoon as we slow into Pittsburg. Everyone in our car is silent; tired of the trip. The novelty of being out of the prison has worn off and we are enduring. Sometime in the early morning, Major Traweek went to his place by General Thompson without saying a word. I hope that will be the last time he and I will be in that close proximity, but during the night it occurs to me that I don't have to worry about him. If he's planning an escape too, he will wait to get further east, closer to Tennessee; closer to Alabama. I will make my attempt in Pittsburg.

Pennsylvania is where Gettysburg is, and Yankee sentiment runs high from the Union victory. I am in the heart of enemy territory, but if I'm going to make an attempt, the further east I let the train carry me, the longer my cover and disguise will have to hold.

At about 3:00 p.m., we arrive at the station. The place is packed with people wanting to see the Rebel officers. As we disembark, there's a swarm around General Thompson, many wanting to see the "great Guerrilla Chief". He is gracious, and the guards are lax in letting him mingle with the crowd, answer questions, sign autographs, and talk to the press. I stick near his side. The guards, seeing my arm band, ignore me.

I do not make a decision to go; it just happens. The crowd moves around and engulfs me. I fear that at any moment a guard will raise the alarm; no one notices. I take off my hat to be less conspicuous. The gray of my uniform is swallowed in the press of the crowd. I am being jostled as those from behind press forward to see Thompson. People push past me and I am shuttled further and further back. Can this be happening? I am holding my breath, afraid to believe my fortune, but I take one small step backward after another. No one is paying the least bit of attention to me. A man, anxious to move closer the General Thompson, elbows me in the stomach as he tries to get past. I bend at the waist and, gasping, back further into the crowd. When I stand, I am on the outside of the crush. There's no one behind me, and from what I can determine without looking around, there's no one looking at me.

I move back as they press forward from me. It's now or never. I will not get another chance like this. I look to my left to the station house. Through the windows, I can see lines and crowds milling at the ticket windows, but no one is looking at me. To my right is the rail yard with many trains on several tracks moving in different directions, but the platform is vacant. There is not a soul in sight. This is it; time to go. I can hardly believe it; after all the time, plans, and disappointment, I have simply stepped out of a crowd and into freedom.

I don't think. If I hesitate, or look confused, someone might notice. I turn, and acting as if I belong, walk with shaking legs down the steps from the platform to the rail bed and slip between rail cars. In an instant, I have vanished.

There is much noise and confusion, and the cars are close together so that there is little chance of being seen. I look down the tracks toward the cars we arrived in and see guards leaving their posts, joining into groups lighting up smokes and joking with each other. After all, why would someone want to go aboard prisoner transport cars? They smell worse than cattle cars.

I step between two cars and find myself in a row where no one is visible. I fling my pack into the first open car I come to. I follow it without looking back.

The car is empty. My heart is pounding, my mouth feels like it is full of cotton, I am panting, and my hands are shaking as I start to pick at the buttons of my gray uniform. I strip off the worn shabby coat, empty the pockets of my orders, journal, pocket knife, and introductory letter and place them on the bag. I sit and pull off my boots, checking to make sure my boot dagger is still in place. I stand up again and strip out of my filthy long johns; find the cleanest spot on them and wipe myself all over to freshen up as much as possible before I put on the new underwear I pilfered from the supply room.

I am shaking as if I am freezing, but it's May, and warm. I begin to have doubts that I am able to do this, but attribute my nerves to the fact that I am naked and alone for the first time in over three years. I do not know if it is joy or fear, but I must get it under control. The thought flashes in my mind, "I'm free!" I force myself to breathe and to calm down, but can't make myself stop smiling.

I put my new underwear, shirt, trousers and uniform jacket on, and feel myself make the transition as I become a medical officer in the Union Army with the rank of Captain. I do not love the blue, but if it will get me safely out of this town and back south, I will tolerate it. The more dressed I become, the safer I feel. I secure my papers and journal inside my new coat, and I am ready.

Carrying my hat in hand, I chance a look out the door of the box car; glance both ways and see no one. With my pack over my shoulder, I jump down from the train. Without rushing, I start back to the platform.

"Hey!" I hear shouted from behind me. I keep walking. "Hey," comes the call again, louder, more demanding. I fight to keep my pace casual and slow. "Oh God, don't let it end now," I plead out loud, but the words are lost in the noise of the yard. I hear foot falls on the gravel of the bed coming up from behind me. I prepare to attack; I've come to far now to be caught so soon. "Excuse me," this time the voice is not as demanding, "sir, excuse me."

I can no longer ignore the hail and turn to face the man, "Yes, what is it, what do you want?"

I am facing a big man, but no one in authority, a yard worker who says, "Excuse me sir, but are you lost?"

"Lost, do I look lost?" My affront stops him and he is at a loss for words, then before he can answer, I say, "The station house is this way isn't it?" I point in the direction I am walking.

"Yes sir, but what are you doing back here? You could get hurt here sir. We are instructed to keep passengers and civilians from the trains. Would hate to have you squashed back here," he says with a big, disarming smile. He is a young man trying to do his job. He then adds as if to increase the validity of his statement, "It happened just last week, a poor old man got confused and …"

"Sir, I am neither confused nor old. I have just left off treating a man that arrived here sick on that transport," gesturing in the general direction of the row of cars behind the young yard worker, "and I am leaving now," I say with as much confidence as I can muster.

"Why certainly sir, I didn't mean no harm or offense."

"None taken; I appreciate you diligence in taking notice of me. Now sir, I am new here, can you direct me to an eatery and hotel?"

"Of course sir, let me show you to the platform and I can give you directions."

I am trapped by the well meaning man, and have no recourse but to say, "You are too kind," then stepping aside and with a sweep of my arm in the direction of our travel, I say, "please lead on."

He steps to the front with a nod and a tip of his cap and starts off with me following. We pass the place where I jumped the platform and continue a good way down the track to an area that is like a wide avenue at the corner of the station. The young giant points down the street and says, "This here street's called Liberty Ave," I cannot control a smile at the thought that I am escaping and the first street I will walk on is Liberty Ave. He sees the smile and says, "Problem sir?"

"Oh no, the name of the avenue has a pleasant sound to my ears is all."

He smiles and pointing down the street toward what I assume is the city center, says, "Down there, just two blocks is the Liberty Ave. Saloon, it has meals, rooms, baths, and all."

"Just what I'm looking for," I say, "thank you for your assistance." I reach into my pocket and extract a coin and hand it to him, "for your kindness sir." No sooner had I done it than I knew it was a mistake. The simple gesture of gratitude will cement me in the young man's memory. I will be missed soon if not already, and if he is questioned, he just might remember me. Although I no longer look the part of a confederate officer, I do have an accent, and he can describe me. I will have to move fast

"Thank you sir, have a pleasant dinner!" He turns and trots back the way we came. I look after him to see if any of his fellow workers are looking our way. They are not. With more nonchalance than I feel, I step down Liberty Ave. a free man.

The Liberty Saloon is a big place. The largest doors, glassed in front and cut in the French style so that they can be converted to the traditional swinging doors in the warmer months, are for the saloon. A drink is tempting, but I must avoid the place, not for liquor, but for the men such places draw; soldiers who like to congregate and tell stories. I stroll past the main entrance to a smaller one opening into the dining room. It is yet early for dinner, but there are a few patrons scattered in the sizeable room. I step inside and stop in the entrance.

The dining room is devoid of military personnel. As I look through the large, open passage to my right, I can see into the saloon where there is a group of union soldiers drinking and conversing at a table, but they do not notice me.

I choose a table opposite the saloon and make my way to it. I am able to sit with my back to the wall where I can watch both entrances. I place my bag on the floor as a nice, middle aged woman walks up with a menu in her hand. I clasp my hands together, hoping she does not notice the shaking.

"Good evening sir, our special tonight is a broiled, split chicken, with potatoes, green beans, and bread; would that interest you?"

"That'll be fine."

"And to drink?"

"Coffee, if you've got it."

She smiles and says, "Of course we've got it! You've been in the field too long. I can tell."

"Oh and how's that?"

"You've just got that tired strained look and the way your eyes lit up when I told you we had coffee."

"Yes ma'am, it's been a long time."

"Where are you from? Your accent isn't northern."

"No ma'am, I'm from Arkansas, near the Missouri border." I figured telling the truth would arouse less suspicion than a lie, and with being as nervous as I was, I didn't trust my voice to tell a lie.

"Oh, really? How nice; I've never been there. Well, you rest up here. I'll bring you your coffee, and your food will be out in a few minutes."

"Thank you," I say, and sit back, trying to relax. I got through that little interrogation without the woman taking a second thought to me. I am free and no alarm has been raised, but I need to get away from the rail station as soon as possible...or maybe not.

I look at the clock on the wall and see it is after six o'clock. Three hours have passed since we arrived. It seems like three minutes. Our train is scheduled to leave at six, and I wonder if it has gone. Just at that moment, I hear a whistle sounding and the steam blast of an engine getting underway. It's distant, but if it's heading east, it will grow faint as it moves. It does, and I relax a little. They must be looking for me now, they will first search the train station and then for a man traveling the back streets or running dressed in gray, not a Federal doctor having dinner in a hotel. If I can avoid other soldiers who like to talk about former commanders and postings, I will be safer in public, taking my time and not running, at least not yet.

My food arrives and the lady asks me, "Where you headed doctor?"

The uniform works; I hope the story does too. This lady has seen many Union soldiers and I have passed my first muster. I answer, "Maryland; I've been assigned to the new prison at Point Lookout."

"No more battles then?"

"No, I hope that's done."

"I'm sure you'll be needed. Those prisons are hell holes."

"Yes ma'am, they surely are."

She looks thoughtful for a moment and then, as if waking from a dream says, "Enjoy your meal. Call me if you need anything. I'm Peggy, I own the place."

"The hotel too?"

"I sure do."

"Can I get a room for the night?"

"Surely; it's a dollar for the room, and another dollar with a bath, and that's the military discount."

"Sounds great," I say around a mouth full of chicken, "I guess you get a lot of soldiers through here?"

"All the time, but just passing; do you want me to get it ready for you?"

"Yes, ma'am, and if you have a spare razor, I would love a shave as well."

"How about a haircut? It looks like you could use one."

"That would be fine, how much more is it?"

"Two bits."

"Good, please take care of it."

"Yes sir, your room will be ready when you finish your meal." With that, she goes to assist other guests and leaves me to myself.

I smile as I drink the coffee and for the first time in months, I am full of good food. It's something I have not had in a long, long time.

I leave the dining room unnoticed and unchallenged as I make my way to my room, bath, shave, and haircut. I try to sleep, but it's fitful. I wake with every foot step coming down the hall. As the dawn breaks, I'm awake, dressed and ready to travel.

I come down the stairs, avoiding the dining room, although the smells are tempting, but I don't want to take too many chances. I make my way west on Liberty Ave. till it intersects with Grant St. and go south on Grant. The irony of the intersection of Liberty and Grant does not escape me; it is Grant and his forces that imprisoned me. Now, Grant Ave will liberate me. It all feels like a good omen to me.

I walk along the avenue through town while it sleeps. I see a lantern up ahead on the right side of the street and horses out front. It's a livery. As I make my way closer, I see five mounts saddled and waiting in front. They have "US" brands and saddles. I spend a few minutes in the dark watching. There's only the stable hand moving about. I wait for him to walk into the rear of the building. I hear a door open and close and figure he's either in a tack room, or out the back door. This is my chance.

I walk up as casually as I can to the larger of the animals and tie my bag to the saddle next to full saddle bags.

I untie the reins talking to the chestnut gelding all the while and swing myself into the saddle, turn and ride away at a trot. It has been so long since I sat a horse that it's dizzying, but I manage. I do not want to appear anxious, but I want to put distance between me and Pittsburg. I listen for a cry of alarm behind me, but hear none and ride the animal at an easy pace until I clear the city and am in open country.

An officer riding alone might be curious, but not suspicious. I keep a sharp eye and ear for anything unusual. I ride the horse hard that first day into Ohio. It makes me nervous riding back into the state of my incarceration, but it is the shortest way.

I ride unchallenged. I stop at an inn along the way and eat, get the horse tended to and ride on. I have Corporal Mather to thank more than anyone else for my security. Dollars open doors with no questions asked.

I spend nights in the woods until I reach the out skirts of Columbus where I find another inn. Again, no one questions me, and the residents are all glad to accommodate my money, but I don't need it. The inn keeper has a little girl who cut her leg with an axe and in exchange for treating her, which amounted to cleaning the wound and dressing it, he allows me to stay in the inn without charge.

I ask about a livery or someone who will trade my tired horse for a fresh one, and he's more than glad to trade. This one is a paint, and a very sturdy, spirited horse. I see a Navy Colt hanging in its scabbard and gun belt by the door and ask if it's for sale. He says he'll take five dollars and I offer him six if he has ammunition and powder and grub for five days. The deal is done with no questions, not even about a soldier riding without weapons.

It takes me four days to get near Indianapolis. I have been successful in trading horses, or exchanging them at various, farms and liveries. In one case, I traded right out of a field near the road. The "US" brand is a ticket to exchange. I want to stay in states that are loyal to the north as long as I have a Yankee uniform, and Yankee orders. It's my plan to cross the Mississippi River into St. Louis, and there all allegiances are questioned. I'll have to be very, very careful. When I get to Missouri, the Yankee uniform can be either target or shield, depending on who I ride up on. As I get closer to the river, I'll have to increase my vigilance.

In the mean time, I'm enjoying freedom and food. I can feel my uniform beginning to fill out as I put on some of the weight I lost in prison. I am feeling good and anxious to get home until I remember that the dangerous part is still ahead when I cross into Missouri.

Riding through Illinois, another land of my imprisonment, I let my mind wander to what is at home. What will I have to deal with? Will I even have a home? Will Lucy Jane be there? Will I have to trail them to Nebraska? I will if necessary if for no other reason than to claim Martha Jane. Will they be with Steven Wayne? Will I have to fight him, or worse, kill him? I know I can, but hope it doesn't come to it. I try to put these thoughts out of my mind. There is nothing I can do about it now, so there's no sense worrying about it. That's my prison training; one day at a time, and "sufficient unto the day is the evil thereof". I'll cross all those bridges when I get to them, but it doesn't hurt to be prepared for the crossing. I'm getting ready for anything, and it's coming.

41) Arkansas

Getting through St. Louis was nerve-wracking and exhausting. I would not have been able to do it without the Yankee uniform and the medical caduceus on the collar. When guards saw a doctor at a check point, they waved me through with a salute which I had a difficult time returning, but I did. I've ridden hard and am now south of Springfield, Missouri where the White River flows northward into this state. The horse and I smell it before we see it. Fatigue and fear shed off me like an old skin as I ride onto a bluff and look over the river into Arkansas. Home.

Its green and lush hills roll away from me like a huge carpet. The water in the river below me has flowed past my home. It is brown with recent run off from rains, but it is beautiful to me. The last time I saw these waters, I was a terrified prisoner headed north into what, I did not know. I smile at the thought I had that night of jumping into the Mississippi and swimming for home. Many was the day that I didn't think I would see these waters again. Yet, here I am.

Free, freedom; what beautiful words, and it's just across that border, but I don't want to cross the river; not yet. It's too wide, too fast, and I need to make some more distance west. I need to see Buck.

Buck will know the news of the area, even in Washington County, and he'll be able to tell me of my family; wife and home. Besides, he's my friend. I want to meet his new wife and get myself ready for the ride home. In truth, I'm afraid to finish this.

I don't know how it'll be, and all the scenarios I imagine are conflicting in my head; some good, most bad. I am frightened of how I will react. This is what I have longed for all this time, yet when it is in sight, I don't want it.

Instead of greeting me with open arms as I have dreamed of, and longed for, I will have to confront my wife and a former commander. Life has twisted and turned on me. How the choices I have made have come to hurt me and others that I love. I am desperate for release from this pain, but afraid of it.

I was selfish when I thought I was being benevolent, caught up in the needs of a woman in distress. I can't blame Lucy Jane; she was the temptation, but I made the choices. I have no one to blame but me, and this hateful war, but who knew; who could have foretold?

I dismount the horse, unsaddle and let her graze in the meadow as I take a much needed rest. I bring out some of my last grub and remember when I was building the cabin and Lucy Jane rode into the yard with her pitiful tale. I see myself as a boy then, infatuated with the lusty woman who begged me to champion her cause. Will she want me? Can we resume our life as before? Should we?

I know the answers; no, we can't go back, and that is Lucy's problem; she wants to go back to the way it was before. It will never be that way, we are two different people who have gone two different ways each doing what we must to survive. We've grown apart.

Whoever said that the first casualty of war is truth was never in one. The first casualty of war is love. The love dies long before the truth. You can't lie to someone you love. I wonder how many broken homes, and shattered lives this war has caused? I cannot conceive of the destruction. There are too many not going home at all, and many who are going home with scars, and many more with scars that don't show. The invisible ones may be the most horrible. They may never heal.

Dr. Allison says time heals all wounds, but I don't believe it. The passing of time covers the hurt with scar tissue and it fades. The pain may diminish, but the wound and how it got there is always part of you.

I am sinking into a dark place, feeling sorry as I think of my dead son James Calvin, and Martha Jane. Will she still remember me? Does she even know I am alive? Has her mother poisoned her to me? I need to ride, I need to get home.

I push the poor horse through some of the most beautiful country on earth. My heart sings as my eyes feast on the hills and valleys of home. I cross into Arkansas and ride along Pea Ridge, the scene of my first combat, my awakening. It all seemed adventurous as we stood here in our shiny uniforms, with our faces glowing, eager to prove ourselves in battle. Those who knew better tried to tell us, but young men can't be told of such things, they must experience it. Here is where the first of many are buried. How many since? I shake my head in wonder as I recall the faces I looked into after battle. They weren't boys, and neither was I, we had changed in the hour. We looked death in the face and had not turned away. We weren't men, but we weren't innocent.

I shake my head and focus. I am nearer my folk's place here than I am to Buck's, but if I push it just a few miles southwest, I'll be at Buck's before nightfall.

The shadows are getting long and the horse is just this side of lame. I have pushed her far and fast, but there is a great deal at stake. The urgency to move on, to stop Lucy from leaving with Martha presses both the horse and I forward. The poor animal can sense my desperation and pushes herself in spite of pain and fatigue.

We ride up the familiar trail to Buck's cabin in the late afternoon a little before sunset and find the place empty. The door is open and the house, yard, and barn show all the signs of being viable and alive, but there are no people. I hurriedly take the exhausted animal to the barn, find a stall, unsaddle, feed, and brush her then go to find Buck and whoever else is here.

I realize in a flash where they are, and smile as I walk fast down a well worn trail. Buck has used this path for years. I can't even guess the number of sunsets he, I, and others have watched from the west facing bluff at the end of the trail.

Up ahead I see them and stop short to take in the scene. In the distance, the sun, like a child's play thing is settling on the horizon looking squat and flattened. It glows bright orange, making you think it will bounce into the sky with its pent up energy. It is lighting the late afternoon thunder heads in shades of yellow to orange, to pink, violet onto purple. It is not possible to capture a sunset in word or picture although many have tried. Every one of them is an individual work of art; a spreading of the glory of God.

When I see the sun dip below the western lip of the world, I want to run to the east to see it come again, but I must wait in faith for the promise that the setting sun gives; that of a new tomorrow. What will tomorrow hold for me and my family; our future? The rising of the sun will tell, but I must wait.

I watch as Buck and others I don't recognize sit on a split log bench. He is sitting on the right with a woman leaning on his left shoulder, his arm around her, his head resting on the top of hers. To their left sits another woman whose shoulders are square to the world, a strong woman, confident, and at peace. Without seeing her face, I know there is a smile there. This must be Sallie Buchannan McPheeters sitting next to Olivia Buchannan, leaning on Buck.

A young man; really a boy, but the way he carries himself, the confidence he exhibits, he seems to be much older, is staring at me, cautious, but unafraid. If I am an intruder, he will deal with me, but he only looks at me with a question in his eyes, no fear; who are you? I guess him to be William McPheeters, son of my benefactor. There are two little girls running around behind the bench with him, who, when they notice him, notice me and become still.

The boy's hand reaches out and touches Buck's arm, not his mother, which speaks volumes concerning the relationships that have grown here. Buck turns to the boy and says something I cannot hear, but it is obvious it is a question, and gently asked. The boy, without taking his eyes off of me points in my direction.

Bucks eyes, still mesmerized by the narcotic of the sun set, shift to me. I see them flare in danger and defense and then dissolve into recognition. He speaks a single word, "Evans."

"What was that dear?" The woman on his shoulder asks. "Did you say something?"

A smile spreads across his face to match the growing one on mine as he repeats the word, "Evans!" This time it is louder and with joy.

Both women turn and look at me. There is no recognition from them, neither has ever met me, but there is acceptance, and joy. This is what I have come home for, those who will take joy in me.

I start to walk toward the gathering, but before I take three steps, Buck, as quick as ever, is on me like a cat, but a cat with the strength of a bear and has me in his arms, lifted above the ground swinging me. "Boy!" He exclaims. "You've come home! Is it really you? Are you really here? How did you get here?"

I don't have time to answer, so I don't. I bask in the moment as I laugh and cry tears of joy. Everyone comes to hug me, even the children. Introductions are made while everyone is laughing and crying along with me. Although I have never met anyone here but Buck, they are as welcoming to me as a man can want. Joy rises in me that I had forgotten existed and wells forth in tears and laughter to mingle with the joy of the others. We make our way to the bench and sit to watch the finale of this day. I sit between the two women who are each holding one of my hands, and feel the gentle power of Buck's hand resting on my shoulder as his arm is around Olivia, I shudder at the warmth. I watch a sunset that I will never forget. It is welcoming me with promise; I am home.

42) Buck's Home

After being held against your will by men who hate you, it is wonderful to sit with people who love you. We talked into the wee hours of the morning. At first, there are rapid fire questions that can only be partially answered before another question is asked that switches the subject and off we go on that tangent. Around midnight, the stories begin to mesh and a cohesive narrative emerges.

Buck catches me up on Martin Wilson. He talks about Ben and Bill as if they're his sons. My parents are discussed and how my father has gone to Texas with my older brother and no one is sure when they will return. He tells of how the Wilson family is doing without their father John, who was murdered. He does not mention Susan.

Sallie tells of her banishment from Missouri and how Buck rescued her and Olivia. Olivia bows her head; she'll tell her own story in time but is bright and cheerful as she teases Buck about how and where they met.

They all tell of how they crossed the state and the dangers they faced. Sallie glows as the story of Dr. McPheeters' appearance at Christmas unfolds, and of Olivia's and Buck's wedding, and the happiness of the place with the two families living there. She's saddened only a little as she tells of her husband's departure. I am impressed with this woman's strength and outlook on life.

I talk until I am so dry I speak in a whisper. I tell as much as I can remember. Some things shouldn't be remembered and aren't told. The escape I tell of in detail from working in the hospital thanks to Dr. McPheeters, to the uniform stealing, to the deep, dark disappointment of failed plans, the snowball war, more disappointment, and the hand of providence that steered me thorough that crowd in Pittsburg, the miracle of getting across Missouri, and on to here. I tell of my sorrow that my dreamed for reunion with my wife and family would not be a reality, but being here has been better than anything I dreamed of.

The evening wears on and the children, one by one, fall asleep. Once they are secured in their hammocks on the big front porch to make use of the cool air of the mountain evening, the two subjects that have been avoided come to the fore; Lucy Jane, and Susan Wilson.

A somber mood falls over us as the lantern is extinguished to keep the heat down in the cabin. "Buck, tell me of Lucy Jane. Is she still at home?"

"Last I heard, but she's sure taken up with Steven Wayne." He pauses, waiting for me to say something. I am silent, he continues, "She's had a baby, a boy, but I can't remember his name. I ain't sure I've ever heard it spoken." I remain silent. "Stevie Wayne wasn't living there full time, but he spent enough time there to get her pregnant. He's stays at his folk's place when not at yours and works at the bank, but Lucy Jane has cast her lot with him." My jaw tightens as I take a sharp breath. "I got to be straight with you Evans; I don't know no other way."

"Go on."

"Boy," it felt good to be called that again, "she ain't worth it. You'd never have a peaceful life with her, and she don't deserve you."

I don't agree, but ask only, "Martha Jane?"

"She's good last I saw her. She's not much more'n baby, but she's old for her years. Lucy Jane and Steven Wayne don't hurt her, but they don't help her none either. Your mother says she asks and talks about you all the time. She spends as much time as Lucy Jane will allow at your folks place. Lucy and Steven Wayne haven't run off yet, but it could be any day now with her recovered from the birthing."

I catch myself clasping and unclasping my hands till they hurt and I'm bouncing one leg up and down with my toe never leaving the floor. Sallie reaches over, even in the dark I can feel her smile, and lays her hand on mine. I unclasp my hands and smooth them over my legs.

"What are you planning?" Buck asks.

"I'm going in the morning to see what I can salvage."

It's quiet in the room. Everyone's afraid of the next question, "What are you gonna do about Stevie Wayne."

"I don't know; it's what's worrying me. I don't have a chance of getting Lucy Jane back with him there, but I don't want to have to get rid of him."

"I can tell you what you ought to do, but I don't know if I'd do it myself."

"What's that?"

"You don't want to hear it."

"I know."

"You need to let it go. Lucy's done made a choice and you ain't it. If you'd been here the whole time, maybe she'd never strayed, but you weren't and she did. It ain't all her fault, but we know her ways now."

"I know; the war..." I let the rest hang; I'm tired of talking about it. They all know.

"She's scared Boy; it did something to her."

"Tell me, all of it."

He did; every detail. I'm angry because I wasn't there to help, but what could I do? I was in prison! The thought makes me madder and madder.

"Calm down Boy; let me finish." I'm quiet, he goes on. "Steven Wayne ain't right in the head. He's dangerous, but there are times when he's gentle. It wouldn't be right to kill him, but when you ride in there, if he's wild crazy, be ready to kill if you have to."

I nod in the dark and say, "I can't let it all go; I have to get Martha Jane. Do you think there'll be a fight over that?"

"No, I don't, but you can't ever tell with Steven Wayne. He's scared a lot of people with his crazy wandering at night and such. Most everyone, including his parents hopes he moves on and quick. My advice is to let it go. Killing him will only hurt you in the community. Boy, she just ain't worth it."

"I'm goin' for Martha Jane."

No one says anything. I'm staring out at nothing in the dark night, and they're all watching me. I have to think.

Pretty soon, the women excuse themselves and go to bed, but not before they give me a long hug and a kiss on the cheek which calms me. Sallie says, "Please don't do anything that would take you from us. It'd kill Buck to lose you again."

I nod and smile. She smiles back and the room gets brighter even in the dark. The women go and leave me and Buck alone.

"I want to walk for awhile," I say and stand up. "You comin', or you got to go to bed with your Mrs.?"

"She don't run me," Buck says, but I can tell from the way he says it he's smiling. I figure Olivia is no woman to take any guff off Buck.

We walk without talking through the moon shadows. The summer cicadas are noisy, even at night. I have not heard them in a long time. "How is she?" I ask.

"Who, Lucy?"

I don't answer.

"Oh, you mean Susan?"

"Yeah, when's the last time you saw her?"

"I saw her at the Wilson place, oh, maybe two or three months back. They'd never met Olivia, and I wanted to show her off. It was one of the Sunday deals, you know, after church."

"How is she?" I ask again.

Buck stops and faces me in the moonlight. "She's fine Boy, she's just fine. She's sweet, tender, stable as a rock, pretty as a picture, smooth as water on a still morning, good through and through, and for some reason; she's in love with you and says she always has been and will be."

"She say that?"

"Yeah, she and everybody else, but I don't know why." He pauses and changes the subject, "Martin still carries that promise about taking care of you. That boy's not gonna rest until you are safe home. I guess he won't have long to wait now." We walk some more, before Buck asks, "Now, tell me true, what are you gonna do about Lucy and Steven Wayne?"

"I don't know Buck, I've thought about that since I got your letter. I've wanted to kill them both and then one or the other, and then want it to all go away. Like you said, my hurtin' them will only do me bad. I just hate to lose all I've got. Maybe I already have."

"You've not lost everything. You'll still have your house when they leave, and if you get Martha Jane, what else is there? Lucy Jane's not the same. I don't think a sane man'd want her, and you sure as hell don't want her back after Stevie Wayne's been around."

"That boy's not right; he's dangerous crazy. You watch his hands all the time. He's gotten almighty strong since you saw him last and claims to kill deer with his bare hands. Many's the tale about him roaming the woods at night. Talk is that only Lucy Jane can handle him. Maybe it's true; maybe they're meant for each other."

"She and I were meant for each other at one time."
"No you weren't. You were thinking with the hot head. You were all wrapped up in lust. Nobody blames you, not even Susan, but it was breathin' hard that you and Lucy Jane had, not love."

I don't want to believe what he's saying to me, but know it's true.
"It grew to love. The babies made it love." We both reflect on it before I ask, "Does everyone know what a fool I was?"
"Hell yeah, ain't nobody blind to it. But they're all willing to live and let live. Hell, we all make mistakes. You forget that we all love you?"

"No, I ain't forgot. That's the only thing kept me alive." We walk some more and I get the courage up to ask, "Do you think she'll have me back?"

"Who, Lucy?" Buck asks as if I had lost my mind.
I don't say anything.
"Oh, you mean Susan. Boy, you're confusing me with all these women," he laughs, then continues, "I don't know Boy. If she does, it'll take some serious courtin', and some serious promisin'. I 'spect she's been waiting for you, but if you don't measure up, she'll drop you like a hot iron and be married to someone who will appreciate her before you hit the floor. She may not love him, but she'll learn to and make it work as smooth as everything else she does."

I know I deserve less than Buck thinks Susan is willing to give, but I'm getting ahead of things even thinking of it. I have Lucy Jane and Steven Wayne to deal with, but above all, I have Martha Jane to get. She's blood, and I'm not letting her go without a fight.

"I'll need to borrow a horse. That poor thing I rode in on is about give out. She'll do good with some rest, but I ain't got time. I wanna go tomorrow."

"You can ride my mare. Come on back to my cabin. I've got something I've been holding for you. It'll put a smile on that sad face."

We walk without talking to the little place Buck has fixed up for himself and Olivia. He says, "Wait here," and goes inside. It isn't long before he comes out with a bundle in his hands and gives it to me. "Remember these?" He asks.

I unwrap the bundle to find my Toothpick and my LeMat. "Where'd you get these?"

"That blue belly lieutenant who had them was wounded and treated by Dr. McPheeters the same day we were. He saw our names on the haversack they's in and took 'em. He gived 'em to me and I've been carrying 'em since. You're gonna need 'em, and that scares me."

I heft and hold the weapons like lost lovers. We've been through it together. There are memories, good and bad in 'em, but they're nice to hold.

Buck's voice is solemn as he says, "Don't waste a minute more of your life on that woman. She ain't worth it. If Susan won't have you, there's others that will. Just take your time. You're home now, there ain't no hurry."

"Yeah, Buck there is; there's a big hurry." We look at the moon light; he knows what I mean, and I know what he's thinking. Tomorrow or the next day will prove out one way or the other the course of my life. I can't lie to Buck, I'm scared, he knows it, but he can't help me. This is my trail to ride, alone.

43) Coming Home

I am ready to ride before dawn. Buck is up with me and puts a whole passel of grub together and makes sure that my weapons are in good order. I leave him the Navy Colt and take only the LeMat and Toothpick. If I'm going to do any fighting, it'll be close in, but I'm determined to not fight unless provoked.

Buck is itching to go with me, but I can't allow it. This is my own.

"I'll ride and meet you at your folk's place Saturday or Sunday."

"Alright; today's Thursday. That'll be about right. If I ain't there by Sunday late, come looking for me. You know where." We part with a hand shake. I ride away in the dark.

The day is a blur. I ride the horse hard as the country flies past, and I can think of little else than the situation I am riding into. Several times I have to stop to give the horse a rest and figure out where I am. Buck's mare doesn't understand the urgency and insists on resting more than I like.

I ride through the valley past the entrance to the Robinson's Spring Dale recalling the just told story of Patricia Anne's wedding. I smile at her circumstance, but it's cruel. My situation's not much different. I'm sure people are laughing at me for what Lucy Jane has done, or am I pitied? I hate pity. It doesn't matter. Those who stayed home will never know the trials of those who leave and those left behind.

It gets late. I don't want to arrive after dark. I camp a few miles out and will finish the trip in the morning. The horse and I both need the rest. I try to sleep, but being this close to the end of my war, to the final problem, to getting on with my life keeps me awake. By fire light, I put pen to paper in my journal:

June 23rd, 1864
Shiloh, Arkansas
Camped near home.

Whatever tomorrow brings will change my life, and the lives of those who are yet to come. Maybe someday, generations from now, someone will read this and find value in these pages.

What happens tomorrow will affect generations. The Bible says that, "the sins of the fathers will be visited even unto the third and fourth generations". I do not want the generations that follow me to suffer for my choices.

I read a quote by a man I admire; David Crockett; frontiersman, congressman from Tennessee, and defender of freedom where it needed defending. He made the statement, "Be always sure you are right, then go ahead." That is how I intend to live my life. At no time in my life has being right been more important.

What if Steven Wayne chooses violence? I will have to respond in kind. I cannot let him hurt me, Lucy, or Martha Jane. What if Lucy wants him to go away and he refuses? What if, what if... There is nothing I can do about it tonight so I should quit worrying. That's easier said than done.

I must rely again on providence to guide me. The Lord has gotten me this far for a reason. I cannot betray that trust and those blessings now. I must follow through and be always sure that I am right, and go ahead. I pray the way is clear when I see it.

I feel better. I put away the journal, lie down on my bed roll and look at the stars. They are the same ones I have seen in Texas, Mississippi, Illinois, Ohio, Missouri, and they give me comfort. In moments, I am asleep and do not dream.

The sun wakes me. I do not want the day to get too far gone before I ride, but I do not want to arrive too early. I make breakfast of bacon and biscuits, put my gear together, saddle the mare, and ride to my destiny.

Up the trail toward my house is as if I ride back in time. I smile as I once did when I knew Lucy Jane would be at the cabin site. She would be eager and ready for me, and I would be obliging to her. We had been happy. That's past, the present makes me worry. I touch my weapons and loathe doing it. It's a habit of war. I hope they will not be a solution today.

I make the last turn of the trail, and there's no more dreaming of the way it was, now only the way it is. I knew it would not be the same, but the place has changed so much I don't recognize it. We all have an image of what things look like and we can't imagine them changing. In our memories, trees don't grow, the garden doesn't expand, and the barn isn't added on to. Children don't grow, wives or ourselves don't age, and a dozen other things. But life does not stand still, it changes with the sweep of the hands of time and that's why I'm here today; things have changed.

Sweat slides down my spine and I wonder if it's from the heat, or my pounding heart. The horse carries me at a walk toward the house, past the shed where Lucy Jane and I first lived, now a full barn. I see no one. All the doors and windows are open. The place is neglected and looks abandoned.

The garden needs tending. Someone made a halfhearted attempt at planting, but left it to nature. The place is in need of repair. It's as if someone has given up; doesn't care. There is neglect everywhere I look. Beside the barn, there's a wagon loaded and covered, ready to roll. They haven't left.

I stop short of the porch. So many times I have dreamed of riding into this yard to a grand and beautiful homecoming. There have been flowers in the beds in front of the house, green everywhere, my beautiful, blonde wife with the enchanting eyes rushing to me with arms open, calling my name over and over while two children, Martha Jane, and James Calvin are trailing behind her, excited as their Mama.

I am greeted with silence, profound sadness; giving up, dying. I have felt it too many times to mistake it.

A baby crying inside the house breaks the stillness. The sound brings rise to bitter thoughts of my passed babe. How dare this child replace my son! I feel irrational anger rise in me and, with all the willpower I have, force myself to accept that the infant is not the cause of my grief, but is a victim too.

I want to flee. I turn the horse and as I do, I see a little girl coming out from behind the barn. She looks tired, is dirty and walks unsteady toward me. I dismount and watch her. I wait and watch. Is this my daughter, my flesh and blood? Is this Martha Jane?

"Papa?" The girl speaks just audible. "Papa, is that you? Have you come? Are you here?" A frail, dirty arm reaches to me with a quivering hand.

"Martha Jane?" I query the waif. She nods, but just. "It's Papa. Yes, Martha Jane, I've come for you." I step toward her.

She runs to my arms as I stoop to her. I sweep her up. She weighs nothing as I hold her crying into my shirt. "Papa, Papa," she says, over and over between sobs. I stand in the yard swaying back and forth, comforting the child. "I knew you'd come for me."

"There you are you little bitch! Where the hell have you been? We've been looking for you for three days! I ought to beat you…" I turn with hate in my heart and flame in my eyes as I look into the face of Steven Wayne Culpepper standing on my porch! Our eyes meet. "Evans, uh, Lieutenant Atwood, uh, what are you doing here?"

"You should be answering that Culpepper. I'm the one with the right to be here."

"You're insubordinate lieutenant; my name is Captain Culpepper and you will be well advised to remember it. You are still in the Army, and I'll …"

"Do nothing! You can do nothing Stevie Wayne. There's no organized unit, you have no authority here." We stand looking at each other. Martha Jane clings to me. There's something very bad here. "Do not ever speak to my daughter like that again Steven Wayne, do you understand me?"

He does not reply. Behind him, in the doorway stands Lucy Jane holding a baby. She is not the woman I left. Just like the homestead, she's worn and unkept. Her beauty is faded. The years and evil have not been kind. There is no love in her eyes, and they have lost their power.

"Evans," she says.

I nod, in disbelief.

"I thought you was dead."

"We thought you was dead," chimed in Steven Wayne with a nervous chuckle.

"No you didn't," I say to both, but looking at Lucy, "you hoped I was dead. You never had any reason to think otherwise. I wrote, and I know you got the letters."

No reply. I look from one to the other; two people I have shared so much with. My wife, the woman I dreamed of those lonely nights on battle fields, and in prisons; the mother of my children, and a man who I had shared the horrors of battle with; a man who I had stood back to back with and admired the ferocity of his leadership. Now he and she are lost; gone to a place I cannot imagine, worse than any prison I was in.

Lucy breaks the silence, "What do you want Evans? Why are you here?"

"I want what's mine, and I'm here to claim it, at least what's left of it." Again, no reply. I look at Lucy, "We need to talk."

"About what?" Lucy asks, puzzled.

"About what we're going to do," as I start up the steps to the house still holding Martha Jane.

"Where the hell do you think you're going?" Steven Wayne demands as he steps in front of me blocking the last step.

Steven Wayne *is* different. Whatever has altered his mind has changed his body too. Although I am standing a foot below him on the steps, I can tell he is larger. I see the bulge of his chest, the strength of his arms and his hands; dangerous hands. He smells of something wild. Looking up and meeting his eye, "I'm going into *my* house Stevie Wayne to talk to *my* wife about what *we're* going to do. It doesn't concern you."

"She don't want you anymore; she wants me."

"Get out of my way Stevie Wayne, you're trespassing here."

"She wants me here, and invited me."

"Her husband's here now and I'm telling you to leave."

"You can't do that." Steven Wayne speaks in a cold, flat, resonating voice that matches the blackness of his eyes and chills the summer air. The transformation unnerves me. I stand my ground and watch his hands. I can see the steel of them. Buck's right; hands kill, not eyes or faces. I'm gambling that he will not get violent with me holding Martha Jane, but with the look that has come over him, and the way he talked to my daughter, I am uncertain of his ability to control whatever drives him.

"Steven Wayne, step aside," comes the calming command from Lucy Jane, "you need to give us some time...alone."

"Alone; you trust him?"

"He's my husband Steven Wayne, holding his daughter. You're the one I don't trust right now."

"Give me my baby then." Steven Wayne does not call the baby by name as he steps toward Lucy.

"No, you need to leave Steven Wayne. You need to go to the woods, get yourself right."

"But what if he tries to..."

"He's got more of a right to it than you do, but he ain't like that; he knows."

"He knows what?"

"Steven Wayne, go."

He is still looking at me with the flat, black eyes, but his voice has changed. Whatever is wrong with him, it seems that Lucy Jane can handle it. He walks past me without a word like I'm not here. I watch him go.

"He's not right in the head since Vicksburg. Sometimes he leaves in his head and it seems that I'm the only one who can reach him."

"Let's go in the house," I say as I walk past Lucy.

The inside is like the outside only worse. There's darkness that opening the windows and firing lanterns cannot drive away. It's something of the spirit. I go to the table, push back the things piled there, and sit down still holding Martha Jane who has not said a word, or moved off my shoulder. Lucy continues to stand. "Sit down Lucy; let's make this as easy as possible." She sits.

"Where have you been Martha Jane?" Lucy asks. The little girl does not say anything, nor does she move from my shoulder.

"What do you mean, 'where have you been'?" I question.

"She's been gone three days."

"Three days! She's been gone three days?! Didn't you look for her?" My voice has risen, and I am angry, but I do not want to lose control.

"Of course we looked for her!" Lucy shouts. "She's the reason we're still here, looking for her."

I move Martha Jane off my shoulder onto my lap. She's stopped crying, but there is fear. "Where have you been baby?"

"Are you staying Papa, are you really here?" She puts her hand up and touches my unshaven cheek. It scratches her palm and she smiles, "You're real! You're really here!" Her eyes dance and sparkle as color flows into her face. She looks at her mother, "I told you he would come," then to me, "Mama said you weren't coming back, but I knew you would and I hid in the woods. I have a secret place."

I look at Lucy and I see tears in her dead empty eyes. It's the first emotion she has shown since I got here.

"Papa, I'm not going to Nebraska am I? I don't want to go; that's why I hid in the woods. Please don't let them take me to Nebraska."

"You're not going anywhere Martha; you're staying right here with Papa."

"I have something to say about that," Lucy says.

"No Lucy, you don't. You don't want her, she knows it, I know it, and so do you. I don't want to get nasty about this, but I will if I have to. Martha Jane stays with me."

Lucy Jane starts to speak, it's too much effort and she stops, looking at the baby in her lap.

I look at the child in my lap, filthy and tired as she is, she's beautiful. "I missed you so much," I say.

"I prayed for you every night Papa."

"I know little one; I could feel it."

"Really?"

"Yes, really. Have you had anything to eat?"

She shakes her head.

"Not in three days?"

She shakes her head again.

I look at Lucy Jane once more, but say nothing. It would serve no purpose. She gets up, puts the baby in its cradle, and goes to the stove to get some biscuits, then to the cool box for milk and sets them in front of Martha who I put into another chair. She eats them very slowly.

It is a myth that starving people wolf food down. That comes later, but the first meal; every bite is savored. I know Martha is absorbed in the food, and will not hear us as I ask Lucy Jane, "Why; what happened?"

"You're back," she says with resignation. She looks down at the baby across the room and says, "I wanted it to be better; I wanted more."

"You've always said that, wanting better; when will it be good enough?"

"I don't know. It was better before you left; it was good, but then…, the war. The war killed more than soldiers," her voice trails off and she looks out the door at nothing. "God help us it's hot," she says. She's a defeated woman. She had it all and let it go; she couldn't wait.

We sit quiet before I say, "I know what I asked you to do was hard. I didn't think it would last... I had no right to ask it, but it's over now, I can't go back and change it. I'm here, and I'm sorry."

"Sorry for what?" Lucy asks, confused.

"Sorry for all of it; sorry for leaving, sorry for being young, sorry for war, and causes; sorry for James Calvin dying without me here."

"But it's changed; all of it, everything's changed. I'm not the same..."

Something in her tone lets me know we are done. There's no arguing, or explaining, or saying sorry, or begging. It's over, and we both know it, and I think we're both relieved.

As if she can read my thoughts, she meets my eyes. "What do you want me to do?"

With no malice or anger, but resolute sadness, I say, "I want you and Steven Wayne to leave. Take your baby, and what you think you have to have and leave." The words are cold. I can't believe I'm saying them and with such conviction, but I feel peace flow over me as I do.

Her eyes never leave mine as she says, "Okay. Are you keeping Martha?"

"Yes, I am."

"Good." We sit for a minute or two and she says, "When you see your parents, say 'goodbye' to 'em for me."

"I will."

She gets up from the table and goes to the door, "He's hitched the team."

I wait.

"It's got to be better... I just want it better." She does not look at Martha or me. She walks to the cradle, picks up the baby and walks out the door, down the steps, and across the yard to the wagon. She hands up the baby boy to Steven Wayne who seems awkward taking him. Lucy Jane climbs aboard, and without looking back, they ride off.

Martha Jane and I, holding hands stand on the porch and watch the wagon down the trail to where we can't see it any more.

"I hope you find it Lucy Jane," I say to the retreating wagon.

"Are they gone?" Martha Jane asks.

"Yes, baby," I reply with a little sob and a catch, "they're gone."

"Goodbye," she says as she looks once more to the spot we last saw them, and walks into the cabin, goes to her bed, lays down, and goes to sleep.

I'll bathe and feed her in the morning. Together we will face a new beginning. We have turned the page. The cabin is brighter already.

44) Sunday, June 25th, 1864

Lucy Jane rode out of our lives and didn't look back. The next day, Saturday, Martha Jane and I rode to the home of my youth. The greeting that I had dreamed of is here. It isn't with the passion, but it is with love from those dearest to me; my family and Buck, and for that, I am glad.

My father and brother James are still in Texas looking at land. We lived in Texas when I was a small boy, and Pa always wanted to go back. I do too after Buck and I did our wandering there. Pa is expected back before harvest.

Mother and Nancy are home along with William who has grown to be the man of the family with Pa gone. He's eager for tales of the war and begs Mama to let him go enlist now that I'm home. Buck and I tell him to drop it.

"Why?" He asks.

We look at him. After a minute, of silent staring, he says, "What?"

We say nothing. As we glare at him, I can see understanding come. "Okay," he says, "okay for now." He never raises the subject of going to war with either of us again.

He can't understand that the family has given enough. It is the plight of young men. To the young, war is adventure, glamorous. Death and destruction happen to others, but others believe the same. War is death, destruction, and pain. It ruins lives; even of those who do not go. Adventure and glamour are for survivors. Our minds refuse the memory of pain, and what is left are good times, and those grow to glory that may not have been.

I do believe in the cause of freedom and our right in the south to choose our own destiny, and I will fight if compelled to, but glory and adventure are no longer there. The only thing that matters now is the safety and security of my family.

We have a good meal that Saturday night, shave and scrub for Sunday. Mama finds clothes for me to wear, and she has sewed a new dress for Martha who is delighted and much more animated than she has been. She will, on occasions, stop whatever she is doing and seek me out. She smiles and says, "Papa" in a way that speaks to my soul.

Our first night together after Lucy left, she had awoke and called, "Papa."

I had come awake calling her name in return, speaking calming and soothing words.

"I'm okay Papa; I just wanted to know you are here."

"Yes Lucy Jane, I'm here baby; I'm not going anywhere."

"Ever?"

"No, not for a long, long time. You'll leave before I do."

After that, it was quiet. I thought she had gone back to sleep and was letting the tension of being startled awake begin to drain away when I heard, "Papa, I love you."

"I love you too Martha Jane." She turned in her bed and I soon could hear the steady, deep, breathing of the innocent. Peace settled on the house. It had been absent for a long time.

Sunday morning there's an unusual amount of energy in the house. Everyone is up and about doing things preparatory to going to church. It's an exciting day; the end of an era, and the birth of another.

Bill asks me to wear my uniform, but I ridded myself of the rags it was miles ago. He is disappointed and goes out to hitch a team to the wagon which we pile onto for the ride to church.

The greetings of the gathered are heartfelt and warm. There are many hugs and well wishes. I get lost in the attention. My face hurts from the smiling. Happy tears are shed. A few ask about Lucy Jane. Most know the story, and are kind enough to be gentle about it. I spend no time at all worrying about how they view me. It's not necessary; I'm welcome here. I fill three roles to these people; the returning war hero, the escaped prisoner, or the prodigal son. I am something different to each person. I can deal with the judgments. I have survived far worse.

Martha Jane is subdued at first, but is soon running with the other youngsters much to the chagrin of their mothers and in this case, grandmother. I am amazed at her resilience, and dare hope for the happiness of my daughter.

Buck is greeted as hero and prodigal as well. He is well received wherever he is unless it is in a fight. He is off with Reverend Claiborne and from the redness of Samuel's face; Buck must be poking fun at him for something; maybe his wedding, or the debacle at Patricia Anne's. I hear Buck's roaring laughter and see Reverend Claiborne turn a brighter shade of red.

The Reverend steps away from Buck and calls to the gathering in his most pious voice, "Children of the flock, it is time for reverence and to go into services," and, still red as a sunburned tomato, leads us in with as much solemnity as he can raise with Buck still poking fun walking next to him.

We sing hymns, pray, and hear a blessedly brief sermon on forgiveness and not judging. I wondered if the subject was planned, or if it were inspired at the moment to coincide with the attendance of Buck and myself. The closing hymn is sung, the closing prayer said, and we are released to once again gather outside it the bright June sun.

The atmosphere is jovial and upbeat. A steady breeze cools and freshens. It brings peace to me. I feel more and more welcome, and cleaner with every passing minute. Martha glows with the joy of family, and if you didn't look at her eyes, you would never guess the trauma the child has endured. Her joy is an elixir to me.

We invite all to dinner at our place, but before we leave, there is a thing to do. Mother takes me by the hand and walks me to the cemetery adjacent to the church; to my son's grave.

A small, white, marble stone cut in an arch, carved with his name and the appropriate dates stands at the head of a small grave. I see the stone and think of all I have missed and was not able to protect, I fall to my knees as pent up grief escapes. The frustration of three long years, loss, death, and helplessness pours out.

Martha Jane comes over and puts her hand on my shaking shoulder and says, "It's okay Papa; James is happier where he is."

I look at her expecting to see a child parroting what parent, grandparents, and friends have taught, but what I see is conviction. She knows where James is and why he's happy. I envy the strength of simple faith and wonder if I will ever have it again. Seeing Martha, I understand what the Lord means when He declared that to enter the Kingdom of Heaven, we must become as a little child.

Martha gives me strength as she hugs me and says, "Papa, I love you."

Those are the most healing words that can be spoken. I rise, she takes my hand and we stand looking over the grave. I sense someone looking at me. I cast my gaze about and lock my eyes with those of Susan Wilson.

She does not avert her gaze, and smiles as if saying, "It's going to be alright." I return her smile as I watch a young man take her by the arm and walk her away.

He steers her through the departing crowd to the Wilson's wagon; assists her up, and she smiles down at him. I watch, hoping that she will look back. She does not, but she knows I'm watching. I see Buck. He gives me an assuring smile which I return. With Martha Jane in hand, I start to walk to our family.

I hear a hale and turn to see a tall, assured man step away from the Wilson wagon and come toward me. It takes me a moment to recognize Martin. Physically, he is taller, and broader of shoulder. He has the face of a man. The things he has seen and done are etched there. I know I look the same. We of the war are not difficult to spot. He is an officer of the Army approaching me, not a boy playing soldier. He extends his hand, and smiles saying, "Welcome home Evans; thank God you are safe."

I take his offered hand and feel the strength not only of body, but of mind and spirit. "Thank you Martin," I say as we embrace. We hold each other in the way that only brothers in arms can understand, "Your promise is fulfilled; I'm home. You did well."

He steps back, smiles and says, "Thank you. I'm anxious to talk to you this afternoon. Find me if I don't find you."

I nod before he returns to his family.

The journey home is short. The further we get from church, the louder Buck and Bill get. I look back on the road where trailed behind us, are wagons and riders following. It's like old times, but it isn't.

I haven't ridden this road in five years. In that time, Lucy Jane is gone, James Calvin is dead, John Wilson is murdered, Pa and James are off in Texas, Martin is a grown man, Buck is married, Susan is not interested, and we are all older. I wonder if we are wiser.

Activity at home is frenzied. Men are tending the meat that has been slow cooking since early, women are setting tables, warming dishes, and making ready for a Sunday feast. The children, including Martha Jane are running and playing all about the yard. Buck, Martin, Bill, and Ben are engaged in an intense game of horseshoes while I sit on the back porch and take it all in.

It feels good to sit and watch. I don't think about where my next meal is coming from, whether or not men on the ward are going to live, whether or not I am going to die. I do not worry about my wife and family. I am at peace. It is all resolved, almost. A cloud is yet over me.

Susan Wilson and the young man from church, come around the corner of the house. With them is Reverend Claiborne. I think dark thoughts about what could, and should have been. My mood falters.

Susan's widowed mother Rebecca steps to where I am sitting in the rocker and puts her hand on my shoulder. I put my hand on top of hers and she squeezes me. We both look over the gathering as she says, "Welcome home Evans."

"Thank you," I squeeze her hand again; "I've missed you."

"You've been missed." She nods her head to the growing group of friends and family around the tables in the shade of the oaks as final preparations are made to begin the meal. There is a pause while we take it in before she says, "I haven't seen her this happy in years."

"Yes, he looks like a fine man."

"Evans Atwood!"

I turn and look up into her impatient, angry face. She glares at me as if I am a dense child unable to grasp a simple concept of math, and shakes her head in wonder before saying, "Men are such fools; every one of you. She ain't happy with that boy. She's happy that you're home, and safe! Son, I thought she was going to bust a gut yesterday trying to act like she didn't care when she heard that Lucy had left you and you had Martha Jane! What is the matter with you boy; are you blind *and* a fool?"

"Yes ma'am, I guess so."

She laughs at my consternation then serious again, says, "Evans, I'm not going to pretend that what you did was right, and that I don't hate it, and what it did to Susan. I ain't going to lie and say that I didn't beg her to forget you, and move on with her life, because I did, even as near as last week, but she, like all kids, don't listen to her Ma. That girl loves you, and always will. You've got to talk to her and see what's there. To tell you the truth, I don't know, but you and she need to get on with whatever it is."

"Do you think she'll have me?"

"God knows I wouldn't! But there's no telling what's going on in her head since she's seen you. I'll tell you this Evans, you'll never know until you talk to her, and son, it's up to you to make the first move. If you don't, I'm gonna take you out back and give you the whopping you deserve! I've never known anyone to love another person like that girl loves you, and I know something else even though it sticks in my craw to say it, I know you love her too, and you two are meant to be."

"I don't know Mama…"

She laughs, "Look at you, the big war hero! Fought in all those battles and locked in a prison with no food, facing death every minute of every day, and scared to talk to a girl!" She snorts laughter again saying, "Men; the lot of you ain't worth shootin'." Then with more force, "Evans you ain't ever going to shoot the squirrel if you don't pull the trigger," she moves in front of the chair and bends at the waist so that her face is even with mine and says with fire in her eyes, "I don't know if she'll take you back or not, but if she does, and you hurt her again, I'll come after you, and if I can't, Martin damned sure will. Do you understand?"

"Yes ma'am, I do."

"Now, you do the right thing, and if you have any question about what the right thing is, go ask her," pointing to Susan working at the tables.

"Yes ma'am," I say as I rise from the chair, "thank you for speaking to me so clear like. I know what I have to do." I hug Mother Wilson and leave the porch to go to Susan.

"Come and get it!" Buck cries and can be heard across the county.

I get to her just as the crowd starts to find places at the table, "Hello Susan."

"Evans, I am so glad you're back and safe. How are you?" She extends her hand which I feel awkward taking.

"Susan, I would appreciate it if you made some time to talk to me before you leave today."

She could have said something hateful and had every right to, but she didn't, she smiled her sweet, calm, peaceful smile and said as smooth as ever, "That would be nice; I would like that very much."

Reverend Claiborne comes to me and asks that I get the meal started by asking him to bless the food. In the absence of Pa and James, I am presiding over the family. I call all to order and turn the blessing over to the Reverend.

We shuffle to our places, me between Buck and Martin, and what a threesome we make as we fill our plates, shove, and jostle each other like school boys. I look to see Susan helping Martha Jane and I turn red with embarrassment. I had forgotten all about her, and get up to try and correct my bad manners and poor parenting.

I go to the two of them and say awkwardly, "Martha Jane, you getting everything alright?"

"Yes, Papa," she says, "Miss Susan has helped me before."

I smile at them both, and say to Susan, "Thank you."

She smiles at me, and says, "You're welcome."

"Martha, do you want to sit with Papa?"

"No sir, I always sit with the kids."

"Oh, yeah," I say embarrassed at forgetting the kid's table and wondering if I don't belong there myself. Susan laughs at my discomfort; I do too.

"It's going to take awhile to become a full time Pa. I've been away for awhile if you haven't heard."

Susan laughs and finishes helping Martha with her plate. After she has run to the table with all the other children, Susan turns to me and says, "You'll do fine. If you ever need any help with her, I'll be glad to do whatever I can."

"It looks like you already have."

"She's a beautiful child. No one should have to go through what she has in the past few months. Your Mama tried...," she quits but adds, "it's none of my business," and busies herself helping another child.

"I would like for it to be your business. We both know it is"

She blushes, "You'd better go eat before your food's cold."

"Yes ma'am, I guess I'd better." We smile and go our separate ways.

After dinner I take a couple of dollars off Buck and Martin at horse shoes, but my heart's not in the game. I watch Susan every chance I get as she works with the other women to clean up, and watch again as she speaks with the young man who is paying way too much attention to her.

"Boy," Buck says. I look to see what he wants, "The game's over here." He sees where I'm looking and says, "You're the biggest chicken in the yard! Why don't you go on over there and talk to her?" He says with all the subtlety of a fog horn.

"Buck, you've got the loudest mouth of any human being I ever did know."

He and Martin grin at me. Martin asks, "You going to go see her or stand here gawking like a fool?"

"I don't know, I…"

"Evans, I didn't go to war and promise Susan to watch out for you just so's you could come home and go all bashful on me. Now, get your butt over there and get on with becoming my brother-in-law!" Both of them go into a riot of laughter.

"You two just want me to go so you don't lose any more money to me."

"Oh, yeah, that's right, we're afraid of your wonderful skills with horseshoes! It's a shame you don't have any skill with women," Buck roars.

By now, most everyone is looking our way. I leave the game; there are smiles from around the yard as they watch me walk toward Susan.

The boy sees me coming, and without looking at Susan, leaves. She dips her head once then meets my eyes as I approach. The same years that were so hard on Lucy have been gentle to Susan. She is beautiful. Her eyes are a deeper, clearer, bluer, her hair blacker, and her curves more pronounced. "How did someone as beautiful as you stay single the whole time I was gone?"

She doesn't blush or blink as she says, "I've been waiting for the right man."

"That boy," I gesture with my head at the retreating young man, "sure seems interested."

"Oh, there's lots interested, but none of them right." She smiles at me unabashed and says, "Are you going to ask to take me for a walk?"

"Miss Wilson, my I have the pleasure of your company as I walk around the old homestead. It has been a long time since I've been here, and longer still since I had a lovely woman to walk with."

"Sir, you honor me."

I offer her my arm, and she loops hers through like we've done countless times before. It feels as natural as the wind blowing. We walk in the direction of Spring Creek. I glance back to see mother and Mrs. Wilson standing on the porch watching. I look for Martha, and they both shoo me with their hands to indicate they'll watch her. I am so pleased that I remembered to look for her and smile.

"What are you smiling about?"

I don't answer; I can't, and smile more. I cannot believe Susan is next to me. It's as if we had never parted and nothing has transpired to distract us. This feels so right, but I am at a loss for words. I feel more awkward with each passing minute, but Susan is calm and peaceful as if this is the grandest thing she has ever done.

Two days ago I still had a wife. It seems like ages, a different time, a different place. Lucy and I were finished years back and what happened at my place was the last act in a long play.

Susan and I come to the creek as if we know where we're going, and in truth, we do. There is a big, flat rock that extends out over the water where you can dangle your feet in the stream. This is where Susan and I both learned to swim as children. The thought of us both naked swimming and swinging out over the pool in the innocence of youth causes a stirring in me that I hope she doesn't sense.

We walk out onto the rock as we have done so many times before. Neither of us has spoken. Susan has a placid, happy, unruffled look on her face, while I'm as nervous as a dog in a room full of cats. She walks to the edge and offers me her hand so I can assist her in sitting; I do, then sit next to her. We take our shoes off, dangle our feet over the edge into the flowing stream and watch water and time pass.

Sitting is worse than walking; there is nothing to distract us. I had asked to talk to her, and now is the time. "I'm sorry Susan, so sorry."

She looks at me, smiles a little half smile and asks, "Do you know what for?"

There are so many things. I'm quiet for a minute or two before saying, "For not knowing how good I had it when I had it." As I say it, I realize that Lucy Jane and I share the same sin.

She doesn't say anything for awhile then asks, "If it had been you and I who had married, would you have still gone off to war?"

"I don't know Susan." It is hard to imagine that time with her instead of Lucy Jane. "Probably."

"Do you regret going?"

"Regret it, no, I don't regret it. I wish it had…, well, there's a lot of things I wish, but no, I don't regret it."

"Why?"

"It was honorable; I did my duty, and I learned so much."

"Like what?"

"Like what kind of man I want to be. Most of it was by seeing what kind of man I didn't want to be, but I learned a lot about who I am and what I want."

"And what kind of man are you?"

"I am kinder, I think of others more. I want to stop hurt where I can. If I hadn't gone to war, I would have never met Dr. McPheeters and learned that I want to be a doctor."

"A doctor!" Susan exclaims. "I thought you wanted to be a teacher. How did this come about?"

That broke the ice. I told her the whole story, and more. I don't know how long it took, but the sun was much lower when I finished. She sat silent and listened, never taking her eyes off me. She made me feel like it was the grandest story she had ever heard. I finish and she continues to look at me.

"You'll make a good doctor."

"How do you know?"

"I could hear the passion in your voice as you talked about your patients. You were possessive and protective. They're yours and you hurt with them."

I made no reply.

"How do you plan on going about this, or have you gotten past the dreaming about it stage?"

"After the war is over, Dr. Allison has invited me to study at the medical college where he teaches in Kentucky. In the mean time, I can study with a preceptor nearby if someone will have me."

"Have you inquired?"

"No, I just got back, but tomorrow, Monday, I thought I would talk to Doc. Hankins in town, or Doc. Black."

"I'm sure either'll have you."

Silence falls on us again. There's something hanging between us and it won't go away. I don't know what to say, so I wait.

Susan cuts to the heart of the matter, "I'm not going to wait forever, but I've waited this long."

"What do you mean?"

She looks at me with the same sweet expression as before and says, "I'm not going to mince words with you Evans; I don't have time. I've waited for you since we swam here as naked children. I've always wanted to swim with you as a naked adult, but... Let me tell you how it is. I love you, and I know you love me, but you're too afraid to say it. You always have been, but I've always known it."

"I'm not going to let you walk back into my life and act like the last five years didn't happen, but I am willing to let them lie in the past where they belong. I will never throw them up to you, and I love Martha as if she was my own, so that won't be a problem, but you've got a long way to go to prove yourself to me, and it's going to take a lot of proving."

I start to speak, but she stops me.

"I'm not finished. I've waited and hurt for five years, and you're going to let me say what I have to say."

I nod.

"I won't lie and say that I'm over the hurt you did to me, but again, it's past and I'm going to let it stay there, but the future is another matter. I'm willing to let you back into my life on the following terms: You will get a job, and in this case with a doctor, and earn a good living. You will clean and rebuild the house that you and I started. You are going to be a wonderful father to Martha, and again, if you need me to help, I will. You will see me as much as is decently possible and hold me as often as we can get away with it, and Evans," she raises a finger to me to make her point, "if you slip up and cause me or Martha any hurt, even a little, then we will be done. Now, the question is, can you live with that; am I worth it?" Before I can start to answer, she adds, "I want things in life too, and if I can't get them with you, I'll find someone else."

My answer takes no thought at all. We sit being serenaded by the flowing water with the late afternoon sun playing in her hair through the leaves as I voice something that I should have said a long time ago, "I've always loved you. Before we swam here, before we were born, and I will always love you. Even if we don't marry I will love you. You've given me a second chance that I never dreamed of having, and I'm not going to let it pass. To answer your questions; yes, you are worth it and a hundred times more; and yes, I can and will live with it. I will not fail us."

"I can't promise you that I won't make you shed a tear or two, but I will never leave you or hurt you as I have; we've both had enough of that. I will get a job as I said, and I will provide and protect you and our children to the best of my ability, and I do have ability."

She smiles and takes my hand in hers. We sit. It is good. At that moment, I realize that if it had not been for the war, if all the ensuing horrors I experienced in prison and battle had not been part of my life, I would never have known the peaceful assuring love that I feel at this moment. It is patient, kind, nurturing, and above all else, charitable.

"How many?" Susan asks.

"How many what?"

"Children," she smiles, "you said you will provide and protect me and our children, how many children?"

We laugh. Hers' is music that blends with the natural symphony of the life in the stream flowing beneath us. "As many as you want."

"I don't want there to be a minute that we are not trying for more."
She looks at me and her eyes sparkle as I look into them. They are a
comforting oasis, full of passion, and love. She leans in closer and we
kiss; the first of thousands.

45) **Sunday, February 17th, 1867**

It is hard to believe more than two years have passed since that June evening when Susan and I took the first small steps on the road that would be the rest of our lives. The war is over; peace of a sort is on the land. There has been much work to do, and it hasn't been easy, but it has been worth it. Today, Susan Wilson will add Atwood to her name. She will be my bride.

The house has been added on to, and rebuilt. Susan has never said so, but I think she wanted the influence of Lucy Jane to be removed. The land has been cleared and planted with two good crops.

Martha Jane has grown into a beautiful seven year old. She is wise for her age, but plays with others and is normal in all but one regard; she will not go into the woods alone. I do not know what she experienced out there, but the woods are not a place of solace for her.

After we got back from the trip to my folk's place, she went off and came back later with a very pale face, breathing hard, carrying a corn shuck doll, and the old picture of me in my uniform that at one time resided on the mantel. It does so again.

I asked her why she was so pale and frightened, and all she would say was "Steven Wayne." I soothed her until she fell asleep. While she was sleeping, I took my weapons and scoured the woods, but never found anything. I was afraid that Steven Wayne had come back, but after several days of vigilance, nothing came of it, and the evil about the place left.

We have had no word from Lucy. I saw her mother one day in town and asked if she had any word of her, but she looked at me and said in a questioning tone, "Lucy Jane?" I do not know if she knew who I was.

Peace has settled over our home. It is a place that holds memories, but only happy ones now. As I built and added and changed, Martha and Susan would approve or disapprove until we got it right. It had to be just so for both of them, and so it is.

The other requirement that Susan laid out for me was that I spend as much time as was decent with her and Martha. I am happy to say that I have fulfilled that requirement. Susan spent days with us at the homestead building and clearing, planting, and harvesting until the place felt like it belonged to her and not history. I worked very hard at making her and Martha happy.

I have worked with Dr. Hankins and Dr. Black and am making a good living. I keep up a lively correspondence with Drs. Allison and McPheeters. I will study this coming fall with Dr. Allison in Kentucky and have taken courses from Dr. McPheeters who is here for the wedding with his lovely family. I am not yet called "doctor" by title, but it won't be long. Susan will be with me and care for our daughter as Martha has become, and I will be able to complete my studies.

We survived the war. There are scars for us all, but we are better people for having acquired them. Some are slower to heal than others, but we are moving on and getting better and better. Lucy Jane would like that. I must stop writing, Buck is calling for me. He is the best man. It's time to take a giant step forward; getting ever better.

46) The Wedding

"Come on Boy, the party's gonna start and all's you're doing is writin' in that book," Buck booms from across the room. I finish my journal entry; my last as a single man…again.

"I wish you would keep a journal Buck. With you and Olivia's three kids and more coming, you have a story to tell."

"Nah, ain't nobody wants to read about an old Keantuck, Arkansas hillbilly," he says with sincere, but misguided humility.

"I bet the McPheeters think your story is worth telling."

"Then let them tell it. Now, come on boy; your bride and her family have been here thirty minutes; let's get this party started!"

I pull out my pocket watch that I have been carrying again since I am an honest working man and check the time; 1:30PM; thirty minutes before the ceremony is scheduled to start. "Buck, you should know by now that a woman's got to have time to get ready. We've got a half hour before we even have to start thinking of getting out there." He paces back and forth in the room. I laugh, "You're more nervous than I am."

He stops his pacing and says, "Boy, I've waited a long time for this, and I want you and Miss Susan hitched, and I mean right now!" Stomping his foot for emphasis. "I've been sent by Martin to make sure you're ready, and get there on time."

"You should be more diligent about watching Reverend Claiborne to make sure he stays away from the shine and all. I don't want a repeat of…"

"You don't have to say it, Bill and Ben have the good Reverend well in hand with instructions that he is to only have water or root beer before the ceremony, and they are to taste it before he drinks it." He pauses, looks at me, and then the floor, shakes his head and says, "Lord, that man does love his drink. Did you know that he thinks he hears angels when he drinks?"

I laugh as I look at myself in the mirror, "I've heard some voices when I drink too, but I don't think they're from angels."

"No, me neither."

I smile at his reflection behind me as I straighten my tie and collar in the mirror. I am wearing a gray coat with tails and black piping at the collar, and on the sleeves. Buck is similarly dressed, but without the piping. We both wear black trousers.

We do not want to appear too military in our dress. We are proud of our service to a cause we still believe in, freedom. It is my hope that freedom from oppression will always be worth fighting and dying for, and if my progenitors learn anything from me it will be that it is.

I have grown a beard since the war. It is trimmed and short unlike the bear look of my friend who is catching a peek at himself in the mirror over my shoulder.

Buck walks to the window and peers out. "It's going to rain tonight."

"So long as it holds off today, I don't care what it does tonight."

"You and Susan will get wet on the ride to your place."

"How do you know where we're going? We might stay in town at the hotel."

"Okay, you're going to get wet riding to the hotel. I don't care where you go."

He does. He's trying to bait me into telling him where we are going for our first night together. The truth is that he's hoping it won't be far to ride to play pranks on us. He doesn't want to get wet.

The Atwoods and Wilsons make a crowd, but with the addition of church and work people and some "out of towners", it's a large gathering. The homestead has seen weddings but this is the first one since the war, and it is a cause to celebrate.

The ceremony itself is to be held under the ancient oak with its limbs almost touching the ground. It seems that weddings are its natural purpose. There is much activity at the tree as the final preparations are made. Music is being played by the musicians who played at Buck's wedding.

I step out onto the porch to listen. The violins, guitars, and banjo are playing a minuet for strings by Boccherini that sounds more beautiful here at home than if played by the grandest organ in greatest hall in the world.

Buck leans to me and says in my ear, "It's time to go Evans," as he guides me down the stairs. I step onto the lawn with my Best Man, and the group breaks into a popular hymn even though it is written by a Yankee and is most appropriate for me this day; *He Leadeth Me* rises from the band. I feel a surge of emotion for He has surely led me these past years. I marvel at the miracles that have led me to this point and am grateful for friends and family who have assisted along the way.

I look at those gathered to honor me and Susan, and am amazed to see not only Dr. McPheeters and his family, but Dr. Allison and his. The real surprise is Walter Mather standing with Dr. Allison!

We exchange greetings and hugs with all except young William, never to be called Bill, who is too much of a man to hug and insists on shaking hands. I get to see Sallie's ever present and powerful smile which calms me and gives me strength. When I get to Walter, he extends his hand which I take and he says, "You owe me ten dollars."

"It's twenty and you know it."

"Yeah, but who's counting. I see that you used them well."

"Yes I did, and thank you."

"It's you who I should thank."

"Oh?"

"For never giving up on me, and always reminding me that there is a future, but most of all, that God loves me and has a plan for me."

"And what of that plan?"

"Dr. Atwood, you are speaking with soon to be Dr. Mather."

"Congratulations!" I cry. I look to Dr. Allison and say, "I suppose you had something to do with this?"

"You more than I; when Walter learned that you would become a doctor, he decided that it was his calling as well, so he will be at the college this fall in the same class as you."

I beam at Walter and say, "You won't be calling me Reb anymore!"

"No, it'll be Dr. Reb."

We have a good laugh and Buck pushes me on. "We'll visit later."

The last notes of the hymn finish as I step to the altar and smile at the very nervous Reverend Claiborne who is flanked by Bill and Ben. I take my place with Buck as the two boys step to be with us. We make a dashing line all dressed in gray. Standing across from us is Olivia, two of my sisters, and two of Susan's sisters dressed in winter dark red that melds with the foliage of the ever green oak.

The *Wedding March* is taken up by the band and we all turn to see Susan stepping down from the porch. She is dressed in the same gown her mother was married in. It is a simple, full length, long sleeved white brocade gown that accentuates every curve.

All eyes are on her, but my attention is divided; for preceding her is Martha Jane clothed in white but in a less formal dress of taffeta and linen embroidered across the bodice in the same red as the bride's maids. She is carrying a red pillow holding two rings. She is enjoying leading the way before her soon-to-be mother who has already earned the title by her good works which make the biology secondary. I look at the two and marvel at how much they have grown to act and look alike although Martha is golden blonde, and Susan's hair is raven black. I could not be happier.

It is sweet to see Susan on the arm of Martin; my brother-in-law and in-arms. I wish Susan's father John was here to give her away, but it is appropriate for Martin to have the honor. He fulfilled his oath with honor and is responsible for me being here in many ways. He is dashing in his gray and of all the veterans present; he has survived war the best although he still does not shoot. He has become the teacher of the local community and I love him for it. He has been my guardian angel all these years, and says he always will be there to pick up the pieces. His task and oath are complete as he hands Susan to me, and says, "It's been a long time coming brother, but if you ever need me…"

"I know, you'll always be watching out for me." Then to Susan, "When are you going to release him of his charge?"

"Never, watching over you is a two person job."

We smile as we take each other by the hand and face Reverend Claiborne. Martha's little hand slides into my other and I stand holding the two most wonderful things I have in this world. Susan's hand in mine feels so natural and I wonder why this did not happen before; why was I so blind? Then I know; some treasures do not come until you have been through the refiners fire to know how to care and use them. Susan is such a treasure.

"Dearly beloved; we are gathered here today in the sight of God and these witnesses…", and so it is that the circle is closed and the better things have come, and will come for years in the future. As I stand holding the hand of my intended from the beginning, I wonder to myself if war has served a good purpose. Some things are worth fighting for.

Thunder rolls in the distance for a fitting finish to the ceremony. The rains can be seen moving our way, but they do not matter, we've said "I do", and we both know we will…forever.

Epilogue

Evans and Susan Wilson were married for twenty years until Susan's death March 2, 1887. Their union produced ten children the second of which is my great grandfather, John Wilson Atwood who passed on to me among other things, my middle name.

There is much to be learned from seeking out ones' ancestors, and not all of it is charming, soft, heroic, or decent. The basic story told here is true, but I have fictionalized events and added characters to fill in the blanks of things that Evans did not record, but must have happened. The afterword will explain the characters and their roles.

I want readers to take from this story that people are real and make mistakes. It is what we do after the mistakes that will define our character. I hope I have shown how these choices can affect generations and we need to be thinking of what is in front of us, and not behind us.

The second thing I want the reader to take away is the importance of keeping a journal and a personal history. You may think that your life is insignificant and will never matter, but you are wrong. The compilation of traits from Evans Atwood, John Wilson Atwood, Clifford Wade Atwood, and Hugh Gerald Atwood, along with their spouses is who I am. What they did, or did not do is the essence of me.

Isn't it sad that Buck elected to not keep a journal? Although he is fictional, his generations would love to know his story as we long to know the story of his parents. Don't leave your family with the same empty pages.

You should want to know who you are and enjoy the discovery. Have you ever wondered why you do a certain thing a certain way, or why you have an irrational fear? I have had so many epiphanies as I have researched and written this book about who I am and why I do the things I do; some of it is "in the blood".

Who are you? Go find out; discovery waits.

Afterword

It is impossible to thank everyone who contributed to this project, but some must be mentioned. First, to my dear wife and First Reader, JoAnne; thanks for patience with all the whining and feelings of insecurity. The same has to go to our daughters, Emily and Gillian, who had me working from home for two years. They have been a tremendous support.

William Brandon "Bucky" Bowman was the first outside my immediate family to learn of my desire to write Evans Atwood's story. He has contributed much in material, love, and support. He had it easier than the others; he did not have to put up with the whining.

George E. Cone, Jr. did his master's thesis on "The Confederate Delaying Action at the Battle of Port Gibson, 1 May 1863". It was invaluable in my understanding of the units and battle plans for the action in which Evans was captured.

Thanks too to the wonderful people at the Claiborne County, Mississippi Court House who treated me like I was one of their own, and likewise to the Port Gibson Chamber of Commerce personnel.

The battle ground and Rodney Road are "undeveloped" and are much as they were at the time of the action. The Shaifer House and grounds are wonderfully preserved and are worth the "off road" effort to see them.

The Characters

Evans Atwood, Lucy Jane Roberts, and **Susan Jane Wilson** are real and are the story, as are **Martha Jane** and **James Calvin Atwood**, Evans' children with Lucy. Little is known of Lucy Jane, so her background and family, other than being from Tennessee, are fictional.

The Atwood and Wilson families are accurate as far as research revealed. **Martin Wilson** is not fictitious, but his rank and relationship with Evans are. There was a Martin Wilson in the 15th Arkansas, and Martin Wilson is one of Susan Wilson's younger brothers, but I could find no indication that the two are the same, so I assumed they are and built the story accordingly.

Steven Wayne Culpepper is fictional. I based his character on a lieutenant I was under in Vietnam who had the same limitations and talents.

Patricia Ann Robinson is fictional as well as is the whole **Robinson** family. I took her name from my first love in the first grade in Levelland, Texas, but did not do justice to the sweet, sweet girl she was and I remember. Patsy, if you read this, I still remember you fondly and apologize for disparaging your name.

The **Yeller** family is fictitious. There was an Archibald Yell who was governor of Arkansas in the 1840's and had nothing to do with the story. Those of my family will recognize the names of **Clifford Wade**, and **Lola Bye** as those of my grandparents.

Nathanial James "Buck" Buchannan is a story in his own right which is told in a prequel/sequel. He is fictional; born of necessity. One of the rules of engagement in the Civil War by both sides was to not leave your place in battle to aid a fallen comrade. Evans was doing that very thing when he was captured. Being an officer, this was more serious, and I wondered about who the man might be for Evans to break this rule and risk his own capture and death. He had to be special to him and thus Buck appeared. Evans did have a traveling companion he refers to often in his journal entries, but there was no record of him being in the army so Buck took his place.

Buck was solidly in place in the narrative and his background of being a Kentuckian was already established when I discovered the very real, heart breaking story of **Dr. William McPheeters** and his family. His wife, **Sallie Buchannan McPheeters,** was from Kentucky. She, and many, many women of Missouri who refused to sign a pledge to the Union were banished and the stories are horrific of losing children, murder, rapes, and other terrors. It seemed natural to me to tie Buck and the McPheeters together as cousins although Dr. McPheeters was never in

Mississippi at the same time as Evans. I was so fascinated with this bit of history that I had to blend it in.

The commanders of the 15th Arkansas Infantry and the unit's history are very real.

The prisons were horrible on both sides. Andersonville is the most infamous and arguably the worst of the lot, but the northern prisons were, in many cases, as bad. The Gratiot Street Prison in St. Louis, Missouri was particularly notorious for its treatment of citizens who refused to sign the aforementioned pledge. From this horror came the character of **Olivia Lacey,** later Buchannan, and her relationship with the McPheeters family.

Major Washington B. Traweek was of the Alabama Regulars, but was not a major. I mention him only because he is recorded prominently in books about prisons and escapes, and I like the ring of his name. He escaped several times and was finally successful. Some of his schemes were inspirational to me for Evans' fictional escape, but in the end, I used none of them. Evans' escape just happened as it does in the narrative.

I had Evans escape because, no matter how hard I tried, having him sit in prison until the end of the war just wasn't exciting and made an already long story longer.

I made every effort to be true to the characters listed here as real. All others are fictional and in no way portray living or deceased individuals. Any similarities to persons living or dead, names, traits, or actions are purely coincidental. All mistakes are mine and mine alone.